PIG

PIG

MATILDE PRATESI

corsair

CORSAIR

First published in the United Kingdom in 2025 by Corsair

1 3 5 7 9 10 8 6 4 2

A CIP catalogue record for this book is available from the British Library.

Hardback ISBN: 978-1-4721-5910-6

Typeset in Garamond by M Rules
Printed and bound in Great Britain by Clays Ltd, Elcograf S.p.A.

Papers used by Corsair are from well-managed forests
and other responsible sources.

MIX
Paper | Supporting
responsible forestry
FSC® C104740

Corsair
An imprint of
Little, Brown Book Group
Carmelite House
50 Victoria Embankment
London EC4Y 0DZ

The authorised representative
in the EEA is
Hachette Ireland
8 Castlecourt Centre
Dublin 15, D15 XTP3, Ireland
(email: info@hbgi.ie)

An Hachette UK Company
www.hachette.co.uk

www.littlebrown.co.uk

PART ONE

Chapter One

London, April 2019

The moment I hear the clunk of the lock I spring into action, lifting my bag from under the counter and grabbing the shutter keys. I need to be out of here by 18.15 at the latest or there's no way I'll be home by 18.30. I check my phone and see that it's already 18.17. This is not good, not good at all. Because she hasn't worked in so long, Clara just doesn't understand that sometimes I end up running late to get it all done.

I've been behind all day. It's not the pigs' fault, but I was thinking of them, again, as I walked into work this morning. I don't eat pigs. If everyone knew how truly amazing pigs were, they wouldn't eat them either. I wonder if people have heard that pigs are smarter than a three-year-old. And if they have, does that mean they could eat a toddler, too?

When I tell someone that human flesh smells just like bacon when it burns, it doesn't seem to put them off. They just give me a strange look and keep eating their sandwich.

First thing this morning, from behind the counter at the bookshop, I looked up to see Ollie walking in. I eyed the paper cup he was holding in both hands.

'Hot choc. I need the extra calories this morning,' he said, swaying

3

a little before sitting next to me. Ollie is tall and thin. He's been in London for a few years but is originally from what he describes as a 'pointless village' in South Wales. He doesn't have an opinion on Welsh pigs – even though I've repeatedly told him they're nearly extinct – and is fed up with talking about them. Ollie only wears tops with writing on them. Today his T-shirt reads . . . *forever?* on the front, while large red letters on the back of his jacket spell out *Rebels Motorcycle Club*. He doesn't own a motorcycle.

When Ollie collapsed further into his chair, I checked my watch.

'Today is all about self-care,' he mumbled, chin resting on his chest.

'Why?' I asked.

He told me he got lost twice last night trying to get home after locking up the shop. He must have taken a wrong turn because he ended up in front of Twickenham Stadium, which is more than a mile away from where he lives.

'Ollie,' I said, 'pigs can remember directions and find their way home from very far away. Their sense of direction is better than yours.' Then I laughed.

He looked right at me as a deep frown creased his forehead. Then he got up, walked over to the travel section, and started loading books onto the shelves.

I could hear the *thud* each volume made as it landed on the polished oak, even when I was in another section of the shop. It's not a big place and the ceilings are low because people used to be shorter back when it was built, so every noise travels around like mad. But the walls are thick enough to keep all outside noises from the nearby high street to a low hum, making you feel like you're in a cave all day, which I like.

The bookshop is in a very, very old building that has been on Church Street for centuries. From the outside, it's rickety – the doorway leans slightly to the left and is shorter than the others on the street. I always think that the black beams and powdery white walls

4

of its front and the bulky shape of its square windows make it look like a German layered cake.

Inside, it smells like dust, glue and paper. The once-red rugs on the floor are bleached pink by faint sunlight and threadbare from consistent walking, so that you can see the outline of the floorboards. There are five small rooms in the shop, connected by dark wooden arches. The shop is packed with books.

The children's book area is at the back, in the largest room, and there are old velvet armchairs in the middle, leaking stuffing. I feel safe and calm in the children's area, as if the outside world isn't quite real.

While Ollie stacked the shelves, I stood by the till and watched a pencil roll off the counter onto the carpeted floor, then disappear behind a pile of books waiting to be priced up. I crouched down low and rolled it carefully back towards me with the tip of my index finger. Once it was in my grip, I took a moment to enjoy the feeling of the smooth, shiny veneer pressed against my skin. It was soothing. I got an irresistible urge to find out what noise it would make if I tapped its end onto the worn patch in the carpet. I tried it but it wasn't great, more of a soft *pft*. I started tapping it harder and faster and eventually got a better—

'What ... erm ... what are you doing?' Ollie was looking at me, his arms crossed so high they were almost hiding the writing on his T-shirt.

'Something got stuck.' I got up and brushed the dust off my trousers.

'So, what do you think?' he asked.

'About what?'

'Should I shave my moustache?'

I leaned in closer to the space between Ollie's mouth and nose. I saw a shadow that looked like a faint smudge of ink.

'No, keep it.'

A customer walked in, making the bell on top of the door ring.

He was a middle-aged man wearing a floppy rain hat and holding a crumpled copy of the *New Scientist*. Ollie and I exchanged a knowing look before I went over to the travel department to continue restocking. About half of the customers that come into the shop behave in the same way. They mostly arrive mid-morning and walk around from shelf to shelf. They pick up the books, look at the covers and take the time to read all the blurbs.

After half an hour or so of this ritual, they select one and hold it in their hand, flip between the front cover and the back and maybe read the first page or somewhere in the middle.

Then they head over to one of the armchairs we have in the back of the shop, settle in as if they're in their own living room and start reading. For an hour, two hours, three. I've had to ask many of them to leave at closing time, and every time it's like you've shaken them awake from a deep sleep. They look at you blankly for a second or so, apologise, then get up slowly and leave. They never put the book back and they never, ever buy it. Ollie says they get it online instead, for half the price and with next-day delivery.

While I put away the new stock into each section, Ollie tapped his fingers at lightning speed across the keypad of his phone. His elbows were planted on the flat wooden surface of the counter and his long fringe got in his eyes when he tilted his head down to read the screen.

I imagined he was speaking to Rafael about their plans for the evening.

Rafael and Ollie met in the shop a while ago and now they spend all of their time together.

Before Ollie started working here, I'd spoken to Rafael maybe once or twice, helping him find obscure Polish poetry books. After the two of them got talking a few times, he started waiting to be served by Ollie even when he was busy talking to another customer and I was free. They must like a lot of the same books because they never seem to run out of things to talk about.

One day I saw Rafael waiting for Ollie across the road at closing time. That's when I realised they had been hanging out outside the shop too. They spend a lot of time going to gigs and to the cinema, and Rafael is now pretty much the main topic of Ollie's daily stories. It never takes very long for those stories to come out as soon as we're alone in the shop.

'Cup of tea?' he asked from inside the tiny staff kitchen.

Before I could reply, I heard the thud of two cups on the hard plastic tabletop and the liquid gurgle of the kettle.

We leaned on the wall facing each other, our hands gripping the cup handles tight, and his voice began filling up the room once more.

'Don't get me wrong, Vale, I don't care about the money stuff, it's not like I'm greedy. But it would be nice if sometimes he paid for something, the drinks, the tickets. I've told him, I said, "Let's try the new place up the road sometime. The one with the big chandeliers near the roundabout?" And you know what he said to me? He said: "That one? Looks pretentious." Pretentious? It's not it being pretentious he's worried about, I know it, it's the bill. He knows I won't pay for the whole thing and he can't get away with it if it's a proper place instead of the usual pub. Well, I like the pub as much as the next person, but it would be nice to go to a place with people our age sometimes and not always be surrounded by old farts, you know?'

I looked at my watch, aware of the hours and minutes left until closing time. I couldn't be late home again.

'Yeah.'

'He says they're "real people", Vale. Well, what am I? Am I not a real person?'

'You are real, Ollie.'

'Exactly. I'm real too.'

He took a sip of his tea, deep in thought.

I never know what to answer when he asks me these kinds of questions. So I mostly either nod or say 'yes', 'no' or 'of course'. But sometimes I can guess the answer right away, like in that case. He is definitely a real person, so it was easy.

7

We spent the rest of the afternoon like this, drinking tea and dealing with customers. Until the time crept up on both of us and we got busy tidying the place after the last stragglers and cashing up.

Ollie and Rafael were going out to see a band, and he already had his coat on when the clock got to six. He sometimes waits around for me to finish my tasks and lock up, but he didn't this time.

'Do you mind if I go? He really hates it when we're late.' He seemed unable to stay still.

'No, that's fine. Have fun. Don't do drugs,' I mumbled, straightening the paperwork on the counter into neat piles. I felt bolts of electric energy shooting through my fingers. He needed to leave now so I could go.

'Yeah, okay, *Mum*, thanks. Ha. See you later.'

And he was out of the door.

But now I'm running late. I've timed the journey a hundred times over and it's never less than fifteen minutes. My leg muscles contract from the adrenaline shooting through my body. I bring the shutter down so fast it slams onto the ground. A group of men outside the pub over the road turn away from their pints to look at me. I ignore them and start walking as fast as I can.

The prospect of being home with Clara, inside the safety of those walls and following the rules and rituals that shape our time together, is enough to put an extra spring in my step. She needs me home on time, and I like to stick to those rules. It may add stress to my day, especially when I'm running late like today, knowing that she won't be happy with me, but the joy of having clear parameters within which to live my life is enough to push me to want to be better. For myself, but mostly for Clara.

18.20. *No, no, no, no.* My feet skip over the cobbles, I angle my body forward and hold my bag against my side to be more aerodynamic against the breeze. I jog past the gift shop, the Fox and Hounds, the ladies' hairdresser's, and the children's clothing shop. I hate getting through the door with my chest burning and sweat dripping down my face but there's no time to slow down.

I reach the big roundabout where rush hour is in full swing. Hundreds of cars crawl up and down the streets like prisoners in a chain gang and the traffic lights seem to switch slower than usual. As I rush towards the zebra crossing, images crowd into my brain: getting hit and dragged under a car. My head smashing onto the rough asphalt.

The images are so complete I can almost feel the weight of the wheels crushing my bones. 'Come on, come on, come on, come on . . .' I say under my breath as I hurry along the pavement. I check my watch. 18.31. *Oh no.*

I can see our street in the distance, the red door, the front garden, the black and green bins. I check again. 18.35. *Shit.*

I grab my keys from the bag and fumble at the front door, opening it as the clock in the entrance shows 18.37. *Shiiiiit.*

I drop my bag onto the polished wooden floor and shout, 'I'm here. I'm here. Sorry! A customer. He just wouldn't leave. I had to push him out of the door and . . .'

The house is quiet.

I look in the living room, but it's empty. No time to check every room. I run upstairs, nearly tripping on the first few steps, and dash into the bathroom. I push the plug down hard and turn both taps as far as they'll go, then, once a little bit of water has begun to fill the bath, I check for temperature. It must not be too hot but can't be too cold either. I grab the large sponge and the small one, the comb and the liquid soap, and line them up along the edge of the tub.

I sit on a stool by the side, take a deep breath and wait. My hands folded in my lap, my eyes fixed on the door, I list pig breeds under my breath:

9

'Aksai Black Pied, American Yorkshire, Angeln Saddleback, Ankamali, Appalachian English ...'

I can hear footsteps coming up the stairs, slow and deliberate, wood creaking underfoot.

'Arapawa Island, Auckland Island, Australian Yorkshire, B-B-Babi Kampung ...'

The steps get closer. I grip the edge of the stool I'm sitting on. My hands start to tingle the moment she steps into the bathroom.

Her long hair is down, and she's wearing a towelling robe knotted tightly at the waist. The contrast between the deep black of her hair and the white of the robe reminds me of tree roots in the snow. I feel dizzy. Her feet are bare, her toenails painted blood red.

'I'm sorry. I'm late. I know I ...' I blurt out, before I realise my hands have risen and I'm holding them up as if praying to the Virgin Mary. Despite everything going on right now, it is a relief to slip back into speaking Italian and the familiarity of us.

'It's okay.' She closes the door behind her and begins to take off her robe, undoing the knot with slow movements.

'Clara. Please, I'll make it up to you, I promise. You know I will.' I lower my hands – she can't stand it when I'm pathetic. I sit on them and wait for a sign. She's still not looking at me.

'Vale, it's okay. You were busy. Had better things to do, no?' She hangs the robe on the hook and dips her toe in the water. She shivers out loud, pauses for a second then lowers herself in with a sigh.

'Is it too cold?' I feel sweat forming on my temples. I turn the hot water back on and start swirling the flow around, trying to mix the new water in faster. 'It's not that I was busy, there was a customer who just wouldn't make his mind up, I couldn't kick him out, I ... I ...'

'Leave it.' She shifts her weight around until she finds a comfortable position, then leans forward, tying her hair up into a bun. 'I'm so tired today. I really don't want to end up catching a cold sitting in this for too long.'

I dip the large sponge into the water, squeeze a big dollop of soap onto it and bring it up to a thick lather with my hands. I move the stool closer and start rubbing her back with the sponge, leaving her skin flushed. I rub her arms, neck and shoulders, careful not to get soap in her hair. I tap her forearm lightly as a signal and she stands up, facing away from me, her arms long and heavy down her sides. I rub her legs, her lower back, her bum and all the way down to her knees, just above where the water laps. Another tap, and she turns around, facing me but still not looking in my direction. Instead, her head is turned towards the window; she seems to be concentrating hard on a cluster of clouds high up above us. Normally, during bath time, we chat, and she tells me about her day: the programmes she's watched on TV, and what the cats have been up to outside the windows. Today she doesn't seem in the mood, and I know that initiating won't help; she will just ignore me. Maybe it's true that she's tired ... It could just be that.

We are in complete silence, and I can feel my unease grow with each movement of my hands. This is not going well. I shouldn't have been late. I've been doing so well in the last month. I was even early a couple of times, and then we laughed throughout bath time.

Laughed! It's so hard to believe right now, when the only noise I can hear is the dripping of the taps.

I clean her stomach, her shins, her knees and begin rising up between her legs. As my hands circle upwards, she turns her face, staring right at me now as I begin running the sponge over the thick, dark hair at the top of her thighs. My eyes are fixed on hers. As the soapy lather grows, I can feel the suds starting to trickle down my forearm and off my elbow onto the mat. An overwhelming warmth instantly blooms over my cheeks and between my legs. I keep a steady movement with my hand, terrified that if I change anything about this moment, it might end. A sigh comes out of Clara's mouth, then a gurgle. Is she enjoying this? Oh, I hope so. Her eyes aren't moving away from mine; it's like she's reaching deep inside my gut through them. The bathtub, the sink, these walls,

11

they're all gone. It's like we're suspended in space. Me, her and the sponge. Another muffled sound escapes her mouth, then she breaks into a guttural laugh.

'What is it?' I ask, alarmed.

She is still laughing. 'It's ticklish. You're tickling me.' She gently moves the sponge away with her hand. Her whole body shudders, but it doesn't look like it's an unpleasant feeling.

I'm at once disappointed that the moment has passed, but happy to see her smile. The previous tension – whatever that was – has dissipated. But her smile makes up for the small void that the end of that moment has left inside of me. I laugh too. Extending my fingers towards her sides and pretending to tickle her again.

'No, stop it.' She giggles.

I do it some more and she laughs again. I squeeze the sponge to get rid of the excess lather and go to rub under her arms. 'I'm going to tickle you,' I say in a silly voice, getting up, sponge in hand. She giggles again. Then, like a sudden thunderclap, her face becomes serious. She takes the sponge and puts it back on the side of the bath.

'Enough. I'm clean. You'll get my skin off with this thing if you keep going.'

She swings one leg over the bath, then the other.

'I'm going to have a lie-down. Let's eat in half an hour,' she says, putting the robe back on and tying the belt into a tidy bow. She opens the door and I watch her back disappear around the corner as her body leaves a Clara-shaped hole in the steam.

I look at the doorway for a moment, my head bursting with thoughts. I have no idea what just happened to make her go from laughing with me, playing even, to just . . . gone. I must have done something wrong or said something I shouldn't have. It was childish to pretend to tickle her, but I only did it because she was laughing. She seemed to enjoy it. And before that, her eyes. The way they were fixed onto mine. She would have looked away if it was wrong. Every second of that moment felt right to me. But I must have messed up. Again. I press my flushed cheek on the cold ceramic wall and close my eyes.

My head is still for a moment, then I continue:

'Ba Xuyen, Bantu, Basque, Bazna, Beijing Black, Belarus Black Pied, Belgian Landrace . . .'

Chapter Two

The house is quiet and cool when I wake up the next morning. Clara stayed up late again last night. I walk into the kitchen and see two paper notes stuck to the marble countertop.

Brown trousers, black scoop-neck top (the older one), light blue trainers, reads the first note in black marker pen. I peel off the second: *One can of fizzy drink (Diet Coke or San Pellegrino) and a sandwich (no meat)*. I fold both into little squares and slide them into the top pocket of my nightshirt. I'm glad she's specified that there doesn't have to be meat in the sandwich. Sometimes she leaves it blank, and I feel guilty if I pick the vegan option on instinct. As if it might upset her. It's such a relief to be told what to eat. It means I don't have to spend ages agonising over the deli counter or at the supermarket near work, paralysed with indecision. Clara knows how tough I find those choices, so she helps me by making them for me. It's great because it regulates my daily life.

I remember when the notes first started. It was not long after I moved in with her.

We had planned to go on a park outing but I was feeling confused that day and I was finding picking an outfit to wear more overwhelming as the minutes went by. So I asked her if she could help me choose something.

'Sure,' she said and sat on my bed while I showed her some of the options I had in mind. As I talked, she picked up each of the garments I had thrown onto the bed and started folding them up and putting them into a neat pile. Once they were all folded, she cleared her throat – I remember it like it was yesterday – and said the next few words in a different voice, lower and deeper.

'Put this one on.'

I hesitated for a second.

'Now,' she said.

I took the top and trousers from her hands and started putting them on. As I did so, I was acutely aware of her eyes on me. It was as if she was trying to look through my skin, to burn a hole through me. I felt elated.

'It looks good on you. Could be an option. Now try this,' she said in the same voice, handing me another top and trousers. I undressed under her gaze and slipped them on.

'Hmm. We can do better. Take it off.'

We kept repeating this, over and over again. Each time she would give me her opinion on the outfit, then order me to take it off and try something else. Throughout this, her eyes were fixed on me. She remained neatly sitting on my bed, her knees touching and the soles of her feet in full contact with the floor. The only movement was in her arms and the occasional tilt of her head. She was concentrated on me and me alone. It was as if we both knew that at some point it had stopped being about choosing an outfit and was now about something else. A game. Bit by bit, we went through every piece of clothing I had in my cupboard, until there was nothing left. We ended up not going to the park that day.

Then, a week later, I started finding the notes in the kitchen listing outfits for the day.

Some included my own clothes, some were a mix of what I had and what she thought would work better. Every time I bought a new piece of clothing, I ended up going for the kind of thing she said she liked on me. Now my clothes are all the ones she thinks suit me better; none of the old stuff is left. I trust her opinion and I know she wants the best for me.

15

The food thing came later. I started doing it like I was doing the clothes thing. It just kind of evolved that way.

Clara also helped me get rid of all the unnecessary clothes I had when I was living alone. It doesn't take me long to find the clothes in my room now as there aren't many left. Just enough to cover the week without having to wash stuff every day. Saves me getting confused and gives me more time to make us both breakfast before I head off.

Everything hangs on a metal rail, the browns with the beiges, and the blacks and greys together. My shoes – a pair of trainers and some leather sandals – are by the door. I choose my own underwear – white and white, although it's more grey than white now after too many washes – then take the brown trousers and the black top and slide them on.

Once outside, I notice how close the weather is today. As I walk past the green, I see that birds are flying low: rain must be on its way. I feel my hands become sticky with humidity. I like it when my body is affected by the changes in the weather. Like the way it can fluff up the top of my hair, or make my legs feel heavier, my mood lower. It reminds me that I am an animal, too.

A flock of geese cross the sky in the distance and my head feels instantly clearer.

Animals always help.

When I moved to London from Rome, my head was still full of chaos and I found it hard to sleep at night. But one day, as I was walking down the road near my old flat in Whitechapel, I came across Stepney City Farm. As I stepped through the gates, I saw a sign pointing to the pig enclosure almost straight away. My heart started racing as I got closer.

Two Berkshires with the most beautiful white and black patches stared up at me and I felt as though a fog had lifted. I breathed in their scent deeply, hungrily. I stood there with my hands on the wooden edge of the pigpen for over an hour. Talking to them, grunting, looking for signs that they were being kept in the correct way. After a while, the pig keeper came up to me and started asking questions. At first, he was curt and serious, but as we chatted, his features softened and he introduced himself as Homer. I shook his hand, and we talked about pigs until he told me that he had to lock up as it was getting dark. I slept like a baby that night. After that encounter, I went to Stepney City Farm every weekend for over a year to look at the pigs and speak to Homer. I haven't been back since moving in with Clara, but the geese, swans and ducks that live around here by the river help me miss those visits a bit less.

As I get closer to the shop, I see that the door has been wedged open. Lauren must be in town. She's the owner of MacGregor's Bookshop; she lives in Scotland and comes down to London occasionally to check on stock, or new releases. She might also make an appearance for special events like book launches and World Book Day, or for 'The Ruby in the Smoke', the author readings series she holds here every few months.

She's American but met her Scottish husband Clyde on a Philip Pullman-themed cruise. They're both big fans of the *His Dark Materials* trilogy. She loves those books as much as she hates rooms being 'stuffy'. She can't resist opening all doors and windows whenever she goes into a place. There's only a small window in the shop's bathroom, so when she visits, she leaves the front door wide open even if it's raining or snowing outside. Ollie and I always bring in a scarf or blanket to wrap ourselves in when we know Lauren is down from Aberdeen. But we didn't get a warning this time: it must have been a last-minute decision.

'*Ciao!* Just the person I was looking for,' she says. She's on her knees looking through the drawers under the counter.

'Hi, Lauren. How are you?'

'You wouldn't happen to know where the labelling gun is? Ollie says you used it last.'

I can see the strip of paper labels sticking out from the top of the maps and travel guides section. I walk over, retrieve the gun with its dangling tongue and hand it to her.

'Amazing. Thanks, sweetie.'

'How's Clyde?'

'He's well ... Annoying. Scottish. Sends his love.' She smiles and winks at me.

'Has he been back to the Turriff Show?'

'I'm not sure about that, darling. I'll ask him when I get back, okay?'

Now she's looking at the computer screen, her fingers gripping at the mirrored surface of the mouse.

I join Ollie in the back of the shop and help him open boxes and restock the shelves. A group of teachers came around yesterday and took large quantities of children's books for their refurbished school library. I hid from the loudness of their voices in the back room while Ollie dealt with them, so it's only fair that I help him out today. By the time we're done, a couple of hours later, blades of sun are slicing through the gaps in the window display.

The storm must have moved on. I wonder if Clara is up yet. She likes the sun.

I heard her until late last night, moving from room to room. She was talking on the phone in Italian for ages. I could only hear a few words of what she was saying – something about money and promises – but I could tell that her voice was terse and that she was first angry, then sad. The sounds of loud whispers and of her slippers dragging across the wooden floor have become so familiar to me that they have blended into all the other noises the house makes at night.

Only a few months ago, she would have been up early, showered and dressed, and we'd have had breakfast together. Now her bedroom door is closed most mornings and the house is quiet.

I run out for lunch to get myself a Diet Coke and a sandwich. They don't have Coke in the places nearest to the bookshop, so I go to the high street and find a shop that sells it. It's best if I do what the notes tell me. Clara has a way of sensing when I've done something she doesn't want me to do. I can't risk upsetting her again. And I find that having to make too many choices confuses me. This way she takes some of them away from me; it's useful.

Ollie seems in a good mood after lunch. He's got plans for the evening again with Rafael and is whistling a tune under his breath as he tidies up the card racks. I join him and we read the cards aloud to each other in funny voices.

He turns to me and says in the deepest tone he can muster, 'With warmest thoughts on your special day, Vale.' Then he takes a deep bow that ends with a hand wave.

When I first saw him do that, I couldn't understand what he was doing. Then he explained that he liked to impersonate the kind of people who would give those cards. He thinks Lauren picks silly cards.

It's my turn to do the same, so I take another one, one with flowers and puppies, and put on a squeaky voice.

'To my wonderful wife, with love on our anniversary,' I read.

Ollie laughs and swats my arm. 'Oh, darling husband, you're such a charmer,' he says.

Lauren watches us from behind her horn-rimmed glasses and occasionally smiles.

She has teased her blonde hair high on top of her head and tied it into a tight knot. I really want to put my finger through it to feel its consistency. I imagine it to be tense but soft to the touch, like a Chinese steamed bun. But I know it's not an acceptable thing to do to someone.

Today she's preparing for a group of reps to come around and present the year's book releases. They usually come in small groups and bring in a box of samples of what's coming up in the next few months. Lauren goes through them and decides if they're what our customers will like and how well they're going to sell.

'Right,' she says, walking over to where Ollie and I are standing,

'I've got the first group coming in soon and I'm going to close the shop for the day. I want to have time and space to deal with everyone without worrying about customers getting in the way. You can leave early.'

Ollie and I look at each other. This hasn't happened in ages. It's more usual for Lauren to ask us to stay later and help her tidy up after a group has been rather than leave her to it. But we know better than to question her decisions.

Ollie asks quietly, 'Are you sure?' but he's already on his way to the kitchen to get his stuff.

'Yup. Go, have fun. Sun's out. I'll be okay.'

He comes out with his jacket draped over his arm. I get mine and we're out in the sunshine before she's had time to change her mind.

'Now what?' I look at my watch. It's still only 4 p.m.

'Now, *my beloved husband*, we go to the pub,' Ollie says, looking straight ahead and steering me down Church Street and towards the riverside. There are a couple of pubs nearer to the shop, but when the sun is shining, I know he likes to head to the one further down the road, by the water's edge.

The tables overlooking the river are still a bit damp from the earlier rain, but the sun should make the moisture evaporate soon. I run my hand over the wooden surface. Wet wood has a quality to it that makes me want to run my tongue slowly over every vein and groove, tasting it. But there are too many people watching right now, so the feeling of it under my fingertips will have to be enough.

After a few minutes inside the pub, Ollie comes out and walks towards me with a pint of beer in each hand.

'Just spoken to Rafael, he's on his way. You want to sit there?' He points at the table I've just been touching.

'Yes.' We sit in silence and look at two swans drifting with the current towards the shores of Eel Pie Island.

'Why don't you ask your flatmate to join us too? She's not working at the moment, is she?'

'Who?'

'Your flatmate. She's called Clara, right?'

I think quickly. There is no way I can ask Clara to come along. She cannot know that I'm out, let alone join us.

'Yes. No. She's got a new job.'

I feel a bead of sweat forming on my temple. I wipe it with the edge of my sleeve.

Ollie turns away from the swans and looks at me.

'Are you two close?'

'Close? Yes, a bit. I mean, we chat. But not, like, super close.'

'You've lived together for what, three years now?'

'Four.'

'Four. And I've only ever seen her once. At the Christmas party. And even then, only for like an hour.'

I shudder, thinking of that time. Clara had insisted on coming to the Christmas party. She said she wanted to meet the people I spent so much time with during the day and that I wouldn't stop banging on about. I was surprised she was interested. I had heard her call them 'geeks' before in the same tone of voice she used for people she didn't like. I told her I didn't think she would want to come, but she said I was being weird about it. I remember being confused. Clara and my bookshop colleagues were my only friends in London; maybe bringing them together was expected of me.

At the party, she had introduced herself to everyone, and had been chatting to Lauren, Clyde and Hermina – a Dutch student with a sharp fringe and spike earrings who worked with us occasionally – for most of the evening. After a few drinks, though, I noticed she had stopped smiling and was walking towards the bar, where I was standing waiting for a round of drinks.

'We need to leave.' She had red circles around her eyes and looked close to tears.

I'd been having a nice time chatting to Ollie about the different nutritional values of corn vs wheat bran vs rice for feeding young pigs

21

and wasn't ready to go home yet. Ollie had disappeared while I was at the bar, so my plan was to go find him and continue our conversation.

'Why?' I asked.

Clara had whispered in Italian that Hermina had been rude to her and that she didn't want to be there a minute longer. She had gripped my hand and we'd left without saying goodbye to anyone. When I asked her to explain in detail what had happened as we walked away from the venue, she told me Hermina had begun asking her questions about her split from Edo, laughing at her Italian accent, telling her not to drink quite so fast.

Clara had been furious. She'd been nothing but nice to her, she told me, and this horrible woman had taken advantage of her kind nature. I knew Hermina to be a little blunt, but she had never been unkind to me. We got on quite well, actually, as we both enjoyed spotting and naming different species of birds from the shop window when we worked the same shift. But being rude and mean to my friend wasn't right. Poor Clara hadn't done anything to receive this kind of treatment. I never had the chance to ask Hermina about it, though, as she went back to Holland early in the new year.

After that night, Clara had made it clear that my being out with work people meant that I preferred them to her and that she found that painful after all she'd done for me over the years. I felt so guilty hearing her say that, and I still do.

Now, Ollie shrugs his shoulders and points at some ducks jumping from the bank into the water.

We both hear his name being called and turn around to see Rafael carrying a pint.

'Skiving off, are we?' he says as he lowers himself into the chair next to me.

'Hardly. Lauren's in town.' Ollie lifts his pint in Rafael's direction, and they clink glasses. 'Cheers.'

They turn to me, and I do the same.

'Cheers.'

Rafael works in advertising. Most of his clients are abroad, so he often has the afternoon free, then works late into the evening.

'What's new, Vale? How are the pigs?'

He always asks me about the pigs. I don't know which pigs he's referring to – I don't own any myself – but I always say, 'Well, thank you,' because it's polite and because I hope all pigs are well.

'I think it's cool that you know so much about them.' He slumps deeper into the chair. 'I wish I had a strong passion like that.'

Rafael likes poetry and horse racing, but he's not *passionate* about them. Wouldn't be able to talk about them as much as I do about pigs, he tells me.

Ollie nods and says, 'Yeah, it's cool.' Which he's never said before.

They start discussing their night out while I sip my beer. They're getting the train into town in a couple of hours and are planning to see a photography exhibition on the South Bank, then maybe the cinema or on to a nearby club. It sounds fun. While they chat, I go into the pub to get us all another round. When I get back to our table, I can see the two of them looking at me and smiling. I don't understand what's going on, which makes me nervous. I put the pints down and settle back into my seat.

'The largest ever litter of piglets was in Yorkshire in the 1990s,' I blurt out. 'Thirty-seven of them. To a sow called "Sow 570". Isn't it sad that she didn't even have a proper name? Just a number.' Words are coming out faster than I want them to.

'That's nice. But we want to know about your love life,' Rafael says, then wipes the foam off his top lip with the back of his hand. Ollie punches him lightly on the arm and mouths, *Stop it*, but he is still smiling.

'Have you ever had a boyfriend?' Rafael asks me.

'Of course,' I say, concentrating on the colour of the liquid inside my glass. On the bubbles and the foam on top. It's not the first time I've been asked this. When it happens, I try to get away with not answering. If they push further, I always say the same thing. I tell

23

them it was in Italy before I moved to the UK. A friend of a friend. I don't like not telling the truth, but I've learned that sometimes a small lie can help me get out of situations I find uncomfortable. I've also learned that telling people the truth – 'no, I've never had a relationship' – makes things much, much worse. I shrug my shoulders.

'Let her be,' says Ollie.

Rafael puts his hands up. 'Okay, okay.'

He flicks his hair back and starts talking about something he saw on his way here. Ollie and I listen to his stories, nodding and sometimes laughing.

I am calm again. The beer has loosened my muscles, the fresh air on my skin feels good and the conversation flows without anyone asking me any more uncomfortable questions. It feels normal.

I feel normal.

After a while, I become aware that the sun is lower, the shadows longer. I check my watch. 18.15.

'I have to go.'

I start gathering my things. The two of them stare at me, then exchange a look.

'We were going to ask you to come out with us. Are you sure you have to go?' Ollie asks. 'Why don't you stay with us this once?'

'Yeah, Vale, you're always running off. Stick around, it'll be fun,' Rafael interjects.

'I really have to go. I'm sorry.' I need to start walking now or there's no way I'll be back home at the usual time.

'Fine. But come with us next time we're out in town.' Rafael says, then tips the last of his pint down his throat. I'm aware of the red flush that must be creeping up my face as I get up and put my backpack on. I try to act as casually as possible.

'Will do. See you tomorrow!'

They both wave back. I don't want them to see how happy this invitation has made me. But the prospect of an evening out in central London with them, strolling down the South Bank, looking at exhibitions, is so enticing I feel like bursting. As I walk back along the path to the main road, my legs are light and my thoughts swim around in my head in a way that is not unpleasant. I'm trying to walk as fast as I can, but I have to concentrate to keep my feet going in the same direction. I trip lightly over a cobblestone but manage to stay upright.

I will tell Clara about having a few drinks during work time when I get back. I will explain that yes, Ollie works with me at MacGregor's and was at the Christmas party that time, but he's nothing like Hermina. He would never have been rude. He was even asking after her! The two of them could be friends. He reminds me of one of the boys from our school back in Italy – Salvo, same gangly limbs, and dark, straight hair. Clara liked Salvo.

Yes. I will ask her if she doesn't mind me going out one day soon with the two of them. I will make sure there's a meal ready for her to heat in the evening while I'm out, and we can still do her bath when I get back. She wants what's best for me – she always says so – and this feels like a good thing for me. Friends. Beers by the river.

All of a sudden, I feel like the future ahead is a little brighter. If Clara sees that nothing bad happens on that one night out, it could even be the first of many more. This could be it. The other side.

As I walk towards the house, I see that the lights in the living room are on. The blurred shape of Clara's silhouette is projected against the curtains. She's standing with her face close to the window. I'm excited as I open the front door.

Chapter Three

I stand in the hallway for a second and take a deep breath. I focus on a small brown spot in the carpet and stay like that for a few seconds, then step into the living room. Clara turns around to look at me.

'You're back, I didn't hear you,' she says, rubbing her eyes.

'Sorry. Did you have a good day?' I begin to tidy up the magazines, cushions and empty cups strewn across the room.

'Not really, my back's been hurting.' She sits on the armchair and goes back to looking out of the window. 'There's a new postman. No idea what's happened to Andy.'

'Maybe he's on holiday?'

'I don't think so. He usually says before he goes.'

'Is the new one nice? What do you fancy for dinner?' I ask as I walk towards the kitchen.

'I don't know, I didn't open when he knocked. Pasta would be nice,' I hear her say, just before I turn the tap on to fill the pan.

I can see from the state of the house that Clara has spent another day on the sofa. Her breakfast bowl is still out on the coffee table with lichen-like grey crusts where the porridge has hardened. Her hair is tied back, but long strands have escaped where her head has been resting on the cushions. The air smells faintly like broth and sweat. My phone buzzes inside my pocket. I take it out and see that it's a missed call and a message from my mother.

How are you?? I haven't heard from you in a month. Is everything okay?? We just want to know how you are. Lots of news from home. Call when you can.

I put the phone back in my pocket and head upstairs to start running the bath. As I wait for the tub to fill up, I try to gather the courage to tell Clara about my afternoon by the river with Ollie and Rafael.

Downstairs, I couldn't see any of the signs on her face that I've learned to recognise as potential trouble, like if her eyebrows are furrowed a lot, or if she chews her bottom lip when she listens. Apart from her being a bit sleepy, she seems to be in a good enough mood this evening.

I call out for her once the tub is filled and rub the edge of the bathmat with my feet as I listen to her walk up the stairs. She stands in the middle of the bathroom and rubs her face with both hands.

'Can you? I'm so tired.'

She lifts her arms up. I walk over and take off her sweatshirt and bra, then pull down her tracksuit bottoms and pants. She shivers slightly even though the room is warm. I watch her get into the water and sit down, her knees hugged tight into her chest. I sit on the edge of the bath and start massaging the skin on her back where her bra has left deep red marks. I press down into her muscles with my knuckles, trying to relieve some of the pain. I continue like this until I've covered her whole back.

'That was nice,' she whispers. 'How was your day?'

I look at the back of her head.

'Good. It was different today,' I blurt out.

'Different how?' she asks, turning around to look at me.

I'm about to tell her, but I just freeze. There's something about the tone of her voice that stops the words from leaving my mouth. I cough and turn to get the sponge.

'Oh, nothing much, just Ollie messing up the orders. We had to send a load of stock back to the publishers.'

'Silly,' she says, turning back around.

I breathe again. I want to tell her, but I'm too scared. I wash her body gently as she stares ahead. When I finish, she gets up and smiles, before wrapping herself up in a robe.

'I'll see you downstairs. Can you make dinner soon? I want to eat early,' she says, then closes the door behind her. I answer yes to the closed door.

Over dinner, Clara tells me a story about when her and Edo, her ex-husband, went on holiday to Malaga and found a tiny place selling tapas in a square away from all the tourists.

She laughs as she remembers how the owner of the place couldn't take his eyes off her and kept getting the order wrong, and Edo told her to stop flirting with him then stormed off when she wouldn't. But once he'd come back, a pigeon had shat on his shoulder and they'd ended up laughing so hard they nearly fell off their chairs. I love hearing stories of Clara having fun.

It doesn't matter who she's with in those stories. In my mind it's always me there with her. Clara and Edo travelled across Spain on their honeymoon. They were young, so couldn't afford to go very far, but they explored as much of the country as their budget allowed.

Clara has endless stories about that trip, and a stash of photographs that she took down a while ago and now keeps in a box at the back of her cupboard.

Now, she opens a bottle of wine and pours us both a glass.

I ask her more questions about the trip and she's happy to answer, giving me as many details as she remembers. Seeing her face lit up and serene gives me a sudden burst of courage. I feel close to her, and I can see she's relaxed and happy to chat. I decide to try telling her what I've been holding on to all evening,

I tip the last few drops of wine into my mouth and say, 'Something happened today.'

'It did?'

I nod. 'Lauren told us to leave early, so Ollie, Rafael and I went to the river for a pint. It's really nice there; we should go together.'

Clara looks at me and tilts her head to one side. 'It's nice, is it?' she asks.

The wine is warming up my stomach and I feel happy. I nod, smiling. 'Right on the river, and there's ducks and swans swimming by your feet.'

'And what were they saying?'

'Who?'

'Ollie and Rafael. I'm not asking about the ducks and swans, am I?'

I go to pour us more wine, but she blocks the top of her glass with the palm of her hand.

'Not much. They were going out tonight so were talking about that mostly. They asked me if I wanted to go along too. I said no, obviously – I wanted to speak to you first – but I thought maybe another time I could join them?'

Words are coming out of my mouth much faster than I'd like. I can't bear to meet her eyes right now, so I stare down at the table surface and start scratching at a raised knot in the wood.

'What did you tell them?' Her voice is monotone, and each word is coming out like it has a full stop at the end of it.

I concentrate harder on the wood knot.

'I said maybe.' It comes out no louder than a whisper.

She slams both hands onto the table. I jump and instinctively move further away from her. I grip the sides of my chair. I shouldn't have said anything. The warmth in my stomach has gone now and my mouth tastes bitter.

'After what they've done to me?' Her face is red, and her eyes are wide open, fixed on mine. 'You must really hate me,' she says, shaking her head.

'Clara, no! Of course I don't hate you. It wasn't them who—'

'I took you in when you had nowhere to live. What was your life before me? Nothing.'

Her head is turned away now, as if she just can't bear to look at me. I feel panic rising in my chest.

'You did. I know you did. I'm sorry.' The biggest clump has formed at the pit of my stomach. My breaths are coming fast and shallow.

'So while I'm stuck here at home, in pain, you go out with people who have treated me badly. Without a thought in your head for me.' She's still not looking at me. 'And on top of it all, you tell them you'll do it again!'

'I only said maybe,' I whisper.

She turns her head to look at me and shakes it once more. Then pushes her chair back and stomps up the stairs. I hear the door to her bedroom slam and let my head fall into my hands.

She is right. I shouldn't have gone out with Ollie and Rafael. It was selfish of me, knowing how upset Clara had been at the party after what Hermina had said to her. I know Ollie and Rafael aren't the ones directly responsible, but Clara doesn't see it that way. I should have respected that. She is my only true friend, and I can't lose her. I make a cup of tea the way she likes it and bring it up to her room.

And then I beg her. I beg her to forgive me. I tell her how stupid I now realise I have been and that it will never happen again. Ollie and Rafael are not my real friends, I cry, she is.

And I will do everything I can to make sure she isn't upset with me ever again. As I speak, tears roll down my cheeks.

She stares at me and listens. Her face is blank once again and I have no idea what she's thinking. Once I'm finished talking, she says, 'I'll think about it. Now go to sleep.'

She picks up her book and starts reading. I close the door behind me, careful not to disturb her, and go to my own room.

I can't sleep during the night and stay up watching the ceiling, hoping for my clenched muscles to loosen, but they never do.

Over the weekend, when Lauren's nieces help out at the bookshop, I do everything I can to get back into Clara's good books. I bring her breakfast in bed and bake her lingue di gatto biscuits dipped in chocolate. I massage her back and keep the radio tuned to her favourite music station, playing nineties dance hits all day long. She doesn't say much at first, but by the end of Saturday, she seems happier and more relaxed.

When she goes to her room to sleep, I lie on my bed and try to get some rest. My heart is still hammering against my chest from the fear of what I could have lost. I pick up my book and try to breathe deeply as I immerse myself in learning how building a pigpen on poor quality farmland can benefit the terrain. As I read, page after page, I can feel my heart slowing down to a more normal pace, and my muscles finally relax.

On Sunday, we go for a walk around the park and feed the ducks. I cook Clara a lasagne, and we spend the afternoon reading on the sofa. I catch her looking at me from time to time. She is quiet, so I can't tell if she's still angry at me.

Chapter Four

On Monday morning, everything is silent when I wake up. I walk down the stairs and find the notes on the kitchen table. I'm relieved that she still cares enough to leave them.

Blue cotton top, grey jeans, sandals (no socks).

Bottle of water (fizzy or not), salad with chicken or tuna.

I find the clothes and get dressed quickly. It feels good to leave the emotions of the weekend behind, but as I walk towards the bookshop, I realise I still feel nervous. I really don't want to get into trouble with Clara any more. I need to be as good a friend to her as she is to me, and if me going out with Ollie and Rafael upsets her, then it simply can't happen again. I take my phone out to check the time and see three missed calls from my mother. Two from yesterday and one from half an hour ago. She will start worrying if I leave it any longer, so I call her back.

'Valentina. Finally. Is everything okay?'

'Yes, all good. I'm sorry. It's been a busy weekend.'

'You're always busy. I hope you're getting some rest and making time to have some fun. How's work going? There's that author who's just come out with her new book. What's her name? She's great. Do you sell her? I bet it's flying off the shelves.'

'I don't know, Mum. Work is good, ticking over.'

'That one. The Irish one. You know? She's always writing about families. So funny. I've got one of hers somewhere.'

'Sorry, Mum, I'm not sure. Marian Keyes?' I say.

'That's it. So funny. Anyways, Dad says hello. His hip is sore today, so I told him to take it easy. He went up a ladder yesterday. I had to shout to get him down. He thinks he can still do everything he used to, but he needs to realise it's time to take better care of himself. And you, too. You always seem so busy whenever I speak to you. Are you sure you're okay?'

'I am, Mum. Promise.'

'Okay, okay. And how is Clara? Has she been able to find a job? I saw Antonio and Marilena the other day and they told me they haven't heard from her in months. Tell her to ring them, will you? They seemed so worried,' she says.

'I will. Sorry, Mum, I need to go now.'

I won't tell Clara to ring her parents. That would put her in a mood so bad it would take me longer than a weekend to fix it. I tell my mother I will call her again soon and hang up.

The bookshop is cool and quiet. Ollie must have just opened the door, as the smell of paper and glue in the air is still strong. It usually gets fainter as the day goes on, but it's so intense it's tickling my nostrils right now. I put the kettle on and start firing up the ancient till.

Ollie walks towards me with a pile of books balanced, palm up, in one hand.

'Hey, Vale. How's things?' he asks, trying to keep the pile from slipping to the floor as he moves his hand up and down.

'I'm okay, thanks,' I answer, not looking up from the till.

'Cool cool. Nice weekend?'

'I was reading about the benefits of keeping pigs in weedy terrain as they can help keep the soil clean and fertilised.' I keep my gaze on the till. I can't look him in the eye, or he might ask me to do the shelf-stacking together as we usually do. And that might lead to more invitations and more trouble. I can't risk that today.

'Right. Sounds fun.'

'It is. I also found out that in Denmark there are twice as many pigs as people.' I walk to the kitchen and start making myself a cup of tea. He watches me take just one mug out of the cupboard and one tea bag out of the glass jar on the counter. He says nothing, but I can see his brow furrow.

'Big on the pig talk today, eh?' he asks, but I can tell it's one of those questions that don't need an answer, so I don't say anything.

I hear him play with the pile of books for a bit longer while I stay in the kitchen. Then he walks away to start stacking while I keep busy at the front of the shop.

The few times he speaks to me, I answer by telling him pig facts. I know he doesn't tend to stick around very long when I do that, so we manage to avoid each other for most of the day. At closing time, he leaves without saying goodbye and I lock up on my own. I feel relieved.

Back home, I find Clara lying down on the sofa. As I take off my coat and ask her questions about her day, she responds with a moan, her hands clutched to her stomach.

'Are you okay?' I ask her.

'I have a terrible stomach ache. All day I've been on the edge of throwing up.'

'Oh no, poor you. What can it be?' I ask, crouching down next to her.

'It's so painful,' she says, closing her eyes as her breath catches. 'I can't have a bath tonight. I'll just eat something light and go to sleep early.'

'Of course. I'll cook you something now.'

I don't want her to see my face and realise how disappointed I am to be missing the bath, so I quickly get up and head to the kitchen to start cooking.

I'm worried about her. Her aches are getting worse and every day there seems to be another part of her body hurting. I couldn't bear it if she was seriously sick, but she refuses to go to the doctor no matter how much I beg her to get herself checked. She says she doesn't trust them.

That evening, as she gets ready for bed, she asks me to help her undress. I peel the layers of clothing away from her warm skin carefully, as though she is a caterpillar shedding its exoskeleton, revealing the vulnerable body underneath.

Just as I'm about to turn the lights off, she whispers something I can't quite hear. I ask her to repeat it and get in closer to hear. She grabs my hand and squeezes it tightly. I can feel the small bones shift painfully under her grip.

'Please can you watch over me tonight? I'm worried I might be sick in my sleep and choke on my vomit and die,' she says, a little louder this time.

'Choke on it?' I ask.

'Yes, it can happen. Please, Vale,' she asks, as tears well up in her eyes.

'Of course,' I tell her.

I turn the lights off and sit in the chair by her bed, watching her sleep soundly through the night. The sound of her light snoring in the quietest hours seems to reverberate against the walls. I'm too worried about her to get any sleep myself, so I sit there watching her chest rise and fall until the sun comes up. She didn't leave a note for me the night before, so I wear what was written on yesterday's one.

I gently wake her up before I leave for work and ask how she's feeling.

'Great. Hungry,' she answers, then stretches her arms, yawning loudly. Although I'm exhausted after a night of no sleep, I'm relieved she's back to health so quickly. I get ready for work and leave the table set up for her breakfast. As I close the door behind me, I hear the TV in the living room come on and a breakfast bowl being filled with cereal. Leaving her alone worries me after she was unwell yesterday. But I have no choice, I must go to work and earn our money. And still feeling bad for letting her down, I just hope that we can put it behind us for good. I feel a shiver of fear run down my spine at the thought that we might not be okay.

Chapter Five

The lunch place near the bookshop has run out of jacket potatoes, so I walk to the high street to see if one of the bigger chain places still has them. The streets are busy, and I feel a bit overwhelmed by all the people rushing past me, so as soon as I manage to find a potato and some fizzy water, I head for the river to eat my lunch near the path. All the benches are busy with people chatting, making calls and eating, but as I get closer, I see a couple stand up and I manage to sit in their place. I turn and am about to murmur a 'thank you' their way when something about the profile of the man stops me in my tracks.

Could it be?

I stare at him as hard as I can, trying to catch a glimpse of his face, but he is looking straight ahead. Then the woman he's with says something, he turns to listen, and I see his face. It's not him. I breathe a sigh of relief.

Edo.

The man's hair and build are the same, but his features are different. Edo's nose is stronger, wider, his eyes darker. This guy's step is faster and his back not as straight. And Edo is in Rome now, there's no reason he would be hanging around here any more. I haven't seen him in years, but it's hard not to think about him when I'm home with Clara. His presence is everywhere in the house, even now that the photographs of the two of them together have come down.

When I saw him again after many years, when he and Clara moved here from Rome, I remember thinking that he looked the same as he did when we were young. The sharp suit and tie fitted him better than the baggy trousers and tight T-shirts of his youth, and the musky cologne he wore showed a belief in his own presence that he didn't have when we were kids.

But his face hadn't changed at all, and he still pushed his mop of wavy brown hair to one side every few minutes like he did back then. I remember my mother telling me that he had been a very shy kid growing up, so *his* mother – one of her best friends – had enrolled him in every possible sports team to get him out of his shell. As a result, he'd grown more confident, and his circle of friends had got wider. And the girls at school had started to notice him.

Especially Clara, of course.

Because boys like him didn't speak much to girls like me, beyond the few social occasions our mothers had organised, I didn't know him well at all. It was only when I ended up living with him and Clara in London that that changed.

I had been renting a flat on Whitechapel Road for a few years, but when my landlord gave me notice because he had decided to sell it, I was left looking for somewhere in a hurry. When I mentioned it to Clara over coffee, she kindly offered me their spare room. I hadn't really wanted to live with the two of them – our shared past was still too painful, and I didn't want to reopen old wounds – but I was desperate. And seeing Clara after all that time – her enthusiasm at this new adventure, the way she smiled when she talked about our teenage friendship – had made me feel like we could maybe go back to the way we were.

So, I moved in. And for the first few months it was good. The two of them would often have people over for dinner – Edo's friends from work and their wives mostly, but also some of Clara's old classmates from her master's at LSE. Edo would often travel for work, and on the days he was away, Clara and I would spend the evenings eating snacks, video-calling him and watching films. When he was home, we would eat Edo's cooking at the dinner table and he would tell us about his travels. Clara would mostly be quiet during those dinners, so he would talk to me, and I lapped the stories up. I haven't travelled apart from moving to London from Rome, and hearing of all the places he'd been and the strange characters he'd met made me almost feel like I was there too.

Now, I finish my potato and drink the last few drops of fizzy water, then get up. My lunch break is nearly over, and I don't like being late. I spend most of my lunchtimes eating whatever food Clara tells me to and either walking up and down the river path or sitting on these benches and looking at the ducks. Being near nature helps me to relax if I've had to speak to too many people at work or if Clara is in a bad mood at home. I watch the ducks paddle around the water looking for worms and bugs on the riverbank, and my head gets instantly quieter.

The afternoon is slow at the bookshop; it's the school holidays, so many families are away, and it tends to be a bit quieter around here. I don't mind it. Ollie and I have split the tasks today and have been working in different parts of the shop. I keep an eye on the clock from time to time, but it seems to move slower than usual. The front door opens, breaking the silence, and I let the customer who has just walked in know that I'm available if he needs any help, like Lauren has taught me. His curly hair reminds me of mine, but greyer. It's wild and unkempt, but his clothes are sharp and his shoes shiny.

He comes closer and asks me for a copy of *The New Farmer*. I sigh and point him to the nature section.

'Not a fan?' he asks,

'Of the subject – yes. Of the book – no,' I answer.

He stares at my face, clearly waiting for me to tell him why I don't like the book.

New Agriculture is a trend that has caught on in the last year, and since then I've heard and read plenty about the many young people who have quit their media jobs to move to the countryside and follow the life their forefathers would have had, raising livestock and tending to the fields. Except too many of them don't do enough research and base their efforts on books that are 99 per cent fluff and 1 per cent useful advice. They end up making many easily avoidable mistakes.

Out of all the New Agriculture books, *The New Farmer* is the most popular and, in my opinion, the worst. Lauren has told Ollie and me to always keep a positive attitude when speaking to customers, but she also encourages us to share our opinions on books we have read, when prompted. I think for a second whether this situation falls on the 'negative attitude' side or the 'giving opinion when prompted' side. I decide it is the latter, but to proceed with caution.

'I don't have an opinion on the people following the trend,' I say, holding my hands up, 'more on the "experts" putting themselves forward to teach them how to do it.'

The man opens his mouth to say something, then changes his mind and just nods.

'It's overly simplified and unnecessarily romantic about the way of life of the farmer,' I continue. 'It puts farming on a pedestal without ever giving practical advice that's worth its salt. It's a book made for quoting on the internet and nothing else.'

The man laughs. 'Okay,' he says, 'which one do you recommend instead?'

'It depends on what you're looking for,' I reply, ignoring Ollie, who is pulling a silly face behind the customer's back. 'If it's a more generic overview of new farming techniques to ease yourself in, then *The Future of Ploughing* is a good one to get you started. If you want to focus more on the livestock side of things, then *From Alpaca to Zebu: How to Raise Livestock Ethically* is more in that direction. It's not the best, but it's the only one we have on the subject.'

'So it's not that good?' he asks, tilting his head to one side.

Usually when I get into any conversation about farming – whether old or new – the customers' eyes tend to glaze over and they quickly make their excuses to go and browse. This guy is still here and asking questions, which is unusual.

'Not really. The pig section, for example, is completely useless,' I answer, feeling my feet tingle with excitement at being asked my opinion on the subject I know the most about.

'How come?' he asks.

I've learned over time that people don't seem to want to know about pigs in the same level of detail that I enjoy. But he's now leaning comfortably on the back of an armchair, his eyes fixed on mine.

So I keep talking.

'Well,' I say, 'I think the author has done a sloppy job at bringing together some of the latest studies on pigs without doing a proper comparison with the older studies, as well as not bringing in the on-field research with the farmers themselves who have been doing the actual work for centuries.' I can feel my heart rate increase with every word. 'Only including newer studies leaves out an enormous amount of information that, although not as appealing to new sensitivities as the more recent stuff might be, means you're missing a massive part of the bigger picture.' I realise I've been holding on to my breath so I say the last few words as quickly as I can. 'Because of this, his advice and conclusions are not only unhelpful but incorrect.'

I breathe in deeply and realise both the customer and Ollie are still looking at me. I lower my eyes and start rearranging a pile of books that has been left to one side. My cheeks feel warm; I imagine they must be red too. I've spoken too much about pigs again and made a fool of myself.

But the customer nods, then asks to see the two books I mentioned. I hand them to him, and he flips the pages from cover to cover a couple of times.

'Thanks, I'll get these, please,' he says.

I ring them up and put them in a bag for him, still thrilled from our conversation.

After he leaves, Ollie walks up to the till and asks, 'What was that about?'

41

'Pigs, mostly. Wanted to buy *The New Farmer* but I told him to get something else instead,' I reply.

Ollie rolls his eyes and strolls away.

I look at the clock and see that closing time is getting near, so I start locking up. The warmth still in my belly keeps me company on the walk back home, all the way until I see our front door.

Chapter Six

Saturdays used to be my favourite day to spend with Clara. When Edo was still around, most Saturdays the three of us would pile into their car and go explore villages and farmers' markets on the outskirts of London. I would spot the local farmers and chat with them while Edo and Clara walked arm in arm around the stalls, choosing vegetables and pastries to bring home for our meals.

On the way back, Edo would plug his phone into the car's speaker system and play Italian songs from our teenage years at ear-splitting volume. He and I would sing as loudly as our voices allowed. Clara would sometimes join in, but mostly she would look out of the window smiling and nodding her head. Then, back home, I would assist her in cooking elaborate dishes while Edo watched Italian league football on TV.

When dinner was ready, we would crack open a bottle of wine and the two of them would reminisce about past trips, parties and nights out.

'Lorenzo got so drunk at that party he fell asleep in the bush outside the French embassy and the guards found him the next day and kicked him out.'

They laughed until their breath came out in bursts.

'And then Anto couldn't remember the address of his hotel and did laps around the town centre in his suit in the rain until an old lady helped him find his way.'

More laughs.

Listening to them, I could almost feel like I'd been there too.

If Edo was away on a work trip, Clara and I would go for long walks. She would loop her arm into mine and we'd go look for a new café she'd heard about, or a shop selling a shade of lipstick she'd seen in a magazine. Being close to her would make me feel like we were teenagers back in Rome again, with the mix of giddiness and trepidation that my happy times with her always brought.

One day, something shifted between Edo and Clara. Or maybe it had started shifting before but I only just noticed it then. We were having dinner, the three of us, as usual. Edo was talking about his day at work and retelling a funny thing that had happened to Kirsten, one of his colleagues. She was about to step into an important client meeting with Edo and a few senior partners and had noticed something on their boss's pristine white shirt. She'd reached out to get it off and had quickly discovered that, rather than some flyaway fluff, she had just grabbed hold of a tuft of his chest hair that had made its way out between two buttons and was still very much attached to his skin.

I burst into laughter at this and so did Edo. But a few moments later I noticed that Clara's facial expression had changed. Where she had been laughing before, she was deadly serious now. Her arms were crossed over her chest and her eyebrows raised. Edo must have noticed too, because he stopped for a second, stared at her, then shrugged and went back to talking.

After a while, Clara seemed to relax and joined the conversation again, telling us about a deli she'd discovered near work that sold the exact brand of almond biscotti she used to devour when she was a child. I was relieved to see her at ease once more and reminiscing. Talking of our shared past in Rome was always a source of fun for the three of us. I brought up the elderly man who used to run the stationery shop near the school, his hair dyed bright red and the dentures that would just not stay in place. Edo laughed and mentioned a couple more funny things that had happened in that shop, like the time he picked up a pencil and the whole display fell to the floor, merchandise scattering absolutely everywhere. He was so embarrassed, he ran out without a second glance. He and I were laughing so hard at that memory that he'd gone red in the face and I was holding on to the edge of the table with both hands. We stopped when we noticed Clara get up and carry her plate to the kitchen. Her face was serious.

'What are you up to?' Edo asked her.

'I thought you and Vale might want some alone time,' she said in a calm voice. 'I wouldn't want to intrude on your fun.' She straightened the flowers in a nearby vase, then turned around and walked up the stairs to their bedroom.

After that day, she started to often leave the table early and go upstairs.

Later, I would hear raised voices from their bedroom when Edo joined her, as I tidied up the kitchen. It was when it started happening every night that things around the house really began to change. I didn't quite understand what was going on, but I could see that something wasn't right. Neither of them would talk to me about it; all I knew was what I could overhear. There were different triggers each time. But even from where I was, behind walls, I could tell that Edo wasn't happy with his life and the way Clara talked to him.

'They're my clients, Clara. It's part of my job to entertain them. It's once a month!' he shouted once, his voice so loud that it felt like he was in my head. I could only just hear Clara's answer. She wasn't matching his tone; hers was so calm it was eerie. I could just about make out her answer. 'Look at you. You've gone all red. Is it really worth getting yourself all worked up over a work dinner? If you really loved me, you wouldn't even care about spending time with them. You'd just run home.' The roar that came out of Edo's mouth then was more animal than human. Like a bear struggling to get out from the teeth of a metal trap. Other times I'd hear her laughing at his anger, calling his frustration 'crazy' and him a 'drama queen'.

45

But I don't think it did much to calm him down. He just retreated into himself.

He stopped telling us his travel stories in the evening and driving us to the countryside at the weekend. He would mostly just sit on the sofa and scroll through his phone when he was home. After a while, it became rare for the two of them to speak directly to each other, and they would often ask me to ask the other one questions instead. Clara also wanted me to report back to her what Edo had said when she was out of the house, which was more and more often. She was working at an interior designer's studio and started staying at work later, missing dinner and coming home long after Edo and I had finished eating. He seemed relaxed when it was just the two of us, chatting or watching TV together, but the moment he'd hear the front door open, his whole body would stiffen, and he would become serious and withdrawn again.

In the mornings, I would often find one of them asleep on the sofa as I was getting ready to go to work and would try to be extra quiet to not wake them up. One Monday morning I found Clara watching TV and eating her breakfast on the sofa at the time she would usually be at work. I asked her whether she wasn't feeling well, but she said no, she was feeling absolutely fine, thank you. When it happened again the next day, and the one after that, I asked her if she was going to go back to work again.

'I've cut the umbilical cord, Vale,' she told me, eyes fixed on the TV. 'Let's just say it wasn't working for either of us.'

'What happened?' I asked.

'A whole load of nothing, that's what happened. Anyways,' she turned the TV off, 'I can do bigger and better things on my own, just you watch.' I wanted to ask more questions, but she walked away saying she was going to have a shower. I got the feeling the matter was closed as far as she was concerned.

Things between Clara and Edo seemed to escalate quickly not long after that. From what I could overhear late at night, Edo didn't want to let the matter of what had happened at the interior design studio stay closed, and they were disagreeing a lot on whether this new phase of Clara's work life was a good or bad thing. I still have no idea why Clara had stopped working there so suddenly, but it sounded like something bad might have happened from the level of Edo's voice when he talked to her about it. I don't think they ever ended up agreeing, as Edo moved out and back to Italy a few weeks later.

Now Saturdays are not so great. Clara has been spending nearly all her time on the sofa, sometimes sleeping on it too. Lately she has been talking about the characters on the shows she watches on TV in the same way she used to tell Edo and me about something funny a colleague had done at work, or if she'd bumped into an old friend on one of their trips back to Italy to visit Edo's family. She uses the same excited tone but quieter voice – as if she's telling a secret – and calls them all by name: 'Gary did this' or 'Then Carole said that ...'

At first I thought she was talking about someone new she'd met, and I would listen aghast to the incredible adventures and tough trials these poor people would find themselves involved in. Then one day, over dinner, she told me about someone called Alyssa who had just discovered that her husband had a secret fruit machine addiction and gambled away all their savings. Now they had to sell their house, even though he still wouldn't admit to having a problem. I felt for this woman – she must have been going through such a tough time – and asked Clara to give her my love when she saw her next. She stayed quiet at that, but I didn't think much of it. Then, later that evening, we settled onto the sofa to watch Clara's favourite show, and the recap of the previous episode showed the exact same story playing out on screen. One by one, I matched the people in her stories to the characters in the shows we watched together. And I got worried.

When I was little, Mum sent me to a doctor who told her that if I kept on spending too much time with the pigs at the farm near our house, I would 'lose touch with reality'. I never understood that. Pigs are real, and, if anything, I was more in touch with reality by being close to them.

But Clara's characters aren't real; she could be the one losing touch with reality.

This morning, I sleep in, and when I get up to collect the sticky note outlining my outfit for the day from the kitchen table, I see that Clara is already lying on the sofa watching one of her shows. On the screen, I can see two heavily made-up women shouting at each other across a table strewn with half-drunk cocktails and tiny bejewelled handbags.

I know that her days have been spent this way for the whole week and at least the one before, while I was at work. The air in the house has been stale and the curtains stay drawn.

Something about this isn't right, and I feel like it's my responsibility as her best friend to help her.

As I make us both a coffee, I remember how much lighter she seemed after we'd come back from a long walk in the park some time ago. Maybe a trip outside to see real people going about their real lives is what she needs. I have to tread lightly, though, to not annoy her with my ideas or suggestions. Her bad moods can appear very suddenly, and I still haven't worked out how to stop her from erupting.

I stroll casually into the lounge and place her cup of coffee on the table in front of her, then walk over to the window and move the curtain aside.

'It's sunny today,' I say, keeping my voice as neutral as possible. 'Looks like it might be quite warm.'

Clara grunts in response, her eyes fixed on the screen.

I walk away from the window and sit down on the armchair.

'A customer told me about a shop that sells those silk scarves you like,' I continue.

There's no need to tell her that it was Ollie who told me about it, not a customer. She would only get irritated if I mentioned him. He went to Brighton with Rafael recently, saw the shop and remembered that I was looking for those scarves last Christmas.

Her eyes flicker in my direction. 'Where is it?' she asks.

'Brighton,' I say, then quickly follow with, 'only a couple of train changes, about an hour and a half in total to get there.'

I take a deep breath and stare at the faces on TV, waiting for her to say something.

After a few minutes of silence, I realise my plan has failed. She clearly has no intention of going out today either.

Still in silence, we watch the credits roll as her show comes to an end. Then Clara picks up the remote, turns the TV off and sits up.

'Is it really sunny outside?' she asks.

I nod.

'I guess Brighton isn't too far to go to find those scarves. They are very nice.'

I nod even harder.

'Check the train times while I get dressed,' she says, walking to her bedroom.

I clench my fists in excitement and smile as I reach for my phone.

It's only once we're finally sitting down in our seats and the train has left the station that Clara seems to relax. Her jaw muscles visibly unclench, and she starts pointing at the scenery as it whizzes by. Crowded places irritate her, and I could see that she was uncomfortable queuing at the ticket gate as we waited to board our train. But her mood seems to have lifted now as she leans into me and asks me questions about the various farm animals our train passes close to. Before we know it, we've arrived at our destination.

Brighton station is loud and busy, but the exit on the side by the last track is a lot quieter – as Ollie told me it would be – and we walk out into the car park. I haven't been to Brighton before, but I've spent hours listening to Ollie's tales of his and Rafael's weekends by the seaside, and I remember a lot of what he said to avoid the bigger crowds. Rafael isn't a lover of them either, apparently.

I get my phone out and find the shop on the map. It's only a ten-minute walk from the station, so Clara and I get a coffee from a kiosk and wander down the hill towards it.

The streets are buzzing with people, and I worry that she might get into a bad mood because of it, but she's still smiling and seems to be enjoying looking at the shop windows.

We stop a few times to get a closer look at various displays, and she takes me into one or two places to browse. Seeing her relaxed and curious after days of dark moods makes me feel ridiculously happy. I am so proud that my idea this morning has worked. We walk past a small café with a handful of tables outside and a long list of delicious-sounding dishes scribbled on a blackboard balanced against the window. Feeling emboldened by her smiles, I ask her if she fancies getting some lunch here after we've been to the shop.

She remains silent for a moment as she reads a poster on the wall, then shrugs her shoulders and says, 'Okay.'

I can't stop a massive grin from stretching across my face. She sees it and laughs.

The shop is tucked away on a side street that peels off from one of the main shopping alleys, only a few metres from the seafront. We walk in and see right away a large display of colourful silk scarves looped through large wooden rings suspended from the low ceiling.

Clara makes a beeline for them and pulls a couple off the rings to try them on.

I walk around exploring the rest of the shop until she calls me over to help her decide on which one to buy. She likes them both, so I buy her one and she gets the other. As we head to the restaurant, I help her knot the more colourful of the two around her neck.

'How do I look?' she asks, as we sit down at one of the few available tables for two.

'Wonderful. Like the finest Highland cow on the prairie,' I reply, taking in with awe how the green and red silk makes her pale complexion stand out even more.

With horror, I see her smile disappear and her eyes narrow.

'Are you calling me a cow? That's not very nice,' she says, the corners of her mouth now pointing downward.

I feel my pulse quicken and my hands tremble. *Oh no, I've upset her.*

'No! I don't mean it in a bad way. Cows are beautiful. And Highland cows are the most beautiful of them all. They're majestic! Sorry,' I say. Then, again, 'Sorry.' I feel the prickle of tears start at the corners of my eyes.

I've messed everything up.

I notice that my hands have automatically joined together in front of her as if in prayer.

She says nothing for an instant, then bursts into laughter.

'You should see your face,' she says, pointing at me. 'You look like you've seen a ghost.' She continues to laugh as I feel a wave of relief wash over me. I haven't upset her. It was a joke.

'Cheer up, Monk, I was having a laugh,' she says, picking up the drinks menu and scanning it.

I pick the menu up too and pretend to read it, trying to hide the fact that my heart is now bursting at the sound of her using the nickname she made up for me when we were teenagers. She hasn't done it in a very long time.

This is a good sign. Today is a good day.

We eat crispy fish and chips and drink a cold local beer. I'm still a bit nervous from the cow scare and giddy about her using my nickname, so I don't say much. I listen to her talk about her holidays by the seaside when she was young. How the smell of salt water and fish always gives her a sense of excitement. She remembers being in her parents' car and the two of them bickering in the front seat while she pressed her nose on the window to catch the first sight of the blue half-moon of water that could be seen from the motorway. I breathe in the sea air and try to imagine what she must have felt.

Clara and her parents are no longer close. They had a rocky relationship for many years, and their on-and-off contact has gone quiet altogether since she moved to London with Edo. Growing up, Clara and her mother had recurrent fallouts over what she calls her mother's 'neediness'; apparently, she would ask Clara endless questions and try to insert herself into all areas of her life. Clara felt controlled and stifled by her. She also told me her father could be abusive. I was shocked – I met Antonio many times when I lived in Rome, and he seemed like a kind and shy man, hidden behind his impressive moustache. I asked her whether she meant sexually. Clara told me that no, it was never sexual, but remained vague about the actual nature of it. Something about raised voices and thrown objects.

I can't imagine him behaving that way. I've witnessed a few conversations between the three of them over the years and they just seemed tense but civilised. But apparently they kept the worst behind closed doors; that was when things really got abusive. Clara told me that they hated seeing her succeed, and that when she decided to move to the UK, they 'dropped' her and now want nothing to do with her. That part has always confused me, because my parents tell me Antonio and Marilena always ask for news of Clara whenever they see them. It could be that they're lying about that, but I can't work out why they would. Either way, I try not to think about the bad times poor Clara must have gone through at the hands of her parents, and focus on her happy childhood memories. Like smelling the sea air from the back seat of the car.

Where we come from, families are either seaside people, mountain people or countryside people, depending on where they spend the school summer holidays. My parents and I were countryside people. I can vividly remember being in the car and seeing the turning where I would start smelling the sweet and earthy manure, then, right after that, recognising the gate of the ostrich farm that would announce we'd truly left the city. Her memory of the sea must evoke the same feeling.

After lunch, we decide to go for a stroll on the beach. I warn Clara it will be busy, but she doesn't seem to mind.

'Don't be so scared of people, Monk, they won't bite.' She laughs and starts walking quicker.

'I'm not scared of people,' I reply, struggling to keep up. When I do, we take in the view together. The noise of the sea, of children playing on the beach, of the many cars driving down the road that runs along the coastline. It's deafening, but joyous. The blues of the water and the sky are so bright they seem fake, and the pebbles on the beach shine with a thousand shades of brown and yellow.

We cross the road and buy ice cream cones from a stall, then start walking alongside the beach. Clara loops her arm in mine and we stroll up and down the seafront, looking and laughing at people, comparing the idiosyncratic ways the British enjoy the seaside to how the Italians do. I feel the warmth of her body against mine and the sound of her voice in my ears, and I'm so happy I could sing. My feet feel lighter than air, and thoughts of a future where this is what our weekends are always like are swimming around in my head.

The two of us, still together after all these years.

Edo is gone now, and Clara is alone. Except she's not, she will never be as long as I live, because I will look after her. I can make her happy. A day like today could happen again.

I just need to be home on time after work and not upset or annoy her, and we could be together like this all the time.

A breeze has picked up and we huddle even closer for warmth. Clara checks the time on her phone.

'It's getting late, we should head back to the station,' she says.

I nod and try to stop the slight disappointment I feel by telling myself that the happiness and closeness we've had today is just the beginning. I need to be patient.

*

The train back is much busier than it was on the way in, so we walk through a few carriages until we find two seats that are taken up by someone's bags. I ask the two ladies sitting opposite if they could move them, and we sit down. Once we've settled into our seats, I take a better look at the women. One of them seems to be in her mid-thirties and has cropped blonde hair and a quiff. The other looks to be a similar age and has long red hair. She's wearing a polka-dot dress and has a small gold ring in her septum. She catches me looking at her and asks me if I know what time the train arrives in London. I tell her. She thanks me and asks me if we had a nice day in Brighton. Clara and I both say yes at the same time. I ask them the same in return and they tell us they're visiting London for the weekend. They have tickets to a West End show, then are planning to maybe go to a club or two in Soho afterwards. They ask me whether I can recommend any good clubs in Soho. At that question, Clara snorts. I'm confused by her reaction but say no, I don't really go to clubs, Soho or otherwise. And I try never to bring up the subject of clubs with Clara anyway.

Back when we were young, she used to be a regular at many clubs in Rome. Some of the group she was friendly with around the time we first met often went to one of the bigger clubs in the centre. They would be there for hours, dancing and drinking until really late at night. And the next day, Clara would tell me all the gossip of what had happened. Who had kissed who, who'd fallen out with who, how short someone's skirt was, and how embarrassing for her that all the boys were staring. Clubs were never somewhere I went to myself, but thanks to Clara's morning-after stories, it's almost as if they are now also part of my history.

She stopped going herself after a while, not long after she got together with Edo. I don't know exactly what happened because we weren't as close any more around that time, but I remember hearing that there was a big falling-out between her and two of the other girls from the group, Beatrice and Elena. Something about one of them messaging Edo on Facebook and Clara hitting the roof about it. After that, I didn't see them hanging around the school corridors and outside the ice cream place together any more. We only got to talk about this once, when Clara and I were reminiscing about our school days – around the time when she'd just moved to London with Edo and our friendship was like a tree in spring after a long freeze, blossoming again. I asked what had happened between her and the girls from that group, and she looked at me for a long moment, then said, 'They betrayed me. I trusted them and they didn't honour it. Simple as that.'

I was confused. 'What does that mean? In what way?'

She huffed in the same way she used to when she was getting frustrated at me back when we were children. The memory surprised me with how fresh it still was.

'Some of them tried to get in between Edo and me. And I couldn't allow that.' She took a long drag of her cigarette – she still smoked then. 'They were jealous. I didn't – we didn't – need that in our lives.'

Years later, when I was living with them, I remember Edo saying once that he missed their old group of friends, and Clara shutting him down, saying that they were in the past for a reason. That if he'd behaved better, she wouldn't have been forced to do what she had to do. He'd rolled his eyes, but made sure only I saw. When Clara was in one of those moods, we both knew not to antagonise her more. She went upstairs for a bath after that, and Edo and I were silent for a while, while he drank beer after beer.

'Facebook,' I remember him muttering under his breath.

'What was that?' I asked.

'They got in touch on Facebook to wish me happy birthday and we chatted. There's nothing to it. She's crazy.'

I didn't know what to say. Of course Clara wasn't crazy. But also, I couldn't understand why he couldn't chat to his friends over Facebook. It was confusing, so I stayed mostly quiet. He got angrier and angrier the more he drank. Then, when Clara came back down after her bath, steam still rising off her and her dark curtain of hair soaking wet, I could tell that Edo wasn't the only one whose mood had got worse. She started telling us that we had to delete our Facebook accounts, that it was ridiculous to be clinging to the past. 'We're here *now*,' she shouted. 'Is it not enough? Is what we've left behind more exciting? If so, then go back to it.' Edo stared at her for a few seconds, then got up and raised his voice even louder, telling her that she was controlling and crazy. That she couldn't stop us from speaking to other people.

I went upstairs, the way I always did when things escalated between the two of them. I was no use to either of them in those moments. I could help the next day when the silence would invariably descend by making myself busy around the house, cooking and cleaning. But in that moment I was only in the way. I deleted my Facebook account that night, though, just in case she asked me about it. I didn't care if it was right or not. Edo could have his battles, but they didn't need to become my battles too.

The two ladies seem to go quiet after Clara's snorting reaction and look outside of the window holding hands until we reach London. As the train stops, they exchange a quick kiss on the lips and stand up to get their bags. I look away and can feel my face burning. I take my phone out of my pocket and stare at the screen closely to try and hide any redness.

'Vale, are you ready?' Clara asks. I quickly get up and follow her onto the platform. She says something else, but I miss it.

'What did you say?' I ask.

'Nothing. I just think it's weird,' she says, looking through her bag.

'What's weird?'

'They were. Kissing and that. Right in front of our faces.'

'I thought they seemed nice. I didn't notice,' I say, walking faster to match her pace towards the platform.

'As if.' She snorts again, shaking her head as she checks the train

56

time on the board. 'I was having a good day and now I just feel uncomfortable. I wish you hadn't tried to make friends with them. It was kind of creepy, actually.'

She visibly shudders. The mix of surprise and grief I feel hearing her words seems to congeal in my throat, and I can't speak.

We walk faster and faster through the connecting tunnels to get to our train; one arrives a few seconds after we reach the platform. We sit down next to each other and look around our carriage: it's quiet apart from a few people who seem dressed up to go out, and a couple of families back from a day of fun. A group of boys in the next carriage start singing a football chant in low and wobbly voices.

I focus on the advert in front of me while I swallow hard to keep the hard lump of disappointment from bursting out of me. I've been here before with Clara; this is not new. But each time it hurts more.

We spend the whole way until we reach our stop in silence. When we get out of the train, my phone comes alive again. I take a quick look and see that I have two missed calls and a few messages from my mother. I glance at the screen and see words framed by plenty of exclamation and question marks. I'm desperate to read them but can't risk Clara getting even more annoyed at me. I put the phone back in my pocket and push the messages to the back of my mind.

Chapter Seven

'I don't feel well.'

Clara is standing in my bedroom. This statement is followed by a coughing fit that lasts a few seconds.

'I must have caught a cold being out in Brighton.' She looks at me as I lie in bed.

I rub my eyes. 'Oh no, I'm sorry. You seemed well yesterday.'

She ignores my comment and sits down on the chair in the corner, breathing out noisily.

'I also feel dizzy. Can you stay home today to make sure I'll be okay?'

'Clara . . .' I start.

I hate taking time off work; it breaks my routine, which makes me feel anxious. It also means that Ollie has to cover my shift, which is especially bad on busy days like Mondays.

I see her eyes narrow, and another coughing fit follows. When she's finished, she folds her legs up against her chest and hugs them. She's not looking at me and seems to be absorbed in her own thoughts. Even though the room is warm, she pulls her sleeves over her hands and hugs her legs even tighter.

I can see that she's not feeling well, and I can't help but want to wrap her up and hold her until she's better. She wouldn't be asking me to stay home if she didn't feel unwell. She knows how much it stresses me out.

'Okay,' I say. 'I'll message Ollie.'

She jumps up from her chair and mouths *yay*, then blows me a kiss. 'Thanks. I'll see you downstairs.'

She's out of the room and walking down the stairs before I've had time to say anything else.

We spend the day watching her TV shows together in the living room, me on the armchair and her lying on the sofa. I check her temperature occasionally, but it never goes above 36.8 degrees. When an episode ends, she turns towards me and mimes the gesture of lifting a cup with her thumb and forefinger, tilts her head to one side and smiles sweetly.

I make her cup of tea after cup of tea. So much so that after a while, she only has to turn around and look at me for a moment and I get up to put the kettle on. She must have got through at least ten cups just today.

When I asked Ollie, he didn't seem to mind covering my shift. He said that he was hung-over so preferred to be busy or he would fall asleep. I thanked him and told him that there were a few studies in which teenage pigs were given alcohol and displayed similar consumption and intoxication behaviour to humans.

He hasn't replied yet.

At bathtime, Clara is chatty and animated. She is excited because a 'For Sale' sign has gone up in front of the house across the road. As I wash her, we discuss who we think could be moving in. She thinks it might be a family with children and a dog, from the type of cars she's seen slowing down to read the sign. I think it could be an older academic couple with friends all over the world who they like to invite to stay over in the spare rooms.

Clara once told me that she saw the previous owners bringing in exotic-looking furniture, so in my mind, the house is filled with art and antiques, and likely to attract people who appreciate those things. It feels good to see her relaxed.

Since our trip to Brighton the other day, she has seemed tense and on edge. But things are back on track today and I feel a wave of relief when she stops by my bedroom before bedtime and announces:

'I feel better now. I think my cough has gone. Night, night.'

The next morning at the bookshop there is a pile of post waiting that Ollie didn't have time to deal with yesterday when he was on his own. I sit behind the counter and go through each letter, one by one. They are mostly bills and invoices, and I sort them out in neat piles for Lauren to deal with when she's next in. Either Ollie or I do this job as and when the letters start piling up. We started doing it occasionally when Lauren moved to Scotland so that she didn't have to get through too much post during her occasional visits, but in the last year or so it has become a weekly task. If anything looks urgent, I take a picture of it and send it to her. I try not to look at the figures too much as it feels wrong, but sometimes I can't help but see things. Things like accounts in red and people who have been waiting to be paid for a long time. The number of pictures I need to send Lauren grows bigger every time I do this, but she doesn't seem alarmed. She always replies with *Thanks lovely! Xx*.

Ollie comes in clutching two paper bags and hands me one, saying, 'Cinnamon buns! Freshly made. The smell in the bakery was unreal.'

I thank him and breathe in the sugary scent with a loud 'Mmmm.'

He flicks on the kettle and makes us two cups of milky tea.

'How are you feeling?' he asks me, handing me my drink.

'Much better, thank you,' I answer, feeling guilty for having lied to him. But he would have asked too many questions if I'd told him I had to take the day off work because my flatmate had a cough.

'Good. Shame you weren't in yesterday. Something happened.'

'What?'

'Well, some*one*, I should say. He came in asking for you.' Ollie is leaning on the wall and smiling at me.

'Who?'

'Marcus.'

I quickly think of all the people I know in London, and in Rome. No one is called Marcus.

'I don't know a Marcus.'

'Yes. Yes, you do.' Ollie is pronouncing each word slowly. 'It's the guy you were having a pig debate with the other day. The guy with the crazy hair who was looking for New Agriculture books.'

'Oh, right. I didn't know he was called Marcus. What did he want?'

'You. Clearly. Well, not "you" you. Your expertise.'

Ollie elbows me in the side, causing my tea to slop around and a few drops to spill. He's looking at me as if waiting for an answer.

I look at his face and feel confused.

My *expertise*? Have I missed something? I know people often say things with their bodies and expressions but not words. This could be one of those times. Still, I really thought Marcus and I were just having a conversation about books, the same way I do with a lot of other customers in this place. Admittedly, it was about a topic I am very passionate about and I might have got more excited than I would if I were discussing, say, brutalist architecture or the art of flower arrangement.

'What do you mean?'

'He came all the way back and asked after you for just another book recommendation? I don't think so.' Ollie is wagging his finger in the air at me. 'No one is *that* into New Agriculture.'

'*I'm* into it. And old agriculture. And future agriculture too, probably.'

'Okay, *you* might be. But you have to admit that not many people are going to be into it as much as you are. The man clearly has an ulterior motive. He's probably a researcher and wants to interview you for a thesis. Or ... a university professor looking for assistants! Can you imagine?'

I let out an involuntary snort.

This is silly.

This man, Marcus, clearly just got a little too involved in my pig

61

chat. I can relate – once you start to know a bit more about them, it's impossible to stop. I should know. I never did and never will.

And yet. Is it possible that I am missing something? It wouldn't be the first time.

'I bet he's coming back,' Ollie continues, nodding, 'and this time, I think he'll offer you a job.'

'Stop it,' I say, but I can't stop the corners of my mouth from lifting up into a smile. It really would be quite exciting to meet someone as fascinated by the topic as I am, who wanted me to say more. It has never happened. The possibility of it makes me dizzy for a second. If there was no one to stop me from going on about it for too long – if, in fact, they wanted to know even more – I could finally set free everything that is in my head. And without having to worry about people getting bored, or annoyed, or angry. Or without them laughing at me and calling me names. It would be so ... liberating.

Ollie winks at me and turns around to start answering the emails that have come through overnight from our website. Before he starts typing, he says to himself, loud enough that I can clearly hear him, 'I bet I'm right.'

We spend the afternoon working around each other in contented silence.

The hours pass slowly and only a few people come through the door. No one buys. I keep an eye on my watch every now and then to make sure I'm not late tonight. Yesterday was a good day with Clara, and I really want to make sure I keep her happy. I'm looking forward to our evening and spending more time together. As closing time gets nearer, I start cashing up and making sure everything is tidied away. Ollie must have heard the till being fired up, because he walks over and helps me with the last few tasks. After a few moments, I can feel him staring at me. Then he touches me on the arm, which is what he does when he feels like giving me a hug but remembers that I'm not too keen on close physical contact.

'What's that for?' I ask him.

'You've been huffing and puffing like a steam train for the last five minutes. You seem a bit stressed. Is everything okay?'

I check the big clock on the wall. Time is running out. If I want to make it home on time tonight – and I really, really do – I need to wrap this up in the next ten minutes.

'I'm fine,' I tell him.

He lets out a sigh. 'If you say so. Hey, do you fancy coming out with Rafael and me at the weekend? There's a new escape room not far from here that just opened. We can do it and get cocktails afterwards.'

No no no. I can't risk a repeat of the other day. If telling Clara about the remote possibility of me going on a night out with Ollie and Rafael is enough to upset her, asking her again will really make her hit the roof. Obviously going is out of the question. But I can't just tell Ollie that my flatmate won't let me.

'No.' The word tumbles out of my mouth.

His brow furrows, and he stares at me. I know I have to give him more of an explanation than just 'no'. But my brain is too busy worrying about the precious minutes passing by to concentrate on coming up with anything good.

'I'm busy. With work,' I stutter.

'This work?' He points at the till next to us.

'Not this work, other work. Housework. Too much to clean at home,' I say, then smile to try and look relaxed.

'Riiiight.'

I can tell he doesn't believe me.

'It's okay if you don't want to come, you know. Escape rooms aren't my thing either; Rafael loves them, though, so we often go.'

I start gathering my things and grab Ollie's coat and mine from the hook behind the kitchen door.

'There's lots to clean,' I mumble as I usher him outside. I can feel him looking at me as we both bring the shutter down.

'Vale, are you okay? Is something going on?' he asks me.

63

'Nothing's going on. I'm okay.' I can't look him in the eyes. 'Everything is fine. I need to clean, I told you. Maybe we can go out another time.' I reach out and touch him on the arm.

He is standing there watching me as I close the heavy padlock and gather my stuff. He says nothing. He looks like he's waiting for me to say something else. I check my watch. I need to go now, or I won't make it on time.

'I'll see you tomorrow,' I shout as I start walking quickly down the road. I turn around and see that he is still there, the crown of his head lit up by the lights outside the pub.

He hasn't moved and is still looking in my direction. I wave at him, turn back around and pick up the pace. I continue like this, half walking, half running, until I'm home.

Chapter Eight

May 2019

A few weeks later, I'm in the children's section of the bookshop, staring at the perfect spirals of a particularly pretty spiderweb I just found, when I hear Ollie call my name.

I turn around and see him jogging towards me with an expression on his face I can't decipher. Today he's wearing a purple T-shirt that reads *Je ne regrette rien* in white blocky letters.

'He's back,' he says, lightly panting.

'Who?'

'Marcus. The New Agriculture guy from the other week. He's asking for you.'

'What does he want?'

'No idea. I just said I'll go fetch you.'

'Okay. Tell him I'll be there in a second,' I say, and he skips over to the front of the shop, to where, I imagine, the guy is waiting.

I delicately place a cardboard cut-out of the Gruffalo over the spiderweb so no one will ruin its beautiful threads, then stop to brush a few specks of dust off my trousers.

I wish Ollie had told the guy – Marcus – that I was too busy to talk to him. But I didn't expect him to come back again. I still worry that he said something during our chat that I missed. Like a turn of phrase that went right over my head.

I wish I was back at the city farm chatting to the animals there; at least I would feel a lot less worried. Either way, Marcus is here now and knows I'm around and free to chat, so I don't have any other option but to go to the front and speak to him.

As I walk, I keep my eyes on his back. He's chatting to Ollie, and from the few words I can catch, they're discussing the benefits of the pub across the road from the bookshop – the Fox – versus the Eel Pie, which is further down and closer to the river.

This seems to be a popular topic around here, but to me, the two places seem almost impossible to tell apart. They both look like they've been here for ever, or at least as long as MacGregor's Bookshop has, and both have that distinctive look inside where everything is covered in dark wood and the beer is pulled from long brass pipes into large, dimpled glasses with a handle. Both places smell like yeast and cleaning spray and have menus written in white chalk on boards hanging off the walls. From what I can hear, they both agree that the Fox is way better than the Eel Pie. I'm tempted to turn around and leave them to it, but then Ollie spots me.

'Here she is,' he says.

Marcus turns around and smiles. 'Hey.'

He thanks Ollie with a pat on the back and looks at me.

'I was hoping to ask you something.'

I can see Ollie winking at me in the background, but I ignore him.

'How can I help?'

'Well, I'm enjoying both books you recommended the other week. I'm finding *The Future of Ploughing* particularly interesting, but I remember you saying that it was only a generic overview of the movement.'

I nod. 'It is.'

'Do you have anything that goes into more depth? Especially around the topic of mixed cropping and all the different techniques. I find it fascinating.'

'Let me check,' I tell him. 'There is something I have in mind that

66

would be perfect, but I haven't seen it on the shelves in a while.' I walk over to the computer and start typing the title into our online database. 'It's less of a manual and more of a history of a particular kind of mixed cropping. But it also has lots of really interesting tips that I think could be helpful,' I tell him as I wait for the results to appear on screen.

'What's it called?'

'*The Three Sisters.*'

'Strange. Why?'

'Corn, beans and squash. That's what they were called by the indigenous American tribes: the three sisters. Back in AD 1000, farmers would plant all three seeds into the same hole. As the plants grew, the corn would act as a stalk for the bean shoots to climb on, while the squash growing low on the ground would protect the soil from weeds and shade it from the harsh sun. They would basically grow together, protecting and supporting each other along the way.'

The computer pings, telling me we don't have any copies left in stock.

'Ah, we don't have it. Sorry. I can order it in for you, though?'

'That would be great, thank you,' he answers. 'It's a beautiful story.'

'*The Three Sisters*? It is.' I smile. 'It's one of my favourite books on the subject. It really shows how mixed crop—'

'Can I ask you something?' he interrupts.

'Okay,' I answer, feeling a little nervous.

'Have you ever considered writing your knowledge and ideas down?'

'As in on paper? Like a book?'

'Yes,' he answers.

I'm confused. I thought we were already talking about a book.

'I haven't, no. I'm not a writer.'

I take notes sometimes, but I *know* books – I practically live among them – and the few pages of scribbled pig facts that I find particularly interesting are very far removed. And anyway, all the knowledge I've gained through the years sits very comfortably in my head; that way I get to choose when it comes out and who to.

I prefer it this way, it's safer.

'It's all in here,' I tell him, tapping the side of my head. 'No need to write it down. I remember everything.'

He stares at me for a moment, then shakes his head very slightly.

'Can you order a copy of *The Three Sisters* for me, please? I'll be back in the area next week, so I can pick it up then if it gets here on time.'

'Yup, no problem.'

I see Ollie moping in the background. I'm hit with the thought that him telling me Marcus had come back was the first time all week I've seen him smile. He doesn't seem like his usual self, and I feel guilty for not having picked up on it sooner. I will ask him if he's okay as soon as we're alone in the shop. Hopefully it's nothing serious and he's just having an off week.

I take Marcus's payment and hand him the receipt. He thanks me and starts walking towards the door. As I close the till drawer, I notice that one of its side panels is coming loose, so I try to push it back into place with the palm of my hand. As I focus on fixing it, I hear a noise and realise that Marcus has walked back towards me and is now looking closely at what I'm doing.

'It's the side panel. It pops out now and then and you need to whack it in the right place to put it back in,' I explain.

'Right.'

'But if you whack it too hard, you risk cracking the plastic. It's a pretty ancient machine and the owner has told us to make sure we don't break it, as if we do, you can't find replacements any more and she'll have to buy a whole new machine.'

'That must be expensive,' he says, raising his eyebrows.

'I think so.'

I give the side of the drawer one more slap and the panel slides back into its hinges.

Marcus claps, and I'm so surprised at the noise I give him a look that must have been scary, because he stops right away. *Why is he still here?*

As if he heard my thoughts, he says, 'I'm back because I wanted to ask you something else. I've enjoyed listening to your opinions, Vale, and I think our readers might too.'

'What readers?'

'Sorry, I should clarify.' He smiles. 'I work for a publishing company – Almastra Publishing. We're quite small and specialise in books about nature, animals, some poetry, but mostly factual. We've watched the New Agriculture wave grow, which is great, but think what's out there in terms of publications hasn't caught up yet with the public's interest.'

He's gesticulating in a way that's making his curly hair bounce in the same rhythm as the rest of his body. It's almost as if he's directing an orchestra, and if I wasn't busy trying to understand what he is talking about, I could get easily distracted by the hypnotic movements.

There's something about the irregular outline of his body, the fluffiness of his head and the piercing nature of his eyes that reminds me of a wild animal – a fox perhaps, or a wolf.

I don't find him physically attractive as a human, but there's something about his animalistic shape that I find strangely soothing.

I catch a glimpse of a silver flash and notice the small metallic pin on the lapel of his corduroy blazer emblazoned with an 'A' surrounded by two birds in flight made to look like inverted commas. It must be the Almastra logo.

'My publisher, Louisa, and I, we've been looking for new literary voices with ideas that haven't been heard before and that can back them up with real knowledge. I can see that you're very passionate about all this and I get the feeling that what you have to say would translate well into writing.' After a moment of silence, he adds, 'I'm usually right about these things.'

I'm confused as to why he's asking me this.

69

He knows I'm not a writer. I've just told him. Surely Almastra Publishing must have real writers on their books who could do a better, more professional job? I know he's saying that they're missing new voices ... maybe he means younger people?

'Have you tried the bloggers?' I ask him. As is the case for most trends of the last couple of decades, there is a small army of bloggers that details every aspect, nuance and sub-trend of the New Agriculture movement online. Ollie calls them 'carrot chasers'. I've seen the books that some of them have written on sale in the shop, but they mostly seem to be made up of beautifully arranged photographs and step-by-step recipes and instructions. You can't really get lost in them and learn anything useful. And, as always, there's nothing about ethical pig rearing – keeping, husbandry, compassionate butchering and the like – in any of them, which is sad and the biggest issue in my opinion.

Marcus shakes his head. 'We have. Some are quite good. But we found that most of them either already have a publisher, prefer to self-publish or ask for astronomical fees. We're only small, it doesn't work like that for us.'

A couple of customers come in, and I can see Ollie trying to speak to them both at once. I need to stop chatting soon and help him.

'Sorry, Marcus, I'm going to have to go to those customers. Is there anything else I can help you with?'

'Yes, sorry. I'll get to the point. Would you be up for submitting some writing to us? Especially your theories on pigs, they're fascinating. I think – I *know*, in fact – that our readers are desperate for a New Agriculture book with more punch. And it sounds like you've got plenty of strong opinions on the topic.'

He runs a hand through his hair to move a curl that has got too close to his eye and waits for my answer.

It takes me a few seconds to register this. In part because I'm watching the customers browsing the shelves, looking out for a signal that they might need to ask me something. In part because my brain hasn't yet caught up with his words. I've never written anything that I would be happy for others to read before, and I know there's no way I could do what the authors of the books on our shelves can do. And no matter what Marcus says, I doubt enough people out there would be interested in my opinions about pigs and their keeping.

In my head, I can almost hear Clara's laughter at the suggestion. Even the people I know sometimes tell me, 'Vale, that's enough. Let's talk about something else.' Why would complete strangers want to know more? It doesn't make sense.

It's all very confusing and my instinct is to just walk away and leave him standing before my head starts hurting. But he is still a customer, and I must be polite to him.

'Thank you, Marcus. I really need to go now. I hope you have a good rest of your day.'

I stretch a thin smile over my lips and start to edge towards a different area of the shop.

I see his face drop and he starts rummaging through his pockets.

'Will you consider it? Please?' he says, handing me a small rectangular piece of card that I can see has his name, number and an 'A' embossed in gold writing on it.

'Okay. Yes. Thank you.' I grab the card and slip it into my trouser pocket, then turn away from him. I stand that way until I hear the door hit the bell and close, then I walk over to one of the customers and ask her if she needs any help. She says, 'No thanks,' so I smile and leave her to browse.

I look for Ollie and find him in the kitchen, scrolling through his phone. He briefly acknowledges me as I go in.

'So, what did he want?' he asks, still looking down at the screen.

'Nothing special. Another book recommendation.' I'm not quite ready to tell him about what just happened, not until I've had some time to make sense of it myself.

Ollie grunts in response. I'm braced for an avalanche of questions

71

trying to get any drop of gossip out of me. I plan to be politely evasive and maybe throw a pig anecdote or two into the mix.

But he has gone completely quiet.

That's unusual.

I stick my head out of the kitchen door to check if any more customers have come in. They haven't. It's just the original couple, who I know will soon wiggle away without buying. We should have a few minutes to chat uninterrupted.

'Cup of tea?' I ask.

The noise he makes in response is a mixture of a huff and a low grunt.

I take it as a yes and switch the kettle on. Something is clearly not right with him.

'Are you okay?'

'Not really.'

'What's going on? Is it to do with Rafael?'

'Yes.'

He gets up and starts pacing up and down the tiny kitchen. His jaw muscles are tensed. All I can hear is the whistling of the kettle. I think I should say something, but my mind is suddenly blank. I'm struggling to read his body language, and his fast movements are confusing me. I reach out and touch his arm. He doesn't move away, so I tap it lightly a few more times, hoping it's enough to let him know he's not alone.

'We broke up the other day. I thought it was temporary, but now I don't think it is,' he says, wrapping both arms around himself.

Oh no, poor Ollie.

'I had no idea. I'm sorry to hear that. What happened?'

'I still don't fully understand. He's been kind of distant for a while, but I didn't want to ask him too many questions in case he accused me of being needy. So I let him be. But then the other day, he just said he wasn't sure he felt the same way about me any more and needed time to think.'

72

Ollie's eyes are glistening as he speaks. I nod while I pour hot water over the tea bags.

'This week I've only messaged him, like, twice, thinking that if I gave him a bit of space it would be enough. Hoping he would miss me. But then he messaged me earlier today and told me it was final.'

'Final?'

'That's what he said, "It's my final decision." I was hoping he'd changed his mind,' he sighs. 'But no.'

At this, tears start to fall from his eyes. I stare at him, frozen. I shift my weight from foot to foot. I tap him a few more times on the arm. My mouth feels like it's full of cotton wool.

'Actually, Vale, do you mind if I leave early today? If Lauren finds out, you can tell her it was my idea. I just need to clear my head.'

I nod again. I'm starting to feel like one of those wobbly-headed dogs that sit on car dashboards, doing nothing useful.

Without saying a word, Ollie grabs his bag, waves goodbye and is out of the door.

The cup of tea he has left behind is still steaming. I pour it down the sink and take mine to the counter, where I start cashing up.

I know he needed more from me. I can tell when Clara needs me because it happens so often and I understand the signs now. But I was caught unawares with Ollie and wish I hadn't just frozen. I should have tried harder – wiped his tears maybe, or said soothing words. I don't know why I find it so hard; it's like there is a barrier that I can't break. I need to try and be a better friend.

During bath time, I find myself thinking about Marcus's words as I soap up Clara's back. I still can't quite understand why he would want me to do the writing. Surely a lot of people know those things already? But if they don't, they should. Maybe I could be the one to write about them after all. It would be a service to the pigs in a way. The thought of it makes me suddenly feel quite excited. And writing might even help quieten my head. It could help take all the facts that are constantly swirling around in there out of it and onto the paper.

'You're quiet tonight,' Clara says, distracting me from my thoughts.

'Sorry, just stuff on my mind.'

'What kind of stuff? House stuff?'

'Work stuff. Some guy said some weird things to me today. I was just thinking about that,' I answer, hoping she'll move on to something else. I don't know how she might react; she doesn't always like me talking about work, and I really don't want to stress her out.

'What weird stuff? Dirty stuff?'

'No! Nothing like that.' I feel my face flush. Luckily Clara still has her back to me and doesn't see. 'Just some stuff about wanting me to write my opinions on pigs and things like that down. Like in a book.'

Clara turns around to look at me. Her face is hard to read, but I imagine she might be excited for me once she finds out more. She knows how much spreading the word about pigs would mean to me.

'A book? You? What does he do?'

'He works for a publisher. I was just thinking it could be good, maybe. I tell people all I know about pigs so that those who don't might start seeing them the way I do too. With more respect.'

'Respect?'

'Yes. And I was also thinking, what if it does well? The guy seems to think there's a demand for it. If it makes money, it will help us. We would be more comfortable, now that it's the two of us.'

I can see Clara's shoulders tighten. She turns around until she's fully facing me.

'We don't need more money, Vale. We are fine on our own. Is there something you're missing?' Her voice is suddenly raised and her eyes narrowed. 'Do we not have everything we need already?' she spits out.

Oh God, oh no. I should have kept my mouth shut. I know the subject of money is still a tricky one for her since Edo left. Why do I always put my foot in it?

74

She takes a deep breath and her chest and shoulders seem to lower. As quickly as she got wound up, she now looks suddenly calmer.

'Sorry, Vale, I didn't mean to raise my voice. It's still hard for me sometimes,' she says, her voice softer again.

'Of course, I know. I'm so sorry. I didn't mean to remind you. We are fine, the two of us. We don't need anything else. I just thought . . . it could be something extra? And the pigs . . . you know how I feel about them.'

'I do, of course I do.' She reaches one hand out towards my face, takes a wayward curl between her thumb and forefinger and hooks it behind my ear. The back of her hand brushes against my cheek as she does so. I close my eyes for a second to savour the feeling.

'But books take a lot of work, focus, time. And you are so busy already. You have your job, the house. Me. I know I can be a burden sometimes . . .' She looks down.

'You're not. Not at all. Not one bit. I love looking after you. Us. And you're right, work does keep me busy, and there's always so much to do at home. Some days I don't actually stop until I realise I'm so tired and it's bedtime.'

She nods. 'Exactly. Where would you find the time for writing?'

She stands up and rivulets of water fall off her in every direction. My eyes are now looking directly into her belly button.

'It's best if you tell him no, okay? I'm sure there are plenty of other people out there who can write about pigs. You just don't have the time.'

I take her dressing gown and help her into it. Rubbing her skin dry as I do so.

'You're right, I don't have the time.'

She smiles at me and we walk downstairs. It's time for me to start dinner and she doesn't like to wait too long for it. I'd better get on with the cooking. There is so much to do.

Chapter Nine

The following day I wake up feeling like the whole thing with Marcus was just a strange dream. I decide I'm much better off concentrating on supporting Clara and doing what I can to get Ollie back on his feet.

Once I'm at work I promise myself to 'be there' for him as he's clearly suffering over his break-up with Rafael. I know that's what he needs as we had a conversation a while ago, after one of their arguments, when he said that he needed Rafael to 'be there' for him more when he'd had a bad day, because Rafael wasn't great at 'being there' for him.

I'm still learning about what that means, because my experience of break-ups is only based on what I witnessed when living with Clara and Edo. I think 'being there' wouldn't have worked so well in that situation. Clara would go silent for days after one of their arguments and Edo would mostly stay out of the house as much as possible. The only time I'd been able to help out was when I noticed signs on Edo's skin while making him breakfast the next day. Like on the morning after the night Clara demanded he delete his Facebook account. He had a bruise on his cheekbone that he didn't have the day before, and I gave him some arnica cream to soothe it and stop it from hurting too much. As I delicately rubbed the cream in, we were both silent. I wanted to ask him how he got hurt, but it was clear he didn't want to talk about it. After he got up and thanked me, the moment had passed, and I never got the courage to ask him about it, although it didn't stop me from wondering.

But I don't think this is the kind of thing that happened between Ollie and Rafael. I've never seen any marks of that kind on Ollie's skin, and I know that if I had, he would be the first one to talk about it.

I also used to think that 'being there' meant something complicated and ephemeral that would turn someone from sad to happy in the blink of an eye, kind of like a magic spell. But I understand now that it's much more literal than that. It just means being *physically* there to listen and comfort someone when they are angry or sad about something, without telling them about yourself and what you're feeling in that moment. And without telling them pig facts, because it apparently doesn't help. Learning fascinating facts like, say, that a sow's gestational period lasts for exactly three months, three weeks and three days doesn't cheer other people up the way it does me when they're feeling low.

Finding a way to make Ollie feel better was on my mind this morning: when I made Clara's coffee, I forgot to put milk in it, which rarely happens, and when I put it in front of her, she pulled a face. I quickly fixed it, but it made me realise that I was distracted, so I tried to put things to the back of my mind at least until I left for work. Luckily Clara didn't seem to notice. In fact, I was surprised to see her washed and dressed so early. She told me that Edo had been in touch first thing for a chat, something that hasn't happened in a very long time. He'd asked her how she was and what she'd been up to and the two of them had caught up for a little while before he got interrupted by a work call that he couldn't postpone, but he'd promised to call back later today. Clara smiled the whole time as she told me this.

Thinking of her happy face has put a spring in my step this morning, and I'm smiling too when I step into the bookshop, with two steaming cups of hot chocolate for Ollie and me.

'Morning!' I trill, expecting to see him already setting up the till and sorting out the post. Instead, Lauren answers in an equally cheerful tone.

'Morning, lovely girl.'

'Hi. I thought you were supposed to be here later,' I say, putting the drinks down on the counter. We have a book launch today that she has organised, and she doesn't usually turn up until lunchtime on event days.

'Am I bothering you?' she asks, smiling. I know from the smile that she's joking, but I still feel my stomach clench with worry at having clearly said the wrong thing.

'No. Not at all. Sorry, I was just surprised to see you.' Then, to clarify in case she still thinks she's bothering me, I say, 'But in a good way.'

She pats me on the shoulder. 'Just joking, sweetie. I've got some paperwork to do here, so I hopped on an earlier flight.'

She grabs a pile of bills, her phone and a cup of tea and takes them to the little table in the children's section at the back, which is usually quiet first thing in the morning. Looking at the size of the pile and knowing how many months it has been accumulating for, I imagine she will be sitting at that table for quite some time. I make myself comfortable on the chair behind the counter and take a sip of my hot chocolate. The sweet liquid has just started to warm my insides when Ollie arrives.

'Evening,' I tell him.

'Very funny,' he replies, rolling his eyes.

'Lauren is here,' I whisper, pointing to the back room.

'Already?' His eyes widen. I mime a pile of paperwork and typing on a calculator. He nods.

I hand him his cup and he grabs it, thanking me and instantly taking a couple of big gulps. He lets out a long sigh.

'How are you feeling?'

'Okay. Not great. But okay, you know?'

I nod. 'I'm here to listen and comfort you,' I announce.

78

He looks at me weirdly for a moment and I worry I've said another wrong thing. But then he sighs once more.

'Thanks, Vale. I appreciate it. I think I just need to be distracted and not dwell on stuff. I'm glad we've got the launch today; it's going to be so busy I'll probably be too knackered to think about anything else.'

I nod again.

'Actually, tell me about Marcus. What did he want yesterday? Was it really just another book recommendation?' Ollie leans against the counter and cups his drink with both hands.

I'm torn. On the one hand, I know that being there for Ollie means not talking about myself but listening to him. On the other hand, he has said that he wants to be distracted so he doesn't have to think about his troubles, so maybe feeling sorry for me might make him feel a little bit less sorry for himself.

'I think so. But it was very odd, to be honest.'

'What do you mean?'

'You know how I told him some of my theories on pigs, agriculture and stuff like that last time he was here?'

He nods.

'Well, he started saying this whole thing about him working for a publisher who's looking for new emerging voices to tap into the New Agriculture trend, and how he thinks I've got interesting stuff to say and I should write it down – as in in a book – and they might publish it, yana, yana—'

'Yada.'

'What?'

'It's yada, yada. Not yana, yana.'

'Is it? Okay, well. He made up this whole story. It was very strange.'

'Right. Then what?'

'Then I thanked him and said goodbye politely because he's still a customer but I didn't have any interest in continuing the conversation. So then he gave me his business card and left.'

79

'It doesn't make sense, Vale.'

'What doesn't make sense?'

'Why would he come all the way here again to tell you that he's interested in your ideas and might want to publish them unless he's *actually* interested in them? Seems like a massive waste of time on his part if he's, what, playing a practical joke on you?'

'You'd be surprised,' I say, but I regret it straight away. Clara has warned me that talking about the bullying I've experienced in the past makes me look pathetic, so I never mention it. But bringing up the conversation with Marcus again is confusing me and it just slipped out.

'What do you mean?' Ollie asks.

'Nothing, I'm just being silly. Now, what do we need to prepare for the event? Shall I go ask Lauren?' I say, anxious to change the subject.

Ollie throws his hands in the air. 'For fuck's sake, Vale. Is it so unbelievable to think that someone might be interested in you?' he yells, as two red streaks creep up his cheeks. 'You're kind. You're pretty. You know lots of random facts. What's not to like about you?' He shakes his head. 'You seem to have no idea how often customers seek you out. You, over everyone else in here. The number of times I've seen it happen since we've worked together ... Sometimes I wonder if you and I live in the same universe.

'And apart from everything you've got to say,' he continues. 'You're a great friend too. Look how hard you've been trying to support me today, and not for the first time. You're a good person, Vale, you should know that. It annoys me that you so clearly don't.'

I'm shocked by his reaction, so I say nothing and just stare at the grooves in the floorboards. Looking at the wood makes me think that I have no idea if grooves work in the same way that trunk rings work to tell you the age of a tree, but I might try to count them to see if that's the case. There should be about a hundred, but probably more. Doing this has an instant soothing effect, and Ollie's frustration at me seems to move further away. A few moments go past where I can feel him staring at me but I can't quite meet his eyes.

'Sorry. I didn't mean to raise my voice,' he finally says, distracting me from my thoughts.

I wave a hand to signal that it's okay. I know he's going through a tough time, and I don't mind him taking it out on me, but it was a bit of a surprise.

'Do you still have Marcus's business card?' he asks.

I pat my trousers and can feel its rectangular outline poking through my pocket. I hand the card to Ollie.

'There you go. Why?'

He walks over to the computer and types a few letters on the keyboard. Then clicks a couple of times, scrolls up and down and makes a noise like 'huh'.

I'm staring closely at a bit of dry skin around my thumb, trying to remember that if Ollie is thinking about me, he's not being sad about Rafael, which is a good thing.

'I knew it.' He turns the computer screen towards me and points at it. 'Look.'

I get closer and see a small, square picture of a guy with curly hair, wearing an open-collared shirt and a confident smile. Marcus. A short paragraph underneath the image reads: *Marcus McGuire, our lead editor specialising in all things nature and poetry. For submissions, email* marcus@almastrapublishing.com. *Please note: Marcus isn't currently accepting any fiction submissions.*

I look at Ollie. 'What does it mean?'

'It means it's real. He does work for a publishing company and is looking for submissions about nature. It also means that he was being serious about you sending him some writing.' He claps his hands. 'This is so exciting!'

He goes back to reading the rest of the Almastra website, making noises like 'aaaah', 'oh' and 'nice' as he scrolls through the pages.

His sweatshirt today reads *Curiosity Killed the Cat*, which seems to be so fitting to this moment I can't help but smile, even though my brain is buzzing with a million thoughts.

Someone being genuinely interested in my opinions on pigs and agriculture is so novel to me that what Ollie is telling me isn't quite sinking in. I'm still trying to look for a different motive. Even though the website I've just seen does seem to show quite clearly that Almastra is a serious publishing house, and that Marcus appears to be who he said he was.

But if that's the case and they could have submissions from any New Agriculture author out there, why would he want to hear from me? I don't know a lot about the movement, and I certainly don't count myself as being a part of it. Most of what I know I've learned from either books or farmers I've spoken to. I retain all the information I've learned since I was young in my head, and sometimes it does feel like I have a book up there, where I can go and dig through my synapses as if they were pages and find the exact facts I'm looking for in a particular moment. I know Clara doesn't want me to do it because it would take time away from the housework and my job at the bookshop. But maybe if I found a way to scrape some more time out of my day somehow, I could still do it and help spread the message about pigs.

'Lovelies, can you come here, please?' Lauren shouts from the back. 'We need a plan for this afternoon.'

Ollie closes the website and shouts back, 'Okay. Shall I make us all a cuppa first?'

Without waiting for an answer, he heads to the kitchen and switches on the kettle.

I'm finding his nervous energy this morning a little overwhelming, but I'm trying to ignore it, as I can tell that me going along with what he's currently saying is keeping him distracted.

While we wait for the kettle to boil, Ollie makes me promise that I will at least consider writing some of my opinions down and submitting them to Marcus. I really can't see myself doing it – it feels far too exposing, and a big part of me still doesn't believe any of this is real – but I tell him that I promise I will consider it, as I don't want to disappoint him. After seeing him so sad and dejected yesterday, I want to make sure I do what I can today to keep his spirits up.

I help him carry the cups of tea to the back room and the three of us sit in a circle around the little table to plan how the launch event will pan out. I spot the pile of bills shoved in a carrier bag next to Lauren's handbag and wonder if she'll mention it.

But she seems to be immersed in the planning of the launch, discussing seating arrangements for the guests coming to watch the reading, working out the best place to position the signing table, and which of our current stock we should move out of the way to accommodate the stand where all the copies of the new book – a biography of the painter Wilhelmina Barns-Graham – will be displayed.

Over the course of the next few hours, we work hard to set everything up, and by mid-afternoon the bookshop starts getting busier and busier. Ollie and I joke that they're mostly here for the free Prosecco, and looking at the rate at which the glasses are getting emptied, we're probably right. Lauren has put on an extra layer of make-up and is busy buzzing from person to person, making sure no one misses the opportunity to buy the book. The author – a tall academic woman wearing round glasses and a long green suede skirt – reads some extracts and answers questions from the public.

After the talk, a group of friends of the Penwith Society of Arts stick around and Lauren invites them to share one more glass of Prosecco with her and discuss their impressions of the event, while Ollie and I tidy up around them. He seems quite cheerful, which means his plan to stay busy in order not to think about his troubles must have worked.

'Have you thought any more about what we said earlier?' he asks me as we sweep the ancient floorboards in the back room.

'Not really.'

I haven't had a chance to think about anything at all since we spoke, apart from making sure every person who wanted to buy the book could do so, and not getting stuck in the middle of any conversation with more than three people at once.

'Remember you promised me you'd consider it. I'm positive Marcus is the real deal. Think about it, the next book launch could be yours. It could be you standing in front of all those people reading the words you've written and soaking up the applause.'

He's sweeping the broom over my feet to get my attention, and the more I move them away, the more he keeps doing it. I jump out of the way enough times that I find myself backed into a corner. Ollie lifts his eyebrows.

'So?'

'I promise, I promise . . . It would be amazing. But it's never going to happen. I'm not a writer, remember? I'm the one who sells the books that writers write. Not the one who writes the books that sellers sell.'

'Very clever, Vale. But you've promised, so now you have to do it. You're weirdly good at all this pig stuff, and now even a professional is saying it. Think about it,' he adds, pointing his index finger at my face.

'Fine, fine.'

It's nice to hear Ollie say he thinks I'm good at the pig stuff. He seems genuinely convinced I can do this, too. It's different with Clara. She knows I know so much about pigs, but she hasn't ever actually said she thinks I could do it. I wish it wasn't so. It would feel wonderful to hear her tell me the things that Ollie is saying.

I move his finger away and head over to the counter. As I look back at him, I catch a glimpse of the clock on the kitchen wall and realise with horror that it's already ten minutes past the time I usually leave to get home. *Oh no.*

This means that even if I run out of the door now, without taking my stuff and leaving Ollie and Lauren to lock up on their own, I'll still be home at least ten minutes late.

I didn't tell Clara I was working on an event today as I thought

84

it would end at closing time, like our afternoon readings tend to. But I hadn't counted on Lauren inviting the group to stick around for longer.

I hurry into the children's section and see that they're still only halfway through their glasses. I don't have time to wait for them to finish.

I dash back to the till and cash up in the fastest way I can while Ollie finishes tidying up the mess left behind by the guests. I manage to slam the till drawer on my thumb and yelp.

'You okay?' he shouts.

'Yup, yup. I need to go. Something's come up,' I reply, struggling to pull my jacket on and drape my bag across my body. 'Cashing up is all done. Can I leave you to wait for them to be finished? Sorry. Please?' I point at Lauren and her merry gang.

'No worries. I'll wait. It's not like I have anything better to do tonight anyway.' He sighs.

'Thank you. See you tomorrow. No, Monday. Bye, Lauren!' I yell towards the back of the shop. Without waiting for an answer, I throw myself at the door and burst out onto the street.

I run as fast as my legs will let me. I dash across the road before the lights turn red, and a speeding van narrowly misses me. My lungs burn and my muscles ache from the effort. I am home in just over ten minutes – which is faster than I've managed before – but I'm still a full fifteen minutes late. I have no idea what state Clara will be in, but I know it won't be good. The fact that she was in a better mood this morning might help, but there are still plenty of hours in the day that could have turned things sour.

I open the front door, drop my bag and run to the living room. I nearly trip on Clara's mobile phone, which is face-down on the floor, with its silicone protective cover half off. She is sitting on the sofa reading a magazine. I drop to her feet and stare into her eyes.

'I'm so sorry. There was an event today and a group travelling from out of London stayed later and I had to clear up . . .'

85

She is staring at the magazine in complete silence. *This is not good.* Silence usually means she's getting charged for something bigger. The temptation to retreat into a corner and repeat pig breeds until everything in my head is quiet again is overwhelming. But that can come later, when I'm alone. First I need to make it up to her, to fix things. I take a deep breath.

'I'm sorry. Please. It was late before I knew it. I've run so fast to get back, I nearly got run over. Please, Clara, forgive me.'

She starts leafing through the magazine casually.

'Please,' I whisper.

The room is silent for a few moments. I keep my eyes lowered.

Then she speaks.

'You disgust me. You're useless, ungrateful and pathetic. I've done everything for you, yet you refuse to do me even the smallest of courtesies.' She spits out each word without looking up from the glossy pages on her lap.

I nod my head slowly.

She turns around to look at me.

'Exactly. You'd be nowhere without me. If I was a less generous person, I'd kick you out of the house right now.' She shakes her head. 'Edo was right, you are a poison.'

'Edo?' I can't remember him ever saying anything like this. But maybe it wasn't me he said it to. And why would he? He never owed me anything; I was always just Clara's childhood friend. I know I was around a lot during their first few years together in London. And the three of us were almost inseparable at some point. It must have been too much for them. And yet Edo was always so kind and welcoming to me. Even when I could see he was stressed out with work, or tense after an argument with Clara, he always seemed happy to have me around. But I don't dare question her words. If he said that to her, then there must have been a reason. *A poison* ... The thought of having hurt Clara and Edo's marriage without realising is too much to bear. I hold my head to stop it from buzzing so loudly.

Clara looks at me with contempt, then gets up. She throws her magazine onto the sofa and walks out of the room without looking back. A second later, I hear the door of her bedroom slam. I'm stunned into silence.

The pain of her words weighs heavy on my chest, making breathing difficult. I've let her down, again. She's right, she's done everything for me, and I can't even do the few things she asks me to do. I'm being ungrateful and I must do better. I'm thinking hard about the ways I could make her happy with me again, but another thought starts to emerge instead.

Useless.

It's not the first time she's called me that; it's one of her favourite insults, in fact. She also says that I'm a waste of space. And I agree. But tonight, I can hear Ollie's voice louder in my ear. *You're a good person.* And I also remember what he told me earlier, when he was sad about his break-up and I was there for him. *Look how hard you've been trying to support me today, and not for the first time.*

What if I'm not useless? I made things better today, a difference. That's the opposite of useless.

And I can see Marcus's face staring at mine while I talked about pigs and agriculture, not with the usual bafflement, but with something different. Maybe I dismissed him too quickly.

What if Marcus is really who he says he is? Spreading knowledge about ethical pig rearing to a new audience is surely something useful I could be doing? My parents used to often tell me I was good at things. And when I was little, I believed them. It was only once I got older that their words stopped sinking in. Maybe because when you grow up, your own internal voice is sometimes louder than those around you, and it's not always very nice.

Besides my parents, I've never had someone believe in what I'm capable of the way Ollie and Marcus do now.

These thoughts run through my head as I'm getting ready for bed. I'm surprised to not be feeling the painful mix of despair and anguish that I usually feel following one of Clara's outbursts. It's as if Ollie and Marcus's words have just got as loud as hers in my head. They're still competing for space, but Clara is losing ground. And that has never happened before. My eyes fall onto my desk, where my laptop is. I look at it, and a surge of energy snakes down my limbs. My fingers tingle with sudden possibility.

I open the laptop and start writing. I push away the thought of what Clara might say if she finds out, and I'm surprised to notice how easy it is this evening.

I have no idea if any of it will make sense or if it will even be read, but emptying my head might help me sleep better tonight. Marcus said he needed something with 'punch' for his readers and seemed interested in what I had to say about pigs in particular. I might struggle in other areas of my life – like Clara keeps telling me – but having punchy opinions on how pigs are a superior species and what that means when it comes to looking after them correctly isn't one of them.

As I type about my beloved animals, I find that my mind quietens down. All I do feel is a steady stream of words flowing from my head, through my fingers, onto the screen. As if a tap has opened. I write and write until I have to stop because my eyes start closing. I don't know how many pages I've written by the time I realise I'm too tired to continue, but it's many more than I thought I would.

I know Ollie will be at home alone, thinking about Rafael. Knowing I've kept my promise might cheer him up, seeing how insistent he was earlier today that I should do it. I decide to send him these pages as proof. If he wants to read them, great; if he doesn't, that's fine too. And at least he'll give me a break on Monday about this whole thing.

I don't read back what I've written in case I change my mind. I type in his email address and attach the file. I go to the bathroom to brush my teeth and wash my face, and when I'm back, I check my inbox before I turn everything off.

I already have a reply:

LOL at your AOL email address, Vale! What are you, 80 years old??

Anyway, I might have just sent your stuff over to Mr Marcus at Almastra.

Oops . . .

See you Monday xoxo

PART TWO

Chapter Ten

Rome, June 2010

The area of Rome I live in smells of hot urine and jasmine flowers in the summer. I breathe it in knowing that I must get through the pungent ammonia notes first to reach the sweet scent. The leashed dogs mark their territory all over these sizzling pavements. The shiny tarmac exhales the fumes back up as the heat rises.

I remember finding it repulsive when we first moved here three years ago. Now I don't mind it so much because it signals to my senses that a new season has arrived.

But the smell doesn't just come from the dogs; the zoo isn't far. I often walk past its huge walls and breathe in deeply to catch a faint whiff of something different and foreign, exotic. The scents tickle my nose and make me dream of being in places that have more odorous plants than cars, more animals than people. At the weekends, I often go into the zoo and wander around the paths furthest away from the cages, looking for ferns, a former passion of mine.

At night, we leave our windows open and listen to the teenagers on tricked-out mopeds race each other up and down the hilly roads and around the manicured squares. The noise used to keep me awake. In the countryside, when something loud and sudden happens at night, it's never good news.

Here in the city it's the norm, and I eventually got used to it.

I was born in the country, in a house on the edge of a small village. My parents moved there from Rome when my mother was pregnant. My father's work with a pharmaceutical company had started taking him all over Italy, and being based in the middle of a big city with a baby on the way and no parking spaces or a lift in the building they lived in suddenly didn't seem like a good idea.

Life outside of the city was supposed to be cheaper, healthier and easier.

My parents didn't want any other children.

'We have enough on our plate with you as it is. One more just doesn't make sense,' my mother told me once. 'Neither your father nor I saw the point of having more than one.'

I think she was chopping some celery for the sauce when she said it. I remember the *tac tac tac* of the knife on the wooden board. The sharpness of the blade as definite as her decision.

I'll never have children, but I don't know if having them needs to have a point. So many other things do, at least to me, need to make sense. And they often don't. But having a second child after you've already had one? I'm not sure it's one of them. I would have liked a sibling, I think, but not as much as I craved to grow up with pigs.

The kids I went to school with in the village would travel to exotic locations like the South of France or Greece during the summer and would brag about it during morning break. I stayed quiet. We didn't go anywhere else in the summer. My parents didn't like mixing with other people and found the hectic beaches with their rows of identical umbrellas and screaming children to be 'too much'.

I didn't mind not going away. Summer was all mine. I would lose myself in the glorious detail of the sprawling garden, building worm forts and ant castles. Scouring the woods for porcupine spikes and pheasants' feathers to make crowns out of. My shoes would come off at the beginning of June and go back on in mid-September when the school reopened. By then, the soles of my feet had gained the appearance of old leather, brown and tough enough to not hurt if I

94

stepped on a wasp by mistake. I would get lost in a world where, in my head, I was just another species of animal hiding in the undergrowth, running away from predators or waiting to pounce on prey. I would follow the traces of the gangs of wild boar that had overtaken the land and watch their movements from nearby, careful not to be seen by the fiercest members of every group: the females protecting their curious young.

I once stumbled across a dead wild boar in the clearing between two rows of olive trees, not far from the edge of the forest. Wolves sometimes roam these lands. They were reintroduced in part to help cull the ever-growing boar population, but they're no match in number. It's like giving an ant a whole baguette to eat every day.

The dead boar was lying on its side on the dry grass and looked small, only just into teenagerhood. It had large gashes on its flank and its neck, which were bubbling with something brown and sticky. Swarms of flies dotted the mucosa of its mouth.

Something deep within me kept me anchored to the ground. I couldn't look away.

The eye I could see from where I was standing was wide open and looking straight ahead. I wanted that eye to turn towards me so badly, to acknowledge my presence. To see that I wasn't scared of its decay, that I knew what would happen to its body, and that I too would return to the soil when it was my turn to attract the flies. I desperately wanted it to know that I was the same. I cared for that dead boar with an intensity of feeling that made my knees buckle and my hands tremble. My face was soaked with tears before I realised they were falling.

I stood looking at it until the sky turned pink, then black. The bats screeched and circled around us, getting lower with each round. When I got home that evening, my mother screamed at me and told me she'd been worried sick. I didn't tell her about the boar and its gashes.

She wouldn't have understood.

*

I looked forward to when my father would have a few days off from his job. His mood would lift and his whole demeanour change. He would walk at a slower pace, make less deliberate movements and take pleasure in stretching his body and yawning noisily.

While my mother spent time in the garden pruning and potting, the two of us would often go to the village to buy the paper and have breakfast at the café in the main square. I would select the largest pastry from the counter and devour the globs of custard escaping from each bite mark, licking the thick dusting of powdered sugar cleanly off while my father chatted about football with the owner.

On those days, my father would often say things like 'Jump in the car, we're going to have a look around. I heard the boars might have messed up the vineyard and I want to check.' The land was owned by a cooperative that was based outside of the village and employed local farmers to tend to it, but they often weren't around. My father and the farmers discussed how to manage it all the time, even though neither of them owned it.

On one of those trips, we drove past the farm – not the small one closest to us; this one was larger, with a row of outbuildings at the front and shiny tractors lined up on a scraggly lawn to one side.

'Let's stop here for a second, I want to show you something,' Dad said, parking the car just outside the outbuildings. I followed him. The closer I got to the entrance of the outbuildings, the stronger I could smell a toasted, earthy aroma that was new to me.

'What's this smell?' I asked.

'Tobacco. Here's where they dry it after they pick it in the fields. Look . . .' He opened one of many large metal doors that were much taller than him. Inside, rows and rows of yellowing leaves hung from metal poles running from one wall to another. He closed it only a few seconds later, but it was enough for a wall of hot air to almost knock me off my feet. The smell was overwhelming but not unpleasant. There was something comforting to it.

'Stop that. You're letting my leaves go moist.'

96

A raspy voice made us whip our heads round. An old lady with sparkling eyes and a blue cotton handkerchief tied over her white wisps of hair was looking at us and pointing a wooden stick in our direction. I hid behind my father, hoping that he had his car keys ready for us to make a quick escape. I remember being terrified in the few moments that followed. I put my hands over my eyes and peeked through two fingers, every muscle of my body ready to start running. I saw the woman's ripped apron starting to shake, then her whole body followed. A growl from deep within escaped her and I nearly fell to the ground with fear. I looked up at my father, expecting him to be as scared as I was, but he was smiling.

Confused, I looked at the woman. She was laughing, a handful of teeth jutting out from her mouth.

'Your faces!' She was struggling to catch her breath.

I was still scared, but Dad looked relaxed. He put his hands up as if being held at gunpoint and said, 'Sorry,' then pushed me in front of him. 'I wanted to show my daughter the ovens,' he told the woman.

Then he turned to me.

'This is Angela. She's the mastermind who runs this whole place. This is Valentina, my daughter.'

I put my hand out and Angela shook it with a surprisingly strong grip. The muscles in her arms were taut and supple under the wrinkled skin. She smiled at me.

'Nice to meet you, Valentina. Forget about the ovens, your old man doesn't know what he's talking about. Would you like to see some animals?'

I nodded. Although still terrified of her, I was too curious not to go.

I let her lead me towards the back of the main building, a large farmhouse with a storage area on the ground floor and a small flat above, much like our own house.

Behind the building lay a sprawling cacophony of home-made cages, paddocks and wire enclosures with small paths in between them. It looked like a maze with walls made of caged animals. Most

97

of the cages were open, apart from those where the animals were at risk of being taken by foxes, wolves or wild dogs, Angela explained, as she hobbled ahead of me with the help of her stick. I was struggling to keep up with her fast pace and had to resort to a slow jog to be able to catch her every word. She pointed to a cage with half a dozen big white rabbits inside, and a large enclosure with twenty or so chickens picking at the dirt floor.

'Like those. They're always closed. I've already lost too many to the fucking foxes.'

My eyes widened. I'd never heard an adult swear before. Especially an old lady. I nodded. *She must really hate those foxes*, I remember thinking.

There was only one enclosure I could see that was made of stone. It had walls that came up to waist height and a gate with a large lock on it to keep the entrance secure. It looked shallow from where we were standing, but as we got closer, I realised that it expanded down into the ground. The walls were made of large cubes of tufo, the local volcanic stone that every building is constructed from in this area. The floor was compacted soil. One half of the enclosure was covered, the other was left open. I looked in but couldn't see anything. The smell was strong, though, animal waste and rotting fruits. Again, I didn't find it unpleasant. It made me curious to see the source of it.

'Daiiiiii!' Angela yelled, slapping her hand against her thigh. 'Dai, dai, dai!'

I looked at her and was about to speak, but she told me to be quiet and pointed at the dark space under the roof. Nothing happened for a few seconds. Then I heard a low grunting sound and saw two shapes slowly make their way out into the sunlight.

They were huge.

'There they are,' said Angela. 'My pigs.'

'Those are pigs?'

'Of course. What did you think they were? Chickens?' That deep, growly laugh again.

I felt stupid.

'No, it's just that I didn't expect them to look like that.'

The two sows were large – Italian Landraces, I would later find out – and their skin was a dirty pink covered in short, thick yellowy-white hair. Their teats hung low, and their ears almost entirely covered their eyes. They were both looking at us expectantly, the dark beads of their pupils framed by two rows of white lashes. The smell was so strong I could almost see it in the air. They were making grunting noises and scratching the ground with their hooves. Angela patted one of them on the head and threw a squash she picked from the ground in between the two. Both sows flung themselves at it and made it disappear almost instantly.

I was shocked. Those two mountains of flesh with their droopy appendages, intense smell and intelligent, piercing eyes were nothing like the cute, bright pink, giggly pigs I had got to know in books and cartoons. They were not made to be cuddled and befriended. They were to be respected.

Their presence had a magnetic quality that I couldn't pull away from. I wanted to go in and smell them up close. To run my hand over their skin and look them in the eyes. I wanted to speak to them and have them speak back to me. I wanted to understand their needs and wants, their passions, their pain. I wanted to know where the piglets that had fed from those teats were. I wanted to eat what they ate and drink from the same trough. I *needed* to live in that dark hut among them. To listen out for Angela's sounds, to fight over the same food. I wanted to press my nose to their snouts, to smell their breath. It felt similar to how I'd felt when I saw the dead wild boar – that same longing and attraction – but a thousand times stronger.

Angela had moved on and was rounding up the geese, who were free to roam around.

I hadn't moved. The two sows had sniffed around for a bit longer, then had retreated inside the hut to lie in the shade. I was desperate to catch another glimpse of them, but they had gone too deep inside. I couldn't see them any more. I felt a deep sense of loss that was new to me.

It was as if a part of me had suddenly disintegrated. I just couldn't bear to tear myself away.

Pigs. There was something about them that buried itself deep inside my being in that moment. I was aware of it as it was happening. It seemed to make sense to me in a way that nothing else had up until that moment. Something in the way they were contained and dependent on the people who kept them, yet totally fearless in how they expressed their instincts. They were considered dirty by the human race, yet their eyes with their thick white lashes contained what to me looked like an ancient knowledge.

There was a before-pigs and an after. And I was now living in the after.

The plan I'd had for years of finding every species of fern was swept away there and then, as if there was simply no more room left in my head. Pigs had burst in and nothing else mattered.

'Valentina?'

My father's voice shook me from my paralysis.

'Come, we need to go.'

I turned around to look for Angela, but she was gone.

I took one last look at the pen and reluctantly tore myself away.

In the car on the way to the vineyard, my father told me about the new crop we'd soon see coming up everywhere – hazelnuts. They were in high demand, and our region, Lazio, was in the perfect position to grow healthy trees. Some of the land around us had already started transitioning to accommodate for the change. He told me they were going to replace most of the current crops eventually as they made more profit.

He didn't sound happy about it.

Normally I would have asked question after question, but I stayed silent on that journey. I was stunned by what had just happened to me in Angela's yard. There were no thoughts racing through my head,

100

no emotions. Just a sensation of change, of sudden focus, of stillness. All happening at once.

A vision of the two pigs bathed in sunlight, looking up at me. That image didn't leave my brain for weeks.

When I walk around the city now, breathing in what its tiny, coiffed animals leave behind and the sweet scents of its surviving plants, the pigs are still in me.

After all these years, they've never left.

Chapter Eleven

October 2010

'What's that smell?'

'It's coming from over there,' the boy answers, pointing in my direction.

He and his friend both have shaved hair that is shorter on the sides and longer on top. They have gelled the longer hair down and carefully divided each strand so that they rest, immobile and compact, over their foreheads. Their trousers are baggy and their colourful T-shirts tight. Their trainers are chunky and immaculate.

'I can't take it. It's too much.' The first boy pinches his nose with a theatrical gesture, while the other dry-retches.

'I'm going to be sick.'

'I might faint.'

'I think I'm about to die.'

They burst out laughing, cross themselves and hold their palms over each other like the priest does at Mass.

This last action confuses me for a second. But then I think that maybe they're imagining the smell as an evil spirit that must be chased away. It doesn't make sense rationally, but then a lot of what they do and say to me doesn't make sense.

The bullies seem quite dramatic today. They haven't involved religion before.

It's not the worst. They've kicked me and pulled my hair in the past or stabbed me with a sharp pencil on the thigh or the back. That felt worse. Physically at least.

But the religious element is new.

School is harder here because people are different. They are different to my old primary schoolmates in the countryside, but mainly they are different from me. It's as if they're from another part of the animal kingdom altogether. I watch the battles of emotions between my peers unfold around me as if I am a visitor at the zoo. I witness the mating rituals and interpersonal relationships in awe, but at a safe distance and without understanding the majority of what's happening. I like to think of the corridors of my school as if I am in one of those immersive animal experiences where families hop onto a jeep and drive through a natural habitat to see animals in captivity up close, but without having to peer through the bars of a cage. I walk around in the same way, watching groups of teenagers who look just like me on the outside as if they were lions, hyenas, gazelles and meerkats. I observe their behaviour and try to re-create it, but so much of it doesn't make sense.

They laugh when the jokes aren't funny, react over the top to things that don't warrant it; they whisper cruel things about each other, falling out one day and being fine the next. What is the point? I don't get it. But if inside I pretend to be a tourist who wants to know more about this human kingdom, then I find that it all feels easier to understand. It's just the way these animals behave, no different to, say, a peacock displaying its colourful train or a mandrill baring its teeth. They're just characteristics of their species. The fact that I don't seem to possess the same characteristics does make me wonder if it's me who's the different species altogether.

I keep chewing my sandwich, concentrating on keeping the mastication number equal with each bite. I find that counting the number of times my jaw clamps down on a morsel of food until it fully pulverises helps me zone out and not be too scared when the boys start

103

on me. There aren't many places for me to run away or hide – the school's courtyard where we go to do PE and eat our lunches is a concrete square surrounded by buildings. There is a door to the gym on one side, and a gate to the entrance to the school on the other. I can't leave the school without a permit and most of the boys tend to hang out around the gym entrance to smoke, so going through there is not safe. I sit on one of the benches alongside the edge of the courtyard and try to eat my lunch without being seen. But I hardly ever manage it.

Of course, I've tried telling them before that pigs don't have a natural smell. That they're clean animals that use mud as a way to protect their skin from harsh direct sunlight. They actually enjoy being washed as much as elephants or horses do.

That was the time I got pushed so hard I hit my back on the edge of the pavement outside the school gates and a green and yellow halo lingered on my skin for weeks afterwards.

I've also tried telling them that it doesn't make sense that I would still smell of pigs – even if they were smelly animals – because I haven't seen them in ages, and I wash almost every day. There is no way the smell would still linger on me after all this time.

None of it makes a difference, though. In fact, the more I speak to them, the worse it gets. So I stay quiet now and look the other way. I chew and count. Count and chew. But I stay alert. I don't like being hurt.

The boys are bad. But the girls aren't better. They're just different. When I first started at this school, a month after my parents and I moved back to the city from the countryside, a couple of girls in my class and I started to walk home together as we lived close to each other. During our walks we'd chat about different topics. They did most of the talking and I was happy to listen. I learned that one of them had recently gone to the coast of Spain with her family and was worried her tan had started to fade and look uneven. She'd held her forearm against her leg and asked us to tell her how bad it was.

'Please be honest!' she'd gasped before we'd even answered. The other girl had told her that it was not true, her tan was still perfectly even. I told her that her legs looked lighter, because they clearly did. I worried that the other girl had an undiagnosed eye condition that stopped her from seeing colours right. They both looked at me, then looked at each other without saying a word.

'What are your interests?' I asked, seeing as they both still hadn't spoken.

'Interests?' The word seemed to confuse the other girl. She thought for a bit, tapped her chin, then said, 'Well, I'm really into make-up lately.' She shrugged. 'I've been experimenting with different colours of eyeshadow. My sister has a palette that's all blues and greys that's to die for.'

'Oh my God, I'm obsessed with this taupe at the moment. It literally makes your eyes look ten times bigger,' tan-girl answered.

'You can see colours?' I asked eyeshadow-girl, relieved for her. She nodded but looked at me in a strange way for the rest of our walk.

I told them I loved pigs. That I missed the ones I used to know near my old house in the countryside and that I hoped to see them at the weekend. I spoke about them until the three of us got to my house. I could feel my heart rate increase with excitement and my words come out faster as I told them the reason why sows are so great at finding truffles is that to their delicate noses, that type of underground fungus smells like boar testosterone.

They stared at me with that strange look again and said nothing. Then we all waved goodbye and I walked up the stairs. I remember feeling glad that I'd found some new friends I could talk to about pigs, and for the first time since the move, I didn't wish I was back in the countryside every waking second of my day. I could hear the two girls laughing as they walked away, and I thought they must be feeling the same way. Maybe the city wasn't going to be so bad after all.

But the next day, everything changed at school.

None of the girls in my class talked to me any more.

It was like I was suddenly invisible. If I'd missed what a teacher had said, I would ask someone sitting next to me if they could repeat it, but they would just turn away. When I walked into the toilets, the group standing and smoking cigarettes by the ceiling window would usually ask me whether the teacher had noticed if they were gone yet. But now, they all just stopped talking and stared at me until I stepped into the cubicle and locked the door behind me. I would hear whispers coming from outside the door but could only make out a few words.

One of them was usually 'pigs'.

The girls I used to walk home with stopped going the same way. I saw them once or twice across the road, walking on the opposite pavement, and called their names. I don't know if they heard me or not, but they didn't turn back.

If at first I missed the countryside, after the bullying started I ached for it with an intensity that had something to do with survival.

Now, I close my eyes and see the yard in front of Angela's farm. The dusty ground never lies still; each car or tractor that goes past lifts a yellow cloud that settles back onto everything – stairs, plants, the lid that closes the well, sleeping cats – and the air is only clear for a few moments until something stirs it again.

After my first encounter with Angela's pigs, I couldn't get them out of my head. I'd always loved animals, but this was different. Looking into their eyes during that visit, I felt an intense surge of energy that reached every synapse of my brain and every atom in my body. I was hooked from that moment on. I've since wondered if seeing the dead wild boar first had opened something in me that had never closed, and meeting the pigs for the first time had solidified what was already happening. Either way, I was changed that summer.

My parents noticed it not long after. It was inevitable. I had been interested in specific topics before – comets, how thunderstorms form, ferns – but never with this intensity. I started asking them questions: 'How long do pigs live?' 'Are they all the same colour?'

'Do pigs live just in Italy?' 'What are female and male pigs called?' 'What about baby pigs?'

I thought of pigs when I ate, when I dreamed and when I was awake. I wanted to know everything there was to know about them. My parents bought me books and tried to answer my questions as well as they could. But it was very quickly not enough. I wanted – needed – to know things that went beyond what I could find in books, especially those aimed at children my age. At the umpteenth request for information, my mother had had enough. She sat me down and spoke to me.

'Valentina. Listen to me. Your father and I can see that you're very passionate about this. About pigs. It's great that you've found something you love. But it's getting a bit intense.' She looked away when saying this. I remember watching her mouth move as she talked. 'Your father has spoken to Angela and she has agreed to answer your questions, but she asks that you make yourself useful around the farm this summer. She says she doesn't have time to chit-chat with a child when there's so much stuff to do. We must respect this, okay?'

'Yes!' The word shot out of my mouth before she'd even finished speaking.

'But,' she held a finger up, 'if at any point you stop her from doing her job or get in the way . . .'

I held my breath.

'. . . she's going to tell us and you won't be allowed to go there any more. Understood?'

'Yes. Yes! Thank you,' I cried.

On the first day, I showed up at the farm at sunrise as arranged. Angela took one look at my sandals and shorts and told me to go back home and get changed into rubber boots and long trousers. I didn't understand why at that moment, but I quickly realised once I started following her in her daily tasks. The jumble of cages, rusty metal parts and old oil barrels filled with rainwater was never too far away from the legs of anyone trying to make their way through.

107

Cuts and bruises quickly became the norm. Having things fall on my feet or getting stuck in translucent puddles up to the ankle also did. And the stinging nettles would have been annoying had I still been wearing shorts. I kept being drawn back to looking at the pigs over and over, but I was also aware that if I didn't do my job correctly, I would lose this incredible opportunity. So I made sure to give the other animals enough attention too.

My main task became doing the morning and afternoon feeding round, for all the animals. As much as Angela was quick on her feet (and walking stick), it was a lot easier for me to climb in between the cages, or stick my arm into the chicken coop to reach the eggs that were furthest away. I was nimble and I didn't mind getting my hands dirty or the odd cut or peck. I enjoyed feeding all the animals and developed a good bond with the six geese, who had realised I was now a source of food and started following me around everywhere. But feeding the pigs was the best moment of my day, of course. I often left it until last so that Angela wouldn't shout at me for lingering if one of the other animals was still waiting.

That summer went by quickly. Before long, it started getting just a little darker each time I made my way over to the farm in the early morning and back home in the evening. I knew I would have to go back to school soon and wouldn't have as much time to spend on the farm. I was worried things were going to change, and that Angela wouldn't have use for me any more.

So once the school year started again, I made sure to be back there every weekend, without fail. I could see that Angela had now started relying on me for some of the tasks she was struggling with, leaving them until the weekend, when I would find her waiting for me with her crooked smile and a list of orders. We had a silent understanding that as long as all my jobs were done, I could spend as much time as I wanted staring at the pigs and tending to their needs. She had also started giving me a little money as the workload had increased.

'What's fair is fair,' she'd told me after a quick conversation with my father, and like clockwork, she would slip me a handful of crumpled notes at the end of each month.

But then something happened that ruined everything.

On my twelfth birthday, after a day of feeding animals, cleaning out their cages and eating a cake baked with that morning's eggs, I was in the living room reading a book. My parents came in and asked me to put the book down for a second. Then they both sat down in front of me and looked at me with serious eyes.

'Listen, there's something that's come up.' My father started picking at a loose thread from his jeans as he talked. 'We know you don't like change, but we both think it's for the best.'

I looked at the thread too, expecting the answer about the change he was talking about to somehow come from there. My mother was quiet and stared at a point behind my right shoulder. I turned around but couldn't see anything worth staring at. I was confused.

'What thing?' I asked.

My father looked at my mother and the two exchanged eyebrow wiggles and brow scrunching. This exchange seemed to get my mother frustrated enough to burst out talking.

'Look, what your father can't seem to be man enough to tell you is that we're moving to the city. To Rome.'

When she'd said this, she sighed loudly and uncrossed her arms, as if she'd been holding on to her breath for too long.

I looked at my father. He nodded.

My head was suddenly flooded with a thick fog of fear. I pressed my hands over my temples. Leaving the countryside? For good? The city seemed like no place to live. There was no way I could walk to the nearest field there, or track a hedgehog, or spot a flock of pheasants, or watch the wheat mature and the neighbour's foals grow into majestic horses. It was cars and walls and people. Shoes and umbrellas and eggs from tortured chickens. And the pigs. There were no pigs in the city. That alone was quickly turning my feelings of fear into full-blown panic.

'Why?' was all I could muster.

'Because it's better for your father's work,' my mother answered. 'More opportunities for growth there. And it means he won't have to travel so much around the country any more. Also ...' She trailed off.

'What?' I asked, looking from one to the other.

They exchanged glances again, and my father shook his head lightly. My mother huffed.

'Also, we think it would be good for you to be with people a bit more,' she continued, 'now that you're growing up. It's not healthy for a young woman of your age to spend all that time with animals. We can come back at the weekends and in the summer. You'll still be able to see them. I promise.'

That evening, I ran up to my room and cried until the moon disappeared. I thought of all the options I had. I thought of running away into the woods. Of asking Angela to let me stay with her (I could sleep in the pigpen). I considered telling my parents that my life could simply not go on if I was away from my animals. I was sure there was a way to change their minds. But in the light of the day, I realised how inevitable it was. I felt powerless and defeated. Deeply sad and still aghast.

We started packing our bags in the middle of the summer. We had to move before the school year started, and there was a lot of paperwork that still needed to be sorted out with the new place.

It felt wrong somehow to put my shoes back on before the skin on my feet had had time to properly harden, and when the figs on the trees were not yet ripe.

I couldn't bring myself to say goodbye to Angela, so at the end of my last full day on the farm, I told her I'd see her soon. That nothing was going to change.

'Go show them how we do things here, and don't forget what I taught you. People are animals too, the same rules apply,' she told me, patting me on the head. I shook her hand and thanked her.

110

I cried when I said goodbye to the animals. I told them one by one what I'd told Angela: that nothing would change.

We moved to the city on a scorching hot day. In the countryside I was used to a light breeze sweeping across the fields to keep things bearable, but in the city streets, the heat gripped every surface like a vice. Our flat was airy and shiny. My parents had done all they could to make it feel like a home. But it never did to me. It still doesn't.

I often think of the promises that were made on those last few days before my parents and I left the countryside behind.

The truth is that things were never the same.

Everything changed once we moved. We went back every weekend in the first few months, and I took up where I'd left off with Angela and the animals. Then winter came and my father's work got busier. My parents made new friends and started having dinner parties and work events to attend. They couldn't drive me there as often as before, telling me it would be cold and wet, that they were too busy.

Things at school were already bad, and I was alone all the time. I was used to it, but it wasn't like being alone in the countryside. Being alone in the city means being truly alone. The walls high and smooth like a prison cell, the noises loud and metallic, the voices strident and human. The zoo nearby with its haunting howls reaching high above the buildings.

Month after month went by and I only saw my beloved fields a handful of times.

'Don't worry, kid, me and the animals aren't going anywhere,' Angela told me once, after I apologised for not having been for a few weekends in a row. 'Just don't forget what you have at the farm. You know better than your parents, the city can never compete.'

Then one day Angela got sick. My parents wouldn't tell me exactly what was wrong with her beyond 'issues of the elderly', and she was in hospital for a long time. Her daughter was staying at the farm, but I didn't know her and she didn't know about mine and Angela's deal with the pigs. She'd tell me to stay away from them, that they were dirty and could bite. I wanted to scream at her: *How can you be Angela's daughter but be so ignorant?* I hated her in that moment, almost more than I hated my parents.

She was the one who rang my parents when Angela died. She told them she was doing the rounds of all the old neighbours to let them know that she'd gone peacefully in the hospital earlier that day. I knew she would have hated not being at home at the farm to die. She told me so many times that she wanted to go face-down in the soil like a chicken.

I always smiled when she said that because I knew exactly what she meant.

Angela's daughter sold the farm, and last I heard, a retired couple bought it and turned it into a private home. All the animals have gone. The countryside is forever in me, flowing into my veins and living under my skin. But I never want to go back there, it's too painful.

I tried once when my parents saw how distraught I was at the news of Angela's passing. I'd stopped eating and couldn't get out of bed for days. But when I stepped into the dusty farmyard, all I could see was my betrayal. How my broken promises were the only things I'd left behind for Angela and my animals. It felt impossible to do anything other than what my parents wanted for me. I didn't have any independence yet and I was too young to live alone. And yet I couldn't stop the overwhelming feeling that I'd let them all down.

And now that their lives were no longer part of this landscape it was unacceptable that mine would be. I stepped back into the car and asked my parents to take me back to the city. They seemed relieved. I closed my eyes until I could hear the noises of the motorway, then I opened them and forced myself to take in the grey of the road, the unnatural colour of the service stations and the regularity of the factory buildings that whizzed by. I didn't deserve Angela's world any more. It was too good and precious for someone like me, who couldn't keep a promise.

Chapter Twelve

September 2011

The ceiling fan rumbles on above me at top speed, swirling the dense air around. I can feel my ash-brown curls growing thicker and wilder, more alive than usual. The humidity is feeding them and bulking them up like rising dough.

Ice cream.

The sudden thought makes me sit up.

Yes.

I can taste its sugary deliciousness on my tongue already. But most of all I'm craving the sheer *iciness* of it. My room is so hot, and dinner was quick and light: a salad of cold rice, peppers and tomatoes. I'm still a little hungry and craving something refreshing and sweet. Pistachio ice cream would be nice, or mango sorbet maybe. Watermelon! Yes, of course. Pigs go crazy for watermelon, they eat all of it, flesh *and* rind; it's their favourite treat. I won't eat the rind as it tastes bitter to me, but I could eat the flesh all day – and as an ice cream flavour, it's *my* favourite treat too.

I smile to myself and put my comic book down on the bedside table. The dystopian vampire quest has kept me gripped, but it's no rival for the thought of ice cream that has just entered my mind. I stick my nose under my arm and take a deep sniff. Oh yes, it's musky all right. But it'll do.

On a Tuesday night like this there won't be anyone out that I'm likely to know – no one from school goes out on a week night, their parents won't let them, and even if they did, they wouldn't go to the ice cream shop. I think they consider it 'lame' and mostly hang out on the square smoking and drinking beer.

I slip into a pair of crumpled beige cargo shorts, sling my drawstring backpack over my shoulder and strap on my Velcro sandals.

The rest of the house is full of noise. The TV blasts out voices at incredible volume – two police officers are arguing onscreen, their faces red and tense. My parents are sitting on separate sofas, commenting on the scene over the noise.

'I TOLD YOU HE WAS GUILTY; I SAW IT RIGHT FROM THE START. SEE?' My dad is pointing at the screen with an outstretched hand.

I stand in front of them and wave, fast at first, then a little slower, and finally I stop. It takes a while to get their attention.

'I'm off, going to get an ice cream.'

'Move!' they answer in unison.

I don't say anything, just move out of the way. There's not much point trying to get their attention when it's TV time; it's all-encompassing.

I grab the keys to my moped from the dish at the entrance and slam the door on the way out. Running down the stairs and bounding outside feels like stepping through a heavy curtain of hot air and humidity that clings to my skin like a damp veil. The trees that line the road seem to droop a little, their leaves thirsty and pale. I jump on my petrol-blue Honda SH and start the engine with a couple of quick twists of the handle.

As I zoom along the dark, quiet roads of my neighbourhood with the helmet shoved back from my sweaty forehead, I push the engine hard to get the breeze to cool me down a little. I love how the air feels on my skin when I drive at night. How it gets under my clothes and puffs them out and around. While I'm zipping fast over tram rails

114

and cobbles, I'm no longer weighed down by humid clothes, but feel tingly and alive, almost as if I'm flying.

As I turn into the street, I can see the sign outside the gelateria glowing, a lurid pink and yellow neon cone as tall as a car, bathing the surrounding pavement in a bright aura. The place itself is nothing special: garish colours outside and bare stainless steel inside. They sell cigarettes and chewing gum behind a plain wooden counter at one end and coffee and ice cream behind a metal counter at the other.

Usually, the pavement outside is empty on a weekday – even though it's so hot, most people tend to come in, get a takeaway tub and go back home. And it's way too late for children to be hanging around as their parents wipe the gloopy mess off their faces. It should be deserted now. But it isn't.

Oh no.

As I approach, I can see a handful of people around my age, with floppy fringes and logo T-shirts, hanging out in a circle out-side the shop.

Why are they here?

They're all holding ice cream cones in their hands and laughing, shouting, pushing each other. I can see three boys – two sitting on mopeds, one standing – and two girls perched on the bonnet of a silver car. My back muscles contract and my stomach knots up as I realise that two of the boys look familiar. They are a year older than me and one of them, Edoardo, is the son of one of my moth-er's friends.

We were forced to hang out together as children and got on okay while playing with Lego, but he lost interest in me the moment he started playing football with a group of boys from school. The play dates stopped altogether soon after. On top of that, his father is my mother's gynaecologist, which is just too embarrassing to even consider.

Edoardo is tall, over six foot, with wavy auburn hair and a long fringe that finishes just above his eyelashes; his nose is large but fits

115

his face well in a way that makes him look almost regal. He's wearing his usual uniform of beige Carhartt shorts and a washed-out green T-shirt.

His friend is shorter and has cropped blond hair. I always see him hanging around Edoardo. I once heard him say 'weird' as I walked past, loud enough for me to hear.

This is not good, not good at all. Shiiiiit.

It's far too late to turn around. The street is narrow, and if I were to do a sudden U-turn, I would attract more attention and look even weirder.

No, there's no other option than to stop, go in fast, get my ice cream and go back out, hoping that no one notices me. I plan to get a cup, maybe balance it on the handle of the moped and go eat it around the corner, alone.

What a stupid idea to get ice cream, I think. I can feel my face getting even warmer, sweat beads now growing bigger and rolling faster down the side of my face. I take a deep breath, then another and stop the moped a few steps away from the group, between two parked cars.

Act busy, pretend you're on an important mission. In. Then out. It's simple, you can do it.

I can feel the group's eyes on me; they whisper something I don't quite catch.

Did I hear them say 'freak show'? Or did I imagine it?

I roll the question around in my head over and over to distract myself from the impending wave of panic I feel in my body.

I walk towards the shop with my head held high, eyes fixed on the open door, my steps slow and deliberate. The group start chatting again, so I dare to take a quick glance in their direction and notice Edo looking at me. He nods my way, and I respond with a brief smile, then look away. After a few painful steps, I'm finally in the safety of the shop; the chill of the air con makes the hair on my arms stand up. I hold on to the cool counter and breathe, looking at my knuckles

116

as they turn white. I stare at the flavours board, willing my knees to get steadier.

'Cone or cup?' the bored guy asks from behind the counter.

'C-cup, please.'

'Flavours?'

'Watermelon sorbet and hazelnut, please.'

'Whipped cream on top?'

'No. Thanks.'

The guy expertly shapes the soft ice cream into spheres and presses them one after the other into the cone.

He passes it across to me and I give him a note in exchange.

As I turn around, I find myself face to face with Edoardo and one of the girls from the group. He's staring at the board, but she's looking straight at me, her mouth stretched into a wide smile.

I take a step back and lose my footing for a second. My sandal grazes her ankle as I'm trying to keep my cone upright.

'Oh ... sorry.'

'That's okay. What flavours did you get?' The girl cocks her head and looks at me with brown eyes lined in black pencil.

She's the same height as me, a little shorter than Edoardo. Her skin is tanned and her hair is dark brown – no, black – and it's straight, cut choppily just above her shoulders. On her wrists there are a load of bracelets, some made of multicoloured cotton strings, some plain metal bangles. Her fingers are long and thin, adorned with silver rings, holding a bunch of keys and a pack of cigarettes. She's wearing loose linen trousers and a short top, the thin shoulder ties doubled by her black bra straps. Her voice is deep, and her lips are the colour of ripe plums.

'I ... erm ... Watermelon and hazelnut,' I reply, looking down at my ice cream cone. *Cone? How have I ended up with a cone in my hand? I asked for a cup. I won't be able to balance it on the moped and eat it away from the group now. This is bad.*

'Tasty. I'm Clara, nice to meet you.' She waves her hand, still smiling.

'Hi, I'm Valentina. Vale.' I smile back, but I can't quite focus on her face, it's too close, so I look down at the floor near her feet.

'Hey, how's it going?' mumbles Edoardo, still staring at the board.

I go to answer, but he says something else before I have time to.

'What you getting, Clara?'

'Guess,' Clara replies, her smile turning into a smirk.

He snorts.

As I watch them chat, all I can think is, *I don't want to be a part of this. I want to be back on my moped and flying home. Alone.*

But my feet feel heavy, my ice cream is beginning to lose shape, and Clara and Edoardo are standing between me and the door. They are discussing flavours now, holding each other's gaze for a little too long. I concentrate on nodding politely, licking my melting ice cream and making sure the whirlwind of my thoughts doesn't show on my face.

Be normal.

Once they both have cones in their hands, they move back out to join the group. I follow them out holding my own cone, my eyes fixed on my moped, only a few more steps away. *I could just run and jump on it. They will see me and give me a hard time for it at school, but at least the excruciating awkwardness I'm feeling right now will end for tonight.*

The rest of the group are still outside in the same positions they were in before. Clara walks over and sits back down on the bonnet next to the other girl, beckoning me to join them.

'Guys, this is Vale. Vale, this is the crew: Anto, Lorenzo and Beatrice. I think you already know Edo, right?'

The crew wave weakly after a quick glance. I nod and wave back in their general direction. I am feeling numb, my brain is frozen and the damp sensation under my arms is getting more intense. *Can they see it?* I need to come up with a good excuse to leave, one that isn't weird, but I just can't think of anything.

'Aren't you, like, Edo's ex-girlfriend?' Anto asks me loudly, smiling

118

broadly but with his eyes narrowed in a way that reminds me of a tiger about to pounce on its prey. Does he really think I'm Edo's ex-girlfriend? The thought of that makes me shudder a little.

The group laugh and look at Edo, who delivers a swift punch to Anto's shoulder. It takes me a second, but I understand from their laugh that Anto doesn't really believe it.

'Shut up, you dick. She's definitely not,' Edo answers.

'Edo, you didn't tell us that. Why are you keeping her hidden?' Beatrice asks.

'Ha ha, very good, Bea. Get off, you.'

Edo pushes Lorenzo off his moped and sits on it instead, leaning right back onto the seat and shaping his ice cream cone with long, lazy licks.

'Hey, Vale, what's he like in bed? Does he let you keep those shorts on?' Anto continues.

'I can see he's not much of a breast man,' Lorenzo joins in. They all laugh as Edo shows them the middle finger.

I'm getting to the end of my cone, which I'm eating slowly to not seem in a rush to leave, concentrating intensely on it. I smile weakly as if I'm in on the joke; reacting to it is only going to make it worse.

I can feel the cold sensation of the ice cream on my tongue, but I can't taste anything.

'I'm not ... We weren't ...' I say in a whisper.

They're all looking at me now, then at Edo, then back to me again, waiting for us to say something else. Lorenzo tries to shove Edo back off the moped, but Edo pushes him away. As I concentrate more and more on the slow and steady motion of my tongue going over and over the freezing ice cream, I've never wished harder for the courage to just turn around, calmly get back on my own moped and drive away, faster and harder than before. I crave the noise of the engine and the wind to drown my thoughts and their laughter so badly.

'Lorenzo, are you jealous or something?' Clara shouts across the laughter.

At this, the group go quiet again and look at her, as if waiting for her next move.

'What are you talking about?' asks Lorenzo, still wrestling Edo.

'Nothing. It's just . . . you seem pretty obsessed with who Edo is with. Sounds to me like someone has a crush,' she says, smiling. That smile again, the big one.

'Whatever, shut up. I'm not gay. Do you want me to show you?' Lorenzo grabs his crotch.

Clara laughs and shrugs. 'I'm okay. Are you sure you wouldn't rather show Edo?' The group burst into laughter again.

'It's true. You do look kind of gay in that top. And you're, like, touching him all the time and stuff,' Beatrice says, humping the air in front of her and pulling a strained facial expression.

They all laugh and point at Lorenzo, making kissing sounds as he looks on, no longer smiling. They seem to have forgotten about me, and the wave of relief I feel is instantaneous. I'm so grateful to Clara for diverting the attention from me that I want to run up and hug her. A warmth in the pit of my stomach replaces the knot. As panic slowly leaves my chest, I know this is the perfect moment for me to go. Their attention might turn back onto me soon, and I want to avoid that at all costs.

I brace myself and speak as loudly as I can, which is just enough to be heard over the laughter.

'I'm off, it's getting late. Nice to meet you all.' I try to sound as casual as I can, as if this is something I say all the time, as if I'm part of the group too.

They all wave distractedly without stopping. Clara smiles at me again.

'Nice to meet you, Vale, see you soon,' she shouts.

I walk away as calmly as I can manage, get onto my moped and zoom off, leaving the noise behind me. The feeling of being alone again and the wind cooling me off is so sweet that I almost start singing. Only the fear that the group might somehow hear me stops me. Instead, I replay in my head what just happened, over and over, each time starting again right after the girl I've just met rescues me and smiles and waves.

Clara. Clara.

Chapter Thirteen

October 2011

One of our teachers has died. The school has organised a special assembly today to 'celebrate the life and work of a truly incredible teacher and human being, whom we will never forget'. They've also told us that it's a chance for us, his students, to share thoughts, stories and cherished memories of our time with him.

Some of the boys in my class are excited to skip class for a few hours because of it. I feel neutral about it. I don't need to be there to remember him fondly.

We got into a conversation about pigs a while back, after he introduced us to *Animal Farm* by George Orwell. I couldn't get out of my head the fact that pigs would never turn into humans, walking on two legs, gambling and drinking, et cetera. They were naturally shaped to be much nimbler on four legs, while their snouts – which they use to understand the world – would be too far from the ground and they would not be able to see well at all if they only had their eyes to rely on. With all these points burning inside of me, I had decided to stay late after class had finished. I asked Professor Bechetti whether he thought the alliance between pigs and humans at the end should have happened or if it made more sense for the pigs to find new ways of ruling that didn't involve becoming so similar to humans. I must have been quite incensed by the thought, because I remember my voice rising as I spoke. He watched me until I finished, then took a few moments to respond. When he spoke, his tone was calm and his voice quieter than mine.

'You know, Valentina, I hadn't thought of that. I can see your point and I agree that in real life it would absolutely not make sense for pigs to turn into humans. In fact, the opposite would be preferable, I would say. Humans would be a lot nicer to one another if they treated each other like pigs do.'

I weighed up what he'd said and agreed that yes, it would make more sense for humans to get on the level of pigs.

'Of course, as we discussed during the lesson, *Animal Farm* is an allegory, so must be read in that light. But nonetheless, if it had been a piece of regular fiction, it would have been difficult to believe indeed.'

I left the class feeling calmer. I remember being worried he might laugh at me before speaking to him, but he'd seriously heard and considered what I had to say before answering. He was a kind man.

The assembly is in the gym. The cavernous space has been tidied up for the occasion and the large boxes and baskets that line the walls are filled with balls, racquets, cones and supportive cushions. The nets have been cleared away, and the court stripes on the floor seem odd without them. The room smells of rubber and sweat. The aroma is entrenched in the walls and floors of this place. No matter how long the doors stay open on a sunny day, I've never known it to smell of anything else.

Our class is ushered into the gym by our history teacher, who makes sure we're standing together and in an orderly row. We're one of the first classes to go in so we're near the front.

I can see the headteacher's shoes clearly from where I'm standing; they're polished leather with a gold-looking buckle on top. One of them has a scuff mark on the side and I can see the dark seam of her tights sticking out of the other.

I try to imagine why the headteacher's shoe is scuffed and picture her tripping in the street and rubbing it against the wheel of a parked car. *She must have not realised the mark is there*, I think. She's usually very carefully put together and doused in perfume. I can't imagine she would leave the shoe looking like that if she knew.

I think of my lovely pigs and wonder, for the millionth time, where they are and what happened to them after they left Angela's farm.

Of course, there is one very real possibility. But I will not acknowledge it or take it into consideration. It's too horrible and heartbreaking to think about and so I refuse to. Angela's daughter might be very different from her mother, but surely even she wouldn't do something like that? I shudder visibly without realising it until the classmate standing by my side looks at me. I feel myself blush and turn the other way.

I need to remember where I am. It's not safe.

Once the whole school is in the room and arranged into neat rows, the headteacher brings her foot down onto the wooden surface she's standing on a few times to get everyone's attention. The sound of her square heel against the hollow box makes a loud, alarming sound.

The room descends into a hushed silence.

'Good morning, boys and girls,' she begins. 'As much as this is a very sad occasion, it is still nice to see all of your faces together in one room.' She pauses to look around with a smile. On either side of her, standing on the floor, are the other teachers, who look serious and composed.

'As you will all know by now, our beloved colleague and teacher Professor Bechetti passed away last week in very tragic circumstances. I don't need to tell you what an immeasurable loss this is for the school and every single one of us here present today. I can see this clearly from looking at your faces and hearing the stories many of you have shared with me and the other teachers in the last few days. It is indeed a tragedy.' She pauses again, bows her head, and takes a deep breath, then looks around the room once more.

'Today we are here to celebrate Professor Bechetti's life. To remember him and honour his legacy. He may have left us, but his teachings, kindness and presence will never be forgotten.'

Her voice goes up a notch to cover the pockets of chatter that have started to rise in the crowd.

'I know that some of you have prepared some readings you would like to share. Could you please approach the podium and get into a line?'

One by one, a few pupils come to the front and line up by the podium. Some are holding printed-out pages, some scribbled notebooks, and a few books of various thicknesses. The first pupil climbs onto the box, helped by a teacher. She seems unsteady on her feet once she gets up there. It's quite high, and it looks like it's making her feel uncomfortable. But when she starts, her voice comes out clear and steady.

'Dear Professor Bechetti, you were the light that shone through the clouds of ignorance. Your presence gave us, your humble pupils, a reason to discover the masterful works of the greats, from the ancient Latins to the contemporaries.'

A few sniggers rise up from the crowd. The girl stops for a second and one of the teachers shushes the congregation with a loud hiss. When everything is quiet again, she continues.

'We will never again witness the way your face would light up when reading a beloved passage or be transported to magical worlds by the joyous notes of your voice. We are, Professor Bechetti, bereft and orphaned by the loss of you. Rest in peace, sweet man, knowing that the world is a richer place for having had you in it.'

She puts her notebook down and smiles thinly. Two fat droplets fall from her eyes as she takes a small bow. She gets helped back down by the same teacher as the crowd claps.

The second pupil to speak is tall and has thick stubble and the darker shade of a moustache, which make his face look older than his spindly body betrays. I've seen him around the corridors before and heard other students tease him for having a hairy back. He takes a moment to steady himself, then starts reading a moving poem.

One after another, students and teachers climb up onto the stage and read something that feels meaningful to them. As I'm standing there thinking about how scary going up in front of everyone must be, I feel something poke me in the side. Pointy but soft, like a finger.

I turn around and recognise the face staring at me. Clara. She's smiling and waving. She's standing a couple of rows behind me so must have stretched her arm past a few people to reach me. Seeing her again in the flesh is surreal. She's occupied my thoughts since we met.

I'm grateful that she stood up for me at the ice cream shop. It could have gone very badly if she hadn't said what she said to the others. She did it so subtly, and it was quick, before it had time to escalate into something too big to be stopped. But it's not just gratitude. Just being in her orbit for those few moments has left my brain flooded with thoughts of her. Her wit and the way she turned the attention of the group away from me and onto someone else with just a few words was mesmerising. I keep thinking about her dark hair and the way it shone under the street light, unlike my mess of dry curls. I can hear the jingle of her jewellery as she ate her ice cream and fiddled with her keys. I can see the way her bra strap was showing under her top, something I would never dare do for fear of others pointing it out or accusing me of being brazen. But her light reflecting onto me has left a trace or two. I walk a little taller since meeting her, and have started using my mother's mascara. I've noticed it makes me look more awake. I'm thinking of using some oil to tame my curls and make them shinier too.

Although she's been always in my thoughts from the day we met, I was fully expecting her never to acknowledge me again – the way it has been with those two girls in my class, or with Edoardo – but now she's smiling at me and waving. If it wasn't happening right in front of my eyes, I wouldn't believe it.

I smile and wave back.

Clara points at the few centimetres of space next to me and starts making her way through to get closer.

As I watch her gently push people out of the way, I'm suddenly aware of my body and its functions. *Am I sweating? Do I smell bad? Are my arms too hairy? When was the last time I washed my hair?*

In less than a second, she's standing next to me. I'm paralysed with fear, but I would die if she realised. I would hate to make her feel uncomfortable.

'Hey, you,' she whispers, eyes fixed on the stage, where the current speaker, a boy with braces, is gripping his printed-out piece of paper with shaky hands.

'Hey,' I whisper back. My throat and mouth feel like they've been stuffed full of cotton balls.

'You okay?'

I swallow to try and get some moisture back into my mouth, but it doesn't work. I nod and smile, looking in the same direction as she is.

'What do you think? Pathetic, right?' she whispers, gesturing to the boy. 'Did you hear Miss "Masterful Works of the Greats" earlier?'

I think she means the first speaker, who read out the piece she wrote herself, which I found quite touching.

'I did,' I tell her.

'So funny. Like seriously? Back there we nearly pissed ourselves laughing. Prof Mariani had a face like a smacked arse looking at us.'

'Yeah, so funny,' I say.

As I look at the teacher Clara has mentioned, I can see her staring back. We must be making too much noise. She holds her finger to her lips to tell us to stop talking and I nod quickly. I don't want to get into trouble. In the past, people who've been caught disturbing the assembly have been called out in front of everyone and asked to leave and go back to their classroom. Clara has noticed the teacher telling us off but doesn't seem to care.

'What about train-tracks up there? He looks like he's about to cry, poor bastard,' she whispers, this time even closer to my ear.

I look up, and the boy does seem to be getting quite flustered. He's wiping his brow and his hands are shaking harder than ever. He's been going for some time, so surely he will be done soon. I hope so for his sake.

I giggle. 'He does. It must be tough, though, standing up in front of everyone. I do feel for him,' I say.

Then I immediately regret it. Clara has stopped smiling and is looking at me.

Have I upset her? I could hit myself. If this is the last time she speaks to me, I'll never forgive myself. The few moments of silence that follow are like torture. She takes a step away from me and looks like she might be about to go back to her row.

But instead, she comes closer again and whispers, 'Yeah, I know what you mean. But he's a creep. My friend said he's always staring at her, and once she saw him touch her desk and then smell his hand. I don't feel sorry for people like that, it's disgusting.'

She's waiting for me to say something back, I can tell by the way her eyes are fixed on mine. It's tricky, I can understand why someone would feel compelled to feel and smell a surface that looks attractive to them. I have done it many times. But on the other hand, Clara seems to think it's weird behaviour.

'That's ... odd,' I answer, careful not to let my voice wobble with uncertainty.

She nods and smiles. The relief I feel is instant.

'Isn't it? Listen, I'm going to have to go back to my row or Mariani will kill me, but have you been to Bamboo's before?'

I remember a few people in my class talking about it; it's a café where everyone goes to smoke, hang out and drink coffee. I've never been.

'Once or twice. Why?' I answer.

'Oh, I've never seen you there. Anyway, I'm going after school on Friday, do you want to come?'

128

I don't even try to hide my happiness at being asked. I smile and say yes before she's even stopped talking. I don't think about whether my parents will let me go or if there might be other people there who might make me feel awkward. I don't want to smoke, coffee makes me jittery, and I've never 'hung out'. I would still much rather be alone, in a forest, listening to the sound of wild rabbits looking for berries in the bushes. But I'm here now, in the city. And being friends with Clara is as close to that feeling as it can get.

'Yes, okay,' I tell her.

'Great. I'll be there at three, come then.'

She squeezes my arm and disappears. I don't turn around for fear of ruining the moment or attracting the attention of the teachers even more than we already have.

We. Clara and me.

She found me and picked me out of the crowd.

And now she wants us to hang out. I smile until I realise everyone around me is either serious or silently crying, so I stop.

We meet at Bamboo's that Friday, and we drink cappuccinos and watch the people around us.

Clara finds us a table in the corner which gives us a perfect view of the whole place so we can see who comes in and who goes out without having to move a muscle. I listen to her talk about her day and how people at school annoy her. She tells me about her recent fallout with two of her best friends and how she caught them saying nasty stuff about her even though she'd been nothing but lovely to them.

She calls them ugly and mean. I nod furiously and tell her that I can't believe how someone could be so horrible. That they don't deserve her friendship, that they must be evil.

I listen to Clara for hours; she talks and talks with hardly a pause for breath. Her stories are all similar – it seems like there have been so many slights against her in the last few months. I feel bad for her. I know what it's like to not be treated well, and it makes me feel good to help her. I try really hard to have my best listening face on. It works, because she keeps on going and going, and I keep on nodding and ordering us more coffee. We chat until the sky turns dark, then she tells me she needs to go home or her mother will get hysterical again.

'I liked hanging out. Shall we do it again next week?' she asks as we're getting ready to leave.

'I'd like that, yes,' I say.

So we do. And the week after, we meet up again, and the one after that.

People at school still call me names, but the ones who have seen Clara and me hanging out at Bamboo's don't any more. Being her friend feels like walking around with armour that makes people look at me in a different way. I'm not her – I never will be – but even just being near her allows me to borrow her shine. She's the sun and I'm her moon.

I still miss the countryside and my animals. But less so now that Clara is in my life. I no longer watch the human species thinking I must be an alien zoomed in from far away.

There might still be insurmountable differences between me and my classmates, but at last it feels like we're on the same planet.

Chapter Fourteen

December 2011

As I zip through the cobbled streets of the old centre on my moped, I notice that people all around me have already begun to celebrate New Year's Eve. People walking to and from places are wearing plastic glasses that spell *2012* in gold and glitter. They drink from bottles in the street and laugh and hug outside bars. It's not even ten yet, but the squares are already packed. You can't stay home on New Year's Eve, apparently, you can't have a glass of champagne with your parents at midnight then go to bed by one; you have to go out and celebrate.

'Live a little!' my mother told me earlier. 'Go out with Clara and get drunk.'

I've only got drunk once, at a family wedding, and it was miserable. My memories of the night are of trying to clean the toilet after throwing up in it, my cheeks damp with tears, the smell of bleach making me retch, the hardness of the plastic seat on my forehead. I'm not interested in getting drunk ever again.

As I park my moped across the road, I can see that Clara is already there, smoking and leaning against a railing. She's looking directly at me, unsmiling, taking long puffs and holding her cigarette pinched between thumb and index finger. My shoulders tense up seeing her pursed lips and dark, fixed eyes. I can't think of anything I might have done to annoy her; we had a good day at Bamboo's only a week ago, when we played endless games of 'Would you rather?' and drank cappuccinos.

Nice and normal. I tell myself not to worry, and concentrate on tying the chain around the wheel and to a lamp post.

As I cross the road, Clara's features soften, and her mouth stretches into a thin smile.

'Hey, you,' she shouts across the traffic noise.

'Hey, you.'

'You good?'

'All good.'

'You ready?'

I still have no idea what the plan is for tonight. Clara has kept it vague and only told me to meet by the old Temple of Vesta.

'I . . . Yes, I'm ready. I think?' My voice comes out as a croak.

Clara smiles and rolls her eyes. 'Don't worry. Follow me. Try not to attract attention or, like, break a bone or something.'

'What . . . Why would I break a bone? How?'

She looks at me and raises her eyebrows. 'You'll see. Come.'

She throws her cigarette on the floor and presses her boot hard on it. Then, without looking back, starts walking towards a high red-brick wall to the left of the railing.

It must be the wall of a monastery garden; there are many of these old buildings on the seven hills Rome was built on, all of them centuries old. The monks file in and out during holy celebrations and on charity duties. Some of them wear sandals all year round and brown cloaks tied around the waist with thick rope. Others dress in plain black or blue clothes and keep their eyes on the ground when making their way through the traffic. This wall is probably the only protection they have between their calm and reflective world and the hordes of tourists that stomp around central Rome's cobbled streets at all hours of the day and night.

We stop after a few steps and I look at the wall next to us, then around, not seeing anything that could give me a clue as to what's next.

'Right. We're here.' Clara's tone is lower, her voice quieter. 'See this crack here? I've tried it, it's easy. You just need to stick your feet in it, one after the other, and grip with your hands in the space between the bricks. Then at the top you pull yourself up. On the other side it's much easier, you just jump.'

I can't believe it. Clara wants us to climb a wall? A wall that is as smooth and straight, and *tall*, as all the other brick walls in the area.

'What? Clara, that's ridiculous. It's impossible!'

I give the wall a closer look and run my hand alongside its ridges and into the red-brick innards as Clara looks around us, smiling. There is a deep crack in it, sure, but it's narrow, and the bricks all around it look so smooth, so much so that they reflect the surrounding lights in places, as if they've been polished.

'There's no way we won't fall. It's really high.'

Clara focuses her gaze on me, and her expression darkens once more.

'Is it? Oh. I thought you wanted us to celebrate New Year's Eve together.'

I notice her eyes shining, her mouth trembling a little as her head hangs lower, her face now directed at the pavement in between us. She appears smaller all of a sudden, like a child who's just been told off.

'I ... I brought a bottle of wine for us to drink. Look, I even got glasses.'

She unzips her backpack to reveal two clear plastic stemmed glasses and a bottle of white wine with a cork stuck halfway in.

'My mamma's wine, I got it from the fridge.'

'Won't she ...'

'She won't. And even if she does, I don't care.'

I can feel my heart racing hard. I don't know what to do. Every part of my being is screaming that climbing the wall is a stupid idea; images of all the things that could go wrong begin flooding my brain. I can picture us both lying on the pavement bleeding out, or Clara bleeding and me shouting for help but no one comes. Or my trousers getting stuck on the top of the wall and tripping me as I jump, smashing my skull against the other side. The splash of blood that it would leave ... The monks finding me the next day ...

It's a terrible, dangerous idea. But Clara is the first friend I've ever had, and the thought of her being upset, angry with me or disappointed makes my palms sweat and my heart race even faster. Before Clara, I'd never gone out for drinks in the evening or met new people or drunk cappuccinos and gossiped for hours. I'd never even done it for a minute. That sense of closeness with someone other than my parents is so new to me, and it feels much bigger. Clara listens to me; she *cares* about me. And now that I've had a taste of being normal, of having a friend, the thought of things reverting to the way they were before makes me feel dizzy with fear. I can't go back to my old life.

'I just ... I ... Okay. Let's do it. If you think we won't get hurt.'

Even though a deep sense of relief washes over me as Clara's mouth opens into a large smile, my body remains tense.

She jumps up and down with excitement and squeezes my arm hard.

'Great! It's going to be so much fun, I promise. Okay, I'll go first. You help me up, and once I'm on top of the wall, pass me my bag. Then you climb up and I'll wait for you on the other side. Got it?'

She looks around for any police cars, then hands me her backpack and begins climbing. It's clear she's done it before; her hands know where to find the right cracks straight away and her feet are steady.

Who has she been here with? I don't like how this question makes me feel.

Clara has lots of other friends, but she always says that I'm her favourite, and from what she tells me, it sounds like the others annoy her all the time.

'Here! Pass it over.'

She's at the top already and is straddling the wall, stretching her arms towards me.

I throw the bag; she grabs it and disappears down the other side.

134

'Your turn!'

I feel dizzy. I've carefully observed the route Clara took up the wall and have a good idea of what to do, but as I put my foot into the first crack and my hand grips a nook halfway up, I can feel my fingers tremble against the bricks.

I put all my energy into pulling myself up and hope that my foot doesn't come out of the crack, as there is no way I could hold myself up with just my fingers. I can't hear Clara's voice any more, but I know that she must be waiting for me on the other side, getting impatient. As I pull myself up the first few metres, I find the second crack higher up the wall and put my free foot in there; this one is larger and feels more stable. I climb up and am now about halfway. Both the top of the wall and the pavement beneath me look incredibly far from where I am. This is a very, very stupid idea. My knees have started to tremble now too.

I don't have time to ponder over the distance too much as I begin to hear voices coming from down the road, getting louder as they draw closer. I cannot let them see me climbing this wall. It's far too late to come off it, as they would notice me climbing down to their level or jumping onto the pavement. They might just miss me, though, if I go further up and away from their line of sight. The sheer panic of getting found out somehow gives me the strength to pull myself up once more, find the next nook and reach the top of the wall with the tip of my fingers. I grip the smooth tiles with both hands, stick the fronts of my shoes into as many cracks as I can find and manage by some miracle to pull myself up enough to be able to lift a leg over and straddle the wall.

'There you are. Come on, it's nearly time.'

'Time for what? Okay, I'm coming.'

I hear the voices underneath me, on the outside of the wall: a group of men and women in high spirits, chatting loudly. I hold my breath and wait. They don't stop and I see their backs move away from me. I surprise myself exhaling loudly.

'Come on, Vale! You can just jump from there.'

I swing my legs towards the other side and notice that the ground is slightly raised. The jump isn't too far and there's what looks like thick grass between the trees on the ground, which should make for a softer landing. I hold my breath and launch myself, landing awkwardly on my feet but without pain. As I brush the brick dust off my knees, I look up at Clara. She smiles at me briefly, then turns around and starts to walk into the darkness.

The garden is surrounded by walls and thick canopies of trees that keep most of the twinkling evening lights out. I follow Clara but can't see anything more than her yellow backpack and the artificially lit city sky above us.

The surrounding sounds seem to suddenly move very far away, with only the odd siren breaking through the tall trees. I wonder whether the monks are already asleep or if they're getting ready to celebrate New Year's Eve too.

I can see a large structure next to us in the dark; it must be one of the monastery's surrounding houses, where the gardeners and house staff base themselves.

We walk around it, careful not to make any noise, and leave it behind as the trees and plants begin to open up onto a dark lawn. Clara slows down and turns to wait for me. As I catch up, I can see her looking at my face intently.

'We're nearly there. Are you ready?'

I nod. I don't know what I'm declaring myself ready for, but it doesn't matter.

The silence of the place, the closeness to Clara and the thought of sharing this experience with her are making me fly high, and I'm enjoying how that feels in the pit of my stomach.

Directly in front of us, the lawn seems to end abruptly, and it's only as we get closer that I can see what's beyond it. The monastery's garden looks onto the most incredible view of Rome that I have ever seen in my life. I can see the dome of St Peter's, its colonnade around the square in front of it; I can see the fortress of Castel Sant'Angelo with the bronze statue of Archangel Michael on top, sheathing his sword. I see the winding streets, the squares, the Forum, the Colosseum shining almost silver in the faint moonlight. Rome at night, lit up and resplendent like an ancient bejewelled queen. I take in a deep breath, which gets caught in my chest for a long moment. I have never seen my city this way. Not from that angle, not quite so much of it at once. It's incredible, and the view fills my head with its beauty. I wipe my eyes with the back of my hand and look at Clara, who is standing next to me, hands on waist, staring ahead.

'It's so beautiful. I can't believe it. How did you find out about this place?'

'I can't remember. I think I read about it somewhere. It's great, isn't it?'

She's now looking through the bag and getting out the wine bottle, the two glasses and a thick fleece blanket. She sits on the grass and motions for me to do the same.

'Here. A little bit or a lot?'

She doesn't wait for my answer; pours a large glug in and hands the glass over.

'Just wait and see when we get closer to midnight. It's going to get even better.'

She takes a long gulp, arranges the blanket across us both and lies back on the grass, resting on her elbows. I take a careful sip and do the same.

We stare ahead at the view and drink our wine for a while. I don't want to break the silence with a stupid remark, so I remain quiet, waiting for her to speak. The wine has begun to make my head swirl a little and my limbs relax. It's not unpleasant. I was feeling cold before, but I'm now fine. The wine, the blanket and my friend's heat next to mine are keeping me warm.

Clara speaks. 'I love it here.' Her voice trembles. 'But I wish I could enjoy it as much as you. You're lucky, you're always so happy.'

137

'I'm not ... Why, what's up? Are you ... not happy?' I'm suddenly worried I've done something that has upset her without realising it.

'It's nothing. Don't worry.'

'Please. I'd like to know. To see ... if I can help. I would really like to help.'

'It's okay. I don't think you'll understand anyway.'

'Please, Clara, I'll try my best, I promise. I don't want you to be sad. Is it my fault?'

At this she turns around and looks at me, her mouth trembling and her eyes filled with tears. I begin to well up too and grip the grass underneath my hands hard. I can't stand it; seeing her like this makes my chest burn with pain.

'Please?'

'It's okay. I don't want to talk about it right now. I just want to drink. Pass me that bottle, don't be greedy.' She's smiling again now and gesturing towards me with her glass.

She grabs the bottle with both hands and pours me another large measure. Then she takes a big gulp and lies on the grass, arms outstretched and eyes to the sky. She lets out a loud burp and we both burst out laughing.

'Oops, sorry, monks,' she loud-whispers.

'Yeah, sorry you're so boring, monks!'

We both start giggling and dare each other to whisper more and more loudly without waking up the monks or their staff. A cat runs past us letting out a startled meow and we repeat the sound, clawing and pawing at the air.

As the first few fireworks begin to break off into the dark sky over the city, we stop and sit back up to take in the view.

'Must be midnight. Have you got the time?'

'No. But it must be if the fireworks are starting.'

'Hey ...'

'Hey what?' I giggle.

'Happy New Year, monks!'

'Hahaha. Happy New Year, you monk!'

'*You're* a monk!'

We hug tightly and clink our plastic glasses together, then go back to looking at the sky, now filling up with thousands of minuscule sparks of different colours and shapes.

'My mother is driving me crazy, Vale. She's a bully,' Clara blurts out, her body visibly stiffening.

'What do you mean?'

'Just that. She's ruining my life. Sometimes I want to end it all, you know? Like, if I hurt myself, she can't continue to hurt me.'

'Clara, I . . . Please don't say that. I don't want you to hurt yourself. Please, promise me you won't. Ever.'

I look at her with wide eyes, searching for clues that she's not being serious, that we're still playing around. But her eyes are still, her face calm and her hands clenched in tight fists. She's not joking any more.

'I mean it. She makes my life hell. I hate her.' She looks straight ahead.

'Well, I hate her too then.'

'Not as much as I do.'

I can feel my legs getting more and more restless, so I stand up, walking up and down in front of Clara.

'I do, I swear. I do. I HATE her.'

'Thank you, Vale, you're a true friend. My only real friend.' Clara exhales loudly.

I'm standing there dizzy and restless, my heart exploding together with the fireworks in the sky ahead of us. I want to scoop her up and make it all better.

'I swear next time she pisses me off I'll stab her,' Clara says with a giggle, miming the motion of a knife going through a person, one, two, three times, stabbing the air in front of her.

'*I'll* stab her! I'll stab her for you, Clara. Stab, stab, stab.' I'm now also gripping an imaginary knife with both hands, lowering it quickly and repeatedly onto an imaginary person in front of me. 'Stab her good.' I laugh.

Clara's face goes dark as she gets up and moves closer to where I'm standing, eyes half closed and legs planted wide on the grass, still gesticulating with my imaginary knife.

She grips my forearms and pushes her face close to mine. My eyes are now wide open as the noise of the fireworks gets louder and louder, the sky bursting with artificial colours. The sounds of well-timed explosions reach us in waves.

She locks her eyes on mine for a long, long second, then pulls me close to her, our cold cheeks sharing heat as they make contact, my heart beating so fast I worry she might feel it against her chest. Her right hand slides down my arm and her fingers knit with mine. Her left hand follows. We stand this way for ages, gripping each other's palms, cheek against cheek, as the world explodes around us.

Chapter Fifteen

February 2012

When pigs are happy, they wag their tails just like dogs do. In different contexts, it can also mean they're ready to fight. But pigs are not usually fighters – unless they're threatened. They're mostly happy to snuggle up to each other, eat food and stay away from the midday heat. If I was a pig, I would not have stopped wagging my curly tail since meeting Clara. My life has been so much better with her in it. The two of us have become a duo and it's clear for everyone to see. At school, when someone is looking for Clara – including people who would never have spoken to me before – they come to me to ask where she is. I know her schedule well, so I always have an answer.

Now that the other students can see that I too have a best friend, I'm no longer invisible. No longer a target. Clara is in a different league around here; younger students look up to her and those our own age know to stay on her good side. She's too quick, too sharp-witted to be antagonised. As long as I'm in her company, I'm safe. It's as if my body, up until now, was something intangible. As if I knew in my mind that I existed and was worthy of respect, but the knowledge didn't always transfer to the people around me. Since meeting Clara, my body feels solid, my feet are planted on the ground and my head is held up higher, without attracting the wrong type of attention.

Clara told me that a few weeks ago, some of her old friends asked her why she wanted to hang out with someone like me. Apparently she got very offended and told them that I'm way better than any of them could ever wish to be.

'You should have seen the look on their faces, Monk, like they'd been eating lemons,' she said, sucking in her cheeks and crossing her eyes. We laughed and laughed.

Now they mostly leave her alone. I watch them chatting sometimes in the school corridors, but she doesn't go to Bamboo's or around town with them any more. It's with me she goes to those places now. My biggest fear is to be left behind like they've been. I still don't understand exactly why she's no longer friends with them, apart from the fact that they've become 'boring'. I'm trying my best to do what she says, hoping that the same won't happen to me.

I took a big step the other day and invited her over to my house for lunch. My parents had been asking me for a while.

'Clara this, Clara that. It's all we hear. The amount of times you've mentioned her she must be pretty special. In my mind she's as tall as a giant and breathes fire,' my father said not long after I met her. 'If I didn't know that she went to your school, I'd think she was a pig! Actually, no, you mention her even more than pigs lately.' My mother laughed and they looked at each other in this complicit way that was so weird. I rolled my eyes at him for the first time ever, but it didn't stop him from saying that kind of thing more and more often. I realised that if they met her, they would probably stop being so curious.

We walked over from school together, and I was so nervous I talked non-stop the whole way. Clara didn't say much but just giggled at my rambling, detailed descriptions of the history of the buildings in my area and theories on why half of it should be turned into farmland. When we got to my front door, my left eye was twitching and my mouth felt like it was filled with cotton wool.

Afterwards, I felt stupid for worrying so much. It went extremely well. Clara sat next to me at the table and put up with the onslaught of my parents' questions – 'Where is your surname from?' 'Where do you go on summer holidays?' 'What do your parents do?' 'Are you enjoying school?' – in the most wonderful way. Each time, she paused for a second or two before speaking, then gave a thoughtful answer. And she was funny!

'School is fine, I don't mind it. My grades are better now than they were at the beginning of the year. Nothing big to report. Except for Prof Mariani. You know how she's cross-eyed?' My parents nodded. 'Well, I got in trouble the other day because I was talking in class while she was explaining something. There was no telling her that I wasn't chatting to my friend; she just wouldn't believe me. I was telling her and telling her, but she didn't listen and was getting angrier by the minute. In the end, I had to reveal the truth.' She paused for a second and looked at my parents' faces, each hanging on her every word.

Unable to contain a giggle, she continued, 'I told her, "I was talking to you, Prof, I wanted to ask if I could go to the bathroom. But one eye was looking at the blackboard and the other at the door, and you must have missed me."'

They roared with laughter, my father slapping his leg and my mother repeating the punchline to herself and giggling. I forgot to laugh because I was too busy looking at their faces, from one to the other, and watching the chemistry unfold. It was so good. Once or twice, she complimented me in front of them too.

'I've never known anyone talk about a subject the way Vale does about nature. She knows everything. The names of trees, birds, insects. Not to mention pigs, of course. It's really quite something. And she's never arrogant with it, just comes out with a nugget of wisdom just at the right time.' My parents nodded and smiled. 'It's as if she has not one, but two brains under those lovely curls of hers.'

She'd been annoyed at me so many times for talking about pigs in public that her words confused me. I'd thought she didn't like it and that it was embarrassing. But maybe she'd changed her mind. I would love to go back to talking more about it with her; I still had so many facts I hadn't told her. I smiled and nodded too.

'What a lovely thing to say. I couldn't agree more,' said my mother, her eyes suddenly shining.

Just before Clara left to go home and study, my father told her that she should come back for lunch again soon. To that, she replied, 'I'd love to, thank you. I had a really nice time. Vale is my best friend and I feel like you are too in a way, as you're such a big part of her life,' My parents both nodded, beaming.

The warmth I felt in the middle of my body lingered until the next day. I still smile to myself when I think about that lunch. Since that day, every time I tell them I'm going out with Clara, their faces light up. 'Tell her we say hi. She's welcome back any time.' Then they mumble to themselves, 'Nice girl.'

Clara's been giving me some advice lately on what to wear and how to style my hair. I'm wearing lots of black now – her favourite colour – and using argan oil to smooth my curls down. My parents have noticed the changes. When I'm dressed up to go out, I can see them looking at my outfits.

'Interesting look you've got going there, Valentina,' said my father the other day when I was searching for my keys before leaving the house. He was sitting on the sofa with the paper spread out across his lap and looking me up and down. 'New clothes?'

My mother came into the room at that moment and told him to shut up.

'I think it's elegant, all that black. You look lovely, darling. Shouldn't you dry your hair a little before leaving the house, though? You might catch a cold.'

'It's dry,' I replied, touching my curls. 'Ah, you mean the argan oil? It helps to keep it healthy and shiny. Clara uses it too.'

'Okay. Maybe go a little easier with it next time, then. There's a lot in there,' she told me, picking up one of my curls and scrutinising it.

I shrugged. I can't expect them to know about the latest trends in beauty; they're old and so are all their friends. Things are different now. Clara is always fighting with her parents. They don't understand her. They never listen and call her selfish and mean. Although I've never actually been to their house, she tells me that they keep the worst of it to when there's no one else around.

How can they know the real her if they don't take the time to listen?

I know her. I spend hours listening to her talking. She tells me about her plans for when school finishes – university in Italy, then a master's abroad in media studies or interior design. She tells me about what happens in her class and how bored she gets during certain lessons. We discuss the outfits the people around us are wearing – she has strong opinions on who should wear what with certain body shapes.

I try to sit up straight and listen to what's right and what's wrong. Then, when I go back home, I can be sure I don't make the same mistakes. She tells me I don't have to worry about being too fat because I have no hips and they're usually a giveaway. But I could do with a padded bra, apparently. I can't bring myself to buy one at the shops, so for now, I've been putting toilet paper in my bralette and smoothing down the sharp corners of the scrunched-up paper to make a realistic shape. I hope Clara hasn't noticed.

She tells me about the boys at school who fancy her and have asked her out for dinner at the local pizzeria. She doesn't like any of them and I tell her that that's fine, they're all beneath her anyway. She deserves the best. She usually smiles and says, 'You're right, Monk. I do.'

The countryside has been replaced in my heart with Clara. I no longer miss it.

She is the sun, and I am the sunflower. Facing, reflecting, searching for her.

But in the last couple of weeks, I've noticed that she's been harder to reach.

She's been busy, so we haven't been to Bamboo's in a while, and she's taken a long time to call me back when I call her. Sometimes

145

she forgets and tells me it slipped her mind because she has so much on. When I ask her what is making her so busy, she mumbles about homework and her parents keeping her in. But that's never been an issue before. She's always given me the impression that she finds school too easy and her parents don't give her many rules. I wonder what's changed.

I've been spending the last few nights trying to get some sleep but finding myself going over and over our last few conversations in my head.

Did I say something strange? Do something wrong? Have I become boring too?

When I asked her the other evening over the phone if I'd upset her somehow, she said, 'Jesus, you're so insecure. I've literally just told you that I've been mega busy.'

'Sorry, I know you've had some crazy weeks. It's just that . . . I miss you,' I told her.

'I miss you too. Don't you think I'd much rather be hanging out than staying at home with my stupid parents doing stupid homework? I'm so bored I feel like crying.'

I apologised again and promised to be less insecure.

But it's so hard. These thoughts niggle at the base of my skull whenever I'm awake, making it hard to rest when I try to sleep.

I can't bear the thought of having done something to push her away, even though I can't think of anything obvious. But then again, I don't always realise when I do something weird or annoying. She usually tells me when I do, though, so if that's the case, why hasn't she told me this time?

I've noticed something is different when we speak on the phone, too. She seems distracted, in a rush. I can hear the rustling of paper in the background, as if she's leafing through a magazine, and the low sound of the TV. Our calls are much shorter. We used to stay on the phone so long that either her parents or mine would get on the line and ask us to hang up. Now she tells me about her day and

146

then she usually has something she must go and do. After another one of those calls last night, I've had hardly any sleep. I've been distracted at school all day and that niggling sensation has now occupied every surface of my brain. I pace up and down my room unable to stay still.

Something isn't right.

I get a sudden wave of energy that makes muscles all over my body vibrate. I feel like the four walls of my bedroom are closing in and about to squeeze every breath out of me. My nerves are tense, and my head is aching.

I need to know what's going on.

Maybe if I speak to her face to face, when it's just the two of us and not at school, I might get a clearer answer.

I grab the keys to my moped and put my shoes on.

It's a school night. She will be at home studying or watching TV. I'll ask for just a few minutes of her time, then I'll leave to let her get on with whatever she's busy doing. I need to know, or I will explode.

I strap my helmet on before I've even left the house. I don't want to spend any more time than I have to feeling like this. I need to speak to her right now. I mumble something to my parents, and they wave without taking their eyes off the TV.

I speed through the streets – mostly empty – as the sun is starting to set. Clara lives nearby, it won't take long. Her building is one of a row of four-storey apartment blocks built in the fifties. The terraces are rounded and wrap around each floor, loaded with flowers. The entrance is sunk low and there's a flight of stairs, then a marble patio before you get to the glass doors that lead to the lift and the ground-floor flats. I park my moped at the top of the stairs and run down them two by two. I press the buzzer with a trembling finger. I still don't know if this is a good idea or not.

Clara's mother answers. 'Who is it?'

'Good evening, it's Valentina, Clara's friend. Could she please come down?' I ask, then add, 'For just a few minutes.'

The intercom goes quiet for a few moments. I bite my thumbnail nervously as I wait.

'Okay. She's coming down.' *Yes!*

'Great. Thank you! Have a nice evening,' I reply, but she's already gone.

I sit on the steps and wait for Clara. I twist and retwist the stuffed pig key ring she gave me for my birthday last year. It has googly eyes and is round and purple. It looks nothing like a real pig. It's a baffling, incorrect caricature of a noble and intelligent animal made from cheap polyester by the underaged and underpaid. But it's a present from her so it's one of my favourite things. I try not to think about what it looks like and concentrate on what it means: friendship.

The door opens and Clara bursts out. Her hair is up in a bun and her face is free of make-up. She isn't smiling.

'Hey?' she says.

'Hey!' I quickly get up and give her a hug.

She stands there while I wrap my arms around her. We sit down on the steps.

Clara pulls out a bent cigarette and a small lighter from her back pocket and lights up. She puffs the smoke out with a big sigh.

'What's up?' she asks.

I can't bear to look at her to try and guess what the answer to my question might be, so I stare at my shoes instead and wrap my coat tighter around my waist.

'Not much. Well, something. Sorry, I know I've asked you this already. But I can't shake off the feeling that I've upset you somehow.'

I kick a small stone; it lands just in front of the glass doors. It looks like it's waiting to go inside.

'God. How many times are you going to ask me? You haven't,' Clara says.

I still can't look at her. I focus deeply on the little stone. *Could it trip someone there? I should move it.*

'It's really not a big deal. I'm probably just imagining it. It's just …
you seem a bit distant. I know you've been really busy, so it could all
be in my mind. I really don't want to stress you more. But you know
what I'm like. Just Monk monkeying around and all that.' I try to laugh
to show her that it's not a big deal, but it comes out more like a croak.

I can feel her looking at me. The glowing tip of her cigarette comes
into my line of vision at semi-regular intervals. The silence from her
does nothing to alleviate the anxiety I feel inside. I need to fill it with
words, or I'll explode.

'So, like I said, probably just something that I've made up. But if
something is up and you maybe are keeping it in and want to let it
out. Or if you want to take it out on me. I don't mind. We're friends,
I'm happy to listen. I'd love to listen.'

I force myself to glance at her.

She's smiling. A strange, thin smile.

'What?' I ask, confused at her expression.

'You're so funny. Look at you, babbling,' she says.

I feel my face getting warm and I know that great big red patches
must be snaking up my neck and face.

'Like I said, I've just been busy. We're not joined at the hip, you
know? I can see other people too,' she says, taking one last puff of
her cigarette, then crushing the butt under the sole of her trainer.

*That's it. She's just been busy. Nothing to worry about. She's allowed
to have a life outside of this friendship. Did you expect that she would
just be with you and not see anybody else?*

But 'other people'? As far as I know, she hasn't been seeing her old
friends outside of school ever since we've started hanging out, and I
would have noticed if she'd made new friends.

I feel uneasy about this. Not because she's not allowed to – it's not
like we're a couple – but I'm worried she might end up liking them
more than she likes me.

*What if they're not scared of doing daring things around the city
like I am?*

What if they smoke and drink as much as she does, not only a little like I do?

I could share her if that's what she wanted, but I can't bear the thought of being replaced. I can't ask her directly or she'll get annoyed and call me possessive. She can't stand possessive people.

'What are you doing with your hands?' she asks.

I look down and realise that I've been clutching the fingers of one hand with the other so tightly that my knuckles have gone white. I let them go and place both hands on my lap. She picks one up, that weird smile on her lips again. Looking me right in the eyes, she starts squeezing it, clutching my fingers softly at first, then a little harder. Then so hard it hurts. I gasp and try to retract my hand, but she is holding it too tight. Her eyes are still fixed on mine. She gives it one last squeeze, then drops it. It falls back on my lap, the heat of her grip still pulsating across my skin.

But even the pain is not enough to distract me. My mind is crawling with half-formed thoughts. I want to know so badly who she's been hanging out with, but I don't dare ask. I open and close my mouth a few times, but no sound comes out.

'Jesus. You're so weird. Is this whole ...' she gestures at my face with both hands, 'just because you want to know who I've been seeing?'

Yet again, Clara seems to know exactly what I'm thinking.

I nod. *More than anything in the world right now.*

She laughs. 'Why didn't you just ask?' she says, as if it's the easiest thing in the world.

I shrug, and she does an exaggerated shrug back at me.

'Well, it's quite exciting. I was going to tell you at some point anyway if you hadn't turned up. You know Edo, right?' she says, trying to delicately dig another cigarette out of her back pocket without breaking it.

'Yes. Why?'

Clara and Edo are friends, or at least they were. As far as I know, the two of them only see each other at school nowadays. I've seen them chat a few times but no more or less than Clara usually does. She knows many people at school and often stops to exchange a few words with most of them. I usually stand back and wait, or tell her I'll meet her outside.

'Why do you think?' She lights up her cigarette and breathes the first puff in deeply, then blows it out above our heads like a steam locomotive.

'Are you friends again?'

'More than that, Monk.'

'More?' I ask, confused and starting to feel irritated by her unusual caginess.

She sighs and mutters, 'Jesus,' under her breath.

'Yes, Monk.' She sounds exasperated now. 'We are D-A-T-I-N-G. We're together. Seeing each other.'

I don't understand.

'Dating? Since when?'

'Maybe a month. Month and a half?'

A wave of helplessness overtakes me. I don't know why my best friend would keep something like this from me. And why would she start seeing him in the first place? She has told me clearly before that during the friendship with Edo and his group, she'd become fed up with the fact that they never wanted to do anything exciting. They just wanted to hang out at the ice cream place, smoke weed in the park or watch films at each other's houses. Clara needed to experience what the city had to offer, she said. If she wanted to stay home, she'd have stayed at her own place and watched the stuff she wanted to watch on TV. Not the stupid sci-fi or horror films that that group liked. Plus, weed had never agreed with her. She said it made her sleepy and slow. Unable to talk properly and way too paranoid. She hated not being in control. Cocaine was much more her thing. On the rare occasions someone at the club had some, she would always ask for a line. The thought of taking it has always terrified me, even though she told me it was like drinking a really strong coffee, but one that made you feel cool and fascinating.

I can't understand why she needs him in her life all of a sudden. She has me.

We're best friends, and up until a few weeks ago, we did everything together, all the time. What's changed now? She knows I would do anything for her. It's always been enough. Why look for more? I can't help but feel like I've done something wrong. Maybe she's got fed up with my weirdness? But she's always said that she likes it, that it's different and more exciting than hanging out with normal people.

Yes, she draws the line at the pig talk, but I've been very careful not to mention them in front of her.

'Oh.' It's all I can say.

But I don't think Clara has heard me. She's looking at a point behind me and grinning.

'He's great. We've been having a really nice time actually. Spending quite a bit of time together. The other day, we went to a pizzeria he knows near the centre. He randomly told the waiter it was my birth-day, so we got free desserts, but then all the other waiters came out and sang "Happy Birthday". Then everyone in the restaurant joined in. I was so embarrassed! You should have seen me. He was laughing so hard he nearly choked on his beer.'

I manage a weak smile. That sounds stupid, saying it was her birth-day when it clearly wasn't. It's months away. Edo should know that. Her eyes have taken on a dreamy sheen. She looks like a child who's just been given a cupcake – excited and giddy. But there's something that's stopping me from being as excited for her as I know I should be. I don't know what it is, but it's making me feel guilty. Like I'm being a bad friend, letting her down.

I try my hardest to match the way she's behaving. Clapping hands, unable to stay still for very long, grinning. But I feel like a wooden mannequin, a puppet being operated by a higher force. I've never felt such a deep gap between the way I feel inside and the way I'm acting

152

on the outside as I do right now. My heart is thumping inside my chest from the effort.

'There's more,' Clara announces, budging in closer to me so that our thighs are touching. She looks coy for a second, then lifts her head and looks me straight in the eyes.

'We've done it,' she says, then grabs my hands. 'Can you believe it? Oh Monk, it was incredible. Everything I had imagined. He's amazing. There's something so good about having sex with someone you know so well. Like, we were friends before, you know? So, I trust him.'

I stare at her and blink a few times. I realise I've stopped breathing, so I force myself to inhale and exhale a few times.

'Oh God. You think I'm a slut. I can see it! I'm not. We're in love. We haven't said it to each other yet, but I can tell it's coming. Aren't you happy for me?' she asks, squeezing my hands hard.

Her words trigger a mental image in my head: the two of them naked, entwined. Her soft, tanned skin shivering under his large hands. He might hurt her, demean her. She smells like cigarettes and the sweetest vanilla. He's hairy, sweaty, too large for his tight T-shirts. I picture him smelling like exhaust fumes and sour milk. His teeth are sharp and too white. His body has no softness to it, no grace. This image of the two of them together that has invaded my thoughts has a dissonance to it that makes me feel sick. I want to wrap her up in a dozen blankets and watch her sleep, safe and protected, away from his clumsy touch. Somewhere even his eyes can't reach her.

But she looks so happy. Her mouth is stretched in an ecstatic smile so wide I can see her pink tongue resting, waiting for the next word.

I nod, and she lets go of my hands.

I know with certainty that I won't be able to speak to her right now. My mind is wiped of all rational thought.

I get up and stumble away from her. Each step feels like a hill I need to conquer. I turn around and force myself to smile at her. I wave weakly and point at my moped, as if to say, *I'm going to get on this now and go.*

'Fine. I need to go too now anyway. I'll see you at school, yeah?' She turns around, opens the glass door and disappears inside.

The pebble is still there, in front of the entrance. It didn't trip her.

I can't face going home. My parents will still be up and might ask questions.

And even if they don't, I need to be alone right now. Something about what Clara has just told me has sent my brain into short-circuit. I have no idea why. All I know is that I must be the worst best friend there's ever been. I should be happy for her. I should want to listen, ask her questions, support her. People think sex is great. Everyone wants to have it.

And my best friend is having it with someone she's in love with. That should be a great thing.

So why do I feel like the floor has just collapsed under my feet?

I ride my moped around the quiet streets. I fly past my house but keep going. I leave it behind, then cross the bridge over the River Tiber and slide into the artery that slices the city from north to south. I have no idea where I'm going, I just know that I need to keep riding. The noise, the wind, the speed. They must continue. I can't bear to be left alone with my thoughts.

After the initial blank, they are now violently muscling into my head.

Clara and Edo. That night at the ice cream shop when I first met Clara and saw Edo again after a long time. The way they were looking at each other, the risky banter, the ease they so clearly showed in each other's company. It was so obvious.

I ride faster, the wind roaring in my ears. I don't recognise where I am. I must be far away from home. The buildings are lower, the shopfronts tatty and half shut.

I keep going.

Chapter Sixteen

April 2012

The days are longer without Clara. The nights too, but in a different way. While I split the days into chunks of time that obey different imperatives – *Hide! Head down! Keep walking! Remember to breathe!* – the nights are all the same. I spend hours just thinking.

I analyse any glimpse of her I might have caught in the corridors, or any words we've exchanged – mostly 'hi', or a perfunctory 'how are you?' – and roll those thoughts in my head over and over again. Now that the protection that being close to her gave me is no longer there, it didn't take long for the bullying to start again. I deal with it like I used to before she came into my life: try to ignore it until it gets physical, then run when it does.

From what I can see, she and Edo are officially an item now. I've lost count of the times I've seen them share the seat of his moped at the school gates. Smoking and laughing with the rest of the gang. I've also seen them kiss against the gym wall until the PE teacher told them to 'stop right this second'. I try my best to hide from my face the daggers I feel slicing at my insides whenever someone mentions her, but I don't always manage. Clara and Edo are on everybody's lips. They showcase their love, and they seem to be all my classmates want to chat about.

There is admiration – 'Have you seen Clara's new jeans? Oh my

God, I love the cut and they make her look SO skinny. I want the same.' There is gossip – 'I've heard they're going to Formentera this summer. His stepbrother owns a restaurant there.' And more gossip, dressed up as genuine concern – 'Professor Mariani has told her if she doesn't improve her grades, she might not be able to graduate. I hope she can graduate with us, imagine how sad Edo would be if she can't!'

I don't take part in these conversations and try not to listen when I hear their names.

But it's hard. Partly because the voices are loud, and they take no notice of me if I'm nearby, as if I'm invisible. Partly because I can't stop myself from wanting to still be a part of her life. If I have a head full of fresh information about her, I can fool myself into thinking that she hasn't moved on. That she's been telling me her latest news and we've laughed and gasped together. But in the evenings, when I'm completely alone, it's impossible to ignore the truth. The phone doesn't ring any more for me, and even my parents' questions have stopped. I've told them so many times that 'Clara's too busy to hang out right now.' They looked at me strangely each time, as if they wanted to ask more, but thankfully they never did. Now they've finally stopped.

I've recently found out that pigs' tongues contain 15,000 taste buds, and thinking about this fact and what that must mean when they taste different foods has kept me from thinking about Clara all the time. Although it doesn't always work.

I told my parents this fact over dinner the other evening and they just looked at me, then frowned at each other. They still wore those strange expressions even after I reminded them that humans only have 9,000, in case they had forgotten. My father just said, 'Pigs, eh?' while my mum stared at me.

The end of school is near, only a few weeks away. I'm not worried about the exams; I've studied enough to know that I will likely pass. But I don't care that much about good grades. I still have no idea about what I want to do. All I love in life is Clara and animals. She has been taken away from me, but the animals will still welcome me, hopefully. And they don't care about grades. I will probably go back to the countryside, find another Angela and help them run their farm. Then maybe they will leave me in charge one day. This thought is the only thing that gives me peace right now. Although I heard a piece of gossip the other day that has put me in a good mood for a while. And I feel guilty about it.

A few girls in my class were chatting at the end of a lesson. I was packing my bag next to them and trying my best to look busy and involved in what I was doing. But I overheard Clara and Edo's names and my attention was immediately refocused on listening in.

'. . . university. Yes, Milan.'

'Why not Rome?'

'Dunno, better faculty maybe?'

'For what?'

'Economics, I think.'

'What about her? Is she going too?'

'I don't know. I don't think so.'

I quickly finish packing my bag and head for the door. I don't want them to realise I've heard them. Or to see me smile.

Edo is going to Milan for university. If what they are saying is true, this means he will be out of our lives for at least three years. Five, if he stays there for a master's degree too.

Clara has always been very clear about where she wants to go: the Sapienza University in Rome, the one that her father went to many years before, to do either architecture or interiors architecture. It's a faculty well known for that subject, with a long and illustrious history behind it. She won't want to go anywhere else. This means she will be here without him for ages.

The thought puts a spring in my step. I nearly skip home.

Without him around, the two of us can be friends again. She will have time to hang out. We can go back to Bamboo's. Maybe even break into the monastery once again. It must be great in the summer.

157

We can catch the sunset and have a picnic on the grass. The thought of being close to her, of inhabiting her orbit once more, with all that it brings, makes me dizzy with joy.

Yes. I am a bad friend. She will be sad to part from Edo. They might see each other at weekends or during the holidays. But it won't be the same. They will have different lives and new friends. Or, in Clara's case, an old friend. Me.

So she will be sad for a while; maybe she already is. I wish I could hug her and tell her not to worry. That she won't be alone. I will fill that gap and she won't ever have to be lonely. I'll make sure she isn't. Maybe I can go to the same university. She and I could share a room so she doesn't have to live with someone she doesn't know, and I'll be right there to cheer her up if she's missing Edo. Soon she will stop thinking about him and realise that she already has everything – and everyone – she needs. I won't let everyday stuff get in the way of her happiness either. I will cook and clean for us and help her with exams so she passes with good grades and our studies don't become a source of stress.

I've never considered architecture as an option – no animals there – but maybe I could think again. Farms need to be planned: storage buildings, tractor huts. They should be the best they can be, and an architect will be able to see to that.

I look at myself in the mirror and say the words out loud: 'Architect Valentina.'

It doesn't feel right.

But it might do eventually.

Clara called me today. She wants to see me! I'm so happy I could skip.

'In an hour at Bamboo's?' she asked. She didn't say anything else. Even if she wanted to, I said yes before she had the chance to change her mind.

I ride my moped over to the café as if there's an emergency, as if oxygen is running out and the only way I can survive is if I make it there. Which is sort of true in a way. She is the air I want to breathe. I step inside the café but can't see her; she must be running late. I grab us her favourite table – down the back and to the side – and arrange the ashtray, sugar sachets and napkin dispenser in an ordinate line as I wait for her to arrive. She's fifteen minutes late in the end, which is fine. I only notice because I've been checking the time almost constantly since arriving. She takes off her helmet as she walks in, and I see right away that her hair is a little lighter than last time I saw it. She must have gone to the hairdresser. I stand up to greet her.

'Your hair. It looks different. It's lovely,' I mumble.

She smiles. 'Thank you. I had it done yesterday. It's a surprise for Edo.'

I ignore the twinge in my gut at hearing his name.

'Has he not seen it yet?'

'No, not yet, he's away for a few days with his family.' She sighs. 'I've been so bored.'

It's so nice to see her. She gets up to order us both cappuccinos and I watch her pay for them. As she returns to the table, she puts her hand in her jeans pocket and gets out a Bacio Perugina, a chocolate kiss.

'Here you go. Great with coffee.'

I look at the silver wrapping, then back at her. A smile splits my face open.

'Thank you. That's so . . .'

She giggles. 'Relax, it's not like I paid for it,' she says, then winks at me.

I must look shocked, because she laughs again. I catch myself and start laughing too. I can't let her think less of me. I don't want to seem judgemental. It's not like the café doesn't make thousands out of us students every day. It's a small crime. A small, delicious, chocolatey, silver-wrapped crime. I hold it in my hand for a bit then place it safely away in my pocket, to savour later.

Clara starts telling me about a trip to the seaside she and Edo took

159

on his moped. They got halfway there but the engine broke down on the motorway and they had to be rescued by the roadside assistance truck. Apparently Edo's parents found out about it and were furious. She talks about it with eyes shiny from excitement. As if she's narrating the story of a prince and his princess stopped on their way to a noble conquest. It's hard to hear her say his name, but the way she leans in towards me and whispers when she doesn't want the people at the tables near us to hear, or reaches out to touch my forearm during a particularly funny part as if to underline it, keeps me gripped and as excited and happy as she is. We spend hours this way. Me listening to stories of her latest adventures; her talking at breakneck speed and puncturing sugar sachets with her spoon.

When it's time for her to leave – it's nearly dinner time and she's promised her parents she'll be home to eat with them for once – she starts to pick up her stuff. I realise that I haven't thought about asking her about her plans for after the summer. I want to know once and for all if those girls were right. I *need* to know.

'Have you signed up for uni yet? I'm doing mine this week; shall we go together?' I blurt out, arranging my face in the most casual expression I can muster.

'Uni?' Clara asks. Her eyes widen for a second, then she starts fiddling with the sleeve of her jacket. 'Look, I don't want to talk about it right now. Can we just live in the moment, Vale? You seem so concerned about the future. But I ...' she's smoothing down her trouser leg now, 'I choose to be here. In the now. With you. The rest can wait.' That wink again. She's never winked at me before. It looks strange on her, as if she's playing a character, someone older maybe.

'Sorry, yes, you're right. Here and now.'

I will know soon enough anyway. Once school is over and Edo has gone, we will do more of this, she and I, in the café, just hanging out. *Then* we can talk about our plans for the future. Once this chapter of her life is over and the new one – our new one – can finally begin.

As we walk out of the café, I trip on a raised cobblestone. I manage to recover myself and don't fall to the ground. But my legs buckle clumsily. A group of kids sitting at one of the outside tables have seen me and are pointing and laughing. I feel my skin flush and hide my face. Clara is only a couple of steps behind me; there is no way she hasn't noticed them mocking me. I hurry my step to get to my scooter, hoping that she is right behind me and doesn't mention it. I couldn't bear it if I saw pity on her face.

'Funny, is it?' I hear. I whip my head back and see Clara, hands on hips pointing at the group who just laughed at me. 'What's actually funny is *your* face and *his* jacket.'

The group look shocked and have stopped smiling.

'My friend might have tripped this once, but you're stuck with those teeth for life,' Clara continues.

At this, two of the guys stand up and start walking towards us. She grabs my hand, and we start running towards our mopeds. I'm scared, but she is cracking up.

'Uh-ho. We better hurry.'

We jump on and speed off down the pavement, then onto the road. We drive next to each other, shouting against the wind.

'Did you see his face? He couldn't believe it!'

'Shouldn't have messed with us!'

We wave goodbye to each other at the junction and Clara drives off towards her house, I to mine. Our future is so clear to me now. This is just the start. The months without her have been painful, but today has shown me that nothing has really changed. Edo is just a blip. A name we won't ever mention again in a few years from now, a small forgotten part of mine and Clara's shared past.

Chapter Seventeen

June 2012

It's a local tradition. Not to the city of Rome as a whole, but just to my school, or maybe a few others in the immediate surroundings. On the last day of school, after the exam papers have been handed in, the teachers have been hugged and tears have been shed, the whole of the senior year head over to the Villa Borghese park, strip off to whichever level of nudity they feel comfortable with, then jump in the fountain in the middle of the park. The fountain is large and round. It sits in a clearing and has shallow light blue waters. The four large sea horses in the centre of it have the upper torso of leaping horses and long scaly fish tails as the lower half.

No one knows where the tradition started, but every year it gets repeated.

I know everyone in my class is planning to go – it's inconceivable not to – so I've decided to go too. I will be keeping my clothes on, but the last few weeks have been heavy with exam anxiety. It will be nice to let that go. Also, I've felt a new kinship develop with my classmates as our general levels of stress towards this final hurdle have grown at the same pace. Any other topics of conversation we might have had in common – or not had in my case – have been replaced with hurried questions half whispered, half shouted from one desk to another.

'Have you finished the history assignment?'

'There's no way I'll be able to do maths. Mariani has told us to be prepared because it won't be easy. I'm terrified.'

'I'm happy if I just get seventy out of a hundred. No, honestly! I literally don't care any more.'

This collective panic has finally come to an end, for good or bad, but the feeling of us all having weathered a storm together must have stuck, because a few of my classmates have asked if I'm going to the fountain today. It will be the last time I see them, as I doubt we'll stay in touch, so I have nothing to lose. A long, empty summer stretches out in front of me; this could be my last chance for a while to have some fun with people my own age.

I haven't heard anything else about Edo's plans to move to Milan, so I'm planning to ask my mother to enquire of her friend, his mother, in a discreet way. Then, once he's gone, I will message Clara. And we'll start hanging out together all the time like we did before, as she will have lots of free time. I haven't made any plans for the summer because I want to be free for when Clara and I will be best friends again.

I can't wait.

The clamour of voices and the roar of hundreds of moped engines is deafening. Mine adds to the noise as we all descend on the Villa Borghese car park.

We abandon the mopeds and start running up the road. The middle of the park is at the top of a hill, so all the roads that lead to it are quite steep. No one seems to mind, though. Weeks of pent-up nervous energy propel us forward with ease. We're all laughing as we look at the faces of the passers-by reacting to us. Some seem surprised, some irritated; most smile back. The heat is intense, even though it's only early June. We're sweating and panting, but still smiling. As we get closer, I see that other students from our school have already jumped into the water. Their clothes are in bundles on the pavement around the fountain. Some have stripped down to their underwear; others have kept shorts and T-shirts on. They're laughing and splashing each other. I'm trying to do what everyone else is doing, I don't want to stand out. So I shed as many of my clothes as I can bear – socks and shoes – and roll up the sleeves of my T-shirt and the legs of my shorts.

The water is freezing and smells like chemicals. I can feel a few rusty coins under the bottom of my feet once I'm in, but mostly it's smooth marble. I get splashed a few times and my curls start appearing in my field of vision, weighed down by the water. I'm enjoying this feeling of freedom and doing something out of the ordinary.

We're all soaking wet and being silly. Laughing at the absurdity of our situation and at the families all around holding their children back from joining us. A crowd of spectators is forming, mainly tourists amused by the unusual scene. But also locals who seem to recognise the tradition. One of them shouts, 'Congratulations!' and we all shout back, thanking him.

As I look around me, I spot two familiar figures on the other side of the sea horses from where I'm standing. Clara and Edo. I knew they would be here and probably together, but seeing them now still startles me. I haven't spoken to her in a while, not since that time at the café when she stood up for me. Once Edo got back from his trip, my phone stopped ringing again.

I can see that they are both wearing just shorts; he's topless and she's wearing a dark bra, rivulets of water dripping down her tanned stomach.

They are both laughing with open mouths. He's kicking water in her direction and she's shielding her face with both hands. They seem so happy. I would have thought that by now – with his looming departure – cracks would have started to show between the two of them. Maybe some moody looks or strained words. But there's nothing of the sort to be seen. They seem as relieved and free as the rest of us. A pang of guilt strikes me once again.

Why would I want my best friend to be unhappy? If I love her, why shouldn't I want her to have everything she wants? It's clear she's happy with Edo; why can't I be happy for her?

I have no answer to those questions, apart from the fact that I must be a terrible friend.

I try to stop staring at them, but I'm finding it hard. It's as if everyone around me has suddenly gone out of focus and the only two people I can still see sharply are Clara and Edo. I glance in their direction once more and see that they're now hugging. I can't see any space in between their bodies; they are wrapped around each other as tightly as the wet clothes on their skin.

Be patient. Just a little longer. Then she will be back.

The crowd gathered around us suddenly parts. I can't see why because everyone in the fountain starts shouting and jumping out of the water. I have no idea what's going on, but I don't want to make a mistake, so I do the same. As I'm lowering myself onto the pavement, looking for my socks and shoes, I see that three policemen are standing around the outer rim, yelling orders.

Soaked students are running down the hill in the opposite direction. In just a few seconds we're out of the water and dispersing all over the park. I turn around to look and see that three students are being interrogated by the officers as they put their clothes back on. Two boys and one girl, who has her arms crossed over her chest. No one seems actually scared, but we're all still running. I knew it was illegal to bathe in the fountain, but I forgot. The police don't always turn up, but there are tales of people being taken to the station and made to wait in a holding cell in sopping wet clothes for hours while their parents fill out the paperwork. I don't want to get caught, so I focus on running as fast as I can.

'Vale!' I hear my name being called and turn around to see who it is. Clara. She's panting and laughing, trying to catch up with me. I can't see Edo anywhere.

'Wait, slow down,' she says.

I stop and she grabs me by the hand.

'Come, I've got a good place we can hide.'

We run hand in hand to the end of the park. Her hand is freezing – just like mine must be – but the feeling of her skin is shooting sparks of excitement up my arm. We're friends, but is this how friends feel? Sometimes I think I know the answer, but then it gets all tangled up in my brain and then I'm not sure if I do after all.

'Where are we going?' I ask. I would let her take me anywhere, so I don't care where we're headed. I'm just enjoying speaking to her again.

'Here. You'll see.'

She opens a small gate, and we step into a tidy orange grove, with two rows of leafy trees and a few rose bushes around the perimeter. She leads me towards a bench, then lets go of my hand and sits on the ground right behind it.

'Come. They'll never find us here.' She pats the stony ground next to her.

I slide behind the bench and sit. I can't stop smiling.

She lets out a loud breath. 'That was fun! God, I can't believe we nearly got caught,' she says, pulling the front of her T-shirt away from her bra to try and dry out the two dark orbs that have formed over her chest. My eyes linger on her body for a second too long. When I look up, I notice her watching me, her face serious. I hold my breath. A flush of heat makes the skin on my cheeks prickle. I worry I have annoyed her, but then she smiles and shrugs her shoulders. I breathe out. These months of near silence between the two of us have been intensely painful. I'm trying hard to not think about everything that's happened and to mimic the same breezy tone and demeanour that she has.

'I know. I bet they're still looking for us,' I say, smiling in a way I hope makes me look carefree. Although it was clear that the police had no intention of running after any of us. They had their three catches and that seemed like enough for them. But I don't say it. I don't want to ruin the moment.

'How have you been? I feel like we haven't spoken in ages!' she says.

As if it's only just occurred to her that we were everything to each other for a while, until it all changed overnight.

I pretend to do the same, I don't want her to know how much I've missed having her in my life.

'Oh, you know, this and that. Busy studying. The exams have been crazy. How are you?' My tone is light, almost bored.

'Same! So busy. God, I'm so happy it's finally over. It's the holidays, can you believe it?' She asks me another question before I have time to answer. 'Have you decided which uni to go to?'

I haven't. I will go to university if it's near her. But I haven't been able to give up on that hope and sign up anywhere else. Of course, I can't tell her that or it will come across as desperate. I keep it vague.

'Kind of. I've signed up to a few places but I'm still deciding. You?' I ask.

She looks me right in the eye, beaming.

'You'll never guess what,' Again, without waiting for me to guess, she continues, 'Edo has asked me to go to Milan with him.'

'He . . . Has he?'

Wait. That's not the plan.

'Yes. A month or so ago. He's going there to do economics – it's the best in the country – and says he doesn't want us to be apart for all that time. So I've applied to the architecture faculty there and I'm waiting to find out if I've got in. Can you believe it? God, it feels so crazy. I've never even been to Milan! They say the weather is awful there. But the fashion? Apparently, everyone is so stylish. I'll have to get a new wardrobe.'

She's laughing and gesticulating. Clearly so, so excited to be going.

This must not happen. I feel a wave of panic rise in my stomach.

'You're going?' I ask her.

'I am! My parents don't mind as long as I take my studies seriously and graduate at the right time.'

She won't look at me but instead is busy picking up leaves from the ground and ripping them along their central rib.

'And – God, you'll never guess this one either – I was speaking to Martina, his sister, the other day. She told me that during dinner the other evening, he asked their mother about their grandma's engagement ring. Like, where it was kept and could he have a look at it. Then they started teasing him about the two of us and asked if he was thinking of proposing ... Look at my hands! They're shaking just talking about it ... And he said, "Not yet, but maybe soon."'

She grabs both my hands in hers.

'It's all happening so fast. But I kind of love it. I love *him*. Married? It's ridiculous – we're so young – but I'm kind of obsessed with the thought. I haven't told him I know about the ring thing, of course, I want it to be a surprise. I haven't seen it, but Martina tells me it's a bit old-fashioned but beauti—'

'No.'

The word shoots out of my mouth like a bullet. It's too late to take it back. It was loud. Clara is looking at me.

'That's fucking stupid.' The words shoot out once again, I have no power to control what I'm saying.

'What's wrong with you? Milan? You wanted to do architecture in Rome, that's what you told me, a million times. You're just following him. You're doing what he wants to do. What about what *you* want to do? I'm here, we can hang out. You don't need to follow him.'

I'm shouting and I'm aware of it. But I can't seem to speak any quieter. The pressure inside my chest is too strong.

'You're way too young to get married. You're making a massive mistake and can't see it. But I'm telling you. As a friend. It's a big fucking mistake. Don't go. You'll regret it. Stay here. You will be much happier here, with me.'

I'm pounding my chest with my hand to underline my point. This is not how things were supposed to go. I can't lose her for good. At least before, even if we weren't really friends any more, I could still see her and hear her voice. But if she's in another city, with different people, living another life, I won't be able to see her at all.

She's staring at me, mouth agape. I've never spoken to her this way. I have no idea what's happening to me. All I can feel right now is this overwhelming urge to make her change her mind. To make her stay here with me, to let Edo go to Milan alone, away from us.

'Don't you see it? It's a mistake. Listen to me.'

My voice is quieter now. I'm breathing too quickly and my heart is slamming against my ribs.

'Don't go, Clara. Please don't go.'

Chapter Eighteen

July 2012

Clara was angry. She shouted back, I think, after a few moments of stunned silence.

But her words didn't sink in.

I walked slowly away from the orange tree garden, unaware if I was alone or if she was following me.

I didn't care. Or rather, I was too empty to feel anything beyond despair. Too numb. I'd never behaved this way.

Despair. Longing. Awkwardness. I know they're all in me.

I didn't think anger was in my armoury, though. It surprised me as much as it must have Clara. It exploded out of me. I spat those words out with a desperation that expanded suddenly, as if it had been waiting for too long.

Then, once I'd said what I'd said, I said it again. This time begging.

There's something about Clara that brings these feelings out of me.

She is – or was – my best friend. Through her, I discovered the world of normality. For those few years we were close, I was the same as everybody else. She was my bridge to reality. It didn't matter then that I had to stop talking about pigs when she was around or she would accuse me of being 'weird'. I could think and talk about them to myself when I was on my own.

I have been wondering if what I feel about Clara is what she feels for

Edo. I can tell from some of the things I've heard her say about him, her mannerisms when they're together, the way she looks at him. It's the same way I behave when she's around. I know that Clara and Edo were friends for years before getting together, so it could be the way friends look at each other. But when we were chatting in front of her house and she was telling me about the two of them sleeping together, she seemed far away, immersed in a dream world that only had the two of them as inhabitants. I understood how she felt right away. I could empathise.

It was the same thing I felt after that night we broke into the monastery. When we hugged and held hands under the light of the fireworks. I was certain, at that moment, that only Clara and I existed in the world. The fireworks were there for us alone. The planet we were on, I felt, was made up of a wall, a garden, an old monastery and the two of us. No one else.

I remember having to concentrate hard on the way back home that night, as I was driving through the streets, dodging the drunk revellers wandering off the pavements. I kept slipping into the same dreamy state. Reliving those precious moments together a million times over.

I've never listened to the other students at school who made fun of our friendship when she wasn't around to hear.

'Where's your girlfriend?'

'Have you broken up?'

It was just another line in a long list of things they would say to me. I learned to let it slide off me. But now I'm thinking about it again.

Did they see something in our friendship – or in the way I behaved – that I missed?

When we were closer, it was easier to guess what Clara's feelings towards me might be. Like in the monastery garden. It was clear she needed me in that moment, as we stood with our fingers knitted together. I was the one who could help her when she felt misunderstood by her parents. I made her laugh after she got sad that night. Maybe one day I could do that again.

171

These thoughts have lingered. Since the end of school and my last conversation with Clara, I haven't been able to do much at all. My parents have asked me multiple times if I have plans for the next academic year, or even any idea of what I'd like to do this summer. Every time, I just stare back at them. My mind blank.

Without Clara, I have no plans.

Now that she has gone from my life – I won't even get to see her from afar any more – all I want to do is be near my beloved pigs. To go to the middle of a field and take my shoes off, feeling the dry summer soil powder my toes. I want to leave school, Clara, her voice, mouth, hands, our memories, all of it, behind. I can't stand the thought of having lost her again. The only thing I can bear to do is go back to the countryside, away from the city and the pain and confusion that being here have brought me. I want to return to being a child, at one with nature, before all of this happened. Things were easier back then. I was an odd child, yes, but lots of children have obsessions. No one thought I was a freak then. But now, things are different.

Pigs will always feel like home to me, the safest refuge in a chaotic world. If it makes me a freak, then so be it. I'm a freak.

My past has disappeared, and now, with Clara out of my life, I don't have my future either, the one I had imagined for the two of us together. The people I went to school with, they've all made plans. Some are going to university in the autumn. They made their choices long ago and have stuck with them. Soon they will be looking for accommodation and new hangouts. Bamboo's will become a hazy memory. They will meet many new faces and, if they're lucky, see some old ones too.

Others will take a year out, go travelling. Find out a bit more about themselves before they embark on years of studying. Others will go straight into work, no time to waste. I seem to be the only one stuck between a past that no longer exists and a future that will never be. Clara will have her fairy tale with Edo. They will go to university in

Milan, get married and have a lovely family one day. I will be just another adoring friend she left behind with school. A distant memory that will need a moment or two to bring back into focus when she visits her parents in Rome. She might drive past the wall we climbed together, or Bamboo's, or my house. And maybe she will think of me for a few seconds and wonder what happened to that odd girl she was friends with for a while back then. The one obsessed with pigs. She might ask around, but no one will know. I will stay a faint recollection that eventually will disappear.

This fog that has descended over everything will not shift. Back in Rome, after the break in the countryside, I spend days lying on my bed, reading academic texts about pig rearing and farm establishing, and nights fretting about the past. I feel responsible for how things went with Clara.

She rang my parents a few days ago; my mother picked up the phone. I don't know exactly what was said, but I can imagine it from what I was told afterwards. My mother walked into my room once she'd hung up and sat on my bed.

'What is it?' I asked her,

'That was Clara on the phone.'

I nearly choked on my own saliva. Hearing her name mentioned out loud in this house made me feel as if my thoughts had been suddenly laid bare.

'What did she say?' I couldn't get the words out fast enough.

'She's worried about you. The way you've been behaving. She said you got angry at her when she told you about her plans with Edo. And that you go into a bad emotional state. She was scared, Valentina. *You* scared her. She said you sounded unstable.' She reached out to touch my leg, but I moved it away before she could reach it. Her hand hung in mid-air while she continued speaking.

'Clara cares about you very much, you know. She told me so. But it sounds like you might have got a bit . . . maybe . . . over-attached?

173

She told me your eyes looked crazed. That's not normal. The poor girl sounded so worried.'

'I never meant to,' I whispered. I felt awful.

Clara is right, I've been smothering her and all she wants is to be happy with Edo. Why can't I just be a good friend and accept things for the way they are? Why can't I just be happy for her?

But still, my thoughts are full of ifs.

If I'd been less needy, maybe Clara might still be in my life.

If I'd been more fun, she might not have gone to Edo.

If I'd never mentioned pigs at all, she might not have thought I was weird and got bored of me.

I've never been easy to be friends with – that I know – but I thought Clara didn't mind. That she even found it a good thing. As if it was a challenge, a mountain she had to conquer. She once told me, 'I like having you all to myself. I'd hate it if you had other friends apart from me.' It made me so happy to think that she felt ownership over me. I felt special. I'm trying so hard to not think about what could have been that I'm exhausted.

My parents check in on me occasionally. They keep on coming up with things I could do this summer. Learn tennis? Go to summer camp? Join a choir? And I can't face any of them. Sometimes I answer, 'Don't have the energy.' Other times I roll the other way and wait for them to leave.

I know they're talking about me. They're worried. I've heard them say her name. In the last few days I've noticed their tone getting more brusque and their faces not as smiley any more when they ask me things. I think they're losing their patience. I can't blame them.

I'm soothing myself by touching the cotton sheets around me as I lie in bed. The weave of the fabric is both rough and soft. The sheets feel fresh against my skin, and I spend hours rubbing my fingertips over the most worn parts, looking for different textures to explore. But there is this wide expanse of nothingness stretching ahead of me. This 'life' I'm supposed to lead. I have no idea how I'm going to do it, or if I can even manage. It's as if I'm frozen in time. I can see myself staying like this for ever while everyone around me grows, matures, evolves.

Tick, tick, tick. All the life milestones getting ticked off.

And me here, in this bed, skin damp and breathing quickly, reading about pigs until eternity and thinking of what I could have done to keep Clara close to me. These four walls and what's beyond them are as far removed from the landscapes of my childhood as can be. I feel out of place amid the concrete. But the countryside has moved on too, without me. It was a moment in time that has now passed. A utopian setting that lives on only in my mind.

A family wedding is coming up – my cousin Andrea is marrying his girlfriend of seven years, Evelina – and my mother has told me we are going, there is no getting out of it. Andrea and Evelina are an odd couple. He's a scientist involved in stem cell research, and has very white, translucent skin and thick glasses. He finds his own jokes very funny and lets out big honking laughs. Evelina is from southern Italy, works as a legal secretary and only wears lilac. From top to bottom. I've never seen her wear anything but. It suits her fine as a colour, but with so many options, I'm always surprised by her accuracy at only finding clothes that fit within such a strict parameter.

I wonder if she'll wear white at her wedding or if the dress will be lilac.

Her parents are traditional, though, which means white is the only feasible option.

But if I know anything about obsessions, it is that it's almost impossible to stray once you've found the thing you truly love.

175

Chapter Nineteen

September 2012

The wedding venue is a stately home only a half-hour drive away from the north of Rome.

It's a beautiful building, white and elegant, with turrets and a clock tower at the very top, surrounded by a large garden. The garden is too tidy, but not so much that the natural way bushes and trees grow has been hidden. An extensive lawn spreads out at the back, where a white gazebo that looks like sails tied together has been installed. It would be very peaceful if it wasn't for the noise of the nearby motorway rumbling in the background.

Waiters carrying trays of champagne and tall glasses of orange juice circle among the guests. I reach out and take a glass of juice to cool down. I'm already feeling too warm in this dress and aware of the two dark half-moons that I can feel forming under my arms.

The ceremony itself is held in a chapel on site, built in the same white stone as the main building and large enough to accommodate around forty people. Those of us who can't fit inside the chapel during the ceremony gather by the door, waiting for the bride and groom to emerge. I chose to stay outside under a tree while my parents went in to find a seat. The other guests are mostly couples of roughly the same age as Andrea and Evelina; I imagine many will be work colleagues and school friends.

176

I can't picture ever getting married, but if for some inscrutable reason I end up doing it, I would have no one to invite beyond family. It would be a very small wedding indeed. But no point thinking about it; getting married is just not something that happens to people like me.

Clara and Edo's wedding – when it takes place – will be a grand affair. His parents are very sociable. His mother is a member of many clubs and associations in Rome and will undoubtedly want to invite back all the people who have welcomed her and her husband to various celebrations over the years. Those people alone will add up to nearly a hundred. Then the extended families, old friends of both sets of parents and work colleagues who cannot be left out for risk of making things awkward. Three hundred guests is my estimate, could be even more. My parents will certainly be invited. I don't know if I will be or not. Either way, I won't go. Clara will enjoy the extra attention, even though both she and Edo are used to it. They will both look beautiful on the day, no doubt. She will wear something off the shoulders, I imagine, the sharp angle of her collarbones caressed by the soft white silk.

A pang of pain clenches my stomach. I shake my head to let those thoughts loose. There is no point torturing myself. I am here now, and she is somewhere else. Happy without me. I must try and allow myself to live a sort of life.

I focus on watching the other guests, trying to guess what they do and how they know my cousin and his soon-to-be bride. Now that I'm not at school any more, I miss the anthropological observation of the human species that I used to do. Near me, there's a couple who look to be in their early thirties. She has poker-straight long blonde hair and a tight green dress; he's wearing a navy blazer and a bow tie. A child I guess must be their daughter is trying to get her mother's attention by pulling on the hem of her dress. This movement is pulling down the front of it, revealing a thin line of beige bra with each yank.

177

The woman hasn't realised and is still chatting animatedly to her partner.

They're both holding on to champagne glasses and sloshing them around. A few drops fall onto the daughter's hair and the little girl looks confused. Further back, an older man is trying to peek through the door of the chapel for a glimpse of the couple but is being blocked by a taller man in front of him. As the tall man sways to the right, the older man moves to the left. When the tall man sways back to the left, the older man moves right. They keep going like this, the tall man unaware that he's taking part in this sophisticated dance that is so irritating to the older man.

Finally, guests start to file out of the chapel. The bells are ringing and everyone is chatting. They form two semicircles facing each other and we wait. The bride and groom come out to a blizzard of uncooked rice. The grains are going everywhere, and the bride stops to remove one from her eye. She's wearing white – the traditions are too strong to break – which suits her but makes her look like a different person. She does have a large lilac sash around her waist, though, which must have been her compromise. They both look ecstatic.

The speeches are short and sweet, and the food is served on a long table, buffet style. I'm relieved when I find out that I won't have to sit next to strangers during an interminable dinner. Instead, I pile my plate high and go find a quiet spot. My dress is not ideal to sit on the grass in, so once I've finished my food, I get up and decide to stand. The guests have spread out across the lawn, and everyone is mingling. I grab a glass of champagne and decide to toast myself for having made it out of my room. As much as I still feel bereft, my skin is itching and my tied-up hair pulls on my scalp, it's nice to be outside and feel the sunshine on my face. Seeing green all around me is soothing.

I watch Andrea chat with a group of people a few steps away from me. His complexion is looking even whiter than I remember it under the sunlight. He seems to be making a joke, as everyone he's speaking to, including himself, is honking with laughter. He must have noticed me looking at him, because he turns around and gestures for me to come over.

'Vale! My little cousin. You're not allowed to stand over there all on your own. Meet this lovely bunch: Esther, Marisa, Federico and Cherise.'

The women and the man wave at me and smile.

'Hey. I'm Valentina. Congratulations, Andrea, great ceremony,' I mumble, aware of too many pairs of eyes on me. Luckily, they go back to whatever they were discussing before I arrived, and I don't have to keep speaking.

I recognise one of the girls – Cherise – as the woman with the green dress I saw outside the chapel. Her partner is here too, Federico. She turns around to face me and staggers a little, hanging on to my arm for balance.

'Oops, sorry! I must have had a few too many.' She laughs.

I smile too. I don't mind her holding my arm, I just don't want the champagne that's swishing around inside her glass to spill onto my dress. I already have two wet patches to worry about; I don't want to add a third one to the mix.

'No problem,' I tell her.

'I'm Cherise.'

'I know. Andrea told me. I'm Valentina. Nice to meet you,' I tell her.

She seems a bit confused. 'He did? Oh, sorry. How do you know the happy couple?' she asks, clearly forgetting, once again, Andrea's introduction.

'I'm Andrea's cousin. I've known him since I was born. Evelina I've known for seven years.'

Cherise nods.

'And you?' I ask her.

'I went to university with Andrea. We went out for about five minutes back in the day but have stayed good friends ever since.

Sometimes people are better friends than partners, you know what I mean?'

It's my turn to nod. I do know what she means.

'So, what do you do, Valentina? Are you still at school?' she asks.

'No, I've just finished,' I say.

'Congratulations. What's next?'

I swallow hard. I don't know how much of the truth to share. She's a stranger who I'll never see again. Also, she seems a bit drunk and distracted. Probably won't remember a thing I tell her. The champagne is making me feel a little looser too, a little braver.

'I have no idea. To be honest, I've had a few bad months. I thought I had it all planned, but it didn't work out. Now I don't know what to do.' I shrug.

Cherise stares at me.

'Anyway, I'm being boring. Sorry. What do you do?' I ask her, wanting to move the attention away from me.

'Oh no, sorry to hear, that sounds horrible.' She pauses for a second, looking at me with kind eyes, though a little bleary. 'I own a company,' she continues, 'that sells personalised school bags for children. Federico and I live in London, but I import the bags from Italy.'

'What's London like?' I ask her. All I've heard about it is that the weather is no good – much like Milan – and the food is nowhere near as nice as it is in Italy. But more and more Italians are moving there, so it can't all be that bad.

'It's great. I mean, not all the time. Sometimes it's tough. But we like it. Lots of opportunities, and we've made some good friends through our daughter's school.'

I nod. 'Sounds nice. I've never been. Is the food really that bad there?' I ask.

She laughs. 'God, no. It's fantastic! You can eat food from a different country every single day if you want. And the Italian food there is great too. Sometimes I think it's better than it is here. Then I remember that the chef is probably Italian, so it makes sense.' She taps the rim of her glass. 'I'm going to top this up. Do you want any more?' she asks, pointing at my empty glass.

'No, but thank you. See you later, nice talking to you.'

She starts walking away before I've finished my sentence. I wave at her back and watch her stumble towards the buffet table.

Andrea is deep in conversation with Federico, so I leave them to it.

I see my parents on the other side of the lawn and decide to join them. My father has taken off his tie and opened the top two buttons of his shirt. His ruddy complexion tells me that he's been enjoying a few glasses himself. He's a happy drunk, luckily. Prone to bad jokes and loud declarations of love.

'Here she is. My beloved daughter. Come sit next to your old father,' he says, patting the seat next to him with an open hand. I roll my eyes and sit beside him. We chat about the latest gossip he's just heard about some family members, and I let him think he's being quiet as he speaks, when in fact the people near us and those near them are also happily listening in.

An announcement over the microphone tells us it's time to cut the cake, so we all gather to watch Andrea and Evelina take massive chunks out of a white-tiered confection entwined with lilac roses. Everyone laughs when Andrea pretends to put his whole face in the cake. Then the music starts and the two of them slow-dance to 'Aurora' by Eros Ramazzotti. Once the song is over, the DJ announces that it's time to party. Everyone joins the happy couple on the dance floor and starts swaying to club tunes.

I step back to give them more space. I don't feel like dancing. The fog is starting to take over my brain again. It could be the champagne or the fact that the excitement of being out of the house and meeting new people is starting to wear off. I watch everyone hug, laugh and celebrate and feel like there just isn't room for me. I don't have a place where I feel at home. I used to – the countryside – but now that's changed. Rome isn't the same any more either, without Clara in it. It never felt like my home and now even less so.

I watch Federico and Cherise twirl messily across the dance floor. They look happy. I wonder what Clara and Edo are doing right now and if they're also twirling each other across a crowded platform under the summer sky.

Cherise spots me and walks towards me with an outstretched hand. 'Come dance!'

I shake my head. 'Thanks, but I'm okay.'

'Are you sure?' She doesn't seem convinced.

'I am. I promise,' I tell her.

She's sweet. I like her. Messy and drunk, but sweet.

'I was telling Federico about you, and he gave me a great idea.' She's shouting in my ear over the music. I can smell her sour breath and her rose-heavy perfume. 'I need someone to come to London to help me unpack and photograph my new stock. Then repackage it to be sent off to customers. It needs to be done soon as the schools are starting to reopen, so I don't have a lot of time left. If you're at a loose end right now, why don't you come and do it? It'll only be a couple of months of work, but then I can help you look for something else if you like the city.' She steps back and looks at me.

I ask her to repeat it, worried that I must have misheard.

She says the same thing again.

'In London? As in work there?' I ask.

She nods, swaying lightly from side to side. 'If you hate it, you can go back to Rome. No hard feelings. Think about it.'

She hugs me and struts right back to the middle of the dance floor, where Federico is pretending to be a whirling dervish with a napkin on his head.

London. It sounds like a terrifying prospect. I only speak basic English after years of mediocre teaching. It's in a whole different country that is a plane ride away from everything – and everyone – I know. I would be working with a virtual stranger, doing a job I have no experience in doing. I would know nothing of the city's streets; the smells would be foreign to me and the sounds alien. It took me a

182

long time to get used to Rome after moving there. And I was much younger then. Now, almost an adult, it would be even harder to learn new things.

A waiter walks by carrying a tray freshly laden with champagne flutes. He slides it towards me with a smile. I take one, thank him and let the first hurried sips loosen the knot in my stomach.

Yet.

London is not Rome, where everything reminds me of her and what I've lost. And it's not the countryside, where watching it all change around me makes me choke up with pain.

London is a big city; there won't be pigs.

But there aren't pigs in Rome either. If I'm destined to live somewhere far away from my animals, then it might as well be anywhere else in the world but Rome.

Across the dance floor, Evelina shows her left hand to a friend, who admires the new platinum band. Andrea watches them with a big smile, his eyes sparkling with joy. I'm trying so hard to see this scene for what it is: my cousin and his new bride starting an exciting new chapter of their life together. But all I can think of is when Clara and Edo will be doing the same. My best friend, who taught me how to exist in a world that has always been hostile to people like me. The one who saved me from myself and is no longer in my life. She will embark on a new adventure beside her fiancé, soon husband, and everything will fall into place for the rest of their lives.

Their wedding will be just the beginning. More milestones will follow, I'm sure. Tears start forming in my eyes. I don't want anyone to see me cry, so I turn away from the party and start walking deeper into the garden. I take my shoes off and step over the dewy lawn. The air is cooler here, the sounds muffled by the thick hedges.

The feeling of grass under my feet is instantly calming. My head is spinning a little from the champagne, but I don't mind it. It seems to be blurring my thoughts and dulling the edge of my pain. I find a stone bench and sit down.

I take a few deep breaths.

For a moment I lose myself in my surroundings. The crickets are still chirping, slower now, a sign that the temperature is dropping after a hot day. Half a dozen fireflies shine intermittently in the bushes, as if sending messages to each other in a secret code. A soft wind agitates the strands of a nearby weeping willow.

The way its branches hang reminds me of Clara's wet hair that day in the fountain. Thick ropes of dark silk that framed her perfect face.

As if freshly hatched, thoughts of her and what could have been come flooding back. My head is filled with painful noise all over again.

I can't take it.

I get up and run back towards the party, holding a shoe in each hand. I step on a sharp pebble but feel no pain. The dance floor is still full of laughing people. I stop on the edge of the raised platform and slip my shoes back onto my wet feet. I scan the crowd until I see the face I'm looking for.

I wave at Cherise and walk towards her, careful not to get in Federico's way as he whirls and whirls. I shout my answer in her ear but I'm not sure she's heard me.

Then I watch her face light up and she starts clapping.

PART THREE

Chapter Twenty

London, July 2019

'Wind the bobbin up, wind the bobbin up, pull, pull, clap, clap, clap . . .'

The entertainer's voice is louder than I'd like it to be and is making my headache worse. It's not her fault; she's only doing what we've hired her to do – sing and play with a group of toddlers during half term so that their parents can browse the shelves in peace – but I wish her voice wasn't drilling into my skull quite so successfully.

I slink into the kitchen and press my hands onto my ears. I stand like that with my eyes closed for a few moments. When I open them, Ollie is standing in front of me holding two empty mugs and staring.

'It's hideous, I know. I feel the same. Tea?' He switches the kettle on without waiting for my answer. 'Luckily there are no other customers apart from that lot right now, so I can hide for two minutes,' he says.

'I don't mind the children so much. It's her. Her voice is making my head feel like a pregnant sow has decided to sit on it.' I press the palms of my hands on my temples. 'Did you know that sows sing their piglets to sleep? They can stretch out an oink and make it sound like a lullaby. It's beautiful.'

Ollie nods and pours boiling water into both our cups. 'Headache, eh? Were you on the booze last night by any chance?'

I roll my eyes. 'I haven't been sleeping well. I get bad headaches when I don't sleep enough.'

'How come?' Ollie asks.

'There's just a lot to do at home.'

The truth is that since the meeting at Almastra a couple of months ago, I've been worrying non-stop about what I'm going to do if Clara finds out I've been lying. I could try to publish under a different name, but I don't know how I would explain that to the people at Almastra. Really my biggest fear is that they might end up thinking I'm too complicated and decide to drop me and the book they have asked me to write. I try my best to keep these scary thoughts at bay and use any free moment I get to write. But there aren't as many of those as I would like. I can't write at work, and I can't write at home when Clara is awake. So that leaves me with a few hours at night when she goes to sleep and some in the morning before she wakes up. It's not enough.

Still, I've managed to write every day and I'm happy with the shape of what I've done so far. I've decided to split it into questions, so every chapter will act as an answer: 'Why is ethical pig-keeping necessary?' 'Who is doing it right and what can we learn from them?' 'What is needed to ensure a happy and healthy life for your pigs?' and so on.

I'm hoping that this way, people like me who might feel confused when they are asked too many questions at once might find some room to breathe – and the clear explanations helpful. I'm really enjoying writing it and I'm often surprised by how many things I still remember. I've also been finding that putting everything I've learned and absorbed through the years onto the page is making my head feel quieter.

I like how it feels.

But since I've started writing, I haven't been getting much sleep, so I'm always tired. The headaches have started recently, and they are making things like standing in a noisy room quite painful. Even worse, in the last few days I've started falling asleep at the keyboard.

I've tried drinking espressos after dinner when Clara is watching TV and I'm tidying up the kitchen, and I've tried leaving the window of my room open to let the cool air in and having all the lights on, but nothing works. I seem to drift off to sleep without realising it and wake up a few hours later with freezing cold skin and the computer keys imprinted on my cheek. It's as if my body is telling me that I can't keep going like this. And because of the missed hours of writing, I'm now slipping behind the schedule I agreed with Almastra. I don't have nearly enough written down as I should at this stage and the worry about missing the deadline is making me feel anxious.

'What do you mean, "a lot to do at home"?' Ollie asks. 'Because of the writing?'

'Yes. Other stuff too. There's just . . . lots to do.' I want to confide in him, but doing so would mean having to explain mine and Clara's relationship. And I can't do that.

'What stuff?' He's leaning on the fridge door, cupping his tea with both hands, clearly in no rush to head back onto the shop floor.

'You know, cleaning, making dinner. That kind of stuff.' I feel my palms getting sweaty, so I shove my hands inside my pockets. The tea can wait. More lying. I seem to be lying all the time lately.

'Can't your flatmate help? Does she know you're writing a book?'

'Yes, of course. But she's busy too.'

'Doing?'

I don't like where this conversation is going. I feel awful for lying to two of my friends, but I don't know what else to do.

'She has lots on too,' I answer, hoping he'll finally drop the topic. But he's not moving. I can see his forehead is corrugated and he's looking at me in the way he does whenever Clara comes up.

'She's strange, this flatmate of yours. It's like she doesn't want to participate in your life.'

'Not at all. She loves knowing everything about my life. She's just too busy to come out or visit me here.' I'm speaking faster than I'd like. 'She's great.'

189

Ollie is still looking at me.

'Then why isn't she helping you at home and taking some stuff off your hands so that you can write in peace? Surely it's not your turn to cook and clean all the time? And what about weekends? Are you getting any writing done then?'

His barrage of questions is making my head spin. I can usually respond a lot better when I have some time to think, but the lack of sleep means that my brain is garbled.

I look at him in silence, unable to get my words out.

He sighs and says, 'I don't mean to stress you out, Vale. But there's something about Clara that doesn't add up. I know you're flatmates, and that it doesn't mean you have to be in each other's lives necessarily, but aren't you friends from way back in Italy? And I remember you mentioning that her husband lived there with you as well, but I haven't heard you talking about him in ages. Is he still there?'

I shake my head.

'Are they divorced?'

'Separated,' I whisper.

Although Edo initially supported Clara financially, the money has started to dwindle in the last year. It is clear to me that he won't be coming back. He is disappearing from our lives like a ghost and soon the tap will surely be turned off completely, then surviving on my wage alone will be hard. Getting the book out and hopefully earning a little more money from it could help us so much.

No matter how much I try and bury my guilt, it rushes out without warning as I hear Ollie's words. I can't bear the feeling of having had a part in breaking up Edo and Clara's marriage. Not so much because I mind them no longer being together – I wanted her all to myself for years, after all – but because of the way it has affected her. Her sadness and anger, it has nowhere else to go to now. I try and help, but I know I'm not enough. Though Clara has made it clear that she blames me for their separation, Edo has never said it explicitly. But I can read between the lines.

During the final few weeks of their relationship, I could almost smell the confrontation brewing. It would usually begin around dinner time, when they were forced to be in the same room and sitting opposite each other. They would gradually build up from cold answer to bitter quip, to then blowing up in a shouting match. I would never stay around for the whole thing, usually choosing to give them some privacy and retire to the kitchen to wash up – and also because their screams would terrify me. One time, after a particularly fiery row, I was busy scrubbing the cooking pans, trying to block out the noise with my thoughts, when Edo stepped in with the dishes. His face looked different, his skin tone flushed, his features ever so slightly out of place. There was a red patch on his right cheek and down the side of his neck. It looked sore. He was almost transfigured by rage and despair.

I looked at him, once again desperate to say something about the signs I saw more and more often on his skin, but too scared to speak up. So I just continued scrubbing.

He slammed a handful of cutlery down on the table.

'She's impossible,' he said, running a shaky hand through his hair. 'It's only getting worse. I can't do it any more.'

'You know she gets like this. It'll all be calm again by tomorrow,' I replied. We both knew Clara's rages and had discussed it before. This didn't seem any different to me. But it must have been to him.

'And then what? What about next time? And the one after that? It's not getting any better. And I'm sorry to say, but you enabling her is only making it worse. I love you, Vale, but you're not being a good friend to her. You're letting her get away with behaviour that is completely unacceptable. And the more you do that, the less likely it is that she will ever get better.' He was panting and immobile. Looking at me with open arms, vulnerable to the point of rawness. I could feel drops of water from the pan in my hands falling onto my socked foot, leaving a cold patch.

'I don't think ...' I started. 'She's not ...'

He growled with frustration. 'God. You are just so blind. Look, I'm getting out of this. Trust me, if you know what's good for you, you should run a mile too.'

With that, he walked out, and I heard the front door close not long after. I know he came back late that night and slept on the sofa because I saw his pillow arranged to one side the next morning. He was gone out of our lives by the following week.

I was confused for a long time after that conversation. Enabling Clara? I had no idea what he meant. I was just her friend. Friends help each other out and weather storms together, no matter what. That's all I'm doing. But the desperation in his eyes, the way his body looked so defeated. He was trying to tell me something else. All I know is that I hurt him. Not only have I caused their marriage to break down by being a bad friend to Clara, I was clearly a bad friend to Edo too. Their words echo in my head like a faraway choir.

'Earth to Vale?' Ollie's voice shakes me out of my thoughts.

'What?'

'Clara. So she's alone?'

I nod.

'Is she the reason you're watching the clock all day every day and running home after work?' he says, his eyes narrowing.

'She's not very sociable. She's been having a tough time. I help her.'

I don't know what else to say that will make him stop asking me all these questions.

'What about you, Vale? Is she helping you as much as you're help-ing her? What if you miss this opportunity because you don't have enough time to write?' Ollie's voice is raised, and his cheeks have got redder.

He must have noticed the tears forming in my eyes because he takes a step back and apologises.

'Sorry. I just hope she's as good a friend to you as you are to her. I see how caring you are, how hard you try to help people. I would hate for someone to take advantage of that.'

192

'She doesn't. I promise. We're good friends. She's just very, very busy,' I tell him.

'Okay, sure. Anyways, my flatmate Craig is moving out in a few months. If you're ever looking for somewhere else to live, you're welcome to his room,' Ollie says, then peers round the kitchen door to check what's happening in the shop. For a second, I allow myself to imagine what it would be like to live in a different house. A quiet room all to myself where I could hang up the pig-related stuff I now keep hidden away in a drawer. Lie on the bed and look around, surrounded by my things. But that would also mean no Clara, and I could never do that to her. She needs me.

'Thank you. But I'm okay where I am,' I say.

He just shakes his head. 'Okay, Vale. The offer is there if you change your mind. I better go and see how much mayhem those little monsters have caused in the children's section.'

Alone in the kitchen, I take some deep breaths and force myself to think about a singing sow and her snoozing piglets. I can see their furry backs rising rhythmically and hear her soothing tones lulling them deeper into sleep. After a few moments, once my chest is calmer, I head back out.

I tell Ollie to guard the till while I clean the back room. The singing session has ended, and a few remaining toddlers are wandering around followed by their parents. I can see a thin layer of crumbs, discarded tissues and misplaced books and toys all over the floor. I take my time tidying up. Most of the noise has now moved to the front as the families ring up their purchases, and I'm enjoying how the muffled sounds don't stimulate my aching head too much. Ollie's words echo in my mind. He doesn't know what Clara and I have been through together, so I don't expect him to understand our relationship. I owe her a lot and it's only right that I support her in any way I can.

But he does have a point when he says that I spend all my time looking after her needs and neglecting my own. I do, I know that.

It's not just that I think it's the right thing for me to do after our past, but it also feels easier somehow. She tells me exactly what I need to do to keep her happy. But when it comes to knowing what makes *me* happy, sometimes I just have no idea. It's like there's this big jumbled mess in my head. He is also right that if I keep on being behind schedule with my writing, I will end up missing out on this opportunity with Almastra. I could tell from what Marcus and his publisher Louisa were saying that they are keen to jump on the New Agriculture bandwagon and get this book out sooner rather than later. Even if they haven't said so explicitly, I know they're taking a gamble on me as someone who's never written a book before. I don't want to disappoint them. I've never thought about writing before, but now that I've been told I can do it and other people are relying on me, I want to prove them right.

I keep thinking of what Clara might say if I told her. I know she would hate having been lied to, but I also wonder if she might be proud of me somehow. She likes it when I cook for her, and when I arrange her hair in intricate ways she often praises me. Those are creative things; this could be similar. If I manage to finish it, I will dedicate the book to her. That way she will know how grateful I am even if I've let her down by hiding the truth of my writing from her for a while. It's a small price to pay initially, for a big pay-off at the end. But none of this will happen if I don't have time to write.

I have my laptop with me today as I was hoping to do some writing in the shop, but the day has been far too busy. I've seen people write in the pub before, so maybe I could go there when we close the shop. This is a big risk because I know Clara won't be happy about my going somewhere after work and I hate letting her down again. But if I told her a white lie and gave her some notice, maybe she wouldn't mind too much. Now that I think of it, if Ollie saw me heading to the pub, it would also put his mind at ease that I'm not living with a bad friend, and he wouldn't worry so much any more. Double benefit.

I wait until a couple of hours after the lunchtime rush is over, then message Clara to tell her that I want to cook her something special this evening, so I'll be going to the big supermarket after work to get some ingredients, and that I hope it's okay with her. Then I will go to the smaller one nearby instead which will only take me a few minutes. The rest of the time I can be in the pub writing. As I send the text, I can see my fingers shaking. There is a part of me that can't believe I'm doing this. Only a few months ago I would have never thought about lying to Clara so blatantly. Yet recently I've done it several times. She's clearly right when she calls me ungrateful and a poison. But there's also another – newer – part of me that wants to write this book so badly I'm willing to lie for it.

These two sides shouldn't both exist in me at the same time, but somehow they seem to. I don't know what it means.

I wait until closing time for a message back from Clara, but nothing comes through. I try not to think about the fact that maybe she hasn't messaged because she's so angry with me she's waiting until I'm back home to have it out. I really hope that the dinner I cook will help smooth things over. We'll just have to eat later tonight, on Italian time.

Ollie and I close up the shop, and as I leave, I tell him, 'I'm heading to the pub to do some writing. I was thinking that I'm going to start doing it when there's time after work. I'll see you tomorrow.' I point at the Fox across the road as I want him to see me going in, so he knows it's true. I walk over there very slowly and keep turning back to make sure he's looking. He is. I see him mouth a couple of words, but I can't hear.

Inside the pub, the air is thick with noise. I make my way to the bar and order a pint of soda, then find a quiet table at the back on which I set my laptop. I'm worried about the levels of noise and whether I'll be able to concentrate. But I manage to somehow block it out and start writing. The next time I look at my phone I realise nearly two hours has already gone by. I've written a lot – and would like to do even more – but I can't tonight, or I'll really be pushing

Clara's patience. I pack my things and head out of the pub, walking as fast as my legs will allow me.

I stop at the supermarket and grab some smoked salmon, fresh pasta and a tub of single cream. Tagliatelle al salmone always puts a smile on her face. Hopefully it'll work this time too.

My legs are burning, but I keep pushing. I speed past terrace after terrace of identical houses until I can see ours. Suddenly I'm not feeling quite as confident as I was earlier about Clara forgiving me for being so late. I also don't think she will believe my supermarket excuse, as who goes to the supermarket for two hours? I try to think of something to say, but my brain is too focused on the pain in my legs to come up with anything useful. I don't know if it's the walking that's making my heart beat quite so fast, or the fear I'm feeling right now as I stand by our front door, but either way, the manic movement in my chest is causing my T-shirt to twitch. But I can't waste any more time. I need to face her now and accept the consequences.

I open the door and listen out for any noises. The house is mostly quiet apart from a low hum coming from the living room. I would usually expect Clara's TV programme to be booming from there, but the television must be off. I whisper her name.

'Clara.'

I don't know why I'm not speaking louder. It's almost as if I'm trying to delay the inevitable. As I get closer to the living room, I hear the hum more clearly. I step into the room, and the first thing I see is a couple of empty wine bottles and an empty glass lined up on the coffee table. In front of it, I see Clara lying on the sofa with her head propped up by a cushion. I can't see her face from where I'm standing, so I get closer. Her eyes are shut, and I quickly realise that the noise I've been hearing is her, quietly snoring. She is fast asleep. I cover her up with a blanket, pick up the bottles and the glass and turn the lights off. I have no idea how long she's been asleep for, but she's clearly been drinking for some time. A thought jumps into my head: *What if she hasn't seen my message yet?*

196

I take a few quiet steps back into the living room and look for her phone. I find it on the floor near the armchair. I type in her passcode – her and Edo's birthdays – and unlock it. I go to her message folder and see that she has a few unopened messages from earlier today. Mine is in there. I delete it and place the phone back where it was, then step carefully away and out of the room. The sensation of relief that washes over me as I head up the stairs to my room to write some more is so intense it almost overwhelms me.

Chapter Twenty-One

'Darling, hi.'

'Hi, Mum, how are you?'

'We're all good, thank you. How are you?'

'Good. I have some news.' I've thought about it and it's time to tell them I'm writing a book. It's not like it will be a surprise to them – they know about my obsession with pigs better than anybody else. But I think it will make them happy to know that I'm finally doing something with it. I know they've worried about how intense my passion is in the past; this should put their minds at ease.

'Exciting. Good news, I hope? I need something to cheer me up. In fact, I was about to call you myself.'

'What's wrong?' I ask.

'Oh, nothing, just got off the phone to Marilena. She was beside herself with worry, poor thing.'

Even though I know I'm more likely than her own mother to know if something bad has happened to Clara, I can't help but be alarmed.

'Why? What's happened?'

'Well, apart from the fact that her marriage is in tatters at the moment – I'll spare you the grisly details – she's also had a long conversation with Edoardo that sent her over the edge. He's just come back from his travels; he was away for ages apparently. He went over there to speak to her and Antonio. She said he looked so concerned, like he'd seen a ghost . . .'

'What did he say?' I ask. Whatever Edo has said about Clara to her parents, I know it won't be good.

'He says that Clara's moods have got much worse. That she's unstable and violent. He said there were times towards the end of their marriage when he was scared of her. She's not doing well at all apparently. Poor Marilena was crying – she has tried to reach out to Clara so many times, but her phone is always off. She thinks she might have blocked her. She hasn't heard from her in so long. She's beside herself.'

'Oh well, Edo is always . . .' I start, although I don't really know where to go with it. Clara's version of the story doesn't feel quite right for a moment.

'Talking to her has got me worried about you, Valentina,' my mother says. 'I know Clara can be difficult sometimes, but I had no idea things had got so bad. Is everything okay with you?' Her tone is dripping with concern. It's difficult to hear, knowing that the distance must make things feel and sound so much worse than they really are.

'I'm okay. Please don't worry. Clara and I are doing absolutely fine. I have no idea why Edo said those things – must be something to do with the divorce. I know they're not on the best of terms, but Clara just wants to move on with her life.'

'Are you sure?' She sounds relieved. 'Anyway, Dad and I would love to come visit you soon if you'll let us. Oh, wait, what was your news?'

I'm about to tell her about the book when a sudden thought occurs to me. If I tell them about it and they end up coming to visit us, there's a very good chance they'll mention it in front of Clara. And that would be disastrous right now. As much as it would be nice to see them, I can't let that happen.

'Look, Mum, I need to go to work now, I'm running late. It's nothing important, just something funny that happened at work. I'll tell you another time,' I say.

She starts saying something else, but I cut her off.

199

'Really need to go now, we'll speak soon. Love to Dad, bye!'

I hang up and jog the last few steps to the shop.

As I approach, I see that the shutters are half up, and I get worried that burglars have broken in overnight. I prepare myself to find a messy scene as I slide under the metal barrier to get into the shop, but all I see is Lauren, standing at the counter wearing a floppy canvas hat and clicking furiously at something on the computer screen. I'd forgotten she was going to be in.

'Oh, thank God it's you,' I say, relieved. I should have known, considering she always leaves the shutters halfway up when she's in early in the morning. I think she likes going through new stock in peace without interruptions from customers if she's on her own. Ollie says that she likes all the good parts of owning a bookshop and refuses to deal with any of the bad parts. Looking at the number of red bills that have been coming through the doors in the last few weeks addressed to her makes me think he's right.

'Why "thank God"?' she asks. She's still scrolling and clicking and doesn't look up.

'I was worried we'd been burgled. Forgot you were coming in. Tea?'

I put my phone away under the counter and notice a missed call and voicemail from Marilena. I don't have time to deal with her drama right now, I'll listen to it later.

'No thanks, I've asked Ollie to pick us all up some fancy coffees and pastries from the café. We're having a staff meeting in a minute, so I thought it'd be nice to share some lovely breakfast as we chat.'

'A team meeting. What about?'

We hardly ever have team meetings. The last time we had one was when Lauren told us she had hired Hermina to come and help out during the Christmas season. She asked us to show Hermina how things worked in the shop because she wasn't going to be around herself. We haven't had a team meeting since then and I don't think we're looking for any more staff as we have very few customers as it is.

Lauren taps the side of her nose, which is weird – but she could have an itch – and says, 'You'll just have to wait to find out.'

Whether it's good or bad news, I don't like surprises, they make me feel uneasy. I stay quiet until I see Ollie come in with one of those cardboard trays holding three tall drinks and a brown paper bag. The yellow smiley face on his T-shirt and the promise of sinking my teeth into something delicious would usually be enough to cheer me up, but it doesn't work today.

'Breakfast delivery!' he announces. 'What's up with you?'

'Nothing,' I say. Ollie looks at me strangely but doesn't say anything. I don't want Lauren to know that I'm worried about getting fired. I'm wondering if she has found out about the time I worked a half-day instead of a full day because I went to meet Marcus and Louisa at the Almastra offices in Soho to talk about writing the book. Only Ollie could have told her that, though, and I don't think he would have.

Or maybe someone she knows saw me walking around central London that day and told her? I can't stand not knowing for much longer, so I take Ollie's drinks and pastries and set up an area in the back room with a low table in the middle and three armchairs around it. I mentally assign each chair to one of us and put a pastry on a plate and a coffee in front of each seat. I sit on mine and wait.

After about ten minutes, Lauren wanders in.

'Ah-ha. You're already here, my lovely. Great, I'll go get Ollie,' she says, then leans her head in the direction of the front door and shouts his name.

Ollie comes trotting in and we all take our seats around the table.

I take a large gulp of my coffee and some of it ends up down my windpipe. I cough and they both look at me for a moment, then Lauren speaks.

'Right, I know we need to open the shop, so I'll keep things brief. Sorry for calling an "impromptu meeting",' she does quotation-marks fingers, 'but things have been moving quite quickly and I wanted to bring you two up to speed with what's happening.'

She pauses to take a sip of her coffee and a bite of her chocolate croissant. Ollie and I have both stopped breathing and are following her every movement.

'You look so worried!' she laughs. I watch a sprinkle of croissant crumbs fall from her mouth onto her lap. She finishes chewing before speaking again. The wait is excruciating.

'Please don't worry, it's actually good news. Great news! Let me get to it. As I'm sure you both must have noticed, business is not exactly thriving. Our overheads are high, and people just aren't buying as many books as they used to. Or when they do, they get them online.'

Ollie grunts.

'I know, love.' Lauren taps him on the knee. 'It's awful. But we can't ignore it any more. And we certainly don't want to close. But it does look like things might be heading that way if we don't do something soon.'

She takes another sip and a bite. I'm gripping the edge of the sofa so hard my fingers ache. I don't know how much longer I can wait to find out what's happening. Losing this job doesn't even bear thinking about. These walls calm me down; not being able to be among the books, cradled by this low ceiling, would change everything. I remember going to our local library as a child and feeling immediately soothed by the smell and sight of its aisles. Scanning the shelves for all the possible new worlds I could immerse myself into. This place gives me the same feeling. I can't let it go. I could try and get another job, but the thought of that terrifies me. Dealing with different customers and their needs, working with new colleagues ... I couldn't do it. My chats with Ollie make me feel normal. Even though he knows so little about the real me, he still accepts the parts of me that I let him see. And doesn't seem to find them as pathetic as the people I grew up with. I feel dizzy.

Lauren smooths her hair down and I can see that she has left a pastry flake on it. Usually it would drive me so mad that I would have to remove it myself, but I want to hear what's coming next so badly that I manage to ignore the urge to pick it off.

'I've been having conversations with a few people I still know in London, some old colleagues – friends really – from my agency days, and something exciting has come up. So ...' she edges closer and looks us both in the eye; we're hanging on her every movement and every word, 'we're going to start a coffee shop. Right here.' She sits back, smiling.

I don't understand. A coffee shop here? Does it mean there won't be a bookshop any more? Where will we work? Do we still have a job? Ollie and I bombard Lauren with questions, each looking as confused as the other. Lauren answers every single one of them without ever stopping smiling.

'It will be here, at the back. No, we won't "become" a coffee shop, we will be both: a coffee shop and a bookshop, just a slightly smaller bookshop to make room for the counter and a few tables and chairs for those who want to eat in. Yes, you both still have a job. In fact, you're integral parts of this evolution. You'll be splitting your time between the two, some shifts at the bookshop, some in the café helping out with making coffee and serving cakes when things get too busy. I've got the plans here; would you like to see them?'

Ollie and I nod. The relief I feel at still having a job here is intense. I'm sure he must feel the same way. Lauren unrolls a scroll of paper and shows us the plan of the room and a computer-generated image of what it will look like once it's all done. The image shows a cosy space with tall plants, a light wood counter and an imposing chrome coffee machine with multiple spouts. There are smooth-looking human figures of all ages, sizes and ethnicities eating, drinking and laughing around the tables and by the counter. We never have that amount of people in here, so it will be strange to see the place full up.

I feel conflicted about this change. On one hand, it's great that Ollie and I still have a job and that the shop doesn't have to close. On the other, I'm sad I'll be losing my quiet room – the kitchen isn't nearly as good at protecting me when the noises outside get too much. I'm also worried I won't be able to use the scary-looking coffee machine that I can see in the image. At home I'm used to making coffee on the cooker in the small Moka machine. That spaceship looks nothing like it.

As if reading my mind, Lauren points at it and says, 'All three of us will have training with the café manager as soon as the machine arrives. So we can all jump behind the counter and help them when it gets too busy.'

'The café manager?' Ollie asks.

'Yes. Kai. They come highly recommended by an old colleague of mine. They've been working in the City until recently but are now looking for a slower pace of life and a shorter commute.'

They?

'Okay, cool. Are they non-binary?' asks Ollie.

'They are!' trills Lauren. 'Isn't it great?'

He just shrugs. He must have sensed my confusion because he turns to look at me and explains, 'It means neither male nor female. They're outside the gender binary and we don't use him or her or he or she when we refer to them, but just *they* or *them* pronouns.'

Lauren nods enthusiastically as he speaks.

'Yeah, I know,' I say, sitting back in my chair. I don't know why I say that because it's the first time I've heard of that concept. But Lauren looks so enthusiastic and things are feeling so uncertain right now that I don't want her to feel like I might struggle to adapt.

'It's very exciting,' I tell them both.

Ollie gives me a strange look while Lauren squeezes my hand and says, 'It is.'

'But were they born male or female?' I ask, still a little confused.

Lauren starts to say something, but Ollie interrupts her.

'When did you say the training will start?' and we're on to talking about something else.

When the coffee machine arrives, two weeks later, I'm shocked by its size. It takes two men to carry it through the shop and install it in just the right spot at the corner of the new counter. I don't know what we'll do if we ever have to move it. The café manager is due to come in shortly to introduce themselves and show us how to use it to make 'delicious drinkies', as Lauren put it.

Ollie has been quiet whenever she's been down from Scotland since she broke the news about the café. He's not impressed by her, he tells me. 'Evolution? More like demolition. She runs the shop into the ground, then sells its soul to make it a "trendy" coffee shop and has the guts to call it an evolution?'

I don't know what to say to him. When Lauren mentioned the possibility of the bookshop having to shut its doors, I felt a bubble of panic form in the pit of my stomach. This is my home, and without it I would be lost. Clara doesn't work any more, and the monthly allowance Edo has been giving her since he left only takes her so far. We're lucky we don't have to pay rent or a mortgage, as he gifted her the house we live in – he has no interest in coming back to London ever again, apparently. Clara says that giving her the house and allowance is the least he can do after abandoning her – 'God knows his family is rich enough, he can afford it' – but I still think it's generous of him. Aside from that, it's my wages that keep the lights on and food on the table.

I feel safe when I'm within these walls. And sane. Anything that keeps this place open and me working in it has my vote, and I'll do whatever it takes to help it succeed.

The builders were in for a few days and worked away in the back room, hidden by dust sheets. Ollie and I piled up all the children's books into the other sections and placed the toys and the heavier books behind the bookshop counter, out of the way of wandering toddlers. I could see that he wasn't happy about these changes because he kept saying, 'This is stupid.'

But when the dust sheets finally came down, even he admitted that the room looked great. Lauren had kept the original floorboards and shelves on the walls, but they had been cleaned and repolished, making the space look bigger somehow. The ancient skylight had been changed for a sleek Velux that flooded every corner with natural light. The counter was large but not too imposing. In the next few days, he helped her decorate the room with plants, rugs and fine crockery. Putting the books back onto the shelves helped to make the space look less separate from the rest of the shop. Now it's ready, and the coffee machine is glistening away in its place.

I'm busy sweeping the floor when I hear Lauren's voice rise and greet someone. Kai must have arrived. I'm curious to see what they look like, but I don't have to wait long because Lauren and Kai quickly walk over to the back where I'm standing.

They are tall and thin with a sharp nose and auburn hair that hangs down in soft chunks around their face. They're wearing a white T-shirt and dark jeans and are carrying a bicycle helmet. I was expecting someone who looked alien, different. But they look … normal.

'Vale, meet Kai, our lovely new café manager. Kai, this is Vale, our book-selling superstar,' Lauren says.

I put my hand out, but they must have missed it because they just give me a brief nod, then turn to look around the place. I stand there with my hand out for a few seconds, until Lauren sweeps Kai away to show them the new room. I observe them both from where I'm standing, Lauren a blur of smiles, nerves and expressive hands, Kai quiet and serious.

I try to make myself busy, but I keep on being drawn back to look at Kai. They catch me staring at one point and I can feel myself blush at being caught, so I stick my face in a publisher's catalogue and pretend to be deeply immersed in it. I don't know what I expected them to look like, I feel silly for even thinking it now. I wonder what Clara might think of the fact that I'm around someone like Kai at work now, seeing how she reacted to the two women on the train back from Brighton. She's never made remarks about Ollie, so it might be fine. But something tells me it would be different with Kai.

Once the tour is over, Lauren beckons me and Ollie over to join them and we all stand behind the machine around Kai.

206

'Right, boys and girls. Oh, sorry, Kai!' She covers her mouth with her hand.

Kai murmurs, 'No worries.'

'I'm a bit old-fashioned, I'm afraid. But I'll catch up, promise. Right, let's kick off this training session. I've locked the shop for a short while so we can all train together. Kai, would you kindly show us how to make delicious coffees with all sorts of milky swirls on top, please?' Lauren clutches her hands together as if praying to an all-powerful God. I've already lost track of how many times I've seen Ollie roll his eyes behind her.

Kai talks us through each function of the machine in a confident and clear voice. They explain how to grind the beans, what consistency to aim for and how much of the fine coffee powder to then load up into the extract bar. We go over what to look for in terms of liquid and how to check that it's not burned. Finally they explain the milk nozzle and how to care for it, then do a demonstration on how to foam the milk up to perfection. It's a satisfying process and I enjoy seeing how a liquid can become foam with the simple application of steam and pressure, and how water and coffee powder brought together at a certain temperature and compressed in the right way can turn into a silky, creamy black liquid. There's a reliability to the process – once all the ingredients are just right – that feels satisfying.

After explaining the differences between each type of milky coffee, Kai asks us all to take turns making a drink of our choice. I pick cappuccino and manage to foam up the milk just like they showed us.

'Well done,' they say, touching my arm, 'you're a natural.' I blush with pleasure. Only a few short months ago, I thought selling books and remembering pig facts were the only things I could do well. Now it looks like I might be able to write those facts down in a way that makes sense, and make a decent cup of coffee too. It feels good.

Ollie and Lauren both struggle to foam the milk up enough and Lauren's coffee is a little burned, but Kai tells them that some practice should fix those issues in no time.

For the remainder of the afternoon, we take turns working in the café and the bookshop. I'm worried about embarrassing myself in front of Kai, so I've been practising in silence as they watch me. I giggle to myself as I'm wiping the milk nozzle and realise that I've made a noise out loud before I can stop it.

'What's funny?' Kai asks.

'Nothing. I was just thinking that it's weird how humans put all this time and effort into making the perfect cup of coffee. I love coffee, don't get me wrong, but it reminds me of the way we elevate our passions to be above all others, and forget how they're not shared by all other species on earth. I was thinking how great it would be to be able to make an incredible drink like one of these that can be safely drunk by us and by farm animals too. And give us all the same amount of pleasure.' As I speak, I continue to wipe the nozzle until it's shiny and spotless.

Kai looks at me. 'Farm animals?'

'Yes. Pigs, for instance. They hate coffee,' I answer.

They smile. 'Ah, yes, Lauren mentioned about you and pigs. That you talk about them a lot.'

I nod. Lauren doesn't always have a lot of patience with my facts, so I'm not sure what she would have said to Kai, but it was probably not great. But I can't deny that it's true. I do love pigs and I'm never tired of learning more.

During my walk home after I leave work, I think about Kai and the whole non-binary thing. I never thought someone could question whether they felt male or female. I thought you were given those labels at birth and it stayed a non-negotiable fact until you died. Ollie said more and more people are challenging those norms and it's not a big deal any more. It's just how the world is going.

It feels so free.

'Have you ever thought about whether you could feel neither male nor female?' I ask Clara as I scrub the back of her legs with a soapy flannel.

'As in transgender?'

'Kind of. But not really. As in if you don't fit in with either gender. Like you're outside of it,' I say.

'No. I'm a woman, obviously. It's pretty clear, isn't it?' She lifts her arms to either side of her naked body.

'Of course. But I think it's more about what you feel like inside your head and less about the sex you're born with.'

'Where did you hear this rubbish?' she asks, with the same tone she uses when I'm asking too many questions or mentioning pigs at a bad moment.

'I . . . I don't think it's rubbish. There's this person at work – Kai – they're the new café manager. They're neither a he nor a she.'

'Oh, for God's sake. You're so impressionable. He – or she – was probably having you on. Anyways, this is boring. Your little café stories are making me want to go to sleep. Can you get a move on with that flannel? I'm getting cold.'

I don't think Kai was having me on. Lauren is the one who told me about Kai being non-binary, and she only knew because her old colleague who recommended them told her. I don't say anything about that to Clara, though, because I know it will only make her angrier. Instead, I just concentrate on washing her faster so she can get warm again.

After I've finished her legs, I stand up and tap her on the shoulder. She lifts her arms and holds them over her head so I can wash her armpits, and as she does so, I hear her sniffling. I move around to look at her face and see fat tears rolling down her cheeks.

'Oh no. What is it? Was it me? Did I upset you?' I ask her, my chest suddenly aching. She shakes her head as her shoulders keep heaving.

'Are you cold?' I quickly grab her robe and wrap it around her. She shakes her head again.

'What is it then? Please tell me.'

I can feel tears filling my own eyes now too. I can't stand seeing her like this. Her pain is my pain.

'Mum left me a message today,' she tells me, her voice shaking. 'Her and Dad are arguing again.' She sniffs. 'You'll never understand what it's like to come from basically a broken home like I do, Vale. Everything is always about them, never me. They are obsessed with drama, those two. It's so tough.'

I hold her tight and wish for my body's warmth to transfer onto her.

She is right, I don't understand. And even though I think it, I don't tell her that a broken home is technically one where the parents are not together any more.

We sit on the side of the bath and stay this way for what feels like hours. She keeps sobbing and I'm just so powerless. I rub her back until, after a while, her sobs start to soften, and the movement of her shoulders slows down. I kiss her head.

'Why don't you get some sleep?' I ask her. She nods and stands up in front of me. She wipes her nose and eyes with her sleeve, then turns around and heads to her bedroom, closing the door behind her. I sit back down on the side of the bath. My heart is still thumping, and I don't know what to do with my hands. *What just happened?*

Her parents not getting on is nothing new. But I've never seen her react this way about it, and so suddenly. Even though it's nothing to do with me, I still feel guilty. I should have protected her from it somehow. As much as I would like to learn to predict them, it's getting harder to know what causes her strange moods. They often seem to catch me unawares. Maybe there isn't anything I can do. Maybe that's just the way she is.

I get up, wipe my own tears and tidy up the bathroom.

I'll speak to her tomorrow, once she's had some sleep.

I go to the kitchen and make myself a sandwich. I don't feel like eating anything else tonight. I take my plate to my room and sit in front of my computer. I should write now that Clara has gone to bed, but my head is still full of images of her crying. I open a new page and try to compose a few sentences, but nothing seems to work. I can't stop thinking about her tears.

Chapter Twenty-Two

I wake up with a heavy feeling that I can't quite put my finger on. Then I remember last night and Clara's sudden tears. I couldn't write anything after she went to bed. As much as the anxiety of being behind schedule with the book is constantly pressing down on my chest, knowing that Clara is in distress floods every inch of my brain with worry. I think she would have told me if it was something I had done to upset her – she always does – but maybe it's something so bad she can't even bring herself to say it.

Has she found out about the book?

The sudden thought freezes me on the spot. I really hope she hasn't. It would make her very, very angry. It's not the writing of the book itself that I think she would mind, but more the fact that I have hidden it from her. She likes to know what I do at all times because, she says, it makes her worry otherwise. And I don't want to worry her.

I give her enough headaches as it is, I don't want to add to them. Yet I'm doing it. I am hiding it from her, hoping she might accept it but knowing there is a high probability that she would go berserk if she found out. Maybe this is what's happened. Maybe she did find out somehow and her anger is so intense it's making her cry, her disgust towards me last night too strong for her to be able to look me in the eyes.

Then again, it could be Edo. I know the two of them have chatted over the phone a few times recently and I'm not sure it's always a good chat, because I often see Clara looking tense afterwards. I wonder if that's why her phone was on the floor the other night, when I came back home after writing in the pub. Maybe they had an argument. I know that she has the habit of hanging up when a conversation isn't going her way – I remember Edo used to hate it – so maybe they've fallen out over that. She doesn't always like to tell me the details and I know that asking her will only make her angry, so I don't. I just know that she thinks he's 'nasty' and 'has changed'.

I feel for her. I thought she and Edo were on good terms, but maybe it's true, he *has* changed now.

I remember when I first heard from Clara after all those years. I hadn't seen her or spoken to her since leaving Italy. She'd sent me a message out of the blue when I was living in Whitechapel, and at first I thought it might have been a mistake.

Guess who? I miss you!

I didn't have her number on my British phone and she didn't sign the text, so I couldn't work out who it was from. Then I looked closer at the small picture next to her name and recognised her long dark hair and wide smile. She had her arms wrapped around someone's back – probably Edo's – and looked to have been caught mid-laugh. Clara.

I had tried so hard to forget that name, but those few words on my phone's screen were all it took to make me realise she was still etched into my brain. It was like those years of distance between us had never happened.

Clara??? Did you mean to send this?

Of course I did, silly. Guess what? We've moved to London!!!

I had to read that sentence a few times before it could sink in. Clara and Edo were living in London. I told her it was great news, of course. That I was ecstatic. But the truth was that what I felt was much harder to understand. I was both dizzyingly happy that she'd thought of me and terrified of getting close to her again. I knew – just like I do now – that her orbit has always been too powerful for me to resist. I also knew that getting close to her again would open me up to more heartache. So I made a pact with myself to welcome her to the city that I now called home, but to be careful not to get too involved in her life. Again.

She wanted to see me and catch up, so we made plans to go for coffee the following week once they'd had time to unpack their belongings and explore the area.

They had moved far away from where I lived but only a short distance from where I worked, by the river. The appeal of living near the river for Italians is that it is both exotic and familiar, as so many of us are used to rivers running through our cities. But the Tiber, Arno, Po, Adige are large when they're near houses, and they flow fast and deep. Where we are – Twickenham – the Thames is narrow and sleepy, the banks low and the animals that populate them easy to spot. There's even an inhabited island – Eel Pie Island – with quirky little cottages and an arched bridge that connects it to the mainland. I can see why Clara and Edo were drawn to the area. It's halfway between the city and the countryside. It makes sense for a young professional couple to want to put down roots here.

I arrived early to our meeting near Liverpool Street. I'd been working hard to try and avoid thinking about it, but Clara had started to resurface once more into my dreams. Clearly occupying my subconscious just as comfortably as she used to. As I sat at the café table, I concentrated on a sparrow looking for crumbs nearby. It hopped and flew from chair to chair with a natural rhythm that would have been soothing if my whole body hadn't been in a state of shaky anticipation. Even nature was powerless to calm my nerves at that moment. I took my phone out and started sending my mother a long, rambling stream of messages about the weather being too hot and my shoes too tight. Her replies were unhelpful, but reading them and typing calmed me temporarily. During our weekly catch-up call, I had told her that Clara and Edo had moved to London. She paused for a second, and I thought the line had gone dead. Then, right before

213

I was about to say 'Hello?', she spoke again. 'I know, I found out the other week.'

'Why didn't you tell me?' It was odd; she usually never missed out a bit of gossip that might be related to me. But she told me that she wasn't sure how I would have taken it. If it would have been difficult to hear or upsetting. I shrugged her concern off. It wasn't like I didn't know all of that already.

'I wish you had,' I said. I would have liked to have been more prepared. 'But it's fine, I'm a grown-up now.'

'Well, yes. You are.' She paused again. 'I know that. Anyway, now that you'll be having fun with your old friend, we'll never hear from you.' We both laughed at how unlikely that was.

I heard a noise and looked away from the bird to see Clara standing in front of me. She looked just like I remembered her. Large sunglasses hid her eyes, but it was easy to see her features underneath. Her hair was longer, and her clothes were brighter than they used to be. A magenta top over light grey jeans and a thin gold chain with a locket charm hanging from her neck.

'Here you are. Wow,' she said, sitting down at the opposite end of the small metal table.

'Yes,' I said, my mind suddenly blank.

I picked up the menu to give my hands something to do, but put it back down straight away once I realised that it made it even more obvious that they were shaking.

'It's been what, four years?' She pushed her sunglasses up onto her head.

'Three years and one month.'

'I've always enjoyed your precision.'

I didn't know what to answer to that, so I said nothing. She told me about why they'd decided to come to the UK. There was not much work in Rome, once they'd moved back from Milan, so when Edo's bosses had offered him a position in the London office of his accounting firm, he and Clara felt it was the right move for their future. She told me that she hadn't been happy for a while at the interior design firm where she worked so didn't think twice about giving in her notice.

'The Brits love Italian style. I'm sure I won't have a problem finding something here. But while I wait to hear back from a few contacts, I can sort out our new home, meet up with old friends and explore the area. Edo has been missing the old gang like crazy. He's so excited to see you again soon. Hopefully,' she added, looking at me with a twinkle in her eyes.

Seeing her in the flesh after all those years felt like an out-of-body experience. She had lived in my mind, buried deep, for so long that it was almost obscene to see her taking up space, exposed to air and sunshine. Like if the creature that lives under your bed in your childhood nightmares decides, out of the blue, to sit down and share a meal at the dinner table with you and your family.

'Let's go, I want to show you something cool.' She placed some coins on the table and grabbed my hand. I didn't have time to think. The feeling of her hand in mine was too overwhelming, so I just followed her.

She pulled me down the narrow streets towards the Thames, alongside old brick buildings and glass skyscrapers. She didn't tell me much about where we were going, just that she'd heard about it on TV and was curious to check it out. As we walked, she spoke of her and Edo's future plans: how they were planning to work hard for four years, then take a year to travel somewhere exotic. Once they'd get back, they would start a family together. Two, maybe even three children who she hoped would go to an international school. She didn't want them growing up being just English or just Italian, but European citizens, maybe even global. She wanted them to be two girls and one boy. She laughed about wanting to call the boy Edoardo Junior.

The more she talked about her plans with Edo, the more I remembered why this was dangerous for me. I could already feel the daggers of their perfect shared future piercing my present. And it still stung.

But I kept my smile on the whole time and asked her questions, so many questions. I didn't want her to ever stop to take a breath or the next thing she might say could be 'What about you? What are you up to these days?' And I wouldn't be able to lie to her face and tell her about the past adventures and exciting future plans I had too, as much as I wanted her to think I did.

'We're close,' she said, before I asked any more questions. We turned a corner and I felt her hand grabbing mine once again, holding it tighter this time.

'There it is. Wow. It's amazing.'

In front of us were the ruins of an ancient church, tucked in between high-rises. What would have once been the tallest tower in the surroundings now looked almost comically short in comparison. But the real beauty of these unexpected ruins was the way nature had repossessed the walls. Trees, bushes and ivy surrounded and climbed all over them. Even though the building's rectangular shape was still evident, inside it was gutted, replaced by luscious greenery and the odd exotic palm tree. Wooden benches were dotted along the perimeter on which a couple of people sat reading quietly in the shade. The air was eerily quiet.

It was beautiful.

'I can't believe this is here.'

'Right?' said Clara. 'St Dunstan in the East. I thought it'd be right up your street. Apparently it was first damaged during the Great Fire of London, then wrecked in the Second World War. I think they gave up trying to fix it after a while and just turned it into a park. It's cool.'

'It's amazing. It shows it doesn't take very long for nature to take over again if left to its own devices. Kind of scary and wonderful at the same time.' It was what I imagine stumbling upon an oasis while trekking across a desert must be like.

'Indeed. Shall we sit over there? My feet hurt.' Clara walked over to one of the benches and sat open-legged, her head tilted back. I sat neatly next to her and looked around.

That was when I made a mistake. I didn't think of another question to ask fast enough. So in the dead space – just like I feared – she asked about me.

'I've been yapping for hours. What's going on with you?'

'Not much.' I told her that I lived alone and worked at the bookshop in the week and went to visit pigs in a nearby city farm at the weekend.

'And what do you like most about living in London?' she asked me.

'That it's not Rome,' I said.

She looked at me strangely but didn't say anything. I didn't know what she was thinking. I didn't want to try and guess. I had run away from our city, we both knew it, there was no point pretending otherwise. I didn't want her to judge me for not having travelled much since leaving Rome, or made big plans for the future, or for still liking the same things. But it was the truth. I hadn't changed that much.

Luckily, she went back to talking about her and Edo's plans pretty quickly. Telling me about how they were planning to get a car to explore the countryside at the weekend. She'd heard that there were lots of pretty villages around and she was looking forward to discovering their surroundings. I nodded and smiled, relieved to get back onto safer ground. After a while, she said it was getting late and Edo would be heading back home soon; she wanted to get his dinner on as he would be starving.

'He misses the long work lunches. Here it's a sandwich at your desk and that's it. So odd! He's always so hungry when he comes home. Do you know how to find your way from here?'

I nodded and smiled some more.

We promised to meet up again soon and hugged by the wall covered in ivy.

'I've missed you, Monk,' Clara said.

'I've missed you too.' It was true, no matter how hard I wished it wasn't.

Sometimes I forget about the Clara of the past as the Clara of the present fills my mind with anxiety and my body with an urge to protect her that is all-consuming. But during her early days in London, it was different. Being next to her and witnessing her enthusiasm for this new start, seeing the city that I knew so well being reborn through her eyes, was intoxicating. It was as if she radiated light. All that time I'd spent trying to forget about her, running away from the past, was obliterated by seeing her eyes sparkle, watching the curve of her back as she walked ahead of me down the streets of Covent Garden, seeing her feet do a happy dance when she found a pair of shoes she liked or saw a painting for the first time at the National Gallery. She was back inside of me. She'd never left.

Clara doesn't deserve to be betrayed by me as well as Edo. I need to tell her.

Of course. It's the right thing to do. I suddenly feel like it's the only possible decision. I need to tell her about the book and deal with the consequences. I know she asked me not to write it, but I'm sure that when I explain how easy it has been and show her that not only does it not impact on us, but it might even bring in some more money, she will understand.

Hopefully she will see that I never meant to deceive her. That it wasn't my idea in the first place – it was Marcus's – but that it's a good one. If an expert like Louisa thinks that New Agriculture needs a voice like mine, opinions like mine, maybe it can convince Clara too and soften the blow of the deception.

I get out of bed and wrap myself in my old dressing gown. *I'll make her some coffee and bring it to her room, then tell her.*

I step quietly into the kitchen and make us two steaming cups of coffee. As I walk carefully back up the stairs, I see a blade of light under her bedroom door. She hasn't been awake this early for a while; it's unusual. Maybe she fell asleep with the light on. As I get closer to her room, I hear a thump from inside. I take a deep breath, then knock lightly.

'Are you awake? I have coffee.'

The door swings open and I see Clara holding a phone charger in one hand and a British-to-Italian plug adaptor in the other.

'Put it there on the desk,' she says.

I look around her room and see her suitcase on top of her bed, open and full of her folded clothes.

'Are you going somewhere?' I ask, aware of the sudden note of panic in my voice. We haven't been apart from each other for more than a few hours in years.

'Yes, I have to go. Rome.' She shoves the charger and adaptor into her suitcase, then a few more clothes that she grabs from the cupboard.

'Why? You haven't been back in ages.'

'I'd much rather not go, trust me. But Edo has decided he wants to ruin my life. So, of course, I need to go and let him do it.'

'Really? Edo?'

'Really. I told you, he's a nasty piece of work. He's manipulated a new woman into being with him, if you can believe it.' She's slamming toiletries into her bag one by one, with a force that makes me worry they might explode all over her clothes. 'I would feel sorry for the poor thing if she wasn't a horrible human being herself. Apparently she's also in on this whole thing. Agrees with him. They want to see me fall and beg, but I won't give them the satisfaction. I will hold my head high and show them that they can't take me down, no matter how hard they try.'

'What do you mean? Why do they want to hurt you?'

'I told you. Because they are nasty. N-A-S-T-Y. Mean. Horrible. They want to see me fall. But I'm done with taking it lying down,' she says, gesticulating wildly.

'But how?' I don't understand. I know Edo, and even though Clara says he's called me lots of unkind names in the past, I've never been able to imagine him doing so. He just doesn't seem like the kind of guy who would go out of his way to be mean to the people around him.

219

'How? He – they – want us to get a divorce. That's how. Make things official. I said to him, "We live in different countries now; how much more official do you want to make it?" but apparently it's not enough. We need to meet with lawyers and formally split assets and sign paperwork and ridiculous stuff like that. I told him I won't do it, but he says, "It's been years, Clara, it's time. You know it's the right thing to do", like it's me who's being unreasonable.' She shouts the last few words, then zips the bag and throws it on the floor where I'm standing. I grip my cup with both hands in case the bag hits me and makes the hot liquid spill, but luckily it lands just clear of my feet.

'When are you leaving?'

'Today. I've left it last minute because, to be honest, I didn't think he was serious. But he's booked the lawyer for tomorrow, so I have to go. It might take a few days, I don't know how long exactly, but I'll let you know. I've written down clothes and food notes for you for at least two weeks, just in case. You'll have to stick to what I've written until further notice. Okay?' she says, handing me a few pages of handwritten notes.

'Yes, of course. Thank you,' I say, carefully folding the notes and putting them in the pocket of my dressing gown.

'I'll miss you,' I tell her as I stand there kicking one heel with the tip of my other foot.

'I imagine you will, yes. But stick to the routine and you'll be fine,' she says, while reading something on her phone.

I nod. I offer to help her get ready, but she says she has a few phone calls to make before leaving and needs space to think. I close the door of her room quietly behind me and head to the bathroom to get myself ready for the day. There is no point telling her about the book right now while she's upset; it will only make things worse.

I will tell her once she's back and hopefully in a happier place.

I help Clara with her suitcase down the stairs and we hug briefly by the front door.

'I'll be checking in on you, so make sure you have your phone always on.'

'Of course. I hope it goes well,' I say.

'It won't. But don't make things worse for me by making me worry, okay? Stay by the phone and stick to the list.'

'I will. Please don't worry.'

The taxi pulls up in front of the house and I put her bag in the boot and give her another hug. As I watch the car leave, I feel like my chest has suddenly imploded and is now just an empty cavity. But strangely, this feeling doesn't last long. Soon, I feel an unfamiliar sense of excitement at the days ahead of me.

I take the food list she has given me to work, and after I lock up at the end of the day, I go to the shop and buy every item on it. I want to get it right. I load up my trolley with two loaves of bread, three blocks of cheddar, plenty of lettuce and tomatoes, seven jars of pesto and seven packs of dried pasta. She has given me the same food for the week as for the weekend. She has told me to eat the sandwiches at lunch and the pasta in the evening at home. She says I can get the sandwiches from a shop if I want to – as long as they contain what's on the list – but I don't want to risk not finding the right ones, so I will make them at home and bring them in.

Tomorrow is Saturday and a long, lonely weekend stretches ahead of me. I miss Clara but I'm not worried. I know exactly what I'll do while she's away. As I strain the pasta and mix it with the chunky pesto that slides out of the jar, I think of all the time I suddenly have ahead of me. This is my chance to get back on schedule with the book. I will tell Clara about it when she's back, but in the meantime, I might as well write as much of it as I can. I might not have this much time to myself again. I take the bowl to my bedroom and sit in front of the computer. The words burst out of my brain and into my hands like water from a mountain stream, and my fingers don't leave the keys until the moon is high in the sky.

Chapter Twenty-Three

August 2019

I write at night. Sometimes I write at work when Ollie doesn't mind taking over for a while, and then in the pub after the workday is over. I write on my lunch breaks on a bench by the river, and I write all weekend. The hours go by without leaving a trace.

I'm powered by pasta al pesto and cheese sandwiches and I write with my mouth full, searching for my lips with the fork without taking my eyes off the screen.

The pages start adding up, and before I know it, I'm right back on track where I should be by now. Then beyond. I only stop for a few hours at night to get some sleep, when I'm needed at the shop, and the few times a day when Clara calls. She keeps me on the phone for ages each time, telling me about how mean Edo is being to her and how his new girlfriend calls him after their meetings with the lawyer and he always picks up, even if they're right in the middle of a conversation.

Sometimes she just cries and won't tell me why, so I whisper that it will be okay, that Edo doesn't deserve her, that soon she will be back in London.

Yesterday she shouted at me when I didn't pick up on the first ring, then told me how Edo has decided to stop giving her an allowance.

'A marriage means supporting each other. His money is my money!' she yelled so loudly her voice cracked.

This morning she told me she had to stay in Rome for a few more days because the lawyers are still going over the paperwork.

'I forgot what Italian bureaucracy was like.'

I could tell from her low monotone that she wasn't happy about it at all. I feel for her and wish I could make things easier. But a part of me is also happy that I have more time to write. I need every moment I can get to make sure I can deliver the book on time.

She also told me she's found out about this app called 'Find My Friends' that allows you to keep track of people once they download it on their phone. She wants to try it when she gets back so she knows where I am and doesn't have to worry unnecessarily.

This is worrying. If she starts tracking me, I won't be able to go anywhere that isn't approved by her. I couldn't go to meetings with Marcus and Louisa, to the pub, or anywhere else that wasn't work or home. I can feel the walls closing in on me already as I listen to her words. Once I have this app on my phone, there's nothing that can stop Clara from knowing where I am.

Telling her about the book is even more important now that I know that soon I will no longer be able to hide it from her. I just hope that she's in the right mood when she comes back from her trip. But so far, I can tell she isn't. It's also even more important for me to do as much writing as I can while she's still away and can't track me yet. I miss her and I'm looking forward to having her back, but the urge I'm feeling to finish the book has been growing and taking up more and more space in my head. It's odd, there used to be only room for Clara and pigs in there. Now this need to put my knowledge down on paper – and for it to make sense and be an enjoyable read – has been growing so much that it's starting to take up its own space too. I'm trying not to think about it too much because the chances that nothing will come of it are still high – whether it's that I don't finish the project because Clara doesn't want me to, or I do finish it but Almastra don't think it's good enough. So it might not matter much in the long term. Still,

I'm putting all the hours I'm awake towards finishing as much of the manuscript as I can.

Every morning at work, Ollie asks me how many pages I've done.

'Let's hear that number,' he says before I've even had time to put my bag down.

'A hundred and two as of this morning.'

'Vale, that's amazing. What's got into you?' he asks, eyes wide open.

'I must have found my rhythm,' I say, unable to hold back a smile. It feels good to be told I'm doing well.

'I'd say so. You're nearly there! When are you sending it to Marcus?'

'I don't know. What do you think? I want it to be perfect before sending it, but I feel like it never will be. I've been rereading some of the earlier pages and found quite a few typos and mistakes.'

'Of course it's not perfect. Nothing is. But that's where the experts come in. I'm sure Marcus or someone in his office will help you get it to a good place. That's what they're there for. You should consider sending it soon,' he says.

I'm just so worried about disappointing Marcus and Louisa; if the faith they've put in me turns out to be misplaced, I almost don't want them to see what I've done.

As Ollie and I chat, a group of pregnant women walk into the shop and head straight for the café. There's a new prenatal group nearby and the women who attend the classes there have started coming in regularly to catch up before and after. I like the fact that, thanks to the café, this place has now become a bit of a hub for the community to get together. It's nice for them and it makes me feel like I'm going out and meeting new people just by listening in to their conversations. I go in to check if Kai needs help and I see them making the coffees while taking the orders.

They don't seem flustered, but if it were me in their place, I would be glad for some help, so I step in behind the till. Once all the women are sitting down nursing hot drinks, Kai and I lean on the counter and take a breath.

'Thanks, Vale,' Kai says. 'Pregnant women scare me. It's a weird thing.' They shudder.

'I like them, actually,' I say. 'I think it's because it shows that no matter how many clothes or jewellery humans put on, nature still finds a way to make itself visible. It's one of the clearer representations of how close we are to animals after all. Nature always pushes through.'

Kai nods. 'I guess I never thought of it like that. It's quite a beautiful way of looking at it,' they say.

I blush before I can turn my face away. I don't know if Kai has seen it or not.

Luckily, they change the subject almost right away.

'Nice and chilled today. I like it. My old job was hectic all the time. And a very different crowd.' They point at the group. 'Ruder and way needier than that lot. I had to leave before I ended up punching one of the bankers demanding their triple-shot black hot Americano,' they whisper.

'Really?' I ask. 'That sounds awful. I can't deal with customers being rude to me. I used to hide in here if someone raised their voice. Like if an order was late or something. Before it was a café, of course.'

'Where will you hide now?' Kai asks. They seem to be genuinely concerned, their brow furrowing, but without a smirk. Their face is symmetrical in a way that makes it hard to look away. Their features are so angular as to almost strain the skin. It's not unattractive.

'I'm going to have to find a new hiding place.'

'You could hide behind the counter?' Kai says.

I nod. 'I could,'

They stare at me.

'What were you and Ollie talking about? I heard him getting emphatic over there,' they ask.

I don't know why, but I don't like talking about the book. Not that many people know about it. Although when I tell Clara, that will be one more person. I just feel like the more people know, the less real it might feel. Like the more it goes into people's brains, the more it's diluted, until it's just a dream. No longer real. I'm terrified of waking up one day and realising that I've never met Marcus and Louisa. That Ollie has been playing along with my delusion, like one of our greeting card games. Sometimes I open my inbox just to check that the emails from Almastra are still in there, that I haven't imagined it all along.

I've been content all my life to keep my pig knowledge as something that I can retreat into when feeling overwhelmed or stressed. I've learned that it's not the kind of thing that people want to hear about. That's another thing I have Clara to thank for: she's always been very good at telling me what people want to hear about and what they don't.

'No one wants to hear about pigs, Vale, it's weird.' We were sixteen the first time she told me that. She has told me many more times since. And about other things I do that are unacceptable. But even though I've only known Kai for a few weeks, there's something about them that I feel I can trust. It's odd, but when I'm near them I feel lighter, happier. I don't know why.

'My book. He was asking me about it,' I tell them.

'Are you writing a book?'

'I am,' I say, gearing up for the weird looks and silences that will inevitably follow.

'Cool. What about?'

'Pigs.'

'Pigs?'

I nod. 'Ethical pig rearing, to be precise,' I say, aware of their eyes on me. I look down, concentrating hard on my shoes.

'That's brilliant. That whole topic is massive right now. I've got loads of friends who've left London to go live on farms or set up agricultural businesses. It's mad.'

Kai's face has a look that I don't immediately recognise. It's not negative, it's more like they're surprised. Or impressed. Or even . . .

interested? How odd. I feel a not unpleasant warmth rise up through my legs and into my stomach.

'I've heard. New Agriculture. We get a few books about it in the shop. But Almastra – my publishers – say there's a need for more. So I'm trying to write as fast as I can.'

'Very cool.' Kai smiles. 'I'd love to read it one day.'

I smile back. 'Okay,' I say.

That was so easy. And it felt nice to see the genuine interest in their eyes. Why can't it be like that with Clara?

Later that day, I get a text from her.

Back tomorrow. Just booked my flight. I'll forward the details so you know. I want steak and roast potatoes for dinner. Sick of pasta.

She has been away just short of two weeks. Although I have been surprisingly happy on my own while she's been away, I know that our routine will be reinstated once she's here. She is planning to track me with that app, which leaves me no choice but to come clean about the book. And this makes me very anxious.

I spend the night writing. No point in sleeping through my last chance to get on with the book. The closer Clara's return gets, the less sure I'm starting to feel that she will be happy for me to continue with it. There's something about the tone of her message that worries me. And I know that her mood can switch very quickly.

My eyes are nearly closing by the time I see the sun coming up over the roofs outside my bedroom window. I watch what I'm typing through the thinnest slit of eyelid, until my thoughts start to blur into one and I know I need to stop.

Clara's flight gets in around the time I finish work, so I'll have to have everything ready for her before I leave this morning. There's no more time to write.

I read the last few pages I've written and make sure there are no typos. I find Marcus's email address and attach to it what I have so far. I don't have time to stop and think about what I'm doing. And my exhausted brain wouldn't understand even if I did have the time.

I type a few words of explanation in the body of the email and move the mouse over the send button. I close my eyes and click.

I can't worry about what I've just done because there is too much to do. I've been writing with the curtains drawn in this house for nearly two weeks. Nothing has been cleaned and no fresh air has come in. I need to get things back to normal before Clara is home. I draw the curtains and open all the windows. I scrub the bathroom clean and wipe down every surface in the kitchen until it gleams. I go into Clara's room and fluff up her duvet and align her pillows. I wipe away the thin layer of dust that has settled over everything. The particles dance wildly in the breeze and sunshine streams in from the open window. Once the house looks like it did when she left, I run to the shop and grab a fillet steak and a bag of potatoes. I buy an apple and blackberry crumble too. If she's sick of Italian cooking, she's going to be happy with a crumble. I run back home and season the steak with salt and pepper, then put it in the fridge to grill later. I peel the potatoes and chop them into small bites, then lay them on a tray with olive oil, garlic and a few sprigs of rosemary. Then I remember what she said and take out the rosemary. Too Italian.

The workday goes in a blur. It's my turn to be at the front, in the bookshop, and we're busy with summer-holiday kids looking for entertainment and teachers shopping for inspiration. I can hear Kai and Ollie chatting and laughing in the café. I'm jealous of their time together. I realise it's childish to feel this way, but I wish I was there with them rather than on my own. I don't think about the book all day, until closing time, when they both walk over and ask me about it. When I tell them I've sent it over to Almastra, they both whoop and jump up and down. We high-five, even though I'm not feeling as enthusiastic as they are about it. I haven't had time to read it through properly since Clara has been away. I've just been so concentrated on writing as much as possible that I haven't been able to stop and make sure it all makes sense. Kai and Ollie's enthusiasm is contagious, though, and I'm feeling a little better about it as I walk home.

I message Clara to ask her whether the taxi I booked for her was on time and if she's on her way, and she messages back right away.

Yes.

I pick up speed. I want to try and get there before she does so that I can make sure everything is ready for her. The house is dark when I get in, so I turn all the lights on. I put the potatoes in the oven and take the steak out of the fridge so it's not too cold when I cook it. I lay the table using the fabric napkins, the good plates, and the silver cutlery that Edo's parents gave them as a wedding present. I move the vase with the artfully arranged dried flowers from the living room to the middle of the table, to add colour.

Everything is ready, I'm just waiting for the sound of the car pulling up outside. I sit on a chair, rest my hands on my knees and wait.

Aksai Black Pied, American Yorkshire, Angeln Saddleback, Ankamali, Appalachian English, Arapawa Island, Auckland Island, Australian Yorkshire . . .

As I get to 'F' – *Forest Mountain Pig* – I hear the taxi stop outside our front door. I go out and get Clara's suitcase out of the boot.

She says, 'I'm starving,' and walks right past me.

I follow her and watch her survey the scene. I see her eyes dart over every surface, taking it in, checking for faults. They land on the table. Her face is dark.

'Why did you use that cutlery?' she asks.

'I thought . . . I wanted to make the table nice.'

'Don't you know who gave me those?' She's looking at me now, her eyes wide open and her mouth tight.

'I do. But we've used them in the past, I didn't think . . .' My voice is starting to tremble. I know it's fear that does that, but I can't allow it. Clara can smell the fear on me like a bloodhound.

'You fucking idiot. You brainless, thoughtless, pathetic piece of shit. You *did* think. You thought, "How can I make Clara's trip even

229

harder, her return more difficult? How can I play with her feelings so that no place is safe for her any more?"'

I try to say something, but she continues, her voice going up in volume with every word.

'I've just spent the last two weeks fighting with my ex-husband about our divorce. Finding out he's engaged and planning to get married next year to that other moron.' She spits each word out as if they were bitter almonds. 'And when I get back, I have to see another reminder of that bastard before I've even taken my coat off?'

She's looking at me. Waiting for an answer.

'What have I done to deserve this?' she says.

I could kick myself. I *am* an idiot. Why didn't I think that seeing their old wedding gift after the time she has had in Italy might make her feel bad? We've used the cutlery many times in the past, whenever we've wanted to celebrate something or make an evening feel more special. We even used them one evening to celebrate Clara's single status and her plans for the future, just before she stopped leaving the house.

But I should have thought harder.

'I'm so sorry. I wanted to make things lovely for you. To celebrate your return. I didn't think . . . I'm sorry.' I feel tears coming down my face. I can't stop them, but I know Clara won't like it.

'Look at you. You're a joke. You're so lucky and don't even know it,' she says.

She takes off her coat and sits on one of the chairs around the dinner table.

She's playing with the cutlery, dragging a fork along a napkin, leaving little lines pressed into the white fabric.

I hold myself tight around my middle. My throat has closed up and I'm trying to stop the tears, but it doesn't work. I wanted tonight to be perfect. For Clara to be relaxed and happy. To tell her all about my book. For us to go back to the routine we had before. Instead, I've ruined things again. I am all the things she says I am.

230

'You're so lucky that someone like me would agree to live with someone like you. To try and help you every day to become a better person. Someone normal. I've been doing this since the day we met, don't you remember? You'd be nowhere without me. I'm all you've got. And you just "didn't think"? You make me sick,' she says, the red halo of rage on her neck creeping up her face.

She takes the cutlery and throws it on the floor then stomps to the kitchen to get a knife and fork from the everyday drawer. She turns on the grill and switches off the oven.

'Wait, I'll do it. Please, let me serve you. Please,' I beg her.

She thinks for a second, then walks back to the dining room and sits back down at the table. I cook her steak, careful to make it how she likes it, medium rare but not bloody. When it's ready, I bring it over to her and load her plate with potatoes. I stand by the side and watch her eat it.

After a few mouthfuls, she says, 'Get out of my face, I can't bear to look at you.'

I tell her that there's a crumble in the fridge if she's still hungry afterwards, but she ignores me. I wait for a moment to see if she'll speak to me after all, but she doesn't. I walk up to my room, careful not to make too much noise.

Chapter Twenty-Four

'That one goes from *100 Facts on Archaeology* by John Farndon to *A Lasting Impression: Coastal, Lithic, and Ceramic Research in New England Archaeology* by Jordan Kerber. Too easy.'

'Ha. Cocky. I like it. Okay, let's see. What about that one over there, by the wrapping paper bucket?'

Kai points at a shelf near the front of the shop, a whole room away from the café counter where we're standing. You can just see a blur of colour on the shelves. It's too far to be able to read any titles.

'Which shelf?' I ask.

'Fourth from the bottom,' they say.

'I believe it starts with *10 Steps to the Boardroom: Climb Your Way to Success* by G. S. Rattan and ends with *Resolving Sexual Issues with Creative Mindpower Techniques: A Self-Hypnosis Self-Help Guide* by Dr Frank W. Lea DD Dip. NLP RPHH APHP. Psychology and Self-Help.'

Kai runs over to check, reads the book spines and bursts into laughter.

'Oh my God. You're right. That's wild,' they say, jogging back to the café.

'I told you. I know them all. Not as well as I know other stuff, but still pretty well.'

'Other stuff like pigs?' they ask.

'Like pigs. Yes.'

I notice that Kai doesn't laugh when I start talking about pigs; they listen and ask more questions. They don't even roll their eyes like Ollie sometimes does.

I look at their face. I've noticed that the angularity of their features softens when they smile. Their mouth is wide and rises all the way up to the corners of their eyes. Thin lines stretch around their brown eyes like sun rays. It makes them look like a lion roaring.

'Well, it's impressive. Especially considering how often Lauren likes to switch things around in this place,' they say.

We're both standing behind the counter, waiting for the morning rush. It's early, and I would usually dread interacting with customers at this time, but I'm growing to like being in the café. There's still a lingering sense of calm that soothes me just like it did when this room was part of the bookshop. Even though the surfaces now are shiny, and everything looks a bit sleeker, I still feel held by its thick, ancient walls and protected from the outside world. I like talking to Kai too. They speak to me in a direct way that I find easy to understand – no strange looks or complicated expressions – and they always take time to explain things if I'm confused. I look forward to our chats and often find myself thinking about what we might talk about the next time we see each other.

Kai and Ollie have become close too. I often hear the two of them laughing when they work together. The café is busier than the bookshop was, which means I have to speak to more people than I'm used to. But I'm finding out that it also helps me to not think too much about Clara and the way things are at home. When I have a good day at work, it's like I'm recharged inside and I can be stronger for when I get home. Clara needs me to be. After the way Edo has treated her in Rome, she's going to need some time to get back on her feet.

'Okay. Let's do one more and then we can heat up the machine and get ready for the coffee horde. What about . . .' Kai scratches their chin and scans the room, 'there? That weird one over there. Next to the children's section.' They point.

'The one with the largish tomes?' I ask.

'Yes.'

'Too easy!' I say, smiling. 'They're all the Philip Pullmans.' I lower my voice. 'That section never moves. Ollie calls it the "holy altar". Lauren is a big fan of Philip Pullman's work. She often dusts that section when she's in, *just that one.*'

'Yes, I've seen her do it. So funny.'

A few customers walk in, and I position myself at the coffee machine while Kai takes the orders.

I suppose it is funny that Lauren does that; I haven't considered it before. I don't like Philip Pullman's books myself because I find fantasy and science fiction very strange. Why would people make things up – worlds, species, facts – when we haven't finished telling everything about our own world yet? Once every single thing that exists in this world has been written about and every animal and plant and species documented, then we can start making things up. To do it before then is like building a house before its foundations are in. It's a job badly done.

There's no point sharing with Kai how I feel about fantasy and science fiction because they might be their favourite genres and I don't want to offend them. So I just smile. I already have enough discussions with Ollie about this topic whenever someone brings up *Star Wars*. He says, 'It's the one thing I can't forgive you for, Vale. The saga is everything.' I don't think it's everything and I've told him so many times, but I've had to stop because he gets angry after a while and starts gesticulating and talking to himself.

He's been on his phone a lot today. From where I'm standing, I can see him leaning over the bookshop counter messaging someone. His thumbs sweep furiously across the screen as he smiles to himself. I wonder if he has a new love interest.

With all the writing I've been doing while Clara was away and the fact that I've been running off home after work as soon as I can to keep her happy, Ollie and I haven't caught up in a while. On top

234

of that, it has become rare for us to work together because one of us is often needed at the café.

Once all the customers have been served, I tell Kai that I'm going to go to the front for a second. Ollie lifts his head when he hears me walking over and smiles. The hooded top he's wearing today reads in gothic letters *Hogwarts Alumni Est. 933*.

'Hello, stranger. How's things in coffee land?' he asks.

'All good. Kai is surprised that I know what book is on every shelf. I told them it's not a big deal, but they seem to think it's very impressive. How is book land?'

He grunts. 'Same as always, Vale. I wish I was hanging in the back with you two.' He lowers his voice. 'I think what's impressing Kai is *you*, not your knowledge of where everything is,' he says with a wink.

This really confuses me. Have I missed something? But before I can ask him, Ollie asks me about Marcus and whether I've heard back from him since submitting the manuscript.

'Nothing yet,' I tell him. 'I checked my email yesterday morning and there was nothing. I've had to stop doing it too often because it was driving me mad.'

'I hear you.' He nods. 'You never know, though, he might have written today.'

I give him a dirty look. 'Now that you've said it, I'm going to have to check again, or it'll eat away at me.'

Ollie laughs.

I look over to the café to see whether Kai needs help, but they seem to be happily chatting with one of the customers.

'Can I?' I ask Ollie, pointing at the computer next to him.

'Of course, be my guest.' He bows deeply, like an actor at the end of a play.

I've found my email inbox empty so many times over the last few weeks that I find it hard to imagine it any other way. While the junk mail inbox is often full, the regular inbox has started to look like a painting every time I see it, immutable in its colours and shapes. Because of this, it takes me a few seconds to register that something looks different when I log in.

'Wait,' I say under my breath.

'What?' Ollie is examining one of his fingernails and doesn't look up.

I point. He whips his head back up towards the screen and his eyes widen.

'What are you waiting for? Click on it!' he says, scrambling to stand next to me. I recognise the sender as Marcus at Almastra. I click on it with a shaky finger. Ollie and I lean in closer to read.

Dear Vale,

I hope you're well.

Louisa – cc'd here – and I have read your manuscript and think it's good. Like we've told you before, it will need some work before it's ready for publication – all first drafts do – but we feel confident that we can help you get there.

We both particularly liked your section on how to boost a gilt's fertility by closely monitoring its cycles and improving its living conditions and natural light exposure. We felt that even though it was data-heavy and had the potential of being too technical, you handled it in a light and empathetic way that made it feel uplifting and informative. Not an easy feat! Also, are pigs feminists? Some food for thought in there, I'd say ;)

We thought we could include some examples of tracking charts in that section for reference, what do you think?

We also loved your chapter on feeding. It was so passionate and uplifting! Who knew that so many roots and vegetables don't agree with pigs?? And your section on salt and

236

how toxic it is reads like a horror story. I'm going to have nightmares about it.

All jokes aside, it's a really enjoyable read. Louisa has asked me to work closely with you in the next few weeks to get things up to scratch. My team here will do the bulk of the editing, then you and I will meet to go over the bigger structural changes and overall picture together. How does that sound? Will you be able to come to the Almastra office sometime in the week for our first meeting?

Looking forward to working together.

Kind regards,

Marcus

Ollie starts jumping up and down and I have to grip the front of the desk with both hands to stop myself from falling to the floor as my knees buckle. My throat has dried up and my brain is scrambled. I have a sudden urge to call my parents and tell them everything. I reach for my phone and start dialling with trembling fingers. But then I remember. If they know, there is a chance it will get back to Clara, and I can't let that happen. I put my phone back in my pocket. Not yet.

Ollie, still jumping, grabs me by the shoulders and starts chanting 'yes yes yes yes yes yes yes' to the tune of 'Twinkle, Twinkle, Little Star'.

The worry that Clara might find out before I have a chance to tell her in a way that won't send her through the roof is so strong. I feel dizzy but manage a smile for Ollie. The excitement on his face is too contagious not to join in.

Kai runs in looking alarmed. 'What's going on, are you okay?' They stare at me.

I nod.

'What happened?'

I still can't seem to make any sound come out of my mouth. I just point at the screen. They read Marcus's email and a massive smile splits their face.

'This is great. Well done you!' They sweep me up and hug me tightly. Ollie looks worried for a second that I might freak out from the sudden bodily contact, but I'm too dazed to fight Kai's embrace. They let me go and all three of us link arms and start dancing in a circle behind the till.

'She's going to have a book. She's going to have a book. She's going to have a book,' Ollie sings.

Soon Kai joins in and I do too. We're chanting quietly so as to not disturb the customers in the café, but our three voices together add up to quite a noise. I see the customers looking at us, amused and perplexed. When we're done, Kai takes up their position behind the café counter once more, announcing loudly to the room, 'All cappuccinos on us. We are celebrating!'

I laugh and shake my head. I've never felt more appreciated and it's an incredible feeling. Like my heart has liquefied and filled every cavity inside my body with warm treacle. This place is my home. These people are my people. They understand me. They are happy for me. They want me to succeed. And they expect nothing in return but my friendship. I look around and feel so light I could take off.

I go to the kitchen to get some water, and while I wait for the glass to fill, I compose my reply to Marcus in my head. *Of course I don't mind the editing. I would be more than happy to collaborate with you on making it the best version it can be. I look forward to working together too.*

I write and rewrite each word until it flows just right.

Then I remember.

Clara's words when she was away. The app she found – Find my Friends – that she wanted me to download onto my phone. She hasn't mentioned it again since being back and I have no intention of bringing it up first. But if she was to remember about it, I would have to do it. This means I would only be able to ever be here – the bookshop/café – or home. Maybe a shop to get groceries if I cleared it with her first. I wouldn't be able to meet Marcus in Soho again, not even once, without her knowing all about it. The only way to avoid this would be if I didn't have to go to his office at all. Maybe we could do a video call?

I know they're possible because Lauren often has them in the café with her financial adviser, and with her family in the US. I could try and ask him, but I worry that it would make Almastra change their mind about working with me if I made things too difficult; they might think I was tricky. But I have no choice. I can't go to Soho with the possibility of Clara finding out about it before we've had the conversation about the book. She isn't ready yet for it. Her mood is very low, and she spends most of her days slumped on the sofa in her pyjamas. I worry that another upset will send her further into despair. I will tell her, but not just yet. And I can't tell Marcus the real reason why I can't meet him at his office.

From the kitchen, I can hear Kai and Ollie singing in unison, 'bub, bub, bub, bub, bubba, bub, bub' to a hypnotic rhythm and cracking up with laughter. My email seems to have cheered all of us and turned the mood from quiet to hysterical. We don't know what to do with ourselves, and for once, the thick walls all around are struggling to contain us.

Ollie and Kai spend the rest of the day skipping from café to bookshop like drunken chimps. I decide to put off the worry about what to say to Marcus until the end of the day and join them. We play tricks on each other, take turns making hot drinks and read aloud passages from our favourite books. The few customers who come in seem to mostly be amused by our energy. It's as if my news this morning has unlocked a new level of ease in our friendships. We are more comfortable with each other than we have ever been.

The hours fly by and closing time comes around before I realise it.

As it's quiet, we close a few minutes earlier than usual. Plenty of time to spare before I need to be home to Clara.

Suddenly I know what I'm going to do about the meetings with Marcus.

Kai, Ollie and I high-five one last time and wave goodbye to each other.

Today has been such a fun day that I walk away from the shop feeling taller. My back is straighter and I can't stop smiling. No matter what is waiting for me at home, I can keep these feelings inside of me to seek refuge in whenever things feel too hard with Clara. I get my phone out and find Marcus's number. I take a deep breath as I hear the ringing tone.

'Hello?'

'Marcus? Hi. It's Vale.'

I can do this.

'Hey. How are you?'

'Okay, thanks. You?'

'All good. Did you get my email? Good news, right?' I can hear from his voice that he's smiling.

I smile too.

'Great news, yes. I'm so happy. Ollie says hello by the way,' I remember to tell him.

'Lovely Ollie. Tell him I say hello back. So, when are you free for our first meeting?' he asks, not wasting any time.

'I can do whenever really. I mean, I work during the week so we'd have to organise it around that. But there might be a little problem with the "coming to Soho" bit.'

He doesn't say anything, so I continue.

'I can't really come there. It's not that I don't want to. It's just . . . I can't. I'm sorry. Is there any other way we could meet?'

I don't want to lie to him, but I don't know what to say if he asks me to tell him why. I cross my fingers and hope that he won't.

'Oh. Okay. What kind of thing did you have in mind?' He doesn't sound angry, just a bit taken aback.

'Maybe video meetings? I know a lot of people are doing those now. I can see if my computer can support them. It's very old but it might be fine,' I say.

'Hmm. I'm not sure video is the best way to do these kinds of meetings, I'm afraid. It's always best to do face-to-face so we can workshop certain bits together if we're stuck. I'm a big fan of Post-it notes. I use them all the time. It's not the same on video. Let's see.'

He pauses to think. I don't want to interrupt him, so I stay quiet. I'm walking along the street with the phone pressed to my ear. I hope he can't hear the noise of the traffic; it's busy and loud around here at rush hour.

'Can I ask why you can't come to the office?' he finally asks.

Oh no. I'm not prepared for this. It's silly, but I was *really* hoping he wouldn't ask.

Now I don't know what to say. I look around me, aware of the seconds of silence ticking away. I watch a cat dart out of a front garden and under a car.

'It's my cat. I can't leave it alone for too long,' I blurt out.

'Your cat?'

I nod. I'm aware he can't see me, but I still do it. I'm fully committed to this lie now, wherever it may go.

'Yes. My cat. He's very old and needs medication every few hours. I usually walk over from the shop to give it to him. I can't be too far away for too long. Sorry.'

The words roll out of me, and I can hear myself speaking them as if I was the one listening to them. I feel guilty for lying and sad about this non-existent cat all at once.

I don't expect Marcus to believe me. I wouldn't.

'Right. I see. I guess I could come to you instead. Do you take lunch breaks at the shop? We could work together then if you don't mind sacrificing that time for the cause?' he says.

I'm shocked. He has believed it after all. Or if he hasn't, he has chosen not to ask any more questions about the cat. I'm so grateful I could jump.

'No. That would be perfect! Thank you. Thank you so much. We could sit in the café at the back of the shop. There's a coffee shop there now, it's different from the last time you were in. We could sit there and work. That's great. It's perfect. Thank you.'

I realise I'm repeating myself, so I stop for fear of annoying him.

Him coming to me works out perfectly. This way, if Clara decides to start tracking me, it'll just look like I've decided to eat my lunch in the shop instead of sitting by the river as I usually do. Nothing to get suspicious about. We decide to meet in a week once the editor has had a chance to work on the first few chapters. I thank him once again and we hang up. The relief I feel makes me skip all the way down our road. I feel like dancing. I thank the pig gods for helping me make this easier. I feel lucky. I *am* lucky. Today has been a great day.

I stop in front of our door. Clara will ask questions if she sees me so happy. Questions that I won't be able to answer. I need to calm myself down. I smile one last time, then relax my mouth to a neutral state. I brush any fluff off my clothes and smooth my hair. *Act like everything is normal. She can't know. Not yet.*

I push the door open and walk in.

Chapter Twenty-Five

September 2019

Since coming back from Rome, Clara has been making small changes to the daily notes she gives me. I don't know why. It started a week ago when she wrote: *Brown sweater (inside out), beige trousers, trainers.*

The following day it was: *Grey top, beige trousers, one sock only.*

There was a notice in *The Bookseller* magazine the other week about my book being published. Marcus rang me all excited and told me about it after it happened. I wish he'd told me before; I could have maybe done something about it. What if Clara has seen it? I'm worried she might know but is keeping it from me for some reason. Or maybe she doesn't and her notes are getting stranger for reasons that I don't understand.

I was a bit uncomfortable at first with my sweater the wrong way around, and one bare foot inside my trainer, but I forgot about it after a while. Clara hasn't mentioned anything about it, but I've seen her look me up and down to check if I've followed her instructions. When she noticed the label of my brown sweater sticking out at the end of the first day, she looked pleased.

I know her clothing instructions are to help me look the best I can. But sending me out with one sock or my jumper inside out doesn't really make sense. She must have a reason for it, though; maybe I just haven't figured it out yet. Left to my own devices, I would have no idea what to wear. I was lucky that she started telling me what I should wear all those years ago when we first met. I used to dress very differently before then. My clothes were brightly coloured and often mismatched. I used to love anything that had animal pictures or patterns on it; I didn't even mind if the animals were fantastical, like unicorns or dragons. The children at school used to comment on them all the time, never in a good way. But after I met Clara, she told me that those clothes were silly. Real women wore black, grey, a touch of beige sometimes. But mostly black. It made you look thinner, and it was always elegant, she said. 'It keeps people guessing about your personality; they can't tell what you're into if you dress in a neutral way. That way you can decide what to let them know about you. It gives you control.' I had no interest in control, but I wanted her to know that I would do anything she told me to, so I wore what she said from that day on.

Sometime after that, one of the girls in my class asked me where I'd got my new black top from. I thought she might have been joking, but she was serious. I told her and she said, 'Cool, I might see if they still have it in stock. I like it,' as if it was the most normal thing in the world. I couldn't believe it. It had never happened before. I was so happy that I wore that same top every day for two weeks.

This morning, Clara left me two notes. One reads: *Blue jeans, grey top, trainers, no socks.* The other has just two words on it: *No lunch.*

I had to reread it a couple of times. But I got the message in the end. She doesn't want me to eat until dinner. It will be difficult – I get hungry when I'm at work – but it's only a small sacrifice compared to what she has to go through every day with her pains and mood swings.

Clara and I have started spending most of our weekends going for walks. I know she doesn't leave the house on her own any more and is mostly in her bedroom or on the sofa with the curtains closed while I'm at work. When I wash her at night in the bath, I can feel her muscles have got soft from lack of movement. I've started giving her long massages to get the blood flowing. She just sits there in silence and lets me do it.

Since Edo no longer pays her an allowance now that the divorce has gone through, we're relying on my wages only, which is not very much. There's not a lot you can do with little money, but I've been trying to come up with creative ways to engage her. I don't want her to worry about money on top of all the other things she has to think about. Walking is a good way to get her out and exercising that doesn't cost us anything.

Even though I've been spending long sessions with Marcus in the bookshop getting my book into good shape, Clara is always my first priority. Her family doesn't know what she's going through here in London; she doesn't speak to them very much. When they call, she always tells them she's too busy to talk, even though she's just watching something on TV. The friends she made when she first moved here with Edo have stopped making an effort. She says it's because they were never really friends in the first place, but I think it's because she cancelled on them too many times. She only has me now.

I set the table in the living room for one and lay out a nutritious breakfast for her to find when she wakes up.

At work, Marcus and I sit in the café at one of the tables right in the middle and discuss the latest feedback that has come in from Almastra. Louisa has said that I need to show a stronger stance about the slaughtering side of pig keeping, and state whether I'm for it or against it, as it currently comes across as unclear in my writing. This is because it's something I feel very conflicted about. On one hand, the idea of murdering such kind, loving and intelligent animals for the mere enjoyment of their meat – the least interesting part of them – is as horrific to me as any genocide you would read about in the papers. If I ever see something like suckling pig on a restaurant's menu, I simply get up and walk out. The thought that the animals

245

haven't even had a chance to live a full life before being killed is too much for me to bear.

On the other hand, I have had many discussions with Homer and Angela in the past about this topic and I know how the farmer community feels about it. They might love and cherish their pigs, but ultimately they are raising them for meat, not as pets. No matter how many times I told them both that pigs make way better pets than dogs, the power of centuries-old tradition is too strong. I have to recognise and honour that.

Today Marcus and I are bouncing around the concept of 'ethical slaughtering', a painless, trauma-free way of killing adult pigs that might bridge that gap. It's a difficult compromise for me, but I can see where Louisa is coming from and can almost hear Angela's voice in my ear telling me to 'remember your place in the food chain'.

Kai is splitting their time between listening in to what Marcus and I are talking about, serving the few customers who come in and cleaning up behind the counter. They have asked to read my manuscript a few times now and I'm tempted to share it with them, but I want to make sure I'm allowed to.

'I've heard so much about this book of yours that I'm desperate to read it now,' they say, bringing Marcus and me our coffees. 'It's like watching those adverts for the yoghurt with the crunchy corner thing. Once you've been bombarded with them every day, all you want from life is a cornery-yoghurt thing. Like "I have to have them now." And they're not even that good!'

They pause.

'Wait. That sounded bad. I'm not saying your book won't be good, Vale. I didn't mean it that way.'

I notice that their face has gone red. It's sweet.

'I know you didn't,' I reassure them.

Marcus is watching us.

'I think you'll like it, Kai. It's very informative. Vale has a way of making difficult concepts sound easy. She's very matter-of-fact.'

246

'That she is.' Kai looks at me and smiles.

I don't have a problem with Kai reading what I've written before it's published. They seem like they would give me their honest opinion. I trust them.

'If you like, I can send you the manuscript as it is at the moment,' I tell them. 'If that's okay with you, Marcus, of course,' I quickly correct myself. *Oh no. I hope I haven't messed things up.* I still don't really know how these things work and I don't want to make mistakes.

He nods. 'Of course. The more the merrier.'

Lauren breezes in, smelling of synthetic figs and powder blusher. I forgot she was coming in today. She waves in our general direction, makes herself a coffee, then heads back to the front of the shop to busy herself with paperwork.

I hear her swear loudly. It doesn't happen often, but when it does, it's never good news.

'Are you okay?' I ask her, jumping up to check. She's standing by the till and Ollie is handing her a plaster.

'Bloody hell,' she keeps saying; her American accent always gets stronger when she says really British things. 'Bloody hell.'

'What happened?' I ask her.

She ignores me.

'It's the till,' Ollie says. 'The drawer was jammed again and Lauren tried to fix it, but it snapped back on her finger and cut her. It's pretty deep.'

I look at Lauren's finger. A bloom of blood is growing wider on the wrap of tissue she's holding over it.

'Ouch,' I say.

'Yes, Vale. "Ouch",' Lauren snaps back, 'Now can you both just take a step back and give me some space? Please?'

Ollie and I both take at least four steps back. When Lauren gets like this – shouty and sweary – it's always best to leave her alone for a little while.

She straps the large plaster onto her finger and starts typing furiously on her laptop.

'In fact, why don't you three take a lunch break together? I'm going to shut the shop while you're out. Get a bit of quiet and finish some work that really can't wait. I can't hear myself think in here today.'

'Okay,' Ollie says without giving it a second of thought. 'We'll leave you to it. Give us a call if you need anything, but otherwise we'll be back in an hour.'

Lauren nods without taking her eyes away from the screen.

'Let's go before she changes her mind,' Ollie whispers in my ear.

In the café, Kai is already wearing their jacket – a canvas one with thick pockets in a shade of light green that makes their eyes look even more piercing – and has put a tea towel over the till, the sign that the café is currently closed. Marcus is gathering his things.

'Lauren says—' I begin.

Kai cuts me off. 'We heard. I'm ready to go. Marcus has to head back to the office anyway.'

'That's a shame,' I tell him. 'Next time you should come with us. It's really nice by the river.'

'I'd love to.' He smiles. 'I'll email you the latest edits and will see you in a couple of days. Sound good?'

'Yup,' I answer.

We all wave goodbye, and Ollie, Kai and I walk down the street towards our usual bench beside the river. The sun is occasionally obscured by the clouds, but when it comes out, it feels warm enough to be just in a T-shirt. We stop at the sandwich shop and Ollie and Kai get their usual choices: a BLT for Ollie and a hummus and avocado wrap for Kai.

'Vale?' Kai asks. 'What are you having?'

'I'm okay, thanks. Had a massive breakfast,' I tell them.

I need to be careful. Ollie might have been either too distracted or too discreet in the past about my idiosyncrasies and avoided mentioning them or asking too many questions. But since Kai has started at the café, it's like the two of them have decided to dig much deeper into my life. Enquiries about Clara have multiplied, so have questions about my behaviour. Like why I always know without a doubt what I will be eating for lunch at the beginning of every day or why I am so cagey about my home life. I used to be able to get away with it a lot more when it was just me and Ollie. But the two of them are like detectives.

Ollie narrows his eyes. 'What, you're just not going to eat at all? Until dinner time? Is it like a diet?' he asks.

I try to laugh to defuse the tension. 'No. I told you, I'm still really stuffed from this morning.'

It doesn't seem to work, they're both looking at me with serious faces.

They pay and we get out of the shop. Ollie and Kai are both quiet for a few moments.

I try to distract them by talking about Lauren and how stressed she looks today, but it's not working.

'Is everything okay?' Kai asks. I notice a few strange looks between them and Ollie. 'You seem to be getting quite thin lately. And distracted. I know things are busy with the book and the edits. But you do know that you can talk to us, right?'

I can't tell them what's going on at home with Clara. They would never understand. They would think Clara was a bad person and being mean to me when the opposite is the truth.

But I know that it can look strange from the outside, our friendship. As much as Kai and Ollie are kind people who I care a lot about, they wouldn't be able to understand what Clara means to me. She is my home. I can't let her down. I need to do what she asks of me to keep her happy and to keep us together. She already has too much to deal with; the least I can do is be a good friend.

'Thank you, I do. But nothing's going on,' I try to reassure them. 'There's a lot with the book, and as I said, I had a mountain of eggs this morning. Just don't feel like lunch.'

Ollie and Kai exchange another look.

'Look, you're free to do what you want and live however you please,' Kai continues. They look frustrated and I feel bad for making them feel this way. I wish I could be open and honest. But I can't. 'And we respect that. But it's just that we're a bit worried. It's like you're not quite yourself and it's clear that something is up. We think it might be something at home, because if it was work, we would know about it.'

Ollie nods. 'We know you don't go anywhere else – sorry, but it's true. So it can only be something that's going on at home. And the fact that we know next to nothing about your life outside of this place, it's a bit, well, concerning. God.' He rubs his face. 'Sorry, that sounds kind of overbearing. You don't owe us an explanation. But we love you, Vale. We just want to make sure you're okay and for you to know that we're on your side, whatever it is.'

'Yes, no judgement here,' chimes in Kai. 'Look at me, I'm always asking my friends for support. They're basically a free helpline.'

They both laugh nervously.

I'm so tempted to tell them about having to hide the book from Clara. It would feel like such a relief to tell someone. And it sounds like Ollie and Kai would be more than happy to support me and give me some good advice. On the other hand, if nobody but me knows about this secret, then the chances of it getting out and somehow reaching Clara are non-existent. I just can't take the risk. I tell them a few more times that everything is just fine, and eventually they decide to let it go. For now, at least. I'm relieved, but this time it was harder to shake off their enquiries than it has been in the past. It's clear they've spoken about me and shared their concerns. I hate the idea of making my friends worry. But I would hate even more to betray Clara. Beyond the fact that she's my best friend and I owe her a lot, the fallout would be too scary to think about.

I need to be more careful next time, come up with a better excuse if this kind of thing happens again, or just decline the offer to all have lunch together. It's a shame, because I love eating with the two of them and watching nature flow by. But I can't risk it.

We settle on the bench and watch a group of ducks and their ducklings attempt to cross from one side of the river to the other in a neat row. The sun is shining and reflecting off the water. It's a beautiful sight. Ollie and Kai chew in silence. Eel Pie Island is having an open studio day for the artists who live there. There are people crossing the bridge and following hand-drawn signs that point to the many colourful cottages in the middle of the island.

I am so hungry.

It's been a busy morning between work and chatting with Marcus and I could really have done with some food to keep me going until this evening. Especially in case Lauren decides to get into one of her reshuffle stints and we need to move all the stock on display to fit some new criteria. Still, I need to be strong.

I can feel my stomach rumbling and get worried that Kai and Ollie might hear it, but I think the noise around us is so loud – with music wafting in from the island and punters chatting outside the nearby pub – that it must cover it, because neither of them says anything.

We sit in comfortable silence for what feels like ages. I once heard that the sign of a good relationship is the ability to spend time with the other person without the need to fill the air with words. This thought makes me smile. I squeeze both their arms and they squeeze mine back.

Ollie's phone suddenly pings, and he gets it out so fast I almost don't see him do it. He reads the message in a flash, then, as quickly as he got it out, he slips the phone back into his pocket.

He's smiling as if he's just been told wonderful news.

'Okay. Enough with the secret smiles, you,' Kai blurts out. 'You've been doing it all week. The people want to know. Who is it?'

'It's just a friend,' Ollie says, but he's not entirely convincing.

'It doesn't look like it's just a friend,' I join in. 'You spend more time messaging this friend than working lately.'

251

I have noticed it too; he's been very absorbed by his phone for the last few weeks. It may well be a friend. But I've never seen him behave like that with any friend before. Not since Rafael.

He looks at us both for a second, blinking, then bursts into laughter.

'You're right, he's not just a friend. Or at least I hope not. We're taking things slowly.'

That explains it then.

Kai and I both smile and clap.

'Ooh, exciting! How did you meet?' Kai asks.

Ollie's whole face is radiating happiness as he tells us.

'We actually met a long time ago. At school. Except he wasn't out then, and I wasn't the irresistible stallion you see before you now.'

We both roll our eyes at that. He laughs and swats us away like annoying flies.

'We kind of knew each other back then but not really. Just to say hello,' he continues, 'but a month or so ago he followed me on Instagram and started liking a lot of my posts. I was like "Why is this straight guy I went to school with liking all my pics? Doesn't make sense," but I didn't think too much of it. Then he messaged me, and we got talking. Turns out he did some therapy a few years ago to deal with some anxiety stuff, and through that he realised that he was bi and spent some time exploring his sexuality. He had a couple of relationships with men but has been single now for a few months. One day he remembers the gay kid from his school and looks him up on Insta to see what's happened to him, and, well, he must have liked what he saw.'

Kai and Ollie high-five.

'So there you go. We're chatting, we've met once, and it was lovely, but he lives in Cardiff so it's not easy to see each other.'

'You should tell him to come visit you soon. I'd like to meet him,' I say.

'Yes! Tell him to come to London,' Kai joins in.

I'm happy for Ollie. Since he and Rafael ended things, he's

admitted that he's been feeling lonely. As much as the relationship between the two of them was 'toxic' – as he says – he misses the companionship that comes with being with someone and relaxing together after a long day at work, sharing some wine and a meal. When I asked him what was toxic about the relationship with Rafael, he said he never got to be his true self with him and felt tied down and unappreciated. There was a lot of jealousy too. I didn't tell him that he sounded a bit overdramatic; it can't always be smooth sailing between two people. But he knows himself, and I'm sure it felt real to him. I hope that with this new man he gets to have all of the good things he's been missing. Although I don't know how they will manage that if they live so far away from each other. Clara and I might not always have a peaceful time together, but we at least have each other. If that's what stops someone from feeling lonely, then I should count myself lucky to have her in my life. I shudder to think what the alternative might be.

Chapter Twenty-Six

Almastra are planning a party to celebrate the release of my book. Louisa emailed me to tell me I shouldn't let it worry me; it's normal for a publishing company to want to introduce their new authors and launch their books to a selected few. I don't know how she knows that I'd be feeling worried about it, but she's right. I do.

Of course, the first thought that comes to mind is: *What will I say to Clara?*

It's an evening party, so will probably end late. Not something I can hide from her. I'm rarely out in the evening, and never for a party. The only recent times I've been out are when Lauren has asked me to help her set up the bookshop for one of her readings or launches. She used to ask Ollie, too, but he told her he was busy so many times that she stopped bothering. Lauren knows I never have any plans so it's hard for me to say no. And I enjoy doing it too; it makes for a different evening than usual.

But it's always hard when I tell Clara. She makes me explain exactly how long I'll be gone for and who will be there. And I have to recount everything that happened minute by minute when I get home. I think it puts her mind at ease to know where I am, always.

It's because she wants to make sure I'm safe.

She used to ask me to share the shop's rota with her in the past so she would know who I was working with every day. But that was back when there used to be more staff in. Now it's just Ollie and me, sometimes Lauren, so there isn't a rota any more. We're in every day, Monday to Friday, and it's always the two of us. At the weekend it's different; there are more people, and they do have a rota, I think. But I never work then. Weekends are for Clara.

The second thing that worries me is speaking in front of people. Louisa says she can do most of the introduction, but I'll have to read at least a page or two.

Talking about pigs doesn't worry me; it's what I know. Doing so in front of a crowd that will be listening to me is a completely new experience, though. Louisa also confirmed the final title of my book: *Rearing Pigs the Ethical Way: Why It Matters and How to Do It*. It's direct and clear. I appreciate that.

I emailed her back and told her I liked the title and that I was looking forward to the party. I want her to think that I'm a professional who won't crumble at the mere thought of saying a few words in front of a small gathering. There should be enough time for me to practise so that I can feel a bit more confident. Maybe I can ask Kai and Ollie if I can rehearse with them a couple of times beforehand.

I still can't believe this is happening. It's all come along so quickly that I haven't had time to let it sink in. Between work, Clara and trying to write the book around her needs, I haven't had a moment to think. But finding out about the party and the fact that it's coming up has made things feel even more real. The fact that there will be people there just to see me speak or to buy my book is blowing my mind.

A team of professionals have been working with the words I have written to make this book the best it can be. It gives the work I've done in the last few months an official status that is in equal parts terrifying and exciting.

Kai and Ollie are very excited about the party. Although Kai will have to leave no later than 9 p.m. to catch the last train home, Ollie has promised that he will be the last man standing, with me until the bitter end. I didn't have the heart to tell him that I will probably leave as soon as I have made my speech. Still, it will be fun to all be out together and celebrating, even if it's only for a few hours. Christmas is far away, and we didn't have a summer staff party this year because Lauren said we couldn't afford it. She says we should treat my book launch party as an unofficial staff event.

'A party is a party. The way things are going, I can stretch to a bag of crisps at the Fox between all of us. But a catered soirée for free in Soho? Much posher!'

Ollie mumbled, 'Why can't we have both?'

But Lauren had already moved on to something else. I don't mind; it takes the heat off me, so I don't feel so anxious.

Hermina is in the UK for a short visit with her boyfriend and Ollie told me she has decided to extend her holiday by a couple of days to come along. I feel strange about seeing her again after what she said to Clara at the Christmas party, but I'll just have to ignore her. I can't let her ruin this special moment.

'Okay. I've got something to say,' Kai tells Ollie and me as we're sitting on the floor of the shop opening box after box of new stock. We both look up. For a reason that I don't quite understand, my heart starts beating faster. Has Kai met someone too, like Ollie has? I never ask people about their relationship status because I don't want them to ask me the same question back out of politeness. Because of this, I don't know whether Kai has someone or not. They've never mentioned it. It's none of my business anyway. But I find myself staring at them waiting to hear what they're about to say.

'Go on,' says Ollie.

'I've read Vale's manuscript. I know not many people have read it yet and I've taken this honour very seriously indeed,' they say.

Kai is the first person outside of the Almastra team to have read it. They might not be a professional editor, but their opinion matters. And they're in their late twenties, the age range most likely to be represented by the New Agriculture movement. I cover my eyes.

256

I want to hear their words but can't bear to look at their face in case it's bad news.

I feel two hands gently grab my wrists.

'Hey, it's okay. I promise.'

I resist Kai's touch and keep my hands where they are.

'Just tell me. What did you think?'

It might be painful, but I need to know.

'Are you okay?' Ollie asks me, a note of worry in his voice.

'I'm fine. Kai, just tell me. Please.' I can't wait any longer.

'I will,' Kai says. 'But only if you put your hands down.'

I lower my hands and see that they both look alarmed.

'I'm fine,' I say again. 'I just want it to be good so badly. Be honest. I can take it.'

'I know you can,' Kai says, sitting on the floor next to us. 'As I've said before, I know nothing about pigs. And the New Agriculture scene is not really my thing. But I do have a lot of friends who are into it, and they won't stop going on about farming and all that. Plus, I like to think I can tell when a book is good or bad. I'm a reader, always have been.'

'So?' Ollie looks impatient.

Kai turns to look at just me.

'I thought it was great. Seriously, Vale. Considering it's not my subject, I found it easy to read, clear and even funny in places. A fascinating read. You should be proud of yourself.'

I scrutinise their face to look for any signs that might tell me they're not sincere. I'm not very good at detecting them, but I've learned through the years what to look for. A smirk, eyebrows raised dramatically or expressions that are more over the top than the situation demands. But I can't see any of those on Kai's face. They appear to be sincere.

'You're telling the truth?' I ask them, just to check if my instincts are right.

Both Ollie and Kai smile.

257

'I am, Vale,' Kai says. 'It's really what I think.'

A warm wave of relief soothes me. Kai is only one person, and it's still possible that everyone else might think my book is no good. But I trust their opinion. They're a keen reader, and the things I've heard them say about other books in the past are always measured and well thought out. They admitted it's not their favourite topic – which I respect – and they haven't given me blanket praise for the sake of it. I look into their eyes and see that they mean it. I allow myself to smile.

'That's great,' I tell them. 'Thank you.'

'No, thank *you*. I really appreciate you trusting me with it,' Kai replies.

'Get a room, you two,' Ollie interjects, rolling his eyes. 'Sounds like soon our Vale will be too successful to hang out with little old us.'

'Never!' I tell them both, offended that he could even suggest that.

'Ollie was joking,' Kai says. 'He doesn't really think that. We know you wouldn't.'

Ollie winks at me, confirming it. The thought that I could lose touch with the two of them after everything we've gone through together is too sad to even consider.

We may not share the history I have with Clara, but I feel very close to Ollie and Kai.

They don't know everything about my life – I know they wouldn't understand my relationship with Clara, for example, and the things she asks me to do – and that puts a slight distance between us. But they like me for who I am, which not many people seem to. And we have fun together.

Which makes my workdays feel lighter at those times when the evenings and weekends at home feel heavy and dark.

'May I offer you a cappuccino to celebrate?' Kai asks me, extending their hand to help me up from the floor. I could do with a hot drink, so I nod. Kai makes cappuccino in an especially caring way, with swirls of milk on top and a light dusting of chocolate that adds a delicious sweetness to it.

'Can I have it the British way, please?' I ask, taking their hand and getting up.

Kai's skin is surprisingly warm, yet dry. I leave mine in there for a bit longer than necessary; it feels nice, and they don't seem to mind.

'Ha, sure. I'll never understand why Italians don't do the chocolate thing as standard,' they say, for the umpteenth time. 'Why deny yourself some extra pleasure?'

I do what I always do when people question Italian rules: just shrug. I find a lot of them unexplainable too. It was only when I moved to London that I realised they could be challenged, or simply not followed. Like wearing black and blue or red and pink at the same time or adding Parmesan to pasta with fish sauce. Or not wanting to sunbathe until your skin starts peeling and stinging.

I have my own rules – always pet a dog that looks like it would like to be petted; never run after birds, because it scares them; never feed pigs food that you wouldn't feed a human; touch any book cover that has raised lettering – and I prefer to follow those instead. If something makes sense to you or makes you happy and doesn't harm anyone else, then why should it ever be wrong? Kai and Ollie may tease me sometimes, but they never make me feel like there is something wrong with me just being me. I follow Clara's rules too; but I know it's best if I'm not myself around her. Maybe it's not just being in the bookshop itself that calms me and makes me happy. Maybe it's also being here with Ollie and Kai that makes my body feel much more at peace than when I'm at home with Clara. Whether it's her rules or anyone else's, I wonder whether it's right for me to blindly follow them. Even though they're meant to be for my own good, it doesn't always feel that way.

We head to the café and sit down on one of the sofas to the side. The shop is quiet right now, and until customers come in, we can take a little break all together. Even Lauren, who's just burst in through the door, grabs a pastry from the display cabinet and sits down next to us.

259

'Here you all are,' she says, spraying crumbs over herself and us. 'What are you talking about?'

'Vale's book. Kai got to read it,' Ollie tells her.

She turns to Kai. 'And?'

Kai smiles. 'It's great. I've already told her. Quirky, interesting, passionate, full of good points.'

'Just like our Vale,' Ollie says, beaming at me.

Lauren nods. 'Yup. I've always known she was a star. From the first day I met you.' She drapes her arm over my shoulders. 'I like to think that working here has inspired you. As you know, I choose a very varied stock for the shop, so we've always had a wide selection of books about nature. It must have rubbed off on you. Also, so many books with pigs on them in the children's section! It all adds up.'

Both Ollie and Kai are struggling to hold in laughter. I scrutinise Lauren's face to check if she's joking, but she looks deadly serious. Does she really think it's all down to her?

I'm lost for words for a few seconds. I talked to Lauren and her husband about my passion for pigs from the first day I started. She must know that it goes back much further than me working here. And the pigs in the children's section are silly, bright pink and googly-eyed caricatures of the real thing. If anything, they could have put me off.

Although luckily, they didn't.

'I've always been into pigs and nature. Since I was born,' I tell her.

'Well, yes. But I know working here has made a very big impression on you. I'm proud of it.'

She doesn't seem to want to listen, so I let it go. Behind her, Kai and Ollie are rolling their eyes so hard I'm worried they might injure themselves.

Luckily, Lauren changes topic before they do.

'The party. It's soon, right? What's the plan?' she asks me.

'I don't know exactly. Almastra are planning everything. It will be in Soho, near their offices, and I will have to read an extract. I don't know much more than that,' I tell her.

260

'Exciting! Do you know who's doing the catering?'

'No idea.'

'Well, tell Almastra they should include things like mini quiches and sliders rather than those sloppy little plastic cones with a spoon that are fashionable now. They get everywhere and are impossible to eat with one hand. Where are you supposed to put your drink?' she says, looking around at the three of us.

We all stare blankly back at her.

'Sorry,' I tell her, 'I don't know about the catering. I'm sure they have it sorted out.'

'Okay, well, let me know in case they don't. Have you thought about what you'll do with the advance?' She holds her hands up in front of me, fingers wiggling back and forth, like a magician trying to conjure a rabbit out of a hat.

I shake my head. 'Not really. Bills and food, I imagine.'

Lauren rolls her eyes. 'God. How boring. Not even a little holiday or a new handbag?'

I can see she's lost interest now. She sucks the tip of her index finger and presses it over the leftover crumbs on the table, then deposits them in her mouth.

'Have you heard of a fuck-off fund?' Kai says.

'Is it something rude?' I ask them.

They giggle. 'It does sound it. But no. It's an amount of money you keep stashed away to give you some financial freedom if you ever need to leave a difficult situation in a rush. Like a job, a country, a relationship. That kind of thing.'

'Yeah,' Ollie pipes up, 'it's for when you need to fuck off out of somewhere in a hurry. Can be handy.'

'It is. I put a little bit of money in mine every month. You never know. But if you have a big amount of money at once, it means you can have a fully formed FOF in no time. You should do it,' Kai says.

'You should definitely do it,' Ollie agrees. The two of them exchange a long glance.

'I can see how it might be useful—' I start, but Lauren, who has been nodding while the other two spoke, cuts in.

'Clyde and I have lots of things in common, Vale. But money isn't one of them. I always make sure I have a little bit put aside in case the proverbial hits the fan.' She taps her nose with her index finger.

I've never thought about putting money away without telling Clara. What I earn goes into our shared lives and it has worked well so far. But the advance is extra money I didn't expect to have, and there's no reason she will find out until I tell her about the book. As long as all our bills are paid as usual and she continues living the life she is accustomed to, maybe I could keep some money for myself. If she doesn't know about it, it won't hurt her.

A fuck-off fund seems a bit far-fetched for my life, but it would be good to keep some money to finally be able to get things like birthday presents for my friends and participate in our local charity fundraisers. And maybe even get a haircut done by one of those places on the high street instead of by Clara at home with the kitchen scissors. It would be nice to look professional in my author's picture.

'Have you thought about who to invite yet?' Kai asks, shaking me out of my thoughts.

That's easy. I don't have many people in my life, but the ones I do will all be invited. With one obvious exception.

'Yup, everyone in this room. Plus anyone you might want to invite along. Is Clyde coming?' I ask Lauren.

'Of course he is, darling,' she replies, clutching her hands together. 'My darling husband wouldn't miss this for the world. Right up his street.'

'What about your new – old – friend?' I ask Ollie. 'What's his name?'

Ollie blushes immediately. He must really care for him; I haven't seen him behave like this about a love interest before.

'Dylan. I'll ask him.'

'Okay, great. Then he's on the list too. There you go, done,' I announce.

'What about Clara?' Kai asks.

Here we go. I knew this might happen. After all, Ollie and Kai know that Clara is a big presence in my life. But I can't tell them that she has no idea about the book, let alone the party. They would ask too many questions that I don't know how to answer.

I can't tell Clara about the party just yet. I'm not ready. But I have to tell her something, especially if my fear that she has seen the article in *The Bookseller* turns out to be justified. I know that she's not happy when I'm out for a work event. In the past, I've managed to negotiate with Lauren to nip home after work when these launches take place. That way I can cook dinner for Clara, prepare her bath and then run back to the shop to make sure Lauren doesn't have to deal with things like sales, chair positioning, drink and nibbles preparation and locking up once everyone has left. She prefers to do the mingling and introduction of authors part and I'm very happy to not have to do any of that. Also, she often has too much to drink on those occasions and is unsteady on her feet by the end of the evening, so it's safer if I lock up the shop and put her in a taxi. I've explained all of this to Clara, and she understands.

I could tell her that it's another one of these launches, and that I will come home to cook her a meal and run her a bath before heading off again. I will have to think of what to say when she asks me all those questions. I can give her details of the party without saying that *I'm* the author being celebrated. More lies.

And now I'm about to lie to Kai and Ollie too.

They know Clara and I grew up together, that we live in the same house and therefore must be very close. Ollie has only met her once – at the Christmas party. Kai has never met her.

I know they already think this is weird. We spend so much time with each other at work and they think it's odd that they know nothing about my home life.

I know because Ollie has told me so, and from the way he and Kai have been behaving recently, asking all these questions and not giving up when they don't get a satisfactory answer. It's starting to make me feel anxious because I know that I can't keep them at bay for ever. There is no way they could ever meet Clara. A few years ago, maybe – when things were a little easier and she was in a better place – but now things are too complicated. I just know they wouldn't understand. I also have no idea how Clara might react if she met them. I can't think of anything good coming out of it. I have no choice but to keep lying. To them – Kai and Ollie – and to Clara.

I feel selfish and cruel. As if I'm letting them all down. I hate doing it. But I can't think of another way to avoid a massive fallout. I keep telling myself that I'm protecting them from knowing things they might not like or understand. But the truth is that I'm protecting myself. The way life is right now, it feels like I'm walking on a hair-thin blade. So thin that any gust of wind could throw me off balance and make me fall. I'm just about hanging on.

The consequences of my two worlds – home and work – colliding would trigger a storm. One that my current life would likely not survive. Luckily, I knew someone would ask why Clara isn't coming to the party, so I've prepared a lie.

'She can't make it, unfortunately. Has to go to Italy for a family matter,' I tell Kai. It comes out so easily and my voice sounds so confident that for an instant I almost believe it myself. But no, as far as I know – and if I'm lucky – Clara has no idea about the book or the party. She will be home watching TV on the sofa as usual that evening. The party is just over two weeks away, but I know she won't have any plans then, or at any other time.

I *will* tell her. But not just yet. I don't have the courage. I know that the longer I wait, the angrier she will be at being told a lie. But I have thought of an idea that might smooth things over. Marcus seems to think that the book might do well with some marketing push in the right direction. He's explained that this means a little

264

more money might come my way. If Clara sees that I'm contributing financially even more than I already am with my bookshop wage, she might forgive me for lying and see the book as a good thing after all.

Kai and Ollie look at me first, then at each other with raised eyebrows. I'm starting to find their looks irritating. Why can't they just believe me? I don't need them to argue with everything I say about Clara.

I am fine.

'Well, Hermina is coming,' Ollie says, changing the subject. 'She's looking forward to it.'

'Oh yes,' Lauren says, 'the old gang back together.'

'If she has to.' I shrug.

My tone is harder than I intended, and I can see that Ollie is surprised. I'm almost never annoyed or irritated at work; it's usually where I come to get away from bad feelings. But the question about Clara has put me on the wrong foot, and the last thing I want is to think about Hermina. Just talking about her feels like a betrayal of my oldest friend, after the way Hermina treated her.

'You don't like her?' Kai asks.

'I don't like what she did to Clara. She was mean to her. At the Christmas party.'

'Vale. Do you really think that's what happened?' Ollie interjects. It's his turn to be irritated now. His face has got darker, his eyebrows are raised and he's staring right into my eyes.

'I do,' I say. 'Clara told me. It was cruel and unnecessary. The teasing, the questions about the split, the rudeness. Clara had done nothing to her.'

'I think you need to ask Clara to tell you the truth.' Ollie gets up to leave. 'I know Hermina, and I spoke to her that night after you and Clara left. She's a good person, Vale. I'm not sure you've been told the whole story.' He walks away towards the front of the shop.

I'm confused. The truth? Why would Clara lie to me about her conversation with Hermina? She was so upset that night, so hurt.

She insisted we left right that second, and we did, without saying goodbye to anyone.

I must admit, though, that I was shocked when she told me what had happened. It seemed like such an out-of-character attack from Hermina.

She can be direct, yes, but she always comes across as a gentle soul who loves animals and is outspoken about their rights. Not someone I would ever think could unleash a torrent of unpleasantness on a virtual stranger. I know that if she had stayed in the country afterwards, I would have ended up speaking to her to find out more.

I've never been able to reconcile the person I thought she was with the behaviour that Clara told me about. It's weird, I just can't imagine her saying those things.

I believed Clara when she told me what had happened that night. I saw how upset she was. But the more I think about it now, the more it doesn't make sense.

Chapter Twenty-Seven

Hey! There's an event at the shop tonight. Lauren needs me to help. Sorry I forgot to say earlier. But I'll come home and cook your dinner at the usual time, then head out.

As I wait for Clara's response, I dial my mother's number. She picks up at the second ring.

'Valentina. How are you?'

'All good. Great, in fact. How are you and Dad?'

'Well, your father didn't sleep very well last night and kept me up with his grumbling. But apart from that, we're well.'

'Ah, sorry to hear that. I've got some good news, maybe it'll cheer you up. I've been meaning to tell you for some time, but things have been so busy. Anyway, I've written a book. And tonight the publishers are throwing me a launch party.'

I hear nothing on the other end for a second.

'A book? And published. Like a real book? In shops?'

I smile. 'Yes, like a real book in shops. It's about pigs. No surprise there.'

'Of course it's about pigs. How wonderful. I am so happy for you. And proud of you! A party? How exciting.' Her tone suddenly changes. 'Why didn't you tell us sooner? We could have come. We would have been there to support you. But it's much too late now. Such a shame.'

That's exactly why I didn't tell you, I think. Having them here would make things way too complicated with Clara. I need those two worlds to be divided for a little bit longer. Once things are out in the open, we will have time to see each other, and I might even bring them to see the bookshop and meet Ollie and Kai. But not just yet.

I apologise a few times and promise to call her again tomorrow to tell her all about the book and how the party went. I feel bad to have hurt her, but it was necessary.

As I hang up the phone, I see that Clara has texted back.

Okay. Make sure you come back after work.

Of course I will. I'll cook your favourite, I reply.

Okay.

That went better than I expected. I thought she would ask me questions. Instead, she seems to have accepted it without too much explanation. Hardly any, in fact.

It's odd.

She usually wants to understand exactly what's going on, then have me promise to make it up to her the following day and tell me exactly how. It's never been quite this easy. If I had more time and wasn't so busy at work looking after customers, responding to everyone – including Louisa and Marcus – asking me about the party and trying to make sure Clara doesn't find out the truth, I would be questioning it a lot more. But I don't have that time, so I'm just going to take it as a glitch or a gift from the universe.

As soon as the workday is over, I run home even faster than usual. I don't want to be late for the party and make everyone wait, but I still need to cook, chat with Clara and run her a bath. Then somehow find a way to go to my room alone, throw a few clothes into a bag to get changed into and smuggle them out of the house without her noticing.

I let myself in and immediately notice that something is not right. There are tea towels all over the floor and broken glass outside the living room. The lights are on in every room, but the TV is off. The air in the house is thick and warm. A smell of rubbish is wafting from the kitchen, and I can hear a tap dripping somewhere.

'Clara?' I call out.

I go to the downstairs bathroom to turn off the tap and notice that all the towels have been thrown onto the floor there too.

'Where are you?' I check the kitchen, but it's empty.

Has something happened to her?

The thought chokes me. She answered my messages only a few hours ago.

Could someone have broken in since? I run into the living room and see her. A huge wave of relief washes over me.

'Oh God. You're here. Are you okay?'

She's sitting in the armchair with her legs neatly folded and her hands holding on to either side of the upholstery.

'I'm great,' she says, her voice a dull monotone.

'What happened?'

'You tell me.'

She hasn't moved or blinked. She's staring right into my eyes, not a hair out of place.

'Are you hurt? Why is there all this stuff on the floor?'

Clara smiles. Lips as thin as scissor blades.

I can feel panic rising inside me. She must have found out about the book somehow.

'You seem stressed out. Not ready to deal with the consequences of your actions?' she asks.

Her voice has a cruel note to it, but her face is rested and calm. That strange smile is still stretching her mouth and she hasn't moved an inch.

'What actions? I don't understand,' I say.

She laughs. 'You thought you could keep it from me? Your little project. Your pathetic effort at making something of yourself.' She spits out each word, rolling her Rs with evident gusto. 'I've noticed you call it a "book". That's a bit too generous, don't you think?'

269

Oh no.

'We both know that "ramblings of a loser" would be a better way to describe it.' I hear that laugh again. 'Don't we?'

'What? Clara ... But I don't ...' I stumble over my words, my brain suddenly scrambled.

'Don't bother trying to deny it. I've read it all: "Oh Marcus, thank you so much!" "You like pigs too now? Aw, that's so great!" Pathetic.' She shakes her head. 'They've been taking you for a ride. And you like a little puppy yapping along for a pat on the head. What a joke.'

I can't believe it.

'You read my emails?'

'Yup. I did. You left me with no choice,' she says, her chin trembling with rage. 'You've had a shifty look for a while. I could sense you were up to something. When I got your text earlier, I knew right away it was a lie. I shouldn't have trusted you. Who knows how many more lies you've been telling me. I found your computer and guessed the password after two tries. ILOVEPIGS. I mean, really?'

That horrible laugh again.

'We spoke about it, didn't we?'

I nod.

'And didn't we agree that you wouldn't write it?'

I nod again. My face feels like it's on fire.

'But you still went ahead and did it. You lied to me. After all I've done for you. All we've been through since we were children. Children! But you still lied. You are no different to all the other people who have let me down. As bad as Edo. And my parents. And all the others. There was me thinking I finally had found someone who would care for me, but no. You let me down and betrayed me, just like everybody else.'

I hear her words but they're not quite going in as they would usually do. The thought of Clara reading everything that has been said between Marcus, Louisa and me in the last few months is too horrifying to let anything else past it. I've opened myself up to them as I felt safe to show them the true extent of my passion for pigs. They've encouraged and nurtured it. I know they mean it when they say that they like my book, that the concept is strong and that it will be a success. I've spoken to them face to face, I have seen their commitment, Marcus coming all the way to the bookshop multiple times a week just to sit down with me and make it the best version it can be. I've watched his face light up when a sentence works well, his brow furrow when the first samples were delayed from the factory. Louisa throwing tonight's party in my honour, inviting everyone she thinks might like to find out more about me and my passion. She wouldn't do it if she didn't believe in it.

I might not be the best judge of character – I can almost hear my parents' voices telling me this – but I know they haven't been stringing me along. Clara might think I'm pathetic and a joke, but Marcus and Louisa don't. She might be my oldest friend and know me better than anybody else, but having her in my life doesn't feel good. Not as much as being in the bookshop with the people who appreciate me.

She doesn't accept me.

This realisation nearly knocks me off my feet. The internal voice that would have usually shouted at me to stop being ridiculous and be grateful Clara is still in my life is quiet right now. All I can hear is a rumble that seems to come from the depths of my skull. The sadness that has overtaken me is tinged with something new that I don't recognise at first. A sensation that starts as a warm grip in my stomach, then travels down to the tips of my fingers, making them so tense that I need to flex them. Anger.

She never has accepted me. When we were teenagers, I did everything I could to be different when I was with her. I downplayed my passion for pigs, I let her dress me a certain way, I disappeared into the background so she could shine. But why can't I be who I am and still be accepted by her? Am I so impossible to love?

The people in my life now do accept me. She used to be my only friend; it's been just her for ever. But not any more. Now there's Kai

271

and Ollie, Marcus and Louisa. Even Lauren. They accept and believe in me. I'm not a joke in their eyes, not a freak. It's only Clara who tells me this.

They care about me.

'I know that the launch is a lie. There's a party.'

She points her finger at my face.

'You think you're going there tonight, don't you?'

I can only nod. My tongue suddenly feels too large for my mouth. I take some steps back in case she tries to grab me. I want to go to the party more than anything else. Everyone will be expecting me, I can't let them down. They have spent money on it, booked the space, organised the catering, invited the guests. My friends are excited to go. They will be getting ready about now. Ollie might wear the top that says *Supreme*, or the one with the cover of the Smiths' first album, both favourites of his. Kai hopefully will wear the shirt with the pineapples that they only wear on special occasions and which I've seen on them once or twice before, but never for me. Knowing that they've picked that particular shirt for tonight would make the evening even more special. I love that look on Kai and I'm so excited to see them and Ollie.

Clara gets up from the armchair.

'You're not going. You're a liar. You don't deserve it.'

Marcus and his team will already be there, setting everything up: the chairs, the PA, the piles of books. The books! I want to see what the cover looks like in print; Louisa says it's great. I've worked so hard. I know Clara feels betrayed right now – she has every right to – but can't she be happy for me? Or even a little impressed by my effort?

'Look, I know you're—'

The impact of her hand on my cheek freezes me mid-sentence. The flash of pain that follows is so intense that I stumble backwards and bang my back on the dining table before crashing to the floor. My vision goes blurry for a moment. I manage to grab at the rug to help me get up onto my knees and crawl out of the way. I know what's coming next.

Clara's face is crimson. She swipes her hand at me again, but I roll on my side and get out of her reach just in time. She bares her teeth and manages to kick my legs a few times before I get up and hop to the other side of the room.

My cheek is pulsating and raw. The pain feels like a knife slicing through my skull. I press my hand on it, still cool from being outside, to try and limit the swelling. The engagement ring Edo gave her, which she still wears, must have hit my cheekbone pretty hard, because as I rub my face, I feel a dip forming in the skin.

I am going. Suddenly there is no other option in my head.

I turn around and run up the stairs to get some clothes to change into and my laptop with the notes for my speech on it.

'Did you not hear me? You're not going!' Clara is thundering up the stairs after me, shouting at the top of her lungs.

I grab my computer and a black top. It's no different to what I usually wear, but it's clean. I don't have any clothes that would work for an evening do, but I can at least smell okay.

I turn around, my things held to my chest, but Clara is blocking the door.

She's looking at me with what seems to be both fear and excitement.

'Put that down,' she says. 'Now.'

Not this time.

I run towards the door and push past her. Her hands give way easily and she is pressed against the wall. The look of surprise on her face is one I've never seen before.

She is shocked.

I expect her to come running after me, but as I fumble to find my keys by the front door, I don't hear her roaring down the stairs. There is no noise coming from her direction.

'Sorry!' I shout, out of habit. 'I need to go.'

I close the door and run out into the soft evening light.

273

Chapter Twenty-Eight

It takes me a while to find the venue once I'm in Soho. I managed to jump on a train, my whole body still shaking, get changed in the disabled toilet and wrestle my curls into shape with water and my fingers. I'm not elegant or fashionable by any means, but I feel tidy and clean. I have chaos in a very deep place in my head right now – the place Clara lives in – but I'm pushing it down. I don't want it – her – to ruin this night for me.

The streets are crawling with people. I walk around turning corner after corner without finding the place I'm looking for.

I stop to ask someone for directions, and they point me to an alleyway that I hadn't noticed before. I run down it, looking from side to side.

Finally, I find it. The bar is the only venue in an alley that otherwise has front doors with golden plaques outside that read *Drop Dead Productions*, *Jo Wilkin Models* and *Brotherhood Inc.*

Once inside, I see that the building has huge corner windows, and bronze ceiling lights that create a warm glow. The sign says *The Library*. I'm a bit confused as to why a place where people go to drink would be called that, until I notice that the walls inside are covered in books. It makes the room look cosy and inviting. I like it. There's already quite a crowd inside and I spot Lauren and Clyde at the bar.

As I walk in, a few faces turn towards me.

'Vale!'

Ollie and Kai emerge from the crowd. I pretend to rub my cheek to hide the sore spot where Clara hit me in case it's still red.

'Fashionably late, I see,' Ollie says and squeezes my arm. They're both holding bottles of beer.

'You look great,' says Kai, smiling.

'Thanks, so do you.' I smile back.

They really do. The pineapple shirt is as great as I remember it. Boxy and bright, a few buttons undone down the front that reveal a triangle of smooth-looking skin and a couple of gold chains. I'm finding it hard to look away.

Ollie has his *Smiths* T-shirt on and is looking back and forth between Kai and me.

'Erm ... I might give you guys a moment to catch up. Drink?' he asks, rolling his eyes and smiling.

'Yes, I need one.'

Kai puts their arm around my shoulders while Ollie heads to the bar. 'You'll be okay,' they whisper in my ear. 'We've got you.'

I know Ollie and Kai have my best interests at heart. They want me to succeed and have supported me all the way to where I am now. I am so happy they are here tonight.

I grab my beer and take a large gulp. The fizzy liquid immediately warms up the pit of my stomach and relaxes me. I spot a table with a pile of books neatly arranged on top of it and make a beeline for it.

It's the first time I've seen the book in real life. My name on the cover is written in discreet letters at the bottom, nothing showy, just like we agreed. The background is shiny white, and on it is a beautiful black and white drawing of an adult Gloucestershire Old Spot taken from a book from the 1880s. The pig is sideways and looking ahead. The ear that is visible is almost long enough to hide its eye. The dark spots are large and cover most of its body, with just a few patches of white peering through. It's a beautiful specimen and as close to life as an image can get. Above it, the title is embossed in black letters: *Rearing Pigs the Ethical Way: Why It Matters and How to Do It.*

It's perfect.

I see Louisa and Marcus and tell them how much I love it. They do too, they tell me, it has come out exactly how they wanted it. Louisa tells me I will have to sign a few copies before the end of the evening. The concept is very odd to me – why would someone want a book that has a stranger's scribble on it? – but if it matters to them, I will do it. It won't take much time.

'Are you ready for your speech?' Marcus asks me. I must look scared because he quickly follows it with, 'Don't worry! It's just a few words. Louisa will introduce you, then you can choose how much of the first chapter to read. Everyone is excited.'

I look around and keep spotting people I've seen before. Mainly customers from the shop. I know Lauren has included a few words about the launch in MacGregor's Bookshop's monthly newsletter; they must have liked the sound of it. I would usually be so nervous in this kind of situation – a crowd filled with many near-strangers – but tonight for some reason I'm not.

I see Hermina walking towards me. She wears a tentative smile and is waving her hand as she gets closer. The way I'm feeling right now, even speaking to her won't ruin my good mood.

'Hey,' I say, making sure to take another sip of beer to calm any residual nerves. I'm not ready to confront her. Tonight is not that kind of night. It may be the atmosphere of support – or drinking when I'm not that used to it – but I find myself no longer angry with her. Clara is not perfect; I certainly am not either. I shouldn't expect Hermina to be. I wonder if what I was told about that night might have been Clara's version of the truth. And I'm not sure if that makes it the real truth.

It's also very kind of Hermina to show up tonight. I do appreciate her taking time out of her trip to show her support.

When she reaches me, she hugs me. I stiffen a little but try to hug her back. It's only polite.

'Hey. Wow,' she says, looking around. 'This is great. I want you to sign a copy for me before the end of tonight. Please?'

'Thank you. Of course,' I reply. 'It's nice to see you here. I hope you're having a good time in London.'

'I am. It's great to be back, even if it's only for a few days,' she says, then steps in closer, peering at my face. 'What's this?'

She reaches out to touch my cheek and I flinch.

'That looks really sore. What happened?' Hermina's forehead furrows with concern.

She must notice my eyes glistening because she grabs my hand without asking any more questions and leads me to the toilets.

Once in there under the fluorescent lights, I find myself concentrating hard on the floor and the filthy grooves between the lino tiles. I can't bear to look her in the eye. What happened with Clara is only just under the surface; I'm not sure if I can manage to keep it to myself if she probes too much.

She rummages through her backpack and takes out a small beige stick. Without saying a word, she opens it, rubs some paste onto her index finger and starts dabbing it over my cheekbone. After a few moments, she clears her throat and finally speaks.

'So, erm, you don't have to say if you don't want to. But . . . is everything okay?' she asks, her finger still dabbing away. I'm trying to ignore the sharp twinges of pain I feel across my face.

I look up and see my reflection in the mirror. Any redness or bruise there might have been is now completely hidden. I look healthy and normal. I catch myself smiling.

'Thank you,' I say.

Hermina shrugs. 'It looks good. No one will be able to tell.'

I feel a sudden rush of guilt for having bad-mouthed her to Ollie. She doesn't deserve it. She must know from him that I've been angry with her – or was until about ten minutes ago – but I no longer think it's fair for me to be. It must have taken some courage for her to come up and talk to me. And now helping me hide my bruise . . . I don't want to judge her for one stupid, cruel thing she did after a few drinks. She is a good person. I used to like her; I need to remember

277

that. And Clara can be cruel too; the things she said and did to me during our fight earlier could have easily broken me if I hadn't experienced most of them before.

'Look, I know you've probably been told that I'm upset with you,' I blurt out. 'About the Christmas party.'

Hermina is now standing very still and looking right at me.

'I was. I was angry that you treated Clara the way you did. I was so confused as to why you would. I thought you were a kind and sweet person. Then I realised that I probably didn't know you that well after all. But I was still angry.' I take a deep breath and another swig of beer, now warmer from the tight hold I have on the bottle. 'But I want you to know that I'm no longer angry. And that I forgive you. You must have had your reasons for saying the things you did. I've realised that although it's not okay to treat people that way, we all sometimes do bad things, but it doesn't make us bad people. I still like you.'

There, I said it. It feels right to forgive her. I'd want people to do the same to me if I make a mistake. Tonight of all nights I want only positive thoughts to surround me. I want – need – to leave all negativity out of this room. I know there is plenty on the outside of it. But I don't want it to reach me right now.

Hermina looks at me for the longest time. Her mouth is a little agape. I take this to be because she didn't expect to hear these words from me. She probably thought I would berate her.

'But . . . but that's not what happened,' she says eventually, scratching her head. She looks really confused.

'I don't understand. What do you mean?' A dull ache is forming at my temples.

Hermina takes a deep breath. Her brow is furrowed and she looks in pain.

'I think you think it was me who was mean to Clara. Yes?'

I nod. *What's happening?*

'It wasn't,' she continues. 'It was Clara who was saying horrible things. It wasn't me. Clyde was there too, he heard her.'

278

'Horrible things? About what?' I ask. I don't understand what's going on.

'You, Vale,' Hermina says, her eyes glistening with pity. 'I'm sorry.'

A voice in my head is shouting, *I knew it.* I push it down until it's all quiet again.

'What . . .' I swallow hard. 'What did she say?'

'Do you really want to know?' asks Hermina. She's shaking her head from side to side. She looks torn.

I consider for a second whether I do want to know. It feels wrong, as if asking for the real version of events – rather than the one told to me by Clara – is another way of betraying her. She might have had her reasons for not wanting me to know. Could she have been lying to Hermina to test whether she and Clyde were real friends to me? Even as I think it, I realise how far-fetched it is. The real truth is a lot simpler than that: she said horrible things about me because that's what she believes. She shouts them to my face often enough; why would she not tell them to other people too? I do want to know exactly what she said. I have no idea why – it will hurt me even more than I'm hurting now – but I want to know.

'I do,' I tell Hermina. 'Please.'

She takes another deep breath.

'I really don't want to do this tonight. Before your speech. It's not—'

'Please.' There's an urgency in my voice that I didn't expect.

'Okay.' Hermina nods, reluctant. 'She was telling us that you had been so nervous before coming to the Christmas party that you'd had to lock yourself in the toilet for an hour. She called you pathetic and said you were a burden.' She can't look at me as she's recalling what Clara said. 'She also said you were creepy and obsessed with her, but that she felt sorry for you, so she kept you living in the house as a good deed.'

She's shaking her head.

'She was laughing when she said all this. I couldn't believe it. She wanted Clyde and me to agree with her. I could tell she wanted to be seen as a charitable friend. Clyde didn't say a thing. Just walked away – you know how awkward he gets – but I saw red. I didn't think it was kind of her to say those things. I wouldn't say them about my worst enemy, let alone a friend.'

'What did you do?' I ask, my voice struggling to rise above the jazzy music being piped in from the main room. My mouth is dry, and my legs suddenly feel too weak to hold my body upright. I grab hold of the back of a chair and lean on it.

'I told her that I thought she was out of order. That you didn't need anyone's charity and that you were a funny and kind person who everyone in the bookshop was very fond of. I told her she should consider herself lucky to have someone like you in her life,' Hermina says, her cheeks flushed with two red patches that look like flames trying to devour her face.

I hold my hand over my mouth. I can't imagine anyone ever speaking to Clara like that. The fact that Hermina did makes me in awe of her courage. There is also a small, indulgent part of me that is pleased to hear that everyone is fond of me in the bookshop. I've always felt accepted there, but to hear that I am liked too . . . It feels good.

'What . . . what did she say?' I ask.

'Nothing. She looked at me like this.' Hermina opens her mouth and eyes wide. 'Then she turned around and walked away. Next thing I hear is Ollie asking me if I know why you and she have just left the party without saying goodbye.'

'Wow.'

It's not Clara's words that shock me. I've heard them all before. Never in public or with someone else present, but I know them all too well. What I don't understand is why she would have lied to me, telling me that it was Hermina who had been mean to *her*. All those stories about her laughing at her and saying rude things about the split with Edo. None of it happened. *So why lie?* She could have just not said anything.

280

Hermina looks pained and is staring at me, waiting for me to say something.

'I didn't know,' I tell her. 'She told me you had been horrible to her. I believed her. I'm so sorry.'

'I know. You're not the one who should be sorry, Vale,' Hermina says, her voice rising high. 'She should be. Speak to her. Ask her why. She's not a good friend. You deserve better.'

Her last few words hit me like a slap.

Could she be right?

The niggling thought creeps up again. Clara has not been looking out for me the way I've always thought she was. If she's telling these things about me to people she hardly knows, what could she be thinking? If she has lied so easily, confident that I would never find out – or believe – the truth, what else has she lied about?

Hermina gets a little closer and points at my face. 'And if she's the one who's done that to you, then you need to get away from her. And quick.'

I'm about to say something back, but Louisa bursts in through the door before I can.

'Here you are. We're about to introduce you, are you ready?' she asks me.

I'm not. I wanted to read my notes once more and get some time by myself somewhere quiet to gather my thoughts before being thrust in front of a room full of people. But Louisa is looking at me and nodding as if to say, *Tell me you're ready. Come on.*

So I say, 'Yes, I am.'

She mouths, 'Great,' and ushers me out of the door into the main room.

I wave at Hermina as I leave her standing on her own and she waves back at me. My head is still spinning from our conversation.

Before I know it, Louisa is tapping on a microphone to create a *thud thud thud* sound that shushes the room down in seconds. Everyone is now watching as she prepares to speak.

'Ladies and gentlemen, welcome to the launch of *Rearing Pigs the Ethical Way: Why It Matters and How to Do It* by Valentina Tessaro.'

Applause rises from the centre of the crowd. I spot Kai and Ollie beaming at me and clapping manically. Louisa goes on to tell the audience how it all started. How Marcus and I got into a detailed conversation about pigs one day at the bookshop, and how astonished he was to find that I had intricate, informed and fascinating theories that deserved to be told more widely than the four walls of that shop. It's Lauren's turn to smile now; she and Clyde whoop at that mention.

Louisa recounts Marcus's enthusiasm on coming back to the office and announcing that he'd found someone who knew more about pig rearing than any of the 'trendy kids out on the streets today'. She does quotation marks with her fingers at this and the crowd laughs. She asks for applause for Marcus for finding me – the crowd gladly obliges, and Marcus bows his head – and then she introduces me.

'Our author will now read an extract from her first chapter, an insightful snapshot of what makes her the exciting new voice of the New Agriculture movement.'

More applause. I'm finding the noise of it all a little overwhelming.

I know that when I'm overwhelmed, my mouth doesn't seem to be able to produce words any more, so I try to calm myself down before I start speaking.

Lincolnshire Curly Coat, Livny, Malhado de Alcobaça, Mangalica, Meishan, Middle White, Minzhu, Minokawa Buta, Mong Cai, Mora Romagnola...

Slowly my breath returns to normal and I feel calm again. *It's pigs. I can do this. It's what I know and love. I just need to read.*

I wrap my hand around the microphone and start speaking into it. My voice comes out loud and pierces the silence that has descended on the room.

'Hi, everyone. I'm Vale, erm ... Valentina. This is the beginning of the first chapter. I hope you like it.'

A sea of faces watches me.

I swallow, then begin.

'The pig – or *Sus domesticus* – is a noble animal. Domesticated first in Asia eight thousand years ago from the wild boar, pigs have lived side by side with humans since the beginning of our existence on earth. We share our history with pigs. We also share ninety-eight per cent of our DNA with them, so next time someone calls you a pig, they are more correct than you may think.'

A ripple of laughter comes up from the crowd. I'm not sure why they are laughing at this – it's a true statement – but I'm glad they are. Marcus said that some of the sections provide comic breaks in between the facts, which is a good thing. This must be one of them.

'In this book,' I continue, 'I set out to share the knowledge that I have gained since childhood about raising these noble animals in the good and ethical way they deserve. My knowledge does not come from degrees or traditional education, but from direct experience, autodidactic learning and a lifelong passion that has led me to source material from a multitude of places. This is the result of all these years of borderline obsession – as others have called it – or "healthy interest in a fascinating subject", which is how I prefer to refer to it.'

More laughs. I spot Marcus's face in the crowd and see that he's looking around with a grin on his face. He winks when he sees me watching him.

As I continue, I get lost in the words. The more I read, the more comfortable I feel. These are nothing but my real thoughts, voiced out loud in front of people who not only are interested in what I have to say, but have taken time out of their lives to come and watch me do it live. It's so far removed from the reactions I've had in the past that if I think about it too hard, it makes my head spin. So I don't think. Instead, I focus on reading as clearly and slowly as I can, without swallowing words or leaving too-long pauses.

The clapping wakes me up from my reverie. I've read the whole of the first chapter without realising it. I smile at the crowd, then turn around and make a beeline for the toilets. I need a moment to take things in and get my breathing back to normal in a place where I can be on my own. On the way there, someone hands me a bottle of beer. I grab it and shout, 'Thank you,' as I keep walking. I close the door of the loo behind me and take a few deep breaths.

I did it. I managed to read out my work – my book! – in front of a crowd of people. There were plenty of familiar faces looking back at me, but many strangers too. I'm surprised I wasn't completely petrified. I take a sip of my beer and look at myself in the mirror. I almost don't recognise who I see staring back at me. I'm standing tall, my shoulders are down, my neck looks longer and my posture is relaxed and confident. My curls have somehow calmed down after my mad dash looking for the venue and are hanging down just the right side of wild. The skin under my eyes looks brighter than usual and I'm smiling, which I didn't realise I was doing.

I think of Clara's words to Hermina about me.

Pathetic. Creepy.

The person I see in the mirror doesn't look like that. She looks ... happy. Loved. Accomplished.

Why can't Clara see me the way the people outside this door can?

Hermina's parting words buzz around in my head, and for once, I choose to listen to them. I *do* deserve better, and maybe Clara hasn't been as good a friend as I thought she was.

I wash my hands and scrub them well. I want this new me to shine even more.

I exit the bathroom with the bottle of beer still in hand and almost bump heads with Kai.

'Here you are,' they say, grabbing hold of both my forearms. 'That was epic, Vale. You read so well. Everyone has been saying how excited they are to be reading your book. It's flying off the table. Lauren has been taking credit for it with everyone who'll listen, of course.'

'Of course,' I say.

We both laugh.

'I'd like to ask you something,' Kai tells me. Their eyes are fixed on mine, and they haven't let go of my forearms yet. One of their thumbs is going back and forth, stroking my skin. I'm surprised by how nice it feels. I would usually recoil from such intimate physical contact, but with Kai, it feels okay somehow. I like them and feel safe when they're around. They've seen the real me – and heard how big my obsession for pigs is – and they are still here. They find it fascinating, even, which is something I didn't think was possible not that long ago.

'Go on,' I say. The look in their eyes is hard to read. I can tell they're a little unsteady on their feet from the beer, but it's not just that. There's something else in there that I can't quite put my finger on.

'I've been meaning to for a while, but I wanted to wait until the book was out.'

They're acting strange, looking straight into my eyes, then to the floor, my eyes again, then the floor. Over and over. I've seen this behaviour before, but I can't remember where or who from. I'm watching Kai's every move to try and guess. But nothing comes to mind.

Then it hits me. Ollie and Rafael. Right at the beginning of their relationship, when they would stand chatting for hours outside the bookshop at the end of the day. That close physical contact, their faces fixed and smiling, then looking somewhere else, as if scared of getting burned if they lingered too long in each other's eyes. I remember noticing how the air around them would suddenly change, becoming thicker, their peripheral vision disappearing along with their surroundings.

It feels just like that. The sudden intimacy, Kai's change in demeanour.

Could it be ...?

'Okay, I'll just say it.' They take a deep breath and let go of my arms. 'Would you like to go on a date?'

I'm stunned for a second. Hearing them saying these words is shocking, but only a little bit. It's like every look, touch and smile has been leading up to this moment. As if a deep, animal part of me has been quietly collecting these snippets and forming a picture in some recessed part of my brain that I don't go in.

'Like, the two of us?' I ask. I think I know the answer, but I'm also scared of getting the wrong end of the stick as I often do, so I want to make sure I'm not misunderstanding them.

'Yes, just you and me. Maybe dinner? Or just drinks. Somewhere by the river if you like,' they say, still looking at the floor.

I think about it for a second. Dates are romantic. I do know that, although I've never been on one. They often lead to more romantic situations. I've seen it happen to everyone around me.

This is my turn.

I won't know how to behave in a situation like this. I might say the wrong thing or do something stupid. Embarrass myself or Kai. What's worse, if I mess things up, I might also mess up our friendship. What if Kai doesn't want to see me any more and things in the bookshop become so awkward it's no longer the oasis of peace it is now?

But then . . . it's Kai. They know me. I've done and said silly things in front of them plenty of times. I've talked too much about pigs, said the wrong thing and made a fool of myself almost daily. They've never once made me feel bad about it. Being around them makes me feel at ease and free. I like watching them move behind the counter when we're at work, and the way their eyes are always smiling. I don't mind them touching me as much as I do with other people, and time always goes quickly when we're together. I like them.

But romantically?

Yes, I think so.

This realisation stuns me. I thought romantic feeling was always desperate and filled with longing. But this is different. It's happy and comfortable, exciting and grounding at the same time. It feels right.

'Yes. I would like that,' I tell Kai. 'Dinner by the river sounds wonderful.'

I see the crinkles on either side of their eyes fan out like sun rays as they smile. I smile too. 'I'll think of a couple of options and text you later. I need to head off now before I miss my train, but I'll see you at work.' They give me a quick peck on the cheek that surprises me, but in a good way, and they're off.

I can't wait for our date. I feel like I'm floating above ground right now. I look around and see nothing but people smiling at me. When I start signing books, they tell me how refreshing my perspective is, how excited they are to read it. Marcus says how proud he is of me, and Ollie just keeps smiling and handing me bottle of beer after bottle of beer. I want to feel like this all the time, it's addictive. It's like there is a new me inside my skin, and it fits just right.

This feeling sticks with me all the way home, long after the party ends. The taxi that Almastra has booked for me is cool and comfortable. I sink into the leather seat as if in a cocoon, and the smooth radio station lulls my thoughts, already blurred by the beer. I watch the city go from tall buildings and sparkly window displays to terraced houses and corner shops. I know I should plan what to say to Clara when I get in. She will still be angry after our argument earlier. Furious, I imagine. But I don't want the glow of the evening to disappear just yet. I want to bask in the looks of admiration, the applause, Ollie's smiles, the feeling of Kai's lips on my cheek . . . for just a bit longer.

But when I catch a glimpse of the river, I know that I can't avoid what's about to happen. The taxi is getting close; I can see the park and recognise the supermarket.

In just a few minutes I'll be home. The thought of Clara's anger makes every fibre in my body feel exhausted. The likely possibility of violence is nothing new, but it is in such contrast with the few hours I've just had that it feels like a bad film I should be able to switch off.

The taxi stops and I get out. I'm a few steps away from our front door and can see that the lights are on in the house. She's probably still up and ready to fight. But there's a small chance she might have gone to sleep and will ignore me for a few days instead. It's almost harder, Clara ignoring me, because I know that the sword will fall – it's inevitable – I just don't know *when*.

My legs feel heavy and my breath keeps catching in my throat. I don't want to go in.

I hear a noise in the house that startles me. A shadow moves past the living room window. Clara is still up. I need to face the music. It will be horrible for a while, but then maybe we can go back to how we were, eventually. She will add more rules and maybe I can remind her about the tracking app if it helps her trust me again. Now that she knows about the book, I can mention the money. It might smooth things over. Not straight away – I know her – but after some time, she will be happy at the prospect of living a bit more comfortably and maybe she'll forgive me.

There are not enough deep breaths or pig breeds to list that will make what is about to happen easier, so I just open the door and step inside.

Chapter Twenty-Nine

I push the door closed behind me, careful to not make too much noise. As there's probably about to be a lot of screaming coming my way, I should at least keep my own noise levels to a minimum. I pause and stand where I am for a couple of seconds, waiting for something to happen. Clara would have heard me come back; I should go look for her, but I'm scared of the mood I'll find her in. It could be anything – upset, furious, totally aloof – I've never been able to predict her moods. The beers I've drunk tonight have not only made my limbs feel looser but boosted my courage too. I feel frightened of what Clara might do, yes, but there's also a part of me that is ready to fight back. To show her that I do deserve better. If the people around me can see it, she should finally be able to see it too.

There is nothing but silence in the house.

I take a deep breath and walk into the living room. I see her right away.

She is lying on the floor, her left arm at an odd angle. One slipper is still on her foot but the other is nowhere to be seen. Her face is turned away from where I'm standing and the skin on her neck looks paler than usual. The dressing gown she wears in the evenings is open, revealing her black pyjamas underneath.

She is completely still.

'Clara!'

A punch of adrenaline hits my body and I run over to her. Crouching down, I hold her face between my hands.

'Are you okay?' I ask her. 'What's going on?'

She opens her eyes for a moment but looks right past me, then shuts them again. Her body goes limp in my hands.

'Clara. Clara!' I'm screaming now. I can see she's struggling to breathe. 'Please keep breathing. I'm calling an ambulance now. Okay? I'll be right back.'

I run to get my bag and grab my phone. My fingers are shaking as I type in 999. I explain to the lady on the phone that I've found my friend unconscious on the floor, that she is not moving and struggling to breathe. I tell her our address and *beg* her to send someone right away.

I run back to Clara and hold her tight against my body. I won't let go until I know she's okay. And if she's not, then I will never let her go.

You can't die. You can't die. You can't die.

Voices are screaming in my head. I kiss her face and stroke her hair. I'm whispering, 'It's okay, everything is fine. The doctors are on their way. We're going to be fine, me and you, just fine.'

Now and then she opens her eyes, but I'm not sure she can see me. I whisper in her ear until I hear the ambulance pull up outside. I run out and lead them in. They check her pulse and pupils and carry her inside the vehicle on a stretcher.

'Can I come too, please? I need to be with her.'

'Are you a partner or family member?' the paramedic asks me.

I think about it for a second.

'Yes, I am,' I tell him. I hope he doesn't ask me any more questions, but if he does, I'm prepared to say whatever I need to say to get in that ambulance. I just need to be close to her, to make sure she's okay and being well taken care of.

The ride to the hospital happens in a blur. I hold Clara's hand while the paramedics keep an eye on her vital statistics. The regular beep of the machines seems to lull us both into a stupor. There's nothing I can do; I need to accept that I can't fix her right now. It's going to be someone else's job for the next few hours. All I can do is hold her hand and whisper that everything will be fine. The truth is that I have no idea if it will be.

She looks so far away, the body that I know so well now lying under a clinical blanket, strapped to alien machines.

I can't lose her.

The thought fills my head; there is no room for anything else.

I just can't lose her.

I try not to let myself indulge in it for fear of making it real. But every part of me right now knows that losing her would mean losing a part of me that is so big it might just be all of me. I thought I'd lost her once and it nearly broke me. Losing her again – this time for ever – would be the end of me. The end of the person I am now, the one I have become because of her presence in my life all over again.

We get to the hospital and rush through a series of doors, accompanied by a nurse with bright red hair and a kind face. As we get to a door without glass panels, the nurse tells me I have to wait outside.

'Your partner is in good hands. Please, wait here.' She shows me to a small waiting area with a handful of padded chairs and a table piled up with dusty magazines. 'I will come back out and find you as soon as we know more.'

I ignore the judder that word – *partner* – gives my heart when spoken out loud.

It feels at once so right and totally wrong.

I kiss Clara's cheek and tell her to be brave, that we'll be home again soon.

She lets out a low moan as they take her through the doors. I stand staring at the spot where she was just moments ago, the yellow of the doors glowing with meaning after swallowing her up.

I drag myself to the waiting area and sit on one of the itchy chairs. I'm on it for just a second, then I get up again. My legs can't stay still.

A million thoughts are running through my head. All starting in the same way: *what if?*

I try to tell myself that everything will be okay, that she will be fine. But the spark of hope doesn't quite ignite. I am so lost, already.

As I pace up and down the drab hallway, I feel my phone vibrate. A message from Kai.

Such a great night. You were majestic. Would next Thursday or Saturday work for dinner? Really looking forward to it xx

I slide my phone back into my pocket.

Not now.

It's like the party happened years ago, rather than just a few hours. The joy and excitement I felt during the taxi ride home have dissipated under the weight of what's going on now. My mind is still recovering from the whiplash of going from one extreme emotion to the other. Elation to despair. Only the moment I'm in – right now – feels real. This artificial light, the synthetic scratch of the seat's fabric, the peeling grey lino of the hospital floor. The headlines on the covers of the ancient magazines shouting about long-forgotten gossip. Nothing else that happened before I saw Clara on the floor, her eyes shut and her white neck, is real any more.

I stare at the doors and will them to open. I need something, someone to tell me that she's going to be fine. Not knowing is pushing my mind into overdrive.

I can't help but worry that the longer the wait is, the worse the news will be.

But thinking like this is not helping anyone. I need to stay strong for Clara. To calm myself down, I start listing pigs alphabetically.

I've got to the Ts – *Taihu, Tamworth, Teacup pig, Tsivilsk* – when the doors finally swing open and the nurse comes out. She must see the agony I'm in because she speaks immediately.

'Please, don't worry. Do you have a drink? I can bring you out some sweet tea if you like.'

'Me? No. But Clara. How is she? Do you have news?'

'We're still waiting for a few test results to come back. But we're happy with what we've seen so far. There doesn't seem to be anything substantially wrong with her.'

I'm incredibly relieved but also a little worried I might have misheard her.

'So . . . she's okay? What happened?'

'We're still investigating, but the results of the main tests are back. They don't show any immediate neurological or cardiac issues. Her iron levels are a little low and she could be slightly dehydrated. She's told us she's taken a few too many sleeping pills, but luckily not enough to cause lasting damage. Otherwise, everything seems to be normal. Without any concrete results, we can only guess what might have happened. Our current line of thinking is around a stress-related episode or panic attack, intensified by the pills. She's mentioned that she suffers from anxiety and depression, which have recently increased. Would you agree?'

I nod.

'Okay, thank you. I'm going to go and check if the remaining results are back, and if everything is still looking normal, we should be able to discharge her soon and you can take her home,' she says, smiling.

I want to hug her, but I know that's not appropriate. So I just tell her thank you a few times until she disappears back through the yellow doors.

I sit on the chair and wait for the moment when Clara will come through them herself. I am so happy she's going to be fine that I could sing and dance along this grey corridor. The colours around me are suddenly brighter, the ceilings higher.

I will do whatever I can to get her back to health. I've let her well-being drop from my priorities for too long; what happened to her tonight must somehow be a consequence of that. I've been too focused on my own interests – work, writing the book, Ollie, Kai – and allowed things to go downhill so much that her system must have had enough. I knew she had anxiety and suffered from depression – the signs were all there: not leaving the house, her mood changes, the violent outbursts – but she's never collapsed before. And the pills. Was she trying to ...?

I can't bear the thought of what might have happened if she'd taken more. I feel guilty, and can't help but think that if I'd never gone to the party, she wouldn't have ended up in hospital. The stress of finding out about me lying to her about the book must have tipped her over the edge.

I've lost sight of my roots in this city; Clara knows me better than anyone else here. Yes, she isn't always kind to me, and her outbursts are getting more and more difficult to bear, but she tells me she does it out of love, and I believe her.

Do I?

Hermina's words rattle through my brain again.

She's not a good friend. You deserve better.

So much has happened in so little time that I just can't wrap my head around it. All I can do right now is what I know best – focusing my attention on Clara and nursing her back to health. And along the way, hopefully, our friendship – the one we had before it all went wrong – will recover too.

Maybe more might blossom.

I try that word, *partner*, on for size. It fits. Maybe not as well as it would have fitted with Kai. Speaking to them tonight, I realised I don't think of them as just a friend, I never have. It's always been more; I've just been a bit slow to understand it.

And they must have felt the same if they asked me out on a date tonight.

If I think about Kai and Clara as items of clothing, Kai would be a bespoke suit, made to work with the way my body moves. Clara is more like a too-tight dress, never quite comfortable enough, bought in the hope that it will one day fit.

But I'm so used to having her by my side, our edges blurring

294

together, that she's the one I see when I picture myself with someone else. I've been hoping for it for so long that it's like a callus has formed in my brain, one that it isn't easy to get rid of. Things have changed in the last few months; maybe my relationship with Clara is something that could too. Friendships evolve to something more all the time for people, as happened for Rafael and Ollie. What if what Clara and I needed was to go through something as traumatic as what happened tonight and come out the other side as different people?

Although the more I think about it, the more I'm confused by exactly what *did* happen tonight. If the doctors didn't find anything wrong with her physically, why was her collapse so sudden? I know anxiety and stress can cause all sorts of symptoms that don't seem to be related, but doesn't it usually build up slowly?

I thought I saw her walk past the living room window when I was getting out of the taxi earlier, after the party. Could she have collapsed right before I opened the door? Maybe the thought of another confrontation was as overwhelming to her as it was to me. But there's something about it that doesn't quite add up.

Still, if there is something wrong with her – and especially if it's been caused by my behaviour – then I'm making it my job to fix it. I can't let the other distractions in my life take any more time away from her.

Chapter Thirty

Hermina's words haven't left my thoughts since the moment I heard them. A lot has happened in the short time since then, but they have stayed right there, nibbling away at my consciousness. As much as I've been told all those things by Clara before, hearing them out in the open like that, shouted over background noise, landing in what was, for a moment, a safe haven of acceptance, has shocked me. Like a poison quickly spreading through crystal-line waters.

Hearing those words spoken by someone else was harder than receiving any slap or kick or beratement. It made me feel deeply embarrassed. As if I'd been caught naked in the street.

The beers had made me feel suddenly magnanimous towards Hermina at the party, after resenting her for so long. But now I feel nothing more than a sense of gratitude for her openness, and grief that she had to witness mine and Clara's relationship as a bystander. It's hard for people to understand why we are the way we are without knowing about all the history we have in common. Clara has taught me how to live. Without her I don't know how, or if, I would have survived my teenage years. I owe her more than anyone could ever understand. She isn't perfect, but neither am I.

Yes, Hermina's words have shaken me up. But that means I need to hide things better. I never should have taken Clara to the Christmas party. It was my fault she unleashed on those around her. I knew deep down that it might happen. She has been drastically unpredictable for years now. I don't know why I thought that night would be any different. It's pathetic the way I keep on hoping that things might change. In a way Clara is right when she calls me that. I know the rules – she has laid them out very clearly – and if I stick to them, everything will be fine. But lately I keep on trying to change them, to break them. To push the limits of my world beyond its boundaries. And that can only end in disaster. The way it almost just did.

But why is it suddenly so hard to stick to her rules?

I shake the thought away.

I've known Ollie for years now, and things with him are never complicated. I'm not scared, or lonely, or sad when I'm around him. He knows about my passion for pigs and has never made me feel like a freak because of it. He teases me about it, of course, but I know he never means it in an unkind way. I know I could never have his life – open, free, happy to be himself – but most of the time it's enough for me to watch him live it.

And Kai. I haven't known them for that long, but there's something about them I can't pull away from. A kind of magnetism that makes me feel secure yet keeps me on my toes. They don't want to change me. They've seen what I have to offer, and they like it. I can be myself with them. And yet they still want to know me better. Ollie and Kai have only ever known the me that I am now. They didn't see who I used to be before. Derided, humiliated, alone. The version they see now is all thanks to Clara. She defended me when I was too vulnerable to do it for myself. Along the way becoming more than a friend. My everything.

Yes, the bookshop is where I can dream of things having gone differently for me. I can picture what life would be like if I did go out with Ollie and his friends in the evenings. The places we would see, the people we would meet. The music, the food, the art. I can entertain the thought of being in a relationship, a real one, with someone as kind, compassionate and cool as Kai. Kai wants to go on a date with me – me! I can be an author, writing about pigs, spreading the love and knowledge I have of this perfect animal to as many people as will listen.

But the bookshop is just a utopia. My life with Clara is my reality. And trying to change things can only lead to trouble. The situation we're in right now shows just that. I need to be realistic and stop pretending that things can ever be different. They can't and they won't. The truth is that trying to lead two lives has left me exhausted. I can't be bookshop Vale and home Vale at once. Keeping the two of them separate has me spread so thin I could disappear. I'm not being a good, honest friend to those who accept me, and I've been so bad to Clara, I almost killed her. Being in this hospital, waiting for her to come back to me through those doors, has given me the wake-up call I needed.

If I can't get Ollie, Kai and the bookshop out of my mind altogether, then I need to store them somewhere they won't get in the way. I can't be with them, see them or think about them ever again. If my own happiness is the price to pay for everything to go back to the way it was, then so be it.

The Clara I met all those years ago, just arrived in London and filled with excitement. The one I thought I had lost for ever. She needs me now. I can't let her go again. I know what I need to do. I send Lauren a message.

I'm going to take some time off work. A few weeks, maybe more. Sorry. It's important.

It's the middle of the night so she will probably see it when she wakes up. I think of her reading it. She will make a meal of it when she announces it, probably bad-mouth me to the rest of the team like I've seen her do with others in the past. You're either with her or you're against her. I can picture Ollie and Kai's faces when she tells them she doesn't know when – or if – I will be back.

A lump the size of an orange lodges itself in my throat at the thought. They may be baffled, probably angry and sad. I expect they will send me messages. I will make sure to silence my phone. I can't read them, not yet. It will hurt too badly to let them down. It already does. I stare at the words on the screen until they stop making sense.

My head is spinning, but I know there is one more thing I need to do. It's stupid really, but as I get ready to write the words, I feel like a mother abandoning her child on the steps of an orphanage.

I send an email to Louisa and Marcus.

Hi Louisa, hi Marcus,

Thank you for tonight, you gave me a very special gift.

My situation has changed, I can't do any more promotion for the book. For a while at least. There are some important things that I need to take care of.

Sorry.

Vale

I laugh bitterly as I press 'send'. That will do it. It ends here.

As soon as she's better, I will tell Clara that nothing and no one will get in between us again. She won't have to worry any more because she will always know where I am. I know it will make her happy and calm her frazzled brain. I will remind her of the tracking app, and I will find a way to make some money to support us that won't keep me out of the house so much. I'm not ready to tell my friends that I won't see them again – it's too painful right now – but it might get easier in time. Once some time has passed, they might even forget about me. I will be like Hermina, someone they used to work with and like who simply isn't around any more.

Even as I think that, I realise it's not true. They won't let me go without a fight, Ollie, and Kai. Everything that's happened in the last few months has been great. I've never felt more confident, accomplished, appreciated.

Facts about pigs don't swirl around in my head so manically any more. They are still there, of course – they always will be, I like it that way – but I don't have the same urge to cling on to them. Like a fear that I might lose them, just as I lost my countryside all those years ago. Pigs will always be my biggest love; now I can honour them by helping others see them the way I do and treat and raise them the way they deserve. With respect.

My other love – Clara – now needs me. And it's only right that the time I have now I'm not working, and the book is out, is dedicated to her. Just her.

Chapter Thirty-One

I hear a noise and turn around to see Clara and the red-haired nurse come through the doors.

'Hey,' I cry, 'you're out.'

Clara manages a weak smile, and I notice the hospital bracelet around her wrist. She's wearing the clothes she came in with and seems ready to go. I give her a hug and she stands there not hugging me back. She must still be angry at me. It's okay, I have all the time in the world now to make it up to her.

'Were the last results all normal too?' I ask the nurse.

She nods. 'Yes, all good. Clara is doing very well. You can take her home.'

I bombard her with thanks once more, and this time she looks at me with a strange expression in her eyes.

'You take care,' she says, staring right at me. 'If things ever get too much or you don't feel safe, you can come here. Our door is always open.'

It's odd for her to say it to me – I wasn't the one who collapsed, after all – but I thank her all the same, then take Clara's hand and we make our way to the exit.

I turn around before we go through the revolving door and see that the nurse is still there, at the end of the corridor, looking at us as we walk away.

'Let's go home,' Clara says, pulling on my sleeve. 'I want a bath.'

*

I trace the bruises on her skin from the medical tests with my finger. I wish I could erase them all. She doesn't seem angry with me any more. She is pensive.

I wash her body slowly, careful not to scratch her or rub too hard. She is telling me about the doctors, how they turned her inside out with tests. Some of them were nicer than others, but she didn't trust any of them. She thinks there is something wrong with her – much worse than what they've said – and she's convinced they were hiding it.

'Why would they?' I ask.

'Because they can't handle it maybe. They're scared it will show them up as being incompetent, you know? Highlight their limits.'

I'm not sure what she's talking about, but I make noises of agreement all the same.

'I think it's this house,' she continues.

'What do you mean?'

'That's making me sick. Edo's curse. It wants to take me down, just like he does.'

'Clara. I don't think—'

'It is. We need to go,' she says, her voice decisive. 'We can't afford it any more anyway.'

She's right, we're living beyond our means here; the bills for such a big house are too steep. But I never thought she would want to leave. She and Edo made so many sacrifices to be able to afford it, and she fought so hard to keep it during the divorce. But with just my salary and whatever will come from the book sales, it's still more than we can afford.

'Where to?'

'I thought about it. The coast. It's cheaper there. And there's the sea. I was thinking Sussex or Kent, where it's warm. The coastline is nothing like in Italy, but it's not bad.' She turns around to look at me. 'I think it would be good for us.'

I'm stunned. The coast? It's a least an hour and a half train ride from London, not a journey that could be done daily. For a visit at the weekend maybe, but I wouldn't be able to keep my job. Thinking this makes me feel like the ground under my feet has given way. Clara must have read my thoughts, because she tells me to stop worrying.

'There will be other bookshops, other cafés you can work in. I might get myself a job in one too. We could spend our lunch breaks together, looking at the sea. It'll be like when we were young, you know? Like that night at the monastery, except it would be every day. What do you think, Monk?' she asks.

The mention of that night softens me. I can still remember thinking, as we sat on the cold grass and watched the sky light up with a thousand fires, that in that moment I had everything I would ever need. That if the world had emptied while we were lost behind those tall brick walls and we had walked out onto desolate streets, I would have been fine with it. Clara by my side, smiling at me, was all I needed to be happy then.

But now?

I'm not sure if that's still the case now. So much has happened since that night.

'What about the house?'

'I'll sell it. With the money I make from the sale, I can get something down there. In a village maybe. You get so much more for your money out of London. We can live on what's left if we don't spend too much. But it's not like we'd be going out to fancy restaurants or drinking cocktails every night,' she says. 'We'd be home. Together.'

If we move to the coast, it will be just me and her there. I will be away from everyone I've grown close to in my years in London. A smaller place means there will be nowhere for me to hide if things get too much at home. A new job won't allow me to write during working hours the way I can at the bookshop now.

I look at her and see my past. One that I know well, yes, but coated with the pain of a rejection that I understand deep down will never change. The version of me that Clara knows is based on the role I've involuntarily played since the day I met her.

I no longer know if playing that role makes me happy – I suspect it doesn't – but what is left if that version of me goes away? A fraction of me that is raw and unfinished. Will I be lost without her guidance?

If I'm left exposed to the world as the true me, unfiltered and unpolished, will I be alone again?

I'm scared.

'Okay, let's do it,' I tell her.

The smile she gives me chills me to my core.

A few days later, a 'For Sale' sign appears by our front door.

Not long now until we're gone.

Chapter Thirty-Two

February 2020

Clara has gone shopping in central London. After that she has a final follow-up appointment at the hospital, where I will go to pick her up once she's finished. She didn't ask me to go with her, which is unusual, but I think the last few months of being home just the two of us has meant she needs a few hours of alone time too. She said that once we move, those big flagship stores won't be within reach any more, so she's decided to go one more time.

It's a good sign. A few months back, when she first brought up moving to the coast, I never would have pictured her going out alone so far away from our area.

She's come a long way since then. Her confidence has visibly improved, and she hasn't had any more collapsing incidents. For weeks afterwards, I kept reliving in my head the moment I found her on the floor, worried it might happen again. But it never has. Her health has been steadily improving since that night. Some colour has returned to her cheeks and her moods seem to be more balanced.

I've made sure she wants for nothing. The better I look after her and second-guess her every whim, the happier she becomes. I do all I can. She doesn't always think it's enough, so I try harder. There are no more secrets, no more lies between us.

She is not my partner, not yet. But I think once we're by the coast

305

it will be different. Maybe she's right, maybe this house does have bad vibes. For now, our close intimacy that culminates in the evening bath is enough for me.

But I haven't been feeling well since quitting the bookshop.

I miss them.

I only dare admit it to myself late at night when I'm finally alone. I can't think about it during the day as it stops me in my tracks and makes my knees wobble. I need to keep going, because if I stop, I will not start again. Clara still needs me, she always will. In the first few weeks after sending those messages from the hospital as I waited to know her fate, I received endless replies from Lauren, Ollie and Kai and emails from Louisa and Marcus. They started coming through daily, then every other day, then once a week. Now I only get Ollie messaging me occasionally. I never reply.

I don't have the answers he's looking for, and anyway, it's too late. I will be gone soon, and they will forget about me eventually.

Ollie and Kai found out that I'm leaving London a few weeks after I cut off all contact. They must have got my address from the employee folder, and they came to the house and rang the doorbell, looking for me. Clara made me lie down on the floor while she crouched behind the sofa. They rang and rang for what felt like ages. They knocked and shouted my name. They must have seen that the lights and the TV were on and guessed that someone was in. After they finally left, Ollie sent me a message with a picture of the 'For Sale' sign and a long series of question marks.

When I still didn't respond, he wrote:

Are you leaving?? WTF. Vale, we love you and miss you. Please get in touch, we're all worried.

I deleted the message straight away. No point keeping it there to reread a million times when Clara is asleep. It only makes my heart hurt more. I've made my choice and I need to accept the consequences. The pain might never go away, but this is my life now and hankering after the past doesn't make getting up every day any easier.

One day I will learn to not regret my choices. I hope that day is soon. In the meantime, I make sure to stay busy.

With the few hours of freedom I have before I need to pick Clara up from the hospital, I've decided to pay a final visit to Stepney City Farm. It was my haven when I first moved to London, and I want to go one last time before I leave. I started this adventure with their pigs, and I want to end it with them too. I don't think there will be many city farms by the seaside. There might be pigs inland, but I would need a car to drive to them and Clara won't let me get one.

'You'll have everything you need in the village. There's no need to go wandering around. Plus, cars are expensive. We won't need one.'

I take the train into central London and change to the Underground to go east.

The carriages are busy and loud. I would usually hate this, but today I soak it all in: the metallic noise, the pungent smell, the crowds. It's as if I'm already nostalgic for something I haven't left yet. I come out of the station and walk towards the farm. I remember the way to get there well and feel the same excitement I used to feel all those years ago as I get nearer and nearer to the distinctive gate. I salute St Dunstan and All Saints Church as if I'm greeting an old friend. I breathe in the air as I get closer and catch a whiff of manure, which makes me almost burst with excitement.

I can see the farm now. It's still there; nothing much seems to have changed. The same metal gate with the multicoloured letters spelling *Stepney City Farm*, and the wooden signs pointing to the café and the shop. They focus a lot of their energy on education and have set up the farm as a place for people to come and get a taste of the countryside without having to go out of the city. In my eyes, it's an exploitation of farm work as entertainment, of course, but I let them off the hook as they need it to survive. Without the petting zoo element, city slickers' volunteer schemes and school tours, they wouldn't be able to do the work they do with the farm animals. I don't approve of it but understand that it's necessary. I'm aware that I'm a visitor too, after all. I like to feel different – like a fisherman watching hordes of holidaymakers descend on his village at the first rays of sunshine – because of my passion and my friendship with Homer, but really I haven't been here in years. I've become the holidaymaker around here.

It's early afternoon on a weekday, so the farm is not as busy as it would be at the weekend or during the holidays. I see now that a few things *have* changed since I was here last: a large barn has been built to keep the animals inside during the winter – wise – and they've added an entertainment centre where children can learn about 'rural arts'. Things like pottery, ironmongery and woodwork. They are trying to bring a slice of nature and ancient skills to this very urbanised area.

When I was growing up, the city and the countryside were always separate in my mind. You had to make a choice on where you wanted to be and travel to get to anywhere else. This brings the two together and I'm glad it exists.

I look around for some time, taking in the soggy terrain, half-eaten feed mounds and busy workers pushing wheelbarrows around. The smell is stronger where I'm standing; I breathe it in as deeply as I can, hoping that some of it finds a chamber in my lungs and settles in there. But I can't wait any longer. I have somewhere to be, and my time here is running out. I walk past the goat enclosure and the vegetable garden as a cold drizzle starts to fall. I zip up my coat and put my hands in my pockets. The cool summers we get in London are great for the pigs, it means a lower risk of sunburn. But the cold winters can be harsh for them, especially for the breeds that are not used to them. I would expect the current lot to be British breeds – Berkshire or Gloucestershire Old Spot – but you never know.

As I get closer, I start hearing their sweet grunts, signalling curiosity mainly, but they could also be looking for food among the soggy grass. I don't have to search very hard to see them. Five Berkshires, with their beautiful black coats. Two are older – five or six years old – but the other three are still quite young; they must have been born only last year. They have white socks and a lick of the same colour going from snout to forehead, high between the eyes.

They are beautiful, and just the right breed to thrive in this climate. I take them in with my eyes as the biggest smile stretches across my face. It feels foreign to smile, like a newly learned skill. I haven't done it in months. I see a face appear from behind a mound of chopped wood and feel a burst of recognition.

'Homer!' I cry. 'You're still here. Hello.'

The same pig keeper who was here all those years ago, my friend. I wave at him, but his expression doesn't change. *Does he not recognise me?*

His skin is lined, and his hair is nearly all gone. What's left is as white as the pigs' socks. He looks older, but the kindness hasn't gone from his eyes.

I walk towards him, smile still plastered on.

'It's me. Vale. The Italian girl who used to come here all the time and ask questions about your pigs. Still Berkshires, I see. They look wonderful.'

I get closer still, but it hasn't clicked. I understand; he must see hundreds of people every week. It was a long time ago, after all.

But suddenly he smiles too.

'Yes. Of course. It's been years.' He rubs his eyes with one grubby hand. 'Sorry, I didn't recognise you there, you look so different.'

'Oh. How?' I ask him. I can't remember the last time I looked at myself in a mirror, but I didn't realise I look any different than I did years ago.

'Your clothes. They used to be so colourful. That's why it's taken me a while to put the old you and this new you together. You're much skinnier too. But now I see it's you. How have you been?'

He plants a shovel in the soft soil and uses it as support.

It's true. The memory surfaces in my head like a bubble in water. I did use to wear colourful clothes. When I first moved to London, I loved looking at how everyone was dressed around Whitechapel, so many different identities expressed so freely. I started experimenting too: red trainers, orange trousers, flowery shirts. The more I broke away from the rules that I had been following back in Rome, the further away those painful memories got pushed. I must have looked crazy at times, with all those clashing patterns and shades. But I remember thinking that if each breed of pig – and there are hundreds – showed individual characteristics when it came to what they looked like, then why couldn't I decide to show the world just as many facets of my personality through my clothes?

When Clara came back into my life, she accepted my style at first. But I could tell from a few comments she made in passing – 'Clown day today, is it?' or 'Move out of the way, please, you're giving me a migraine with that outfit' – that she didn't like it. And as has often been the case with her, it was easier for me to comply than to fight it. She always wins.

I didn't realise I had lost weight too, but it makes sense. Her notes have been more and more restrictive in terms of how much food I'm allowed. But it doesn't really matter. I haven't felt much like eating anyway. And it's not like we have a great deal to put on the table now. I'd rather keep what we do have for Clara.

The money from the book did come through, but because I stopped taking part in any promotion, it wasn't as much as everyone at Almastra was hoping. They told me next Christmas might help to pick things up again, but it's a long way away. We'll be better off once we're by the coast and Clara's house money has come through. Not for very long, though. We'll have to find jobs as soon as possible.

'I'm okay,' I tell Homer. 'I wrote a book. About pigs.'

'You did? What's it called?'

'*Rearing Pigs the Ethical Way: Why It Matters and How to Do It*. It came out a few months ago.'

'That was you? I heard of it. People loved it, didn't they? Well done, you should be very proud of yourself. I always wanted to write a book, never had the time. These guys take it all up.'

310

He gestures towards the pigs with a look of pure love in his eyes that I recognise as the same as my own. He cares deeply for them and I'm glad he's the person who has looked after generations of pigs here at the farm; he's the living embodiment of what I preach in my book. I just theorised it on paper, but he puts it into practice every day. I used to see him all those years ago looking after the animals with empathy, kindness and knowledgeable care. I'm sure he hasn't changed.

He's right, though, I should be proud of what I have achieved. Writing the book was something I never thought I could do. And not only did I do did it; I did it well, too.

'Thank you,' I tell him. 'Although it feels like a long time ago now. I'm moving to the coast in a few days, starting a new life.'

'You are?' He looks at me with surprise in his eyes. 'Not many pigs by the sea.'

I nod. 'I know.'

After I pulled out of my book engagements, Marcus sent me an email filled with good reviews and sales figures. The book was starting to do well, and people liked it. He told me there was a definite appetite to have me on for more interviews and readings, and would I reconsider my decision.

I never replied. There was no point. My life has taken a different path, one that I have decided on, and it's too late to go back.

Or is it?

As I watch Homer tend to his pigs, cleaning up their pen and calling each by name as if they are his children, I imagine what I could have said to him instead, standing here, had I made a different decision. But not just a few months ago; way back when I first met him, all those years ago. When I lived nearby and came here most weekends, just like I had done at Angela's farm when I was young. If I had never responded to Clara's message when she'd moved to London. If I had ignored her friendly tone and enthusiasm and just remembered the pain. If I'd been better at protecting myself, who would I be now, standing here in front of Homer?

311

If I'd had the strength to fight for the life I wanted, I might have found myself in a different place now. I might have left the bookshop to work here, at the farm, like I always wanted to do.

But the thought of never getting to know Ollie and Kai is a painful one. For the first time in months, I allow myself to grieve the loss of them, to recognise the void of love and acceptance that has opened up in me since I left them behind. The guilt that soaks my every thought since then, knowing that I've made them suffer, leaving them with so many unanswered questions. Every time I leave the house now – which is not often – I'm inexorably drawn towards the bookshop. My body wants to walk there, retrace the steps I still know so well. My thoughts rush ahead, desperate to find solace between those thick walls.

The instinct to go there is so strong, almost too much to bear.

Homer hugs me goodbye. I feel his sharp cheekbones press against the side of my head; his papery skin somehow still soft after a life spent outside. I hold him close, knowing that I won't see him again. The hug I give him is the hug I couldn't give Ollie and Kai. Tight, desperate. He is my happy past and I'm leaving him – and the pigs – behind. Tears fall down my face before I can stop them. I wipe them with my sleeve, but Homer has noticed.

'You're always welcome to come back. The pigs will always be here, even if it's a different lot. This is their home.'

I smile at him and look at the pigs once more. Their shiny black coats are twinkling under the low sunlight and their busy snouts are buried in straw, looking for scraps. I wave once more, then turn around and walk away.

I reach the gate and take one last look at the farm. Soon nature will wake up again and the leaves will come out. New animals will be born, and another cycle will begin. Nature goes forwards, never backwards. And sometimes it heals itself and grows stronger.

The sun is getting lower. I check the time and see that it's later than I thought. Clara will be nearly done. We have a busy evening of packing ahead of us. The new owners will start moving their things in two days and we need everything ready to be loaded in the removal van by the end of tomorrow. I have done a lot already. I have packed most of the large items away; only the smaller things and the essentials need to be carefully wrapped so they don't break on the way there. We are going to be renting first, while we look for the right place. Clara has done plenty of research on areas and pricing. I've let her make all the decisions.

I take my phone out of my pocket. It has been quiet for ages now. Even my parents haven't called in weeks, maybe months, after I just stopped answering. I dial my mother's number without really thinking. I just want to hear a sound. Her voice. Or even the dialling tone. The phone rings out. She must be away from it. The voicemail message begins, and I lose myself for a moment in the familiar tones.

The beep shakes me out of it. After a brief silence, I speak.

'Mum. I'm sorry it's been so long. Things have been strange here. Difficult to explain. I . . . I miss you. I'm sorry. I love you both.'

My finger shakes as I hang up. Guilt doesn't even begin to describe it.

I hurry towards the station and take the train the few stops to the hospital. I feel heavy, as if the very structure of my body is soaked through.

Chapter Thirty-Three

The hospital stands defiant against the grey sky, as if nothing happened last time I was here. I hurry past the A&E entrance, hugging myself to stay warm. It looks busy there, more so than usual, with large groups of people standing both inside and outside the department, waiting to be seen. I've seen in the news that a new virus has been spreading all over Europe. I wonder if it has hit London too.

I feel better once I've left the building behind. I still remember the journey in the ambulance too clearly to be comfortable around here. I follow the signs to the outpatients department and look for the place Clara told me she would be. I am to wait for her in the room to the right of the reception. I walk around the corridors searching for it. The yellow of the doors between departments still makes me feel sick. It's a shade I never want to see again in my life. To think that less than an hour ago I was at the farm, with my beloved animals. And now back in this place. Still, hopefully not for too long. Clara should be done shortly, then we can head home and begin our new life.

Corridor after corridor stretches out in front of me, but as much as I follow the right arrows along, I seem to miss the reception. I need to ask someone, or I'll end up being late. And we don't want that.

I see a nurse come out of one of the consultation rooms. I move closer and wave to try and catch her attention.

'Hi, sorry, do you know where I can find outpatients reception, please?'

She looks at me and I recognise her at once. The red hair is a bit duller than it was then, but the kind face is the same. She seems to recognise me too.

'Hi.' She smiles. 'I know you. You came back.'

I nod quickly.

'I'm just trying to find reception. Do you know where it is?' I'm trying to keep a casual tone but finding it hard, as Clara could be coming out of her appointment any moment now and I need to be there when she does.

'Sure,' she says, pointing towards the end of the corridor we're standing in. 'Go all the way down, through the metal doors and you will see it on your left.' She pauses for a second. 'It's nice to see you again,' she says.

I nod. 'Yes. Well, my friend is in today, so I came to collect her.' I want to get going, but she's kind of standing in the way.

'Does she have an appointment?'

'She does.'

'Interesting.' She breathes out deeply. 'How have things been?'

What's with all the questions, and why is she still in my way? Time is running out.

'Sorry.' I step towards her hoping she'll move, but she doesn't budge.

She's looking at me in a strange way. Her eyes seem kind of sad but they're also wide open. There is an urgency to her demeanour that clashes with how she's pronouncing each word, slowly and calmly. 'As I said last time, if things ever don't feel right, we can help. Our doors are always open. Come talk to us any time.'

I take another step towards the corridor, and this time she moves out of the way. I mumble a thank you and start walk-running towards the metal doors.

What a strange woman. Telling me, again, the same odd words that she told me last time I was here. Why is she focusing on me when Clara was the reason we were here then – and now, too? Is she confused? The way she looked at me reminded me of how my mother did one of the last times I saw her when I went to Italy, now more than a year ago. Those strange eyes, hiding something I can't quite grasp. Is it concern? It looks like it. *But why?*

I find the reception, but I don't see Clara anywhere. What a relief. She must still be in with the doctor. I sit down and try to get comfortable. But the nurse's look and her cryptic words keep rising up to the surface of my thoughts. I feel like I did when I was younger, talking to people but not understanding the space between the words. Not catching the stuff left unsaid. In this case, though, I can tell there was something on her mind when she was speaking to me. Nurses don't usually say those things to their patients, as far as I know, and definitely not to those who accompany them. She must meet hundreds of people every week, yet she clearly remembered me and Clara. What did she see in me – us – that I can't see? The questions roll around in my head like pebbles on a riverbed. My body won't sit still either. I can't seem to stop tapping my foot, and my fingers are twitching.

I stand up to try and use up some energy, but as soon as I'm on my feet, they seem to direct me back down the corridor. I let them take me. I need to find that nurse and ask her these questions. I feel like I might go crazy if I don't.

I walk back to where I saw her, but she's no longer there. I walk a bit further and turn the corner towards a different reception and waiting area. I see the red-haired nurse right away. She's talking to the receptionist and handing him a stack of paperwork. I stand there, unsure how to approach her. Do I go up to her and ask my questions or do I wait for her to notice me first? I remember that I don't have much time. Clara will be done any minute now and will come looking for me if she can't see me. I have to make this fast.

I walk up to her and stand right behind. I go to tap her on the shoulder, but the receptionist sees me first and gestures towards me. The nurse turns around.

'Can I help?' she asks.

'Yes. Sorry. I just wanted to ask you a question.'

She looks at me and nods. We move a few steps away towards a quiet corner.

'How can I help?'

'I don't have much time. I just wanted to know why you kept telling me that thing. About things not feeling right and that you can help. What does it mean?' I realise I'm hopping from one foot to the other, but I can't seem to stop it.

She shakes her head, pushing a strand of red hair behind her ear.

'I'm sorry, I shouldn't have said anything. I really can't do this.' Her feet are pointing away from me and I can tell that she's about to walk off. 'I wish you the best of luck, but I need to go now. It's a really busy ...'

She stops talking. Perhaps it's because she's noticed the tear I can feel rolling down my cheek, but something has halted her in her tracks. I hold my hands up in front of me as if in prayer.

'Please.'

She's quiet for a few seconds, frozen to the spot. Then she gestures for me to follow her, further away from the nearby patients.

'Right. Did your friend tell you much about what we discussed when you both came in that night?'

'Not really. She just said she was told her collapse was due to stress and exhaustion. It's because I was putting her under a lot of strain.'

'You were?'

'Well, yes. It's a long story. But things are better now, she's not so stressed any more.'

'And you?' she asks.

'Me?'

She nods.

'I'm ... fine.'

She puts a hand on my shoulder. My first instinct is to flinch, but I don't want her to stop talking to me. She opens her mouth a few times, as if she's unsure whether to continue. Then finally speaks.

'Please listen, I'm going to be honest with you. I could get in trouble for this but I'm going to tell you anyway. We don't think there was anything wrong with your friend the night she came in. We couldn't find anything. Stress can cause a wide variety of symptoms, but she was completely normal once we'd taken her in for monitoring, away from you. Chatting, laughing, cracking jokes. A different person. The switch was fast. I think she lied to you about being sick. Do you know why she might have done that?'

I shake my head. Lied? No. She looked – was – so sick. I nearly lost her. There is no way it wasn't real. But then she has lied to me before.

'I've seen this before. And when I met the two of you, I thought I recognised a particular type of dynamic. I told you that thing then, and again today, to let you know that if things aren't okay at home, you don't have to suffer in silence. You're not alone. You can come here and someone will help. That's all.'

She takes her hand off my shoulder and smooths down the front of her uniform.

'But you've told me you're fine and I respect that.'

I nod, but I don't move. Her words have frozen me into place. I need to understand.

'Seen it before,' I whisper.

'Pardon?'

I clear my throat. 'You said you've seen it before. That you recognise it. What do you mean?'

She looks around us, then moves closer.

'My sister,' she sighs, 'had a boyfriend a long time ago and the two of them never went anywhere on their own. They were always together. It wasn't like that at the beginning, it happened gradually. When you saw one, the other would always be there. And she began to change, my sister. The clothes she wore were different all of a sudden, her hair changed, she started to look more and more like someone else. Like she was becoming grey after being in full colour, if that makes sense.'

'But we—' I start to say.

318

'Wait. Let me finish. Then we stopped seeing her. Every time I called her, the boyfriend would pick up. I would ask him to tell my sister to call me back, but she never did. What I realised after too many months of this was that her boyfriend had started controlling her. Everything was decided for her: what to wear, who to see. Everything. And because it happened slowly, over time, my sister didn't see it coming. She was right in it and ended up stuck. Like the frog in the boiling water. Boiled alive without realising. Do you know what I mean?'

I nod again.

'Anyway, the whole family got so worried that we decided to intervene. We went to their house one day and found her there, so skinny you wouldn't believe it. With eyes so sad and her face a mask of fear. There were bruises too. But she didn't want to come with us. She was fine, she said. Told us we didn't understand their relationship, that they were happy. Long story short, we asked her to come with us just for a couple of days to help with a family matter. It was a lie, but it worked to get her out. It took us a long time to make her see that things weren't good and that she needed to break it off. She got so angry with us at first. Then desperately sad. But eventually it sank in, and she found the strength to end it. It wasn't easy. And it took a long time. But she's great now – she met her husband two years later. And the two of them are the happiest, silliest people you've ever met. They love each other so much, but most of all, they really respect each other.'

I'm shaking a little and there's a faint buzzing sound in my ears. The tips of my fingers feel numb as I look at her face.

'Look, I might be getting it wrong, but I don't think I am. What I saw that night. The bruise on your cheek. The things your friend told us about you, the look on your face when you saw us come out. The way you clung to her. It really reminded me of my sister during that dark time. Queer relationships can be as toxic and controlling as straight relationships. People are people. And sometimes they are really, really bad to one another.'

I feel my tongue getting colder. Then I realise my mouth is hanging open a little. I close it.

'No,' I say. I shake my head. There's a fight in my mind. I realise it hasn't stopped since the nurse started talking. It's like a storm that keeps picking up pace and I'm powerless to control it.

'I'm sorry. It's a lot to take in, I know. And you might not be ready to hear it. But I struggled to forgive myself for a long time for not talking to my sister sooner. And I'm glad I saw you again.'

I shake my head again. Once. Twice. Then I realise I can't stop shaking it. I think I'm trying to push out the thoughts invading my mind after being buried deep for too long; now made bolder by the nurse's words. I mumble something back to her.

She smiles sadly and whispers, 'Please be careful. It's never too late to get out,' then moves out of the way.

I walk slowly back down the corridor. As I stumble through the metal doors, I see Clara chatting to the outpatients receptionist. She turns around and sees me.

'There you are,' she says. 'I was starting to think you'd forgotten about me. Shall we go?'

Chapter Thirty-Four

I pick up Clara's shopping bags and we make our way to the exit. I can hear her talking to me as we walk, chatting about a rude shop assistant who ignored her in a shop earlier, and how the doctors still wouldn't give her a straight answer about what had happened to her back in September. She's worried it means she's sicker than we thought, and they're just trying to protect her from the truth. I can hear her but I'm not listening. I can't get the nurse's words out of my mind. Just like after my conversation with Hermina at the launch party, there's something about what she said that I can't shake off.

Clara's behaviour has been getting worse in the last few years. It's time I faced that. Edo tried to tell me many times when things between the two of them were disintegrating. And back then, I thought he was doing it because that's what people do at the end of a marriage, bad-mouth each other to whoever will listen. Even then I knew that sort of thing wasn't his style, but I explained it away by filing it in my head under 'things about people's relationships that I cannot understand'. I think I can now see that he was trying to warn me not to drown in Clara's world. To get out while it was still possible.

I didn't listen, of course. I was resolutely in Clara's camp. And for years felt guilt for having broken up the marriage, like the 'poison' I was. But what if it wasn't actually me who broke it up? If it was down to Clara and Edo alone.

321

Something in my gut is telling me that he never actually blamed me for their demise like Clara said. It was something she made up. Just like she lied to me about her conversation with Hermina. It was never about a bitchy workmate being rude to another party guest after a few too many cocktails. It was much simpler than that: just Clara being Clara. After all, it's in line with the things she says to me behind closed doors. I knew deep down it didn't quite add up with the Hermina I knew. I just wasn't ready to listen. All these old thoughts are now flooding through, but this time there is nothing in the way to stop them from registering.

I know now.

I've known all along.

'Clara,' I say, stopping her mid-sentence.

'What?'

'Were you ever actually sick? That night when I came back from the party. Were you just pretending?' My voice is shaking a little. But it's not with fear this time. It's rage. A pure, incandescent rage I've never felt before.

I need her to say it. I want to hear the words come out of her mouth.

'What are you talking about? Of course I was sick. You were literally there when it happened.'

'I wasn't, though. I arrived afterwards,' I tell her.

Clara shrugs as if to say 'same thing', but I'm not ready to stop yet.

'I saw you through the window that night, just before I opened the door. You were standing and moving fine. Then a second later, you're on the floor and unconscious. It doesn't add up, Clara. You've been lying to me. And this is just one example. You've been lying to me for years.'

She's walking ahead of me now, rushing towards the exit, not looking at me. Her face has gone red the way it does when she's about to explode with rage. But I swear I can see fear in her eyes.

I'm doing my best to keep up with her. I need her to listen to every single word I say.

'I know what really happened the night of the work Christmas party with Hermina. I know what you told her about me. How horrible and mean you were and how she defended me. You couldn't take it, though, someone sticking up for me. So you turned her into the villain and you the victim. Just like you did with Edo.'

The mention of his name stops her dead in her tracks. We're out into the car park now, and cars are circling all around us, looking for spaces.

'Don't you dare,' she hisses, turning to look right at me.

'He never said I was a poison, did he? That it was my fault you two broke up?' I raise my voice to be heard over the roar of the engines.

'You're embarrassing yourself.'

'Did he?' I ask again. I'm not letting her off the hook this time.

'You've lost your mind. I knew it would happen one day. Clearly here we are.'

Her voice is calm again. Her lips separated into the thin smile I know means bad things are brewing for me. I don't care any more. I have nothing left to lose.

'Did he, Clara? Tell me!' I yell.

Her eyes widen. 'No, he didn't. There you go. But who cares? He might as well have. You were always there. Like a kicked puppy begging for attention. How was I supposed to cope having to look after you and him at the same time? Two pathetic losers under one roof. And me trying to elevate you both. What a drag. I've carried you since day one. You've lived off me for decades, and now you come to me with this crap? Pipe down. You used to know your place. What's happened to you? You write a stupid pig pamphlet and all of a sudden you forget where you come from? Give me a break.' Particles of spit coming from her wide-open mouth land on me. She is bright red, and her arms are gesticulating wildly.

It's the first time some of her viciousness is out in public for everyone to see. And it's causing quite a show. A few people nearby waiting for their taxi rides home are openly staring at us. A couple of cars have

323

slowed down and are watching us, blocking the line and causing a traffic jam in the car park.

As I look around us, Clara seems to become suddenly aware of what she's doing.

She grunts and gets her phone out of her bag. Taps a few times, then puts it back.

'I'm getting us a taxi. I suggest you stop being ridiculous and making a show of yourself and we go home. We still have a lot to do before we leave, and this is definitely not helping,' she says, enunciating each word.

'I'm not going anywhere until you tell me the truth. We're not starting a life somewhere else based on lies. I love you, Clara, but this time it's different.'

I surprise myself with how determined I feel. It's just her in my life now; without her there's nothing left. But I need to know that things can change. That when we get to the seaside, it will be a new start. One in which we're equals and we care about each other, like my friends cared about me. I want her to talk about me the way Ollie talks about his new boyfriend, light up the way Clyde does when Lauren gets on stage. And I want to blush with pride and happiness when she does. But none of this can happen until everything is out in the open.

'For fuck's sake, Vale, what truth? There is no other truth. You know everything. It's me and you. The way it's always been.'

A white Prius stops near us.

'Clara?' the driver asks. She nods and opens the door.

'Get in, it's late. We need to go home. Come on,' she says, keeping the door open for me.

I shake my head.

'Vale. Get in. I'm going to leave you here if you don't come now.'

I open my arms and smile bitterly. 'All I want is the truth, Clara.'

She growls with frustration. 'Enough with this. The only truth there is is that you need me. Without me you're nothing, don't pretend you don't know it. Come on, stop being ridiculous, get in.'

324

I shake my head again. Now I know there's nothing I can say that will make her tell me what really happened.

So I say nothing.

'Okay.' She gets in the car and slams the door.

Then lowers the window and looks me in the eye.

'You can walk then. See you at home.'

The white car drives off, leaving me behind.

Chapter Thirty-Five

Iwatch the taxi disappear around the bend. I'm not surprised Clara didn't tell me the whole truth in the end. But in a way, it makes no difference. I know with absolute certainty now what really happened, whether she owns up to it or not. The veil I had over my eyes when I looked at Clara has been lifted. I see her for who she is. A broken, callous, manipulative woman who has never truly cared about me. I have no idea why it took so long for me to realise. But here we are. How did it – she – get this way? I suddenly remember the voicemail from Marilena, the one she left me after Edo spoke to her and Antonio when he came back from his travels. I never listened to it. I search for it and find it right away; not many people call me any more, let alone leave voicemails. I play it and I can tell right away from her voice that she had been crying.

'Hello, Valentina, how are you? I'm sorry for calling you out of the blue after all this time, but I don't know where else to go. Edoardo came to see us earlier today and he told us some things that were quite scary. About Clara, I mean. Look, I don't know if they're true, it's hard to tell when two people divorce. Sometimes they say horrible stuff about each other. I've definitely said some nasty things about Antonio and him about me through the years. So it wouldn't surprise me if they weren't entirely accurate,' she sniffs, 'but I know Clara, and I recognised some of what he said. It sounds like she is not well, Valentina. And that she hasn't been for some time. That she has been cruel and mean, that she treated Edoardo shockingly badly. And you too. He is scared for you and feels terrible for leaving you alone with her in London. Truth is, she was always a bit like this, even as a child. Maybe she kept it from you and her other friends, but it was tough at home. She was this strange, unreachable child. Like, a bit damaged, if that makes sense. I'm sure we didn't do a good job at dealing with it, and maybe we even caused it. Who knows . . . Anyway, I do hope you're okay. Your mother tells me that you're fine when she speaks to you. Hopefully Edoardo was wrong about that then? I can't seem to get through to Clara's phone any more, it always just rings out. Will you please call back and tell me how she is? I'm worried that things have got—'

The message ends there. There must have been no more space.

I stand in the car park, aware of people coming and going all around me but not really seeing them. My body feels cold and immobile. I have no idea what to do. Marilena's shaky voice is still clear in my ears. Clara is all I have; there is no one else who will have me now. Nowhere for me to go. I burned all the bridges I created – in Rome and in London – and now it's her or . . . what? Nothing.

I no longer believe that things will be different once we go away. Why would they be? She is still going to be the same Clara. She always was. I will still be . . . But maybe not. Maybe I'm not the same any more. Everything that has happened in the last few months has probably changed me. I definitely don't feel the same. But I'm not sure if it's a good thing or not. It doesn't change the fact that my home is with her. That I will be on that van tomorrow morning, taking all our boxes to a town by the seaside I've never even been to.

A town with no pigs.

The reality of it hits me, sending an ice-cold shiver down my back. A town with no pigs is a town with no connection, no release, no understanding. No matter where I've lived, knowing that there were pigs nearby has made me feel safe, not quite so alone. But a town with no pigs is a place with no hope. What will I do when it all gets too much if I can't find refuge by their pen, hear their noises, watch them rest? They are what keeps me from losing myself. Without them I am adrift.

I start crying and don't even bother wiping away the tears. No one notices. A person crying outside a hospital isn't such a strange thing after all. I take my phone out and look at the map to work out the way back to our house. It's long but doable. I should be there in an hour if I walk fast. I try to take a few steps, but my legs feel like they're moving through honey.

I look at my phone, still in my hand, and open my messages.

I read Kai's last text, one they sent a few weeks after the party. They hope I'm okay, and they promise to leave me alone now, but they're there if I ever need anything.

As I read their words, an iron fist grips my heart so tight I struggle to breathe for a moment. The memory of what could have been is as fresh now as it always was.

Before I can stop them, my fingers start typing.

That dinner, by the river. Can we still go?

I read it back and delete it. What's the point? Soon I won't be here any more. I turn off the screen, then turn it on again. Kai's last text is still there, as a reminder of what I – we – could have had. I should put my phone back in my pocket and start walking towards our home. But my feet don't move. I'm still here, aware of the time passing. I stare at the screen.

Again, my fingers press the buttons to form a message to Kai.

Our dinner by the river. I still want to go. Can we?

This is silly. After all this time, they might not want to hear from me. I disappeared without a word, after all. They might be angry at me, and who would blame them. I go to delete the message once more. But for some reason, I don't.

Instead, my thumb hovers over the send button for a moment, then presses it.

The ping that follows tells me it has been delivered.

328

A burst of electricity rushes through my fingers. I look around, almost expecting someone to run over and grab the phone out of my hands. But no one does. I grip the hard plastic case even tighter.

I smile. If everything is already lost, what else is left to lose?

I find Ollie's name and type a message to him too, with trembling fingers.

I'm here. I'm sorry. The room in your house, the spare one. Is it still free?

Acknowledgements

I've always loved pigs for their intelligence and resourcefulness and found the way they are often misunderstood by humans to be sad. So creating a character who shares this passion – although admittedly to a more intense degree – was easy. But that's where that ended. Writing a book is a long, laborious task of love and I can honestly say I couldn't have done it without the support of the following people, who I would like to thank.

First and foremost the incomparable Laura Joyce, who's enthusiasm for Vale and her pigs has matched mine from the very beginning. This book would not exist without their guidance, patience and support.

And Jodie Kim for putting us in touch, as well as for her valuable advice during the early days of my time on the Creative Writing MA at Birkbeck. I've been a part of many similar courses all over London and online, none shaped the first chapters of this book as much as my time there.

My teachers and classmates at Haringey Literature Live for their feedback and encouragement when Vale and her pigs were still in embryonic stage.

Wendy Bough and her team at the Caledonia Novel Award for their enthusiasm for *Pig* right from the start. Getting shortlisted for the 2023 award was the best starting platform I could have asked for.

My wonderful agent Thérèse Coen who never tires to answer all my questions and champion *Pig* wherever she goes. Her insightful observations after she first read my manuscript not only showed how clearly she had understood Vale and Clara's characters and the story I was trying to tell, but were fundamental in refining it. The book you are holding is a testament to her passion and hard work. I am so fortunate to have Thérèse, Una and the rest of the team at Susanna Lea Associates representing me.

My brilliant editor Olivia Hutchings who further wrangled this book into shape with wisdom and grace and her kickass team at Corsair – Katy Brigden, Lucy Martin and Alice Watkin – who welcomed me into the Little, Brown family with open arms and worked tirelessly to bring *Pig* in front of you, my dear readers. I couldn't wish for a better and more knowledgeable bunch of people to handle Vale's story.

The eagle-eyed Jane Selley, who copyedited *Pig* in record time and was a joy to work with.

Kathy Gale for the invaluable tips and tricks on how to navigate the rollercoaster that is the querying and publishing process.

Chris W. for being exactly who I needed at exactly the right time. You are a rare human being.

Kate Sullivan for being my first reader, Brona C. Titley for the unwavering support and enthusiasm and Nick de Semlyen for being not just a friend, but an inspiration.

My friends in the UK and Italy who have held me up and kept me sane throughout this, you know who you are.

Anna – the OG – who has been putting up with me and my pig drawings since 1988.

Iolanda for imprinting onto my brain from childhood how powerful a woman can look riding a tractor through a field at full speed.

My family in London, Brussels, Rome and Milan – in particular Olympia and William – for their patience, love and kind words. I am proud to be a part of this huge, chaotic and never-dull group of wonderful people.

My parents, Fabrizio and Marguerite, for being my ultimate cheer-leaders and because 'books are never a treat, they're a necessity'.

Stephanie, my love, my rock and ultimate inspiration. May we never run out of laughter, ideas and cocktails.

And to Margaux, the sun that brightens up our every day. This book is dedicated to you.